"STORYTELLING AT ITS BEST . . .
From page one, Louise Voss gets you hooked into
the world of Helena Nicholls."
—*Now* magazine

"[This] funny debut about surviving fame and friendship
is a sort of Gen-X *Anne of Green Gables*."
—*Blender* magazine

"A really original idea executed with buckets of style and
confidence, head and shoulders above the drippy Bridget
Jones imitators clogging up the shelves. *To Be Someone* is a
funny, moving, and fabulous debut. Louise Voss hooks you
from the first page and doesn't let go. This is chickfic at
its best—with heart, soul, and lashings of attitude."
—LAUREN HENDERSON, author
of *Strawberry Tattoo* and *Black Rubber Dress*

"A superb book . . . Moving and touching . . . This is
a truly mesmerizing story."
—*What's Happening South* (UK)

"This debut novel paints a life story so
touchingly that you never want *To Be Someone*
to end. . . . Poignant, tender, and never sappy."
—AmericanEagleOutfitters.com

"Impressive . . . Louise Voss has hit on a smart idea."
—*The Times* (London)

"Beautifully written."
—*OK* magazine

to be
SOMEONE

✳ A NOVEL ✳

BALLANTINE BOOKS • NEW YORK

Louise
Voss

Grateful acknowledgment is made to the following for permission to reprint previously published material:

BMG Music Publishing: Lyrics from "To Be Someone" by Paul Weller. Stylist Music, Ltd. (PRS). All types of royalties worldwide claimed by BMG Music Publishing, Ltd. All types of royalties in the U.S. administered by Careers-BMG Music Publishing, Inc. (BMI). All rights reserved. Used by permission.

Universal MCA Music Publishing: Lyrics from "This Is a Low" by Alex James, Damon Albarn, David Rowntree, Graham Coxon, © 1994 Universal Music Ltd. Administered by Universal MCA Music Publishing, A Division of Universal Studios, Inc. (ASCAP). Used by permission.

Library of Congress Control Number: 2003091266

ISBN: 0-345-44378-0

This edition is published by arrangement with Crown Publishers.

Originally published in Great Britain by Bantam Press, a division of Transworld Publishers, in 2001.

Manufactured in the United States of America

First American Edition: October 2001
First Ballantine Books Trade Paperback Edition: June 2003

2   4   6   8   10   9   7   5   3   1

*Dedicated with much love to
Jackie Graham (1966–1995),
who inspired not only
this book but everyone who
was fortunate enough
to be close to her.*

Acknowledgments

Thanks again to all the same people I thanked in the UK edition of this book, including Errol Kolosine, Regina McBride, and Don Fleming.

Thank you also to Patti Norman, Amy Welch, Christina Foerst, Cindy Maguire, Lida Husik, Brad Koehler, and the women of Regina McBride's Writers' Voice workshop circa '96–'97, including Naomi, Lydia, and Phyllis.

Thank you to everybody at Crown, especially Kristin Kiser, Steve Ross, and Claudia Gabel.

As before, biggest thanks of all to Matt Voss.

to be someone

PROLOGUE

Helena Nicholls
c/o Ron Pickett
Pickett Management Services
14a Gloucester Place
London W1

Geoff Hadleigh
Program Director
New World FM Radio
59 New Cavendish Street
London W1

6 August 1998

Dear Geoff,

Thanks for visiting me in hospital back in May. Sorry it's taken me so long to reply to your kind offer of a nighttime show for New World. I've been thinking things over and the answer's yes, I'll take the job, if it's still open. I'm better now, thank God. After a few months of having the Sword of Damocles hanging over me—well, the Penknife of Damocles, at least—I've finally been given the all-clear and both ears are once more fully functional. I could start work in a few weeks. I understand that we're talking about the two A.M.–four A.M. show.

My only condition is no advance publicity. It's humiliating enough for the breakfast show DJ to get demoted to the graveyard shift, without having to go through that "how the mighty fall" thing from the tabloids again—I'm sure you recall what it was like after my accident.

Since it obviously won't be practical for me to play requests, not at two A.M., please find enclosed the proposed playlist for my first show back on air. I know it's a little unusual, not to mention overzealous, to submit a playlist ahead of time like this, but I just wanted you to know that I've put a lot of thought into each record. Believe me, this show will be GREAT for New World FM, you wait and see.

All the best, and thanks for the lilies,

Helena Nicholls

Playlist

THE BALLAD OF TOM JONES
Space with Cerys of Catatonia

I GET THE SWEETEST FEELING
Jackie Wilson

(GET YOUR KICKS ON) ROUTE 66
Sandie Shaw

WICHITA LINEMAN
Glen Campbell

SUNDAY GIRL
Blondie

SITTING IN LIMBO
Jimmy Cliff

HOME AGAIN
Carole King

OLIVER'S ARMY
Elvis Costello and the Attractions

THERE THERE MY DEAR
Dexys Midnight Runners

GHOSTS
Japan

TO BE SOMEONE
The Jam

SHIPBUILDING
Robert Wyatt

DEEP BLUE DREAM
The Big Blue OST

LOVESONG
The Cure

KINKY AFRO
Happy Mondays

I'LL BE HOME
Randy Newman

SAFE FROM HARM
Massive Attack

NOTHING COMPARES 2 U
Sinead O'Connor

I CAN'T STAND THE RAIN
Ann Peebles

THIS IS A LOW
Blur

WAKING UP IN HOSPITAL

THERE WAS A STORY ABOUT A DRUNKEN SEVENTEENTH-CENTURY shepherd I discovered in a book at school once, when Sam and I were doing a history project about Salisbury Cathedral.

When I awoke in hospital a day after the accident, I was oblivious to the operations that had removed my damaged eyeball, reconstructed my nose, wired my jaw, and stitched my cheek, and I did not realize that I was deaf in one ear, but I clearly remembered that legless peasant.

It was the annual Whit-Week fair in the cathedral close, cattle and sheep for sale in rickety wattle pens, urchins peddling ribbons and knickknacks, a well-patronized ale and cider tent; merchants, farmers, and the usual cast of pickpockets and tricksters milling around. Anyway, a local shepherd patronized the ale tent so thoroughly that he convinced himself and his friends that he'd suddenly learned to fly. Before anyone could stop him, he bolted into the cathedral and up the little staircase hewn from the thickness of the nave walls, right to the top of the tower. At the point where tower meets spire, there was a room with doors that opened out onto all four vistas of the surrounding valley. He opened the door overlooking the festivities beneath, spread his arms wide, and leapt into the void, planning to sail away over the cattle pens and maypole dancers. Predictably enough, he couldn't fly. But the memorable part of the story was that, because he was so drunk, he staggered away completely unhurt. A little dazed and confused, probably, but then he was that *before* he jumped three hundred feet to the ground.

Though I couldn't remember at first what had happened to me, I knew that I'd had some kind of fall, because all I could think about was that peasant plummeting down to earth, headfirst. In the past I'd always imagined him sort of floating down to the soft green grass of the cathedral close, a soporific smile on his pissed face, falling in slow motion like a Disney character drifting off to sleep on a pile of feathers. Now, however, he fell through my mind like a boulder, gathering speed, leaving a crater in the lawn outside the north front.

I envied him the miracle of his intact skull. I didn't know what state my own was in, but I had an unbelievable headache, and my whole face hurt like hell. Hazily I remembered something else I learned at school: that if you dropped an egg off the top of the cathedral, it wouldn't necessarily smash, not if it landed the right way up. I began to envy the egg.

In my morphine-sodden mind, I saw an image of my nose breaking on a dark floor like a wrong-way-up egg; and then like a flour-bomb, a great cloud of cocaine spilling out on impact. This was more information than I felt able to handle, so I went back to sleep again.

The next time I opened my one remaining eye there was a familiar face peering anxiously at me, wavering in and out of focus.

"Another flagon of ale, wench," I mumbled, but all I heard was "Mmmh, mmmh, mmmh." It seemed that someone had their hand over my mouth. Not funny, I thought, trying to shake it off. The movement set every nerve in every cranny of my skull jangling and pulsing with yet more pain. Christ, have I ever got a hangover. Or did I fall off a roof? My brain couldn't fully articulate the scenario, but I had an embryonic vision of myself having performed some vastly heroic action, saving someone from a fire or something. Goody, I thought vaguely. That'll do my public profile good.

I reached a hand up toward my face to try to wrest away the joker who was preventing my speech, but someone restrained me gently.

It was my mother, her face looming into mine, lips moving but no sound. She looked awful, red-eyed, with her normally immaculately coiffed hair all whooshed messily upward and to the side, as if she'd just spent an hour with her head stuck out the window of a moving car.

It wasn't until she shifted position so her mouth was near my right ear that I could actually hear what she was saying. "Don't try to talk, darling, your jaw is all wired up because you broke it in the fall."

Oh, a broken jaw. Well, that would soon mend, I thought. But it must be serious if Mum had flown over from New Jersey (she'd hardly been back at all since we emigrated there in 1980). Besides, judging by the throbbing, I thought it must be my nose that was broken.

I gave a pathetic whine and pointed toward it. Mum stroked the back of my hand with her finger as if I were a newborn kitten. Her voice was strained and distorted, as if she were speaking to me from the bottom of a fish tank.

"You broke your nose as well, sweetheart."

This was getting worse. I tried to glance across the bed, to see if Dad was there, too, but there was something heavy resting on my left eye, and I couldn't turn my head far enough to see out of my right. Oh, no. Not my eye, too.

Mum read my mind. "I'm so sorry, Helena darling. You got some glass in your eye, and the doctors had to operate. Don't worry about it for now, though. Just try and get some more sleep."

My free eyebrow crumpled up with consternation. Even through all the painkillers I could tell she was keeping something from me, but I didn't feel ready to find out what. This all felt like a weird, horrible dream. Perhaps the cocaine had been laced with PCP or something, and I was hallucinating.

Oh God, the coke.

Oh God, the nightclub.

Oh *God,* the seesawing with Justin.

Shit. What had I done?

A big nurse with hoofy shoes came in and stuck a needle in my arm, without asking permission. I wondered if this was how it had been for Sam at the end, this awful swirly painful feeling, as much emotional as physical, knowing and yet not knowing what was going on. Seeing details but not the big picture. Other than to visit Sam, I'd never been in hospital before. It was a disturbing shift of perspective, for me to be the one lying propped up in Sam's place. She'd lain there for so many weeks, white on white, a tube in her throat to breathe through. As I floated back off to sleep, I imagined that I had become Sam—a comforting feeling, because it meant that she was still alive. Or maybe I was dead.

The doctor officially broke the news about my eye, very gravely and slightly patronizingly, as if I were a small child whose hamster had died. I half expected him to say, "Your eye has gone up to live with Jesus," but instead he began to talk about "options"—prosthetics, breakthroughs in medical science, blah, blah—until I cut him off. I'd always been really squeamish about eyes in general, to the point where I'd nearly passed out when Sam once explained to me how the doctors had operated on her cataracts, so the thought that my eyeball had actually been *removed* was too much to bear. Denial was clearly the only sensible option.

After a week in hospital, once I was vaguely *compos mentis* again, I made them move me to the second floor. My original ground-floor room came complete with paparazzi jostling about on stepladders outside, and I couldn't stand having the blinds pulled down day and night. It was bad enough having only one eye and one working ear, let alone dwelling in permanently artificial light.

Apparently the police came regularly and moved them on, but they were constantly hassling the receptionists and nurses, claiming to be relatives, friends, therapists. One even tried to convince the staff nurse that he was my personal tarot card reader. I hadn't had so much press attention since Blue Idea broke up, and I'd almost forgotten how hideous it was.

I couldn't understand why the press was so interested in my accident. Yes, I was still pretty well known in London, since I had the New World breakfast show, but I tried to keep a low profile, and didn't really go out to the groovy places much anymore. Then I found out. One of the hospital cleaners slunk into my room about a week after I arrived, clutching a blurry tabloid, all soft and graying from too much handling.

"Didn't want to bother you before, Miss Nicholls, what with you being so bashed up an' stuff, but wouldya autograph this for me sister? She loved Blue Idea, cried for days when you all split up—a nasty business, weren't it?"

I couldn't believe my eye when I saw the headline and accompanying picture. SEEMED LIKE A BLUE IDEA AT THE TIME! it pulsated at me. And the picture—oh Jesus, the shame. Me on Justin's back, legs kicked in the air, stockings and a flash of knicker showing, eyes closed and a goofy expression. To think I'd believed we looked cool.

A few too many at the UKMAs, chaps? Shortly after this picture was taken at Britain's top music industry award show, these high jinks ended in near tragedy for Helena Nicholls of former chart-topping band Blue Idea. Nicholls, 31, now a DJ at top London station New World, is in intensive care with extensive facial injuries, including the loss of her left eye. Her fellow band member and now successful solo artist, Justin Becker, 33, escaped unharmed. . . .

The piece rambled on about Justin for a couple more paragraphs and then concluded with a firsthand account that we were both "off our trolleys on drugs." I was outraged, until I remembered that it was true.

I screwed up the paper in fury, trying to scream as loudly as I could through my wired-up jaw at the hapless cleaner to get out, leave me alone, fuck off. But the only sound I managed to produce was a high-pitched groan, like a rutting dolphin or a ferret in a trap. Thankfully it was enough to summon a passing nurse, who realized what was going on, ejected the cleaner, removed the tabloid, and administered a sedative.

So it was no great surprise when I received a visitor a couple of days later. It was Geoff Hadleigh, the boss of New World. He brought me an enormous bunch of white lilies, and I didn't have the energy to tell him that I couldn't stand them, their sickly perfume and funereal smell, and their nasty, staining orange pollen.

Thankfully my jaw had been unwired the day before and I could talk again, after a fashion, although it was really embarrassing. One of my front teeth had broken in half horizontally, and the other one had split vertically, resulting in a ludicrously thick spluttering lisp, as my tongue couldn't decide where to put itself (I didn't even want to think about the aesthetic effect). It all just added to the humiliation.

Geoff was a weaselly, gummy sort of man, skinny and loose in his jeans in a manner indicating underendowment. We'd never really got on; his deputy program director, Gus, had originally hired me for an evening shift, so I wasn't one of Geoff's "people." Plus Geoff had obviously never thought that in just a few months I'd build up such a big following. Eventually, when the slot had come free, he'd been pressured by Gus, the other board members, listeners, and production staff to promote me to the coveted breakfast show, where I'd worked to prove myself day and night: researching, broadcasting, writing, taking hardly any time off.

My "trademark" as a DJ was to take requests on air from the public, but I would play their selected record only if they could give a valid reason for why it was so important to them. What they were doing when they heard it, what they'd felt, wore, ate, touched, said, and why this was memorable.

I was tough, too. My listeners knew it wasn't enough to ring up and say, "Please play 'The Power of Love' because my girlfriend and I were dancing to it when I proposed"—oh, no. I wanted to know what her exact response was, what kind of party they were at, what sort of shoes she was wearing, what brand of perfume.

People confessed secrets, scandals, tragedies to me. They sometimes cried, or said how much better they felt for getting whatever it was off their chest. The press had in the past compared me to a disc-spinning Frasier Crane, or "Claire Rayner in a DJ booth."

Damn, I was good at it. "God is in the details," I always said, and, "It's not just about the music." It was so important to set the scene, get people to dredge their minds for even the tiniest little piece of extra information. It made the record even more precious to them, while giving them a few minutes of fame and a Londonwide audience.

At first I worried that people would find it all too self-indulgent, and get bored listening to strangers' stories of woe, but I was wrong; the format was a runaway success. Listeners really did want to know why "Only You" by Yazoo reminded Sharon from Herne Hill of how she once hid behind a crumbling car-park wall, in school uniform. When they found out it was because she was two-timing her boyfriend with an amber-eyed sixth-former, and that the amber-eyed sixth-former was killed in a car crash six weeks later, there were tears all round the M25.

But my novel format was another reason Geoff Hadleigh wasn't my biggest fan. Commercial stations had strict quotas of records to stick to, playlists A, B, and C. He thought I'd never be able to fit requests in around the morning rituals of news, travel bulletins, ad breaks. But I had. We'd struck a deal whereby I could get away with sixty percent playlisted tracks and forty percent requests, unheard of on a breakfast show. It hadn't made me popular with the other DJs, but I didn't care. I knew I was a good DJ.

It felt so different from being in Blue Idea, where, even though I'd written the songs, I'd never felt that it was truly my achievement, because it was a group effort. New World was a whole new and revelatory ball game, where I'd succeeded because people liked my personality. Plus I didn't have to go on tour for months at a time. It had come to mean everything to me. And my hard work had paid off— I'd doubled the station's breakfast-show listenership in less than a year.

"Hello, Helena, you look . . . um . . . well, you *have* been in the wars, haven't you?"

"I thuppothe you're here to fire me, aren't you, Geoff?" I said, as if my mouth were full of peanuts.

He sat down on a chair next to the bed, pulled a capacious handkerchief from his jeans pocket, and blew his nose with a squeaky sound like a balloon deflating. I wondered if I was supposed to think he was crying.

"Of course not, Helena. We at New World would hate to lose you!"

"But?"

"But—you're going to be recovering from this . . . accident for quite some time, aren't you? You must realize that we can't just get a *temp* to cover for you. Our listeners need continuity in their DJ, especially in the morning-drive time. By the time you're well enough to come back—if ever—they will have gotten used to—"

I cut him off. "What do you mean, if ever?"

"Well, um, I understand that your hearing is damaged, as well as you being, erm, physically impaired. If that didn't return to normal, then . . . to put it bluntly . . . there's no such thing as a deaf DJ. I'm afraid you couldn't possibly drive your own desk anymore."

For someone so nervous, he went straight for the jugular. Bastard. It was hard to disguise the loss of my eye, but I hadn't wanted anyone to know about my deafness. Obviously there was no such thing as patient confidentiality, no matter how high the hospital bills were.

"Whoth doing my thow at the moment?" I asked jealously.

Geoff picked up and replaced several of my Get Well Soon cards, without looking at the messages. "Ralph Porter," he said, almost defensively.

I exhaled with disgust. Ralph Porter couldn't DJ his way out of a wet paper bag. I was about to inform Geoff of this, but he plowed on.

"So I've come here with a proposal for you, Helena. You take as much time as you need to get better, and then when you are, there'll still be a job waiting for you at New World. I can't let you go back to the breakfast show, but I'll give you a regular night slot."

Oh no, not the graveyard shift after all my hard work. No.

"But if my hearing returnth to normal, then thurely . . . ?"

I tried hard not to plead, but failed. How could I do a request show at two A.M.? The big audience was what made it work so well—telling your stories to the whole of London. I even had bumper stickers saying HELENA LET ME TELL LONDON MY SONG. Who would care in the middle of the night, when the only listeners were night watchmen and drug-addled losers? It just wouldn't work.

But Geoff was getting into his stride, possibly becoming used to the dreadful sight of my scarred and bruised face.

"I'm sorry, Helena, but it's not as simple as your health. You wouldn't believe the amount of flak I've had from the press and the watchdogs, about allegations that you and Justin were on cocaine at the UKMAs. Frankly, you're lucky I'm *not* firing you."

"You can't prove anything," I muttered sulkily.

"Let's hope not, for all our sakes. Personally I don't need proof—I was at the same table as you that night, remember, I saw what you were like."

He got up, still holding the flowers. They dripped a spiteful puddle of water onto the floor.

"I'm sorry, Helena. I know how hard you've worked. I'll give these to the nurse to put in a vase on my way out, shall I? Let me know if you want to take the job, whenever you're ready."

A BEACH AT LOW TIDE

TODAY I LOOKED IN A MIRROR FOR THE FIRST TIME. INTENTIONALLY, I mean, not just the accidental glance in the reflection of the window at night, or like when the towel covering the mirror in the bathroom slipped as I was washing my hands (I made Nurse Grace rig it up there as soon as I was well enough to get myself in and out of the en suite). I'd turned away instantly without letting myself get a proper look, but even that split second was enough to inform me that, yes, I was in fact a dead ringer for the Elephant Man.

But that morning Grace had said, "Ooh, Helena, you look so much better. The swelling's really gone down. Once the stitches are out, you'll almost be back to normal."

I had more movement in my jaw every day, and the dressings on my face had been reduced to one big one where my eye used to be. Physically, I was on the mend.

The better I got, the more my vanity began to return. I made the nurses wash my hair (even though it hurt like mad to lean my head back) instead of tying a scarf over it, because it had gotten greasy enough to fry eggs on. Plus I became aware that my breath smelled foul. I hadn't been able to clean my remaining teeth—ugh—since the accident. Mouthwash alone didn't quite seem to hit the spot. I didn't think anyone except me would care (Mum—well, she used to wipe my ass, so I was sure a spot of halitosis didn't bother her; the nurses—ditto), but that wasn't the point. Thankfully a dentist was booked to come in and cap my stumpy teeth at the end of the week, which meant I'd be able to talk normally again, too.

This sudden resurgence of interest in my appearance made everyone very pleased with me, including the psychotherapist whom Mum summoned to my bedside twice a week to tell me that a spot of depression was Normal and To Be Expected. They all thought that it meant my gloom was subsiding and I was returning to my old self. But I was depressed *before* the accident! I felt like shouting.

Once or twice, though, I did allow a minnow of optimism to flash in my chest. Perhaps it would be okay, perhaps I could be normal again. But the minnow always swam off again instantly. I'd always be half-blind and scarred, my deafness still hadn't healed, and Sam would always be dead. Sorry, folks, I thought. It's only vanity.

I'd been afraid to look at myself before, but now I felt that I had to know how bad it really was. On some people scars could look quite distinguished. Suitably psyched up, I shuffled into the bathroom and closed the door. Pulling the cord to switch on the light, I held my breath and moved toward the towel veiling the mirror. I remembered my old face with affection and regret, like a lost love. How my only previous gripes about it had been the beginnings of those lines that Homer Simpson has, the ones that run down from nostril to mouth on each side, and faint wrinkles on my forehead even when I wasn't frowning, like a beach at low tide.

Feeling like Dorian Gray, I closed my eyes and twitched the towel down.

Oh. My. God. If that was an improvement, I must have been unrecognizable before. Tears flowed down my bumpy, discolored face as I stared at it; it was bristling with stitches and striped with skin grafts. My formerly wonderful nose looked like the model for a Cubist painting. One of my eyebrows had all but disappeared, and I didn't even dare examine the ridiculous teeth—the ulcers peppering my tongue told me how jagged they were.

The whole effect was as if someone had taken all the bits of my face off and then reassembled them without following the instructions properly. And my forehead was more wrinkly than ever. Basically, I was pig-ugly.

I did not stop crying until just before my doctor's visit two hours later. When he came in to check my progress, I made a last-ditch attempt at optimism.

"So, once all this heals up, I will look *kind* of how I looked before, won't I?"

The doctor gave me one of those rueful upside-down smiles and took my wrist between his fingers to monitor my pulse.

"Well, yes, of course," he said doubtfully. "*Kind* of."

THE PLAN

I'D BEEN LYING IN BED, LISTENING ONE-EARED TO RALPH PORTER'S breakfast show through my Walkman headphones, but after only five minutes I couldn't stand it anymore. The show was testosterone-soaked rubbish, and hearing it in mono was making my head ache. I clicked off the radio and instead stared one-eyed at the dust motes sailing around in the morning sunlight, wondering how old flecks of carpet, dandruff, and naval fluff managed to look so sparkly and beautiful. I wished I could shrink down to that size—pure, uncomplicated, free. I couldn't think of anything better.

Then the dust motes reminded me of my favorite movie soundtrack, *The Big Blue*, which was my "touring album" in 1988, at the height of Blue Idea's success. It was such a wonderfully mellow record; I'd played it through headphones on tour buses and private jets across the world whenever I wanted to transform from a world-weary lump of exhaustion to a tiny light atom, floating blissfully about in space.

I imagined myself phoning up my own breakfast show and requesting "Deep Blue Dream" from *The Big Blue*. Would I play it for me? Yes, I thought, if I described to London exactly how I'd felt back then, reclining in all those luxuriantly upholstered velour seats, being waited on hand and foot, in the days when I was unscarred and in demand. I should have been reveling in the attention, but Sam had been lying ill in hospital at that time, hovering wraithlike between dreaming and death, and there'd been nothing I could do except worry.

In the remembering, I tasted the bubbles of American Airlines's mimosas on my tongue, felt the slippery texture of the linen napkins at the Four Seasons in Tokyo, saw the sun rise and set through so many airplane windows. I heard the screams of fans in fifty different countries, how they made my name sound new in each different language. And I remembered how nothing had mattered to me except Sam's recovery. Behind it all, the tape of "Deep Blue Dream" spooled softly, nostalgically, in my head.

The pain of my losses stabbed me suddenly. My eye, my Sam, my job, my looks—all gone. It surprised me how much it hurt to lose my job. Only Sam's death hurt more. I didn't want to do a two A.M. show. I didn't want to do a show that wasn't about people's memories, their music.

But I couldn't just slink away in disgrace. I don't *do* disgrace, I thought. There had to be some other option. I thought about what I really wanted out of life, what exactly it was that I'd been working toward all these years.

Eventually, what I came up with was me, Helena Nicholls, *being somebody*. Not as a songwriter or band member or even as a DJ, not as a friend or girlfriend or daughter, however important all those things were, but as me. I wanted people to remember my name with admiration, not scorn. Not "Oh, her, she was that DJ who got high and smashed her face up—and didn't she use to be in some eighties band?"

And right now I was in serious danger of meeting that "didn't she use to be" fate. Helena Nicholls, made a prat of herself and was never seen again.

So the situation required drastic measures.

A plan started to form in my mind, gathering its genesis around itself like a snail shell's twirl, tighter and tighter, until all my ducks lined up, quack, quack, quack, in an orderly fashion, and I thought, Yes, now I know exactly what I'm going to do.

I'll tell Geoff Hadleigh I'll accept his offer of a job, I decided, and I'll tell him that my hearing has recovered, whether it has or not. Starting from now, I'll make a list of all the records that have played behind my life, *my* requests, and write down, in detail, exactly why I've picked them. A life's soundtrack will take more than just a five-minute explanation—if I talked about it on air, I'd never have time to play the songs themselves. Hence the accompanying manuscript.

When I come to broadcast all the songs, even though it will be two A.M. and the show's ratings will be minuscule, it will make radio history. Once everybody realizes what I've done, what I'm going to lock myself in the bathroom and do immediately after the show. I don't know what method I'll use yet; pills, probably. But it's not important *how* I do it.

The point is that it will make me a legend. Bigger than I ever was in Blue Idea, or as a hip breakfast DJ, and certainly bigger than the silly tart who broke her face on a dance floor. Justin's career will skyrocket. All our old records will be rereleased. It'll make all the papers. Hopefully I'll get a publishing deal for the book, and the New World show could be released on a compilation CD. Perhaps even a Hollywood movie . . .

I got out a pen and a pad of lined A4 (which Mum had brought me, hoping in vain that I might cheer up enough to write some song lyrics) and prepared to take the plunge. I can do this, I told myself. I can write. I'd won awards for my songs; I'd written hundreds of letters to Sam; kept a diary for a little while. In fact, I'd already been published, if you counted the abysmally puerile *Bluezine* (a fanzine the record company made me churn out from the road).

Hell, I'd been meaning to write my autobiography for years. This would just be a different way of doing it. Using the songs would help me focus—I didn't want to do one of those all-encompassing tomes that subscribed to the "more is more" philosophy, and besides, I'd never be able to remember it all without thinking of the records that went along with it.

It felt so weird, not having to think in rhymes and verses, no breaks for middle eights or guitar solos. This was my life; it needed to be fluent, complete, yet selective. No choruses or intros. No neat bite-sized chunks.

I was going to begin at the beginning, me and Sam, but then I thought—no. Start with the accident, then you'll get it out of the way and not have to think about it again. It had its own record, very definitely: Space with Cerys of Catatonia—"The Ballad of Tom Jones." It was a pity, really. I always loved that song, the humor and harmonies and sexy Cerys to boot. Now I loathed it. For days after I regained consciousness it kept going through and through my battered head. It was such a bizarrely chirpy song to induce such terrible memories.

Space with Cerys of Catatonia
THE BALLAD OF TOM JONES

IT HAPPENED ON THE NIGHT OF THE U.K. MUSIC AWARDS, THE biggest of the annual music business backslapping events. I'd been to the UKMAs six times altogether, and Sam had come with me as my guest three times.

This time it was all different. I wasn't at the Ringside Records table anymore, no longer in one of the planet's bestselling bands, nor with a solo career like Justin. Worst of all, Sam wasn't sitting beside me starry-eyed, because she was dead.

I suppose I should have been thankful that at least I still had a career. I was with a new set of colleagues, my fellow DJs and other assorted top brass from New World FM. The DJs mostly cold-shouldered me, but I was used to it—they were just jealous.

I was determined to have a good time regardless, thinking that a night out might cheer me up a bit, take my mind off Sam. But of course that was stupid. I wanted her there so badly that I felt sick.

To my joy and relief to see a friendly face, I bumped into Justin later. It was the first time I'd seen him in over two years. He had a mad glitter in his eyes, and his shirt was rumpled, torn out of his trousers by the teenagers who'd waited hours for him outside, on an unseasonably chilly spring night. When I'd arrived they were there, all pressed up against the barriers lining the red carpet, not even noticing the cold night air, which sent their star-studded breath cloudy. Not that they'd paid much attention to me, though.

Justin looked gorgeous, of course. It was funny how I'd never seriously fancied him, apart from a two-minute crush when we first met. I was possibly the only straight woman on earth who didn't. I think it must have had something to do with rank socks, transit vans, audible bodily functions, and other such traumatic memories from the band's early days.

He told me I looked beautiful, too, and I really knew it. It took a tiny edge off the fist of grief in my chest, to see myself as everyone else was seeing me. I was wearing my backless velvet dress, soft folds of burnt orange caressing my breasts, tight across my belly and hips, and swirling erotically around my legs. The chill of air-conditioned air, which occasionally skittered up and down my bare spine, turned me on like a lover's fingers.

I remembered how Sam had once said that, that even the air-conditioning was making her feel sexy. Sam adored the UKMAs, for the sense of spectacle of the whole event. She used to bang on about it being "an awesome collision of the huge and the tiny," pointing everything out to me as if I couldn't see it myself: The enormous venue; the tiny sparkling lights winking and blinking across the ceiling like stars. The massive banks of speakers; small performers onstage blown up huge by video screens. Little reedy voices making industry small talk around big tables. Glitter every-where, on the women's cleavages and cheekbones, in the men's eyes as they sized up the talent. Sam didn't miss a thing. And when Blue Idea won Best International Group (we were an American band—I was the only Brit) two years in a row, she was embarrassingly pleased for me. Even when we didn't win, she wouldn't shut up about how proud she was of me. "It's because I can see the respect in everyone's eyes when they look at you," she'd said. "And these aren't your fans, they're your peers. That makes it even better."

Justin knew Sam, I thought, a long time ago. I'd better tell him.

"Justin," I said. "I've got some bad news, I'm afraid."

Justin looked anxiously down at himself to make sure his fly wasn't undone, and then wiped under his nose in case the news was that something horrible had crawled out of his nostril to alight on his upper lip.

"No, not about *you*," I said crossly. Honestly, he was so vain.

"My friend Sam died, a couple of months ago."

Justin arranged his face in an expression of vague condolence, without a flicker of recognition.

"Sam, you know, my English friend who used to visit me all the time. You shagged her. Gorgeous, tall, gray eyes, long legs."

My voice quivered with the pain of describing someone I'd never see again.

Light still didn't dawn in Justin's eyes, but he made a good pretense of remembering.

"Ohhhh, right! Now I know who you mean. Oh, Jesus, H, that's terrible. You poor baby! Such a cute girl, too. What a bummer. Come here."

He tried to envelop me in a bear hug, but I pushed him away. I didn't want to start crying among all the sparkly people.

"Okay then, Ms. Nicholls, only one thing for it—and it's in a small packet in my top pocket. Come on, a flat surface and a credit card await us."

I tutted irritably.

"You know I don't like cocaine," I said.

"Wrong," replied Justin, frog-marching me toward the backstage loos. "I know that you actually *love* cocaine, and that's why you never do it. You're afraid of getting hooked. Well, I think that's totally sensible and mature of you—but give yourself a break, just this once. It'll make you feel much better."

He was partly right about the fear bit, but it wasn't the only reason I abstained. I'd spent years enduring the company of bug-eyed, bollock-talking, coked-up prats the world over, and I had no desire whatsoever to join their chopped-out ranks. Plus Sam hadn't approved.

But Sam wasn't there.

We ended up in a cubicle in the ladies', Justin sculpting two huge chrysalises on the toilet lid with his credit card. I wondered how many lines he'd previously ingested, since he'd suddenly become totally paranoid, grumbling sotto voce throughout the entire operation.

"What if someone sees us?" he asked.

"So what? Everyone else is doing the same thing. Listen."

I angled my ear toward the thin partition of the cubicle next to ours, and pointed down toward the heel of a man's boot, which could be seen underneath the wall. The sound of sniffs and gruff mutters was clearly audible.

"Not everyone. I have to be so careful, Helena. People might not recognize you anymore, but I could end up with my face splashed all over the papers. It could ruin my career!"

"What do you mean? You're the one with the eighth in your breast pocket, so it can't bother you too much. And besides, you aren't the only one with a career—I've still got a face to get splashed and a career to be ruined, too, you know."

How prophetic. The papers weren't all my face ended up splashed over. But all I was concerned with at that moment was the fat tapered line of cocaine camouflaged before me on the white porcelain altar. I knelt in worship, not even caring that my beautiful dress was trailing on the sticky tiled floor.

* ❋ *

The UKMAs eventually wore down to a tired crawl. People were beginning to huddle around their tables in a jumble of black ties and diamanté, like affluent refugees waiting to be rehoused. The mini–fairground rides no longer had to be queued for, and there were puddles of vomit in discreet corners of the arena.

At two A.M. Justin and I decided it was time to move on, and so we managed to fight our way through the hordes of drunk and fractious A&R men milling around outside, to claim Justin's pre-booked limo. We headed back into Soho to a club where his promotions company was holding a private party. We were both wired, and we knew that this was the Place to Be Seen. I wanted so badly to be seen. I was suddenly fed up with the more low-key fame of being a DJ, hungry for the old thrill of adoration I needed to justify my existence.

The air in the club was muggy with cigarette smoke and overly subtle lighting, claustrophobic after the vast hangar of the Docklands Arena. It was a tableau of studied and strained chic, everyone dressed up to the nines, but well the worse for wear, trying to hold it all together.

Jus had a crowd of acolytes constantly hanging around him, and I felt put out. Although he'd always been the focal point of the band, as the token female and songwriter I'd usually received more than my fair share of adulation, too. But it had been a while.

It was a boring party, dull music, drunk people. I was considering going home, but then it all changed. After a lot of worthier-than-thou trip hop, "The Ballad of Tom Jones" suddenly came blasting over the PA, perking me up more successfully than the previous three lines of coke had.

"Let's dance," I said, dragging Jus away from his sycophants toward a raised area of the dance floor, empty except for the swirling lights swooping and glancing over its blackness, giving it the appearance of a deep murky pool.

"To this? You never dance! And besides, no one can dance to this!" he protested, trying to shake off my hand as we climbed up the three steps at the side of the stage.

"I never threw my knickers at you, Tom Jones, Tom Jones," Cerys warbled innocently.

Justin was right. It must have been the coke talking, since I had never been much of a dancer, other than a bit of jigging around onstage with my bass, and the song was about as impossible to dance to as "Come on Eileen." My one big chance to show off: a whole four hundred square feet of media possibilities, all to ourselves, like the old days of the band, no competition—but in this case no inspiration either. There was no way I was going to shuffle around halfheartedly and then skulk sheepishly off again in defeat.

A memory came back to me of an old playground game Sam and I used to play, the junior school's equivalent of drugs, I supposed. A head rush of shifting gravity and stretched boundaries, the scary exhilaration of having no choice but to trust your partner implicitly, blood pounding in your ears and rushing scarlet around behind your eyeballs.

"*I* know," I said, like the ten-year-old me. "Turn around, put your back against mine. Now link arms with me from behind."

Jus obliged, puzzled. We were still alone on the stage and already people were shooting glances at us from the bar area, wondering why we were standing back-to-back. I noticed, and the buzz in my head intensified. I began to bend forward, trying to pull him up onto my back. He twigged what I was proposing and twisted away from me.

"Stop it, Helena! You're crazy—you can't seesaw me in the middle of a stage! Besides, I'm way heavier than you!"

I was mortified. To stop now would make me look ridiculous—just when I was beginning to attract some attention, too.

"It's cool." I grabbed his arms behind his back and relocked them in mine. "Please, let's have a go. It'll be a laugh. What happened to the old daredevil Justin that we all knew and loved? You'd have done this five years ago—people will think you've lost your nerve!"

I knew all the right buttons to push, and it worked a treat.

"Go ahead, then, Wonder Woman," he said. "Jeez, talk about putting me in some embarrassing situations. I'll never live this down."

I could feel the warmth of his sticky skin through his thin silk shirt, and the way his shoulder blades nudged me just below my own. It felt nice, safe and familiar on my bare back. We were actually around the same height, but that night in my three-inch wedge heels I was taller. The hairs on his forearms tickled mine as we wriggled around a bit to get comfortable.

"Ready?" I asked, over one shoulder. "I'll go first!"

So right there, in front of a half-amused, half-aghast crowd of minor media personalities, we began seesawing each other up and down, my legs flying in the air as I balanced on his back, then my own creaking spine taking the weight of the somewhat heavier Justin. He held back at first, worried that I wouldn't be able to support him, but soon we got into a groove. Up and down, blood rushing to my head as I leaned forward to swing him up, and then my own cocaine-enhanced flight into the disco night, serenaded by Cerys. Then he began to relax and enjoy it, too, and we were laughing, harder and harder. I saw a blur of grinning faces below me and I thought they were laughing with us.

But then the laughter and the exertion and the drugs suddenly all took their toll on my body, and my knees gave a tiny little tremble as I hoisted Jus horizontal for the last time. The tremble ran down my right leg and into my ankle, which twisted slightly. It was enough to make me lose my balance, and I began to lurch heavily to the right, toward the edge of the stage. But at the same time, Jus was in full flight. The second before I stumbled, he gave a joyful whoop and kicked his legs as high as he could, his full weight pressed along my back.

I fell. But I didn't *just* fall, the way you do when you trip on an uneven paving slab or down a step. My arms, you recall, were tightly pinioned to my sides, and worse, at that particular moment, pulled even further away from the ground by Justin's joyous ascent.

I slipped off the stage and fell three feet, literally, flat on my face. Look, no hands, nose impacting first. All one hundred fifty pounds of Jus landed on top of me, mashing my head still further into the dance floor.

But it got worse. In the six or so inches of sprung wooden floor with which my head collided, some other careless reveler had recently dropped his champagne glass. It had broken, of course, and yes, it was still lying there in wait for my tender face.

Over the ringing in my ears, I was aware of a distant crunching sound. Immediately before passing out, I noticed several jagged pieces of ivory swimming sedately past me in a bubbling puddle of blood. Good-bye, expensive teenage dental correction work.

The last thing I remember was little Tommy Space confirming, *"I don't come from Wales . . . ,"* and thinking, Sam, oh Sam, please help me.

INTRUSION

"DADDY! DADD-DEEE! MUMMY!"

I'd been lost in writing about my first meeting with Sam, and the cry nearly made me jump out of my patchwork skin. All my misaligned facial bones rubbed painfully together, and I stopped scribbling, irritated. The voice came from my left, near the door. I couldn't see anybody, although if I turned my head as far as possible, I could tell that the door was ajar.

A storm of histrionic childish sobbing ensued. By rolling onto my left side, I could see a bundle of purple and pink fun-fur crumpled pitifully on the floor by my bed.

"Er—*hello*?" I said, trying to make my voice as laden with sarcasm as possible, despite being aware that this probably wasn't the most effective method of dealing with a stray distraught toddler.

The crying intensified, and my head started to throb. Honestly, couldn't I even plan my suicide in peace? So much for my privacy and protection—if theatrical two-year-olds could wander in and out at will, then what was to stop a *Sun* photographer, or a deranged stalker? I began to feel very put out.

Gingerly, I slid out of bed and got to my knees on the floor, where I stretched out my hand and poked the little girl's furry shoulder.

"Where'th your mummy?"

She looked up at me then, and the sight of my stitched and bruised face caused her to leap to her feet in one move, like a vertical takeoff. Recoiling with horror, she ran and hid behind my visitor's armchair. At least she was shocked into silence, though.

"I like your coat," I mumbled encouragingly. It was true, I did. I contemplated asking her where she'd gotten it from, on the off-chance they did it in grown-up sizes.

"Pink flowerth," came a hesitant reply. I saw a small finger stroke one of the said pink flowers.

"Very nith," I said. "Will you come and talk to me now?"

"NO! You got panda bear face like my mummy! I want my mummy!"

I tried hard not to be hurt or angry, deciding that a frosty "Do you know who I am?" might not do the trick here.

"Where ith your mummy?" I asked again.

"No more nap, Mummy! Wake up now!" The finger wagged accusingly, and the tone became quite stern.

"Would you like a thweetie?" I ventured.

Pathetically, I was by now quite enjoying the distraction from my project. It was much harder work than I'd imagined, writing with only one eye to mediate between brain and paper. In slow motion I reached for the tin of travel sweets my mother had forgotten on her last visit. (Very insensitive of her, too, I thought. My jaw was still very tender, and I was enduring meals whose consistency my current visitor had probably outgrown at five months of age.)

Mutely, the hand stretched out.

"Well, come on, then, I won't bite . . . although the chanth would be a fine thing."

She sidled out, eyes downcast. Apart from the chubby red face clashing with her pink and purple coat, she was pretty cute. Skinny little curls sprouted vertically from her head, and her teary eyes held worldly-wise blue depths.

I handed her a wrapped sweet.

"Tankoo," she said politely.

"You're welcome."

She had just crinkled off the paper and popped it into her mouth when my least-favorite nurse, Catriona, knocked and stuck her head round the door.

"Oh, thank heavens, there she is!" she said crossly. "Ruby, your daddy's been looking everywhere for you!"

Catriona retreated and returned almost immediately with a blond curly-haired man, gray around the eyes with exhaustion and what looked like abject misery. They marched into the room, ignoring me completely.

"What am I, chopped liver?" I said to no one in particular. I was still kneeling on the floor in my nightie, suddenly vulnerable.

"Ruby Middleton, what have I told you about wandering off?" said the man, halfheartedly.

"Daddy! My daddy!" came the ecstatic reply as Ruby hurled herself at her father's kneecaps. Suddenly we all heard a very strange noise emanating from the depths of the fur coat, a kind of gurgling, hawking sound. Alarmed, the man prised her away from his knees and peered into her puce face.

"Oh my God, she's choking!" he yelled. "Nurse!"

Catriona, who had just left the room, hurried back in and grabbed Ruby. Inverting her briskly, she slapped her lengthily and enthusiastically between the shoulder blades.

A small green boiled sweet dislodged itself from Ruby's windpipe and flew across the room, bouncing against the far wall and finally coming to rest under my bed. Ruby, howling, was turned back up the right way, and clung to her father. We all looked silently in the direction of the offending travel sweet, until Catriona spoke.

"Well, for heaven's sake! Who on earth was daft enough to give a boiled sweet to a toddler?! Some people have absolutely no sense. I mean, really!"

At that moment she and Ruby's dad simultaneously spotted the tin of sweets on my nightstand.

"Thorry," I muttered, climbing back into bed, furious with myself for feeling so guilty.

Catriona sniffed and left the room, and I was alone with the man and Ruby. I waited for him to give me a piece of his mind, and was preparing to tell him to sling his hook and leave me in peace, when he suddenly grinned at me. I was totally disarmed.

"I really am thorry," I said again, more genuinely this time. I felt confused—what was the correct etiquette for receiving unintentionally visiting strangers in hospital?

The man looked as though the same thought had just passed through his own head.

"No, I'm sorry," he said, "on behalf of Trouble here. It's terrible of us to barge in when you're trying to recover in peace and quiet. We'll get out of your hair now."

All of a sudden I didn't want them to leave. Apart from Mum arriving from the U.S., hideous Geoff Hadleigh, and a quick embarrassed fly-past from my production team at New World, I hadn't had any visitors. Justin had sent flowers but hadn't shown his (unblemished) face, which really upset me, and the other band members were all in the States, too. I was devastated to realize how few friends I really had now that Sam was gone.

"Would Ruby like a drink?" I heard myself ask.

The man hesitated.

"Orringe, pleathe!" said Ruby enthusiastically.

At that moment, Rosemary the tea-lady hove serendipitously into sight with her trolley.

"You could have thome tea with me, too, if you like," I said, cringing at how needy I sounded. Billy No-Mates, indeed.

"Well, that would be nice," the man said uncertainly. "I'm Toby, by the way. And you've met Ruby, obviously."

He stretched out his arm and we shook hands tentatively.

"Helena," I replied, relieved and embarrassed that he was staying. Strangely, once I looked properly at him, he seemed slightly familiar.

Rosemary poured us both a cup of tea, handing Toby his with a faintly censorious, "There you go, Mr. Middleton. White, no sugar."

"Thanks, Rosemary," he replied.

The thick plottens, I thought. Does he work here or something?

"There'th thome cartonth of Ribena in that cupboard there. Would you like to give Ruby one?"

I pointed to my locker, and Toby obligingly extracted the juice, unwrapping the straw and piercing the carton's foil hole with a pop.

Ruby sidled over and took the drink silently, obviously cowed by her recent near-death experience. With her free hand she spent the next five minutes opening and closing the locker door to hear the magnetic click of its catch. It was irritating, but better than listening to her howling.

"Pleathe, thit down," I said to Toby, pointing to the shiny armchair. The whole situation felt horribly awkward.

"So, what are you in here for, then?" asked Toby politely, looking away from my Technicolored puffy and stitched face.

"Oh, my varicothe veinth are playing me up again," I managed, as airily as I could. He smiled, and again I thought I recognized him.

"Actually, I, er, had a fall," I said, feeling like an old lady who'd fallen off a curb. "Onto thome broken glath. My teef were knocked out, too, which ith why I thound like thith."

Toby winced sympathetically. "Ouch," he said.

"Ouch," echoed Ruby. "Me kith it better."

"I with you could," I said, with feeling. "Thankth for the offer."

"I kith Mummy better, but she still seeps," Ruby added conversationally. We were definitely speaking the same language.

Toby's face scrunched up with pain. "My wife's in Intensive Care in a coma," he said, looking at the floor. "She's been unconscious for ten days now—bad car crash."

"I'm tho thorry," I said again. My lisp was irritating the hell out of me. It made everything sound so trite. There was a short silence. I stared at the wall, noticing the silhouette of a small long-legged insect that had been carelessly painted into the emulsion. It made me even more depressed. When I looked back at Toby, he had that same empty expression of desperation on his face that I recognized from my own, when Sam was so ill.

Eventually Toby spoke. "Rubes just can't understand why she won't wake up. It's terrible. She gets so frustrated. I wonder if I'm doing the right thing, bringing her here at all, especially since Kate's face is still so swollen, but I'm sure it helps her to hear Ruby's voice. . . ."

"My friend jutht died, a few month ago," I blurted out shamelessly, unable to help myself. Suddenly it felt as if both our sorrows had sparked and ignited into one great big furnace of hot grief. When I looked up, we were both in tears, embarrassed and overcome.

"Don't cry, Daddy," said Ruby, her tone suggesting that this wasn't something new. "Don't cry, lady," she added, slurping her drink noisily through the straw. She climbed onto Toby's knee and threaded an arm around his neck. He hugged her back, and I had never felt so alone.

"Ith all tho unfair!" I bawled, not really knowing whether I was crying for Sam, for Toby's wife, for Toby, or for myself.

Toby wiped his eyes and moved over to hand me a box of tissues, Ruby still clinging around his neck. I couldn't blow my nose on account of it being broken, so I dabbed delicately above my top lip instead.

"I'm sorry about your friend. Had you known each other a long time?"

We managed watery grins at each other, acknowledgment of the bizarreness of the situation.

"Yeah, thince we were about five. Tham wath my betht friend in the world. I don't know what to do with mythelf without her. . . ."

My watery grin drizzled away. Toby's head suddenly shot up.

"Oh, no! Sam died? Jesus, that's terrible!"

I stared at him and gulped with shock. All my old steel shutters clanged down to the ground around me, bang, bang.

"How do you know Tham?" I hissed.

Ruby's eyes grew like saucers as she followed the exchange. Toby groaned. A blush crawled up his neck, into his cheeks, and over his ears.

"I knew I should have admitted it straight away, but I thought you wouldn't want to be recognized. I don't—didn't—know Sam, but I do know you. We met years ago, when Blue Idea was on tour in London. I interviewed you for *Melody Maker,* and you told me all about Sam, and the charity record, and how she had recovered from the leukemia. You were so happy she was better."

I thought I was about to explode.

"I don't believe it! You're a . . . *journalitht!* You complete thcumbag, how could you do thith to me? Did you thend her in firtht, to get into my room?"

I pointed at Ruby, who shrank back, terrified.

"Wath thith whole thing planned? Ith there a photographer out there? Who'th the piece for? Or are you auctioning it to the higheht bidder? Get the fuck out of here, now, before I call the polithe!"

Toby stood up, clutching Ruby, panic and grief printed across both their faces.

"No, Helena, please, you've got it all wrong. I didn't even know you'd had an accident, honest! I swear it's not a setup. I didn't even recognize you at first, until you said your name. Please, I—"

"Jutht get out!" I yelled feebly, completely unable to think straight.

They shot through the door in a blur of fake fur and curls, Ruby gripping her juice carton so hard that Ribena sprayed up through the straw and across the carpet in their wake.

I cried and cried, even though it made my face throb with pain. I didn't care. I wanted it to hurt. All I could think was, How soon could I make this stop? How soon could I do the show?

And the answer was . . . as soon as I got it all written down.

Jackie Wilson
I GET THE SWEETEST FEELING

SAM GRANT WAS FIVE WHEN WE FIRST MET, AND I HAD RECENTLY turned six. I was in the backyard playing on my swing, a dangerous-looking contraption with frayed green nylon ropes and a plank for a seat, which my father had rigged up for me from a sturdy low branch of the big chestnut tree. The tree itself was in our garden, but the branch holding the swing wandered out and stuck over the fence into a separate paved area where our garage was.

I was swinging mightily back and forward, with my back to the garage. Humming tunelessly and kicking my legs to make myself go higher, I was enjoying the sensation of the wind flapping my skirt up and catching underneath my hair. I was at the apex of the swing's trajectory, eyeing the bloomers hanging on next door's washing line, when a massive, metallic *boom* rang out in front of me and almost caused me to plummet off my seat. I managed to hang on, but listed heavily toward the left-hand rope, which made the swing twirl around, out of control. I hadn't noticed the two figures standing nearby, until I rotated limply to a halt. Then I heard the sound of scornful laughter.

"Not very good, are you? Let's have a go," said a voice.

I turned to see a boy and a girl in the yard. The boy was holding a football and had a mean expression on his less-than-clean face. He looked to be a couple of years older than me. The girl was smaller, and thin. She had her fingers in her mouth and was lagging behind the boy, looking anxious. She was jiggling her legs, perhaps from nerves, although it looked to me more like the sort of fidgeting brought on by having wet one's knickers. Her red woollen tights sagged in wrinkles around her skinny ankles, and I could see their low crotch showing underneath the hem of her short purple-and-red-checked pinafore dress. Then I looked back at the boy and realized what had startled me on the swing.

"Did you just kick that into the door?" I asked, pointing indignantly at the football.

As if to demonstrate, the boy drop-kicked the ball again, sending it crashing into the pale green metallic up-and-over garage door. I was outraged. "I'm telling my dad on you. Buzz off! You nearly made me fall off of my swing!"

The boy swaggered toward me threateningly. I felt a little nervous.

He moved closer and retrieved his ball. "Give us a go on your stupid swing, then."

"No! Buzz off!" I had heard some bigger boys say this in the playground the week before, and had been saving it up for a suitable occasion. This most definitely was a situation calling for strong language. The girl still lurked behind the boy, not meeting my eyes. I was glaring at both of them, hating the intrusion, when a woman's voice yelled from the end of the street: "Dylan! Sa-am! Where are you? Tea's ready! I'm not telling you again!"

To my relief, the boy started to turn away. "You'd better let me play on it next time, fatso," he said menacingly, and ran out of the yard. The girl stayed in her spot, fidgeting even more. We stared at each other. Eventually she took her fingers out of her mouth and said, "That's my brother, Dylan. He's often a bully. Can I come and call for you later?"

I was taken aback, but disarmed. In retrospect I don't know what endeared me to her—I must have been a fairly intimidating sight, standing there guarding my territory with an aggressive scowl on my face and hands firmly planted on hefty little hips. Possibly it was the lure of the forbidden swing. Anyhow, I graciously conceded that she could, if only to spite her awful brother.

It transpired that the Grants had just moved to Salisbury to run the pub on the corner, the Prince of Wales. By happy coincidence, Sam also ended up in my form at school (although there was almost a year between us—I was the oldest in the class, and she the youngest).

This put the final seal on our friendship. For the duration of our primary-school years we pretty much lived in each other's pockets:

We played at the pub, in my bedroom, or raced unsteadily through the terraced streets around our houses on our baby bicycles, first with training wheels, and later without.

Mostly we tried to avoid Dylan, who by the age of nine had acquired a worrying head for business. He used to round up a few of his friends on a regular basis and charge them 5p each to see Sam and I reluctantly show them our underwear. This weekly ritual was known locally as "Bum Time," and I believe that for double the admission fee we'd actually pull down our knickers for a quick flash to the more affluent of the group. I don't recall what Sam and I got out of this arrangement—none of the takings, that was for sure. A deep and permanent feeling of mortification lasting into adulthood was more like it. Dylan threatened to give us Chinese burns if we refused to oblige.

The fact that Sam's parents ran a pub made her something of an icon at school—everyone thought it was the coolest thing that parents could possibly do. In the early seventies, the Prince of Wales was a standard locals' pub, open at lunchtimes and in the evenings only, in accordance with the restricted licensing laws of the time. Sam and I were allowed to sit downstairs in the bar after school, before the evening session began. It was the biggest thrill—sliding around on the leatherette benches, learning how to flip beer mats from the edge of the pockmarked tables, revolving the wheel on the jukebox to make the selections clunk laboriously around. Sometimes Mr. Grant gave me 10p to put a record on, and I always chose "I Get the Sweetest Feeling" by Jackie Wilson, because it was just such a happy song. I loved the *plink, plink, plink, plink . . . hmmmm* of the introduction, and the fat, deeply satisfying brassy noises going on in the background. To this day, it's one of my favorite records.

The jukebox was only one of the gadgets that made the Prince of Wales an Aladdin's cave of technological wizardry. We didn't even have a black-and-white television at home until I was eight; the Grants had two color sets, one in the bar, stuck high up to the wall with a bracket, and one upstairs in their sitting room. They had the first microwave oven I'd ever seen, and pinball and slot machines (which we weren't allowed to touch). Sam even had one of those kiddie synthesizers with the colored piano keys, as well as a record player and a radio. I was so envious.

During business hours we were not allowed to set foot in the bar, and so we played upstairs in the residential part. The Prince of Wales was a very old building, a public house since its inception in the eighteenth century, and was full of appealing little features. As a child I failed to appreciate them, but in retrospect I remember the sloping floors and ceilings, wood-paneled walls, odd cupboards everywhere, and narrow hallways interspersed every few yards with two or three crooked steps up to another level and around a new corner.

These passageways were the venue for one of our favorite games: the Great Continental Quilt Bob-Sleigh Race. Continental quilts, as they were called in those days, were in themselves a total novelty. I had never seen one before, and begged and begged my mother to buy me one, explaining at great length how labor-saving they were—no more constant bed-making or sheet-ironing. Unfortunately, she regarded anything Continental as being French and therefore somehow sweaty and unhygienic, and it was a few more years before she capitulated and bought duvets for *"toute la famille."* My fascination was such that I would drag Sam's quilt off her bed and into the sitting room—initially, I suppose, so we could both lie on it and watch TV. Then one day it became a method of transport.

"I know," I said. "I'm Cinderella going to the ball in my carriage. You be my horse, and pull me." I plumped down in the middle and gathered up the edges around me, leaving the two front corners for Sam to pick up. She neighed obligingly, bared her teeth, shook her mane, and hauled me with difficulty out of the sitting room and down the long hall back to the bedroom doorway. I remember catching sight of myself in a hall mirror and noticing with pleasure the regal air about my demeanor, the queenly tilt to my chin, and my gentle poise as Sam bumped me slowly forward to meet my prince. I was visualizing the adoration of all the lords and ladies at the ball, not just the prince, but everyone. That was the first time I was aware of craving the spotlight.

Sam dragged me back again, faster this time, so I could drop my glass slipper on the way home. That, however, was done less gracefully: I fiddled with the strap of my scuffed blue T-bar Clark's sandal, pulling it off with a jerk, which made me lose my balance and lurch over backward. I then lobbed the shoe over my shoulder, and it hit the wall with a jingle of its buckle, leaving a dirty mark.

"If that was real glass, you'd have broken it," Sam told me disapprovingly. I did a quick role switch from princess to prince, retracing my steps down the corridor to tenderly retrieve the bulky-soled sandal, holding it to my chest and then my lips, looking wistfully back toward the bedroom door for my princess. The drama was lost on Sam; she was too busy trying to rub the scuff mark off the wallpaper by spitting on her doll's dress and wiping it on the wall. The doll was wearing the dress at the time, and the friction from Sam's rubbing only caused the doll's porcelain fingernails to add little scritchy marks next to the original scuff.

But we kept refining the quilt scenarios, and over time they evolved into more of a sport than a charade, which we practiced zealously when Dylan wasn't around to laugh at us. One of us would sit in the quilt, wrapping its back and sides around us for padding, and the other would pick up the front and drag it plus passenger down the hallway from the starting line of the sitting room. Because the hall was so narrow and sloped gently down, with the little sets of stairs and turns breaking up its length, it made quite a respectable bob-sleigh run. We managed to get quite a speed up. The idea was to get to the finish line (the kitchen doorway) without the passenger falling off or the "puller" falling over.

The only problem was that our weights were not well balanced enough to get the maximum momentum. When I was the puller, I'd gallop full tilt for the first flight of steps, charge down them, hurtle round the first bend—and more often than not be left holding an empty quilt, Sam having been catapulted screaming into a cupboard door, or picking splinters from her palms further back up the course. And when she pulled me, she would puff and pant, heaving with all her strength to drag me to the top of the three little stairs, where gravity would kick in and I would invariably cascade down faster than her, catching her in the back of the knees on the way. We once heard her mother commenting in puzzled tones to her father about how quickly their new hall carpet had developed a nasty shiny streak down its center.

DAISIES AND THE GUINEA PIG

IT WAS A SLIGHTLY BETTER WEEK. I HAD MY TEETH CAPPED, WHICH was a huge relief, and I received two new cards. The first was from Toby and Ruby, a simple Get Well Soon card with their names inside. The card had a big white daisy on the front and was followed, within minutes, by a delivery of an enormous bunch of Michaelmas daisies. My favorite flower. I was finding it increasingly tough to feel hard-done-by and cheated by that sunny couple with their curly hair and serious eyes. But I kept trying to dismiss the memory of their visit. Toby obviously had a guilty conscience, I told myself; otherwise, why hadn't he brought the flowers to me in person?

The second card was from Cynthia Grant, Sam's mother. She'd sent it to my home address, and Mum, who was staying at my house, had brought it into the hospital with her.

I recognized Cynthia's writing on the envelope and immediately got a tense, choked-up feeling in my throat. It was so nice of her to think of me, but I almost resented hearing from her simply because she wasn't Sam. We'd kept in touch since Sam died, but had only seen each other once. I'd called on her and we'd sat in her homely front room, knowing that underneath our feet was Sam's abandoned basement flat, both of us wishing we could be down there having tea with Sam instead. And the worst thing of all was that Sam's name never once came into the conversation. We both knew she was the reason we were sitting there together over the syrupy flapjacks and the Earl Grey, and I'm sure we were both aching to talk about her, to get into one of those "Do you remember when Sam . . . ?" conversations, but we didn't. I assumed we were both afraid of upsetting the other, and we avoided the subject of our loss studiously, as if the mention of her name would have incurred some embarrassing forfeit.

"Who's it from?" asked Mum.

"Cynthia," I replied dully. "She says she might come and visit."

"Oh well, if she's not too busy, I guess that would be nice for you," Mum ventured, looking disapprovingly at a postcard David and Joe from the band had sent me. It was a cartoon depicting two doctors examining a man with a camera jammed up his bottom, under the caption: "Yes, Doctor, it's one of the worst cases of media intrusion I've ever seen." On the back they'd written: "Get Well Soon, little Sis. Wish we could be there for you, but we're just about to start a Bowie tour—well, it pays the bills. Can we come stay with you next time we're in the U.K.? Love you lots, D&J."

Mum propped the cards back up on the window ledge with the dozens of others, moving the offensive "camera-up-bottom" one to the back. There was so little space left up there that she had to slot Toby's card inside another one, which irritated me. What was the point of bothering to put it on display if no one could see it? All those supposed well-wishers clogging up my windowsill with cheap sentiment, because they couldn't be bothered to actually visit me in person. (Well, except for my production team, but I didn't think that them shuffling in for ten minutes really counted.)

I made her move the daisy card back into my line of vision.

"No, it won't be nice," I said. "She'll just sit here and torture me by looking and sounding exactly like Sam, and we won't even be able to talk about her. I hope she doesn't come. In fact, I'm glad I'm not getting any visitors. I look like a freak. My life is over. I wish everybody would just go away."

Mum took my hand but I shook her off and looked away. I didn't want her sympathy.

"I heard the nurse mention that Toby was asking after you again," she said casually. "Is that the Toby who sent that card?"

I ignored her and opened my notebook. I'd started writing about my blissful childhood, when Sam and I were first friends, and it had become almost an obsession. It was the one thing that kept me sane, and kept the black dog of my depression in his kennel.

"Who's Toby, Helena dear?" Mum's hopeful tone made my skin crawl with irritation.

"Nobody, Mum. He's just a journalist trying to get a story on me. He says his wife's in Intensive Care, but . . ."

But what? Of course, I knew deep down that Toby's wife really was in a coma somewhere down the corridor. Nobody could be calculating and callous enough to invent a story like that. Not to mention the child. *Me kith Mummy better* echoed in my head, and I suddenly felt a deep and long-overdue wash of shame. Did I really think he'd put Ruby up to that? I remembered Toby quite clearly now, from our one meeting all those years ago. The thing that had most impressed me about him, apart from his disarming smile, was his obvious openness and honesty. I'd really fancied him.

"Well, the flowers he sent you are pretty. And why would he be bothering to write a story on you if his wife is that sick, for pity's sake? I think you're being rather overdramatic, and unfair on the poor man. He's got plenty enough on his plate without you slandering him."

Mum sounded quite cross. I realized she'd probably already gleaned the sad tale of my meeting with Toby from Catriona the nurse and was just fishing to get my point of view. For once I didn't jump down her throat and defend myself. I just nodded miserably.

"Have you even thanked him for the flowers?"

"No," I whispered, feeling about six years old and in disgrace.

Mum tutted and rose to leave, tucking the stiff tortoiseshell handles of her handbag firmly over her forearm. She was clearly enjoying exercising a different emotion with me, not one pulled from the tired old selection grab bag of Pity, Sympathy, Patience, and Understanding, all much overused since my accident. No, today we had Displeasure, and boy, it was a refreshing change for her.

"Well, honey, I'll leave you to your . . . *memoirs*," she said disapprovingly. "I need to get back and ring your father. Heaven knows how he's coping over there on his own. I expect the house has gone even more to rack and ruin. He told me last week that he put dishwasher salt into the salt cellar—and he expected me to be pleased with him for using his initiative! Honestly, he is the limit."

She kissed the top of my head and tried to get a sneaky peek at the writing on my pad. Preempting her, I turned it upside down on my lap so the words weren't visible. Mum was torn between being pleased that I was doing something creative to keep myself occupied, and being absolutely paranoid that she'd been cast in my "memoirs" as Mommie Dearest. We didn't exactly have a very close mother-daughter relationship—not that it was bad, just very distant, in all senses of the word.

After Mum finally left, I tried to get down to work. But being in hospital was not dissimilar to being on a promo tour, waiting ages for room service while an endless succession of people wanted things from you, and I found myself constantly interrupted. There was an orderly asking me to check off what I wanted for dinner from the menu list (although why bother, I thought—it all tastes the same when it's pureed); a nurse wanting to change my dressings; the doctor checking on my skin graft; Rosemary the tea lady; and finally, when my patience was about to snap, my mobile phone rang.

Sighing, I put down the notepad and wriggled laboriously across the mattress toward my locker, to reach the illicitly switched-on phone. Wriggling gradually was less painful than the direct lean-over.

"Yes?" I snapped, holding the phone out of habit to my damaged left ear and wondering why I couldn't hear anything.

"Who is it?"

Through my right ear and over the top of my head I could hear a faint guinea-pig squeak from the receiver, which alerted me to the problem. I transferred the phone to the other side, and the guinea pig turned itself into Justin.

"Oh. It's you," I said unenthusiastically. I was still deeply hurt that he hadn't called or visited.

"H, Jesus, I'm so, so sorry. I can't believe what's happened to you. I came in the ambulance with you, you know. It was a nightmare— paps everywhere, people screaming. I'll never forget the sight of you lying there on the floor with blood coming out of—"

"*If* you don't mind, Jus, I'd rather not know, thanks," I interrupted stiffly. It was too humiliating even to contemplate.

"Listen, baby, I'm totally cut up that I haven't been able to visit you since, you know, but I've been doing PAs and a couple of TVs in South America. I told you I was flying out the day after the UKMAs, didn't I?"

First I'd heard of it. But I gave him the benefit of the doubt—after all, my memory of that night was probably not all that it should have been.

"So why didn't you call me, then?"

There was a brief pause.

"Man, H, I didn't think you'd wanna hear from me. It was all my fault. You wouldn't believe how shitty I feel about it."

He really did sound sincere, and I felt for him.

"Oh, Justin, please. Of course it wasn't your fault—it was my idea, wasn't it? I talked *you* into it. Don't give yourself a hard time. To be honest, I'm more gutted that you haven't been in touch."

"Do you mean that?" I could hear the relief in his voice.

"Of course, you moron."

"So how are you now, then?"

"Still in hospital, but better now that I've had my teeth capped, thanks. I broke both the front ones in different directions and it made me sound like Daffy Duck. And I expect you heard I lost my eye. I'm still deaf in one ear, I've got skin grafts on my face, a ton of stitches, and a broken nose. Oh, and a concussion, obviously." I couldn't face the prospect of more ham-fisted commiserations, so I plowed on. "But that's almost better, and hopefully I'll be going home next week. So when are you next in London?"

"Not for a while now. I'll be doing a bunch of promos in the U.S. for the next two months, and then I'm out on tour. Why don't you fly over for a visit soon?"

"I don't think I'm up to flying. Besides, I've got . . . stuff to do here."

"Oh, right, of course. I forgot you're the top DJ now. Well, duty calls. I'm sure London's hepcats can't stand to have their morning coffee and muffins without your sexy voice telling them what's what."

I didn't have the stomach to tell him I'd lost my job. "We don't eat muffins for breakfast here."

"Eggs and bacon, then. Whatever. Listen, babes, I have to run.

I've got a photo shoot for some Brazilian mag in twenty minutes. Did you get my flowers?"

"Yeah, thanks, Jus. They were lovely. Take care, okay? And don't feel guilty about anything."

"Okay, love you, honey. Get well soon," said Justin, hanging up happily. I knew that I'd be forgotten again in an instant—being Justin Becker was a full-time job, one that didn't leave room for unproductive emotions like guilt and remorse. But that said, he was, like the other two former band members, a good mate and a warm-hearted person, once you scratched beneath the vinyl of the pop star. I was glad that we had at least talked before I got to implement the Plan.

Funny how *his* career hadn't been harmed by allegations of drugs, though.

Justin's suggestion of a visit to the States gave me an idea. I dialed the number of my agent, Ron, and listened to a lengthy answering machine recording inform me that the offices of Pickett Management Services were currently closed, and if I left a message, they'd get back to me pronto.

"Ron, it's Helena. Thanks for the card. I'm still in hospital, but I'm on the mend. I just wanted to tell you that I'm going to go and stay with my folks in New Jersey for a few months, until all the fuss dies down. Geoff Hadleigh's fired me, but I feel like a break from work, anyhow. So please could you keep all my mail and any messages for me until I get back? I don't know exactly when that'll be, but I'll call you. The main thing is to please not tell anyone where I am—just say that I'm away. Thanks. Bye."

That should keep the press off my back, I thought.

Sandie Shaw

(GET YOUR KICKS ON) ROUTE 66

A FEW MONTHS AFTER SAM AND I FIRST MET, I SAW MY FIRST snowstorm. I'd woken up and opened my bedroom curtains to be startled by huge, fat, whirling flakes, bouncing off the glass and bumbling silently down to land on the place where the garden path used to be. And it wasn't just the garden path—everything had been swallowed up: houses, trees, our street, and even, oh no, the spire of Salisbury Cathedral! I ran along the landing in a panic to tell my parents, but as was often the case, their bedroom door was forbiddingly closed.

"Mummy, Daddy, it's snowing, and the spire's gone! Let me in!"

There was a long pause. I rattled the door handle and it opened a fraction and then stopped, which meant that they had flicked across the catch. I caught a glimpse of its skinny upside-down beckoning finger on the other side of the door. A finger whose sole job it was to tell me to go away.

"Pleeease can I come in? I'm scared!"

Then my mother's voice, blanket-heavy and slow, like the snow. The voice she used before she put her makeup on.

"Don't be silly, Helena, the spire hasn't gone. You just can't see it because of the snow. Be a good girl and get yourself some cereal, would you? Put it in your Peter Rabbit bowl, and mind you don't spill the milk. We'll be down soon."

"But why can't I come in?"

This time Dad spoke. "Your mother's terribly tired, Helena. Please just do as she asks and go and have breakfast."

I leaned my head on the door with frustration.

"I *hate* it when you lock the door!" I said, and stomped down the stairs, slapping each banister as I went.

After breakfast, once I'd had a bit of time to get used to the dizzying blur outside the window, I went to stand in the living room to get a better view. I traced the flakes' descent with my finger down the windowpane until my fingertips became numb with cold. I could see my breath and it made me shiver.

I had dressed myself in my favorite cardigan, fuzzy yellow wool. It made me feel like an Easter chick, but even this didn't keep out the cold from the window. The fur of my sleeves stood upright like hairs on gooseflesh, and I felt like the cardie was colder than I was. So I took two steps back into the warmer center of the room to warm us both up.

Eventually the snow-intensified silence became too oppressive, so I gave in to the forbidden game of switching on the big wooden radiogram on the low shelf. One of my favorite things to do was to twiddle the radio's tuning knob and see the green fluorescent needle rush from left to right across the dial, past all the numbers and dots and markings. The language I could make it speak was fascinating; I imagined a country where everyone talked in those strange jumpy fragments of sentences, interspersed with blasts of jazz trumpet, organ, or soprano, and the scratchy hiss and fuzz of static fading in and out, linking words. Perhaps I was even tuning in to God's language.

That day, however, I got a song straight away, a song I recognized because my dad had bought the LP just a few months ago. It was Shelley Beach, my favorite singer! It was a bouncy, jolly sort of song about—well, actually I wasn't quite sure what it was about. Getting your kicks on root 66. I remembered last year's church fete, where the table with the prize-winning vegetables and things had all had numbers on them. Perhaps it was like one of those sideshows where you queued up to throw wet sponges at people who couldn't move, only this was queuing up to kick large vegetables. Which seemed a strange choice of subject for a song. They were usually about kissing and stuff.

I liked Shelley a lot. I imagined she was right there in the room with me, ready to come outside and help Sam and me build a snowman, although she'd need to wrap up a bit warmer. On Dad's record, I remembered her wearing little more than a gold bikini and a crown.

"That was a smashing number for you," said a man when the song finished, "the very lovely Sandie Shaw singing '(Get Your Kicks on) Route 66,' a song from her last record, *The Sandie Shaw Supplement.*"

Through the floor of the bedroom above my head, I heard the muffled thump of a parent getting out of bed, and hastily turned off the radio. Sandie Shaw? I thought. No, he must have got it wrong. That's Shelley Beach.

Dad used to listen to that record all the time, although come to think of it, I hadn't heard it recently. Not since the night that Mum went a bit wirey-lipped and accused Dad of fancying Shelley Beach. I had a quick flick through the records in the LP box, a thick, square green box with a flip-up top, which smelled of dusty paper and sweet vinyl, and sure enough, *The Sandie Shaw Supplement* was missing.

So was her name really Sandie Shaw? I preferred Shelley Beach; I thought it suited her image better. The picture had shown her lolling on a chilly-looking beach. Maybe that was why I'd misremembered her name.

All was quiet, above and below. The snow against the window seemed to press the silence further into the house. The only sound in the room was a clock, ticking robustly on the mantelpiece above the square brick fireplace. Even though I couldn't tell the time properly, I liked to watch the gleaming hands trace their slow path.

I soon got bored. There were none of my toys in there, it was too cold to be by the window, and it was no fun to watch the snow if you couldn't feel its chill. I wondered if it was worth the risk of getting shouted at by going upstairs again. Really, even by their standards, my parents had been up there for ages.

I decided to give it a few more minutes. I noticed that yellow fluff had got onto my tartan kilt and tried to pick it off, frowning with concentration as my small hands grappled with the microscopic fibers. There was too much, so I gave up and stared at my shoes. They felt like part of my body, as if I had shoes instead of feet—actually, they looked similar to my legs: sturdy, scratched, and reddish-brown with mottled white patches. Like my cardigan and myself, my shoes were also cold.

Finally, eventually, I heard my mother tread heavily downstairs in her fluffy mules.

"Mummy!" I cried, running out to meet her and trying to leap into her arms as she stepped off the bottom stair. But her arms stayed by her sides, and she didn't even try to catch me. She was wearing her quilted nylon dressing gown, a garment so shiny that I slipped right down her, landing painfully hard on her foot.

"Ow! Goodness, Helena, must you be so boisterous? You're far too big and heavy for me to carry you these days! Have you had breakfast?"

She opened the front door to take the milk bottles off the step, and a flurry of snow whirled into the hallway, making everything even colder, as if the Ice Queen herself had driven the milk float that morning.

I squeaked and ran into the kitchen. "Don't let it in! Don't let it in!"

Mum followed me, limping slightly, and put the milk bottles on the kitchen counter.

"I asked you a question, dear. Have you had breakfast or not?"

I nodded, still dancing around her as if my surfeit of energy could help boost her lack of it.

"And look, Mummy, I got dressed all by myself, too, shoes and everything."

"So I noticed," she said, rubbing her toe. "You're a good girl, really. I'm sorry Mummy's so tired this morning."

I watched as she stuck the spout of the kettle under the cold tap, filled it up, plonked it on the stove, struck a match, and lit the gas ring. She shivered as the blue flames licked around the kettle's sides, and when she turned around to get a bowl out of the cupboard, her face looked like another square of her dressing gown—taut, shiny, and puffy.

Fattypuff, I thought, making a mental note to ask Sam if she agreed with my diagnosis. We had discussed the strange fluctuations in my mother's girth, and referred to the two extremes as either Fattypuff or Thinifer. I liked Mummy best when she was neither, when she was just in the middle. Then she let me pretend she was my pony, or made biscuits with me, or showed me how to glue strips of paper together into multicolored chains. Her makeup stayed on all day, and she was happy.

"Will you help me make a snowman later, Mummy?"

We weren't into an advanced Fattypuff condition yet, so I was reasonably hopeful of an affirmative answer. But it was not to be.

"Why don't you wait till Sam comes over? I'm sure she'd like to build a snowman with you."

"What about Dad? Will he help us?"

Mum pressed in the silver foil top of one of the milk bottles with her thumb and tried to pour the milk into the flowery milk jug. Nothing happened.

"Oh, for heaven's sake!" Mum said, much more crossly than I thought necessary. "The wretched milk's frozen!"

I heard the sound of the front door opening and then closing again before I had time to run into the hall.

"Where's Daddy gone?" I asked, trying not to think of my father being swallowed up by the snow.

Mum sighed and sat down, as if the milk and I were in some kind of conspiracy against her.

"Nowhere, dear. He just popped down to the shops to pick something up for me from the chemist, that's all. So about this snowman: I'll get you a carrot for his nose if you go and fetch two pieces of coal from the coal scuttle for his eyes. How about that?"

It would have to do. I hoped Sam knew how to construct men out of snow, because I had not the first idea. On cue, there was a scuffling outside the back door, and a timid knock.

I brightened. Mum unbolted the door and admitted a chilly Sam, making her stand on the mat and stamp the snow off her little blue wellies first, before allowing her in properly.

Sam looked like a stuffed toy animal, with numerous layers of coats and woollies, scarves, mitts, elasticized waists, cuffs, and neck bands. Her outer coat was so thick that her arms were forced unnaturally away from her sides at forty-five-degree angles to her body. A red face peered out at me through swathes of nylon parka fur.

"Coming out to play? It's nearly stopped snowing," she chirped at me.

I looked at Mum, and she nodded, as happy to see Sam as I was.

I submitted to the swaddling routine and trotted nervously out into the back garden with Sam, leaving Mum slumped on a stool at the breakfast bar with a steaming cup of black tea.

It was a bit like seeing the ocean for the first time ever—scary to begin with, and then completely exhilarating when you got used to it. I noticed with surprise that despite the chilly flakes on my face, I felt much warmer outside than I had earlier in the sitting room.

I looked at the orange nose and black eyes in my hands.

"Do you know how to do snowmen?"

Sam shook her head. "Like sand castles?"

I shrugged. "Maybe. But we haven't got a spade."

"And it's a bit cold, isn't it, snow?"

Sam pointed at the frost sparkling on a tree branch above our heads.

"Let's do dancing instead, like at a ball. We can pretend that the tree is the chand-*liere*—you know, the big lampshade things they have with candles and stuff."

I had no idea what she was talking about but obligingly dropped my carrot and coal, reached one gloved hand around her waist, and pressed the other woolly mitt against hers. We waltzed clumsily around the garden, trying to step in a fresh patch of snow at every twirl.

"I think Mummy's going Fattypuff again," I said.

Sam nodded knowingly but changed the subject. "Oh, dear. Who are you going to be today? I'm going to be Valerie Singleton."

I considered for a minute as we trod the light fantastic. The garden seemed much bigger when it was all white, with no edges.

"Sandie Shaw, but I call her Shelley Beach. She's a singer, you know. I really like that song she does about church fetes."

Sam nodded again, equally knowingly. "Yes. That's my favorite, too."

We did a few more circuits of the lawn, dancing further and further out until we were almost at next door's fence and our footprints had claimed every bit of pure snow.

Mum opened the back door and stuck her head out. "Keep off my flower beds, you girls, or you'll squash my crocuses!"

MAKING AMENDS

THERE WAS A TAP AT THE DOOR. GRACE, THE NICEST NURSE, STUCK her head in. "Are you up for a visitor, Helena?"

"Who is it?"

"It's Toby Middleton. He's asking to see you."

I hesitated. Time to mend a few bridges. "Okay."

I reached for my dark glasses and hastily smeared a slick of Burt's Bees lip gloss over my chapped and bumpy lips. Funny how there was once a time when I wouldn't let anyone see me without extensive makeup. That all seemed kind of pointless now.

Toby sidled into the room, alone. "Hello," he said nervously.

"Hi," I replied. "Please sit down."

"Thanks. Oh, hey, you aren't lisping! And your teeth look great."

"Thanks."

He sat and waited for the apology we both knew he was due. Inwardly, I commended his courage—a lesser man wouldn't have risked another ear-bashing. But I supposed if your wife was in a coma, you didn't really care about getting abused by a battered old harridan like me.

"Listen, I'm really, really sorry about what I said before. You're not a scumbag or anything, of course you aren't, and thank you so much for the card and the daisies, you really shouldn't have, after I behaved so appallingly. I feel like a total shit, with your wife so ill and stuff. . . . How is she?"

"Still the same, but thanks for asking. I wanted to apologize to you, too. I think we both felt a bit vulnerable that day. I should have been honest with you from the start."

Toby took off his glasses and polished them on his shirt. I noticed his thick, textured wedding ring. Rugged and solid, like him.

I nodded. "It all just got too much for me. I've been so paranoid about the press after that hideous picture of me they got right before the accident. And then when I started to cry like that—I suppose I assumed the worst, that you were going to expose me again—"

"What do you mean, again? That piece I did on you was very complimentary! 'Blue Idea's Green-Eyed Dear'—terrible headline, I know, but it wasn't exactly an exposé."

Toby sounded quite hurt, but when I looked at him, the corners of his mouth were twitching upward.

"No, not that *you'd* expose me again—actually, I quite liked your article, even though my eyes aren't green at all, more swamp-colored really—but that I'd get exposed again. It's all been so humiliating, and I've lost my job, and—oh God, I'm doing it again. Going on about me when you've got such awful problems."

Toby grinned properly. "Well, as Bette Midler said, 'That's enough about me; what do *you* think of me?' Actually, it's quite refreshing to hear someone else's woes. I get sick of talking about mine. Have you really lost your job? What do you do these days? I'm sure I'd know about it if you were in another band."

Somewhat huffy that he wasn't aware of my DJ incarnation, I told him about the New World breakfast show.

"Cool. A DJ! Yes, that figures. I bet you make a brilliant DJ. I don't live in London anymore. We moved to the country so Kate could have a bigger studio—she's a potter—and we don't get New World out in Hampshire. Otherwise I'd definitely have tuned in to your show."

"But I'm not a DJ anymore. At least—oh, well, it's a long story. So why is Kate in hospital here if you live in Hampshire?"

Toby took a deep breath, and I winced at the thought that I was being insensitive.

"Sorry. Listen, you don't have to talk about it if you don't want to. . . ."

"It's fine. It's really quite nice talking to someone who isn't upset about her, too. She had the accident here in London, one night—I didn't even know she was in town. She'd told me that she was going to see someone about a commission in Portsmouth, but I suppose the meeting must have been moved up here. So when they phoned to say there'd been a crash, I didn't believe it could be her.

"Anyway, they moved her to this hospital because it's private—we've always had BUPA, thank God—and it has an ICU and plastic surgery. When she's better she's going to need some work on her face—she's got a major facial fracture, running from her eyebrow down to her jaw. They'll have to put in a titanium staple. . . . It seemed silly to have to move her again when this hospital's so good, so Ruby and I have been staying with my sister Lulu in Fulham. That's where Ruby is today."

I nodded sympathetically, my face aching at the memory of my own recent plastic surgery. My injuries suddenly felt trivial in comparison—a few dozen stitches, a couple of strips of skin relocated from thigh to face. At least I had had no truck with titanium staples, whatever the hell they might be.

"So are you still a journalist?" I tried not to spit when I said the word.

Toby noticed and took me to task. "Hey, there's a bit of a difference between a journalist on the *Melody Maker* and a tabloid hack, you know. Don't tar us all with the same brush. Anyway, no, I'm not. I never made very much money from my writing, so I jacked it in and eventually set up my own Internet music company. It means I can work from home and be close to Ruby and Kate—well, Ruby, anyhow. . . . Kate hasn't been around much recently—she's taken on quite a few big commissions, and organizing those seems to take more time than actually making the pots. God knows what's going to happen with them now. . . ."

He stood up abruptly. "I really should go and see Kate. I just wanted to check that you're okay and feeling better."

He rammed his hands into his jeans pockets as if he thought I might grab them and beg him to stay.

"Thanks," I said. I had been wondering if I dared ask him to come again, but his gesture decided me against it. Besides, he had enough on his plate.

Toby opened the door and looked back toward my bed. All of a sudden he seemed fascinated by the jug of water on top of my locker.

"Um . . . would it be okay if I popped back again tomorrow? It's, you know, really nice to have a conversation with someone when I come and visit Kate. It gets quite hard to, er, just sit and talk to a person who doesn't reply. Would you mind?"

"No," I said. "I wouldn't mind."

Glen Campbell
WICHITA LINEMAN

THE HEL-SAM BOX OF IMPORTANT STUFF!
KEEP OUT!! UNLESS YOU ARE
HELENA JANE NICHOLLS OR SAMANTHA GRANT!!

In the event of the untiemally death of either of us,
this box is to go immidiatally to the other one's house and stay there.
No-one else is ever, ever, allowed to look inside.
It's all completely Top Secret.

I sat back on my heels and admired my handiwork, purple felt-pen blotches all over my hands. Sam was lying on her stomach next to me, laboriously gluing shiny paper flowers onto an old hat box, her tongue sticking out of the side of her mouth.

"What do you think?" I waved the piece of card at her.

"Needs some glitter," Sam replied.

"Give us the glue, then." I grabbed it and squeezed twirls of Bostik around the edges of my cardboard notice. I shook generous quantities of silver glitter over an area approximately sixteen square feet, some of which managed to land on the intended target.

"Watch it!" said Sam crossly as I frosted her flowers, the whole hat box, our hands and faces, and the carpet. "Your mum will kill us if she sees the mess in here."

We were illicitly camped out in my parents' bedroom, because later that day a new, extra-specially comfortable bed was going to be delivered, to help Mum sleep better. It was to be a surprise for her from Dad, who had dismantled the old one and gone to take it to the dump. Its departure had left a brighter, lusher, thicker square of blue carpet, protected from years of harsh sunlight by the darkness of the bed's cool underbelly. Impossible for us not to play on.

"This is our magic carpet, to fly us away," I'd said as we crept into the room.

We had adopted Ali Baba positions, kneeling up, arms folded across horizontally, imagining the square slowly lifting up and out the window, carrying us to a place where Dylan's Chinese burns and homework didn't exist.

However, the carpet's stubborn refusal to levitate eventually became a little disappointing, so we had transformed it into a stage instead, and choreographed a *Guys and Dolls* dance routine to show my mother on her return from the doctor's, a sort of "Welcome New Bed" ceremony.

We were all set: hair blow-dried into monster flicks; as many plastic necklaces as we could find in Mum's jewelry box; me, a Guy, sporting Dad's bright green best shirt, its flared collar flapping around my neck like Dumbo's ears; Sam wearing a matching (or as close as we could get) chartreuse towel round her waist as a skirt. She always got to be the Doll because she was more petite. (Actually, I wasn't much of a fan of *Guys and Dolls*, but I went along with it, because Sam would have to do the Carl Douglas "Kung Fu Fighting" routine with me later.)

But ages had passed, and still we hadn't heard the sound of Mum's key in the lock. So to while away the time, we decided to decorate the hat box, which had been designated the Hel-Sam Box of Important Stuff.

"Can I keep it at my house?" Sam asked when I had finally succeeded in sticking the decorated label on its lid.

"Okay. For a while." I was frantically trying to brush glue and glitter off the sleeve of Dad's shirt. By this stage I was quite keen to be rid of the evidence. "I'd better sweep this carpet—stay there, I'll be back in a minute."

I was just galloping down the stairs to retrieve the carpet-sweeper when the front door began to open. I could tell immediately, before Mum had even entered the house, how uptight she was—it was a Thinifer period, and I had developed a kind of sixth sense about the state of her moods.

"Hello, Mummy, come and see—me and Sam have got a dance for you," I said nervously, helping her out of her swing coat.

"Sam and I," Mum corrected automatically. Several beads of sweat had managed to struggle through the thick blanket of face powder covering her forehead, and she stopped in front of the hall mirror to pat them away with a tissue.

"And we've decorated the hat box you gave us. It's going to be the Hel-Sam Box of Important Stuff. We're not watching telly, like you said. We're amusing ourselves."

I took my mother's hand and tried to drag her upstairs, and for the first time she noticed my appearance.

"Helena—what *on earth* are you wearing? And what's that all over the sleeves? Felt pen? And glue? You're covered with glitter! How could you be so naughty and thoughtless, to do gluing in Daddy's best shirt!"

My head drooped. "But I had to wear it; it's part of your surprise," I said in a small voice. "Come and see."

I was miserably aware that Mum was working herself up into a full Thinifer rage. Her eyes were bugging out, and a drop of the escaping sweat on her forehead was making a bid for freedom down the side of her cheek.

"For heaven's sake, Helena!" she snapped. "I told you and Sam to play quietly until I came back. I did not tell you to root through your father's wardrobe and then get his best shirt all mucky. And if there's that much glitter on you, what sort of state is your bedroom floor in, might I ask?"

"It's perfectly clean," I said truthfully, my heart sinking further. Mum bustled past me and up the stairs.

"Good. I'm sorry, Helena, but I'm too tired to watch you do anything at the moment. I'm going for a lie down in my . . . *Oh!*"

I raced up after her, to find Sam standing in the middle of my parents' bedless room, clad in necklaces and a green towel, hair in a flick that could put your eye out—but thankfully with no incriminating signs of the box, glue, felt-tip pens, or colored paper. Even more fortunately, the sun had gone behind a cloud, making the glitter in the carpet invisible.

"What have you done with the *bed*?" screeched my mother, as if Sam and I had personally carried it, iron bedstead, mattress, and all, down the stairs and into the coal shed.

"Nothing," we chorused.

I didn't want to let out the secret, but some explanation was obviously required.

"You're getting a new bed. It's a surprise from Daddy," I admitted reluctantly.

"It certainly is," said Mum, tight-lipped. "Now just go away, you two, out from under my feet. Put that towel back in the airing cupboard, and that shirt'll have to be washed. If the glue doesn't come off it, you'll be buying Daddy a new one from your pocket money. And who gave you permission to put on my necklaces and use my curling tongs? *Go!*"

Sam shot out of the room, but I lingered for a moment. "But why can't we do our dance for you, Mummy?"

She flopped down on the vanity stool in front of her dressing table and fanned herself with a copy of last week's *Radio Times,* which she'd picked out of the wastepaper basket for that purpose.

"I'm sorry, love," she said, making an effort. My mother always seemed to be apologizing to me. "Maybe later, eh?"

I lost my temper. Hot tears of frustration burst out of my eyes, and I stamped my foot on the magic carpet. "You're always sorry, and you're always telling me to go away! Well, one of these days I'll go and I won't come back! In fact, I'm going to go and live at the Grants'—Mrs. *Grant* never tells me to go away! In *fact,* I wish Mrs. Grant was my mother instead of you. So there!"

I ripped off the necklaces and the gluey green shirt, just catching Mum's stricken, defeated look as I flounced out of the room.

Sam was waiting for me at the bottom of the stairs. "Come on, Augenbrau, let's go to my place," she said sympathetically, putting an arm around my neck as we went through the back gate and toward the Prince of Wales.

Augenbrau was one of our many code names for each other. It was usually accompanied by sweeping a forefinger slowly across one's eyebrow while looking shiftily from right to left, and could be used in any language, although it sounded best in German. We already knew the word for *eyebrow* in about six different languages.

Raking a glittery hand across my eyes and sniffing unattractively,

I said in a tremulous voice, "Where's the Hel-Sam box? And how did you hide all the bits of felt and glue and stuff?"

"It's all in your room. I swept up most of the glitter with your mum's hairbrush," Sam said sheepishly. "As long as she doesn't want to do her hair until you've had a chance to clean the brush a bit, we should be all right."

I smiled at her, ruefully giving the Sign of the Eyebrow to show my gratitude.

"Thanks. You're one hell of an eyebrow, girl."

Arriving at the pub, we cut through the bar. Mr. Grant looked up from wiping beer mugs to give us a cheery wave as we headed up the stairs. Dylan was sitting at the kitchen table when we arrived, leafing through the pages of *Shoot!* magazine and picking his nose. "What's the matter with you, then, fatso?" he said to me without looking up.

"Get lost, moron," I retorted as we passed through the kitchen in search of Mrs. Grant. She was in the living room, ironing shirts and dancing around to the Jackson 5 on the tinny transistor that dangled by its plastic handle from the doorknob. "'*Oh no, no no-oo no, never can say good-byeeee,*'" she warbled to herself. Fascinated, we watched her fluorescent polyester-clad hips shimmying to and fro, until she spotted us in the doorway and wiggled to a halt.

"Oh, hello, girls! What are you up to?" she asked in a cheerful voice. Unlike my own mother, Mrs. Grant always seemed to be in a good mood.

"Helena's had an argument with her mum because her dad's taken the bed and she wouldn't let us do our dance for her and she's all cross and Thinifer," gabbled Sam.

"I can't do anything right. I don't think Mummy loves me," I said dramatically, making my eyes tear up again with self-pity.

Mrs. Grant smiled faintly and propped the iron up on its base. She leaned across the ironing board to talk to me, the contours of her breasts puffing out sympathetically across its scorched surface. "Listen, sweetheart. Your mummy loves you very much. I think she just gets tired a lot of the time, doesn't she?"

"But why?" I asked. "*You* don't."

She laughed. "Oh, I do. It goes with the territory. Maybe not quite as tired as Mummy, though. Just try and be a good girl for her—I think that's all you can do, really. She often doesn't feel well, and it's very hard to be jolly when you're poorly, isn't it?"

"But Mum," Sam joined in. "Mrs. Nicholls is really scary when she's cross! Even more scary than the witch in *Pufnstuf*!"

Mrs. Grant gave her a look, and picked up the iron again to attack a recalcitrant crease in one of Mr. Grant's sleeves. "Don't worry about it, Helena, love. Why not do something extra-nice for her later? Make her one of your super cards or something."

"All right," I said, feeling fobbed off. "Thank you, Mrs. Grant."

"Oh, good gracious! How many times have I told you to call me Cynthia?"

Many times, it was true—but I just could never bring myself to call a parent by her Christian name. Somehow it didn't seem right. I loved that she always asked me to, though. It made me feel very grown-up.

Just then a different song came on the radio. Mrs. Grant immediately turned up the volume. "Listen, girls, it's the Wichita Lineman!" she said. "I love Glen Campbell!"

Sam rolled her eyes and looked bored, but I began to listen. It was a bit confusing: Glen needed me more than wanted me, wanted me for all time—but what did that have to do with tennis?

"Um, Mrs. Gra—er, *Cyth*-nia, is Wichita like Wimbledon, you know, where they have the tennis tournaments?"

I pictured Glen as a lanky thirteen-year-old dressed in a purple shirt and green shorts, crouched at the side of a tennis court, poised to run out after stray balls. Perhaps he was in love with Billie Jean King, and that was who he was singing about, although he did sound a bit old to be a linesman. . . .

Mrs. Grant looked askance at me. "I don't think so, poppet. It's just a place in the middle of America."

It was no clearer to me than Root 66 had been three years earlier, but the tender sentiment of the song sent a sudden wave of emotion funneling up inside me, and I began to cry again, for real this time.

Mrs. Grant seemed concerned. "Aaah—come here, duckling, and give me a hug!"

She came out from behind the ironing board and gathered me into her arms, bracelets jingling. She smelled of Chanel No. 5. I knew that's what it was because Sam and I had often sneaked into her bedroom for an illicit squirt while she was working in the bar downstairs.

I buried my face in her generous bosom and wept. Right then I really did wish she was my mother.

RUBY'S TOES

"Toby," I said, next time he came in. "Do you feel sorry for me?"

Toby looked surprised. "Of course," he replied.

"Well, I don't want your damn pity." I looked away from him. I had the distinct feeling that he was rolling his eyes. At least he had two to roll.

"*You* feel sorry for yourself, don't you?" he said. "I don't see why everyone else shouldn't, too. If you don't want me to visit you anymore, just say so."

We sat in huffy silence for a minute. Then he spoke again. "Ruby said good-bye to all her toes this morning, individually, before they went into her socks."

I was determined not to smile. What difference was that going to make to me? Perhaps it would be better for him not to come again. I had masses of work to do on my manuscript, and Mum's visits were more than enough distraction.

"Listen, Helena. I know what you mean. I get that, too, you know. That look in people's eyes when they talk to me—'Oh, that poor, poor man, wife in a coma and a toddler to look after.' It's the same sort of thing, and it's a nightmare. But you've got to keep remembering that they do care, most of them, and are genuinely horrified that you're having to face something so awful."

My lip trembled. "But what happens when I leave here and go home? Then it's just going to be weeks of photographers trying to stick lenses in my face, jumping out at me from behind bushes, that kind of thing. The whole country is going to pity me. I don't think I can stand that."

Toby reached over and picked up my hand. "You're strong,

Helena. You've got through so much. You can get over this, too. 'Over This,' right?"

I groaned. "Over This" was the title of the song I'd written for Sam when she was first ill with leukemia. It later became a huge hit for Blue Idea.

"You asked me about that song in your interview, didn't you?"

Toby laughed. "Yeah. I was terrified you were going to break down and cry, or punch me, or something, but you were strong then, too. I was really pleased it went so well. Best interview I ever did, actually."

"Really?" I realized that he was stroking my hand in a—well, a *caressing* sort of way. The more I concentrated, the more sexual it felt, as he rubbed tiny circles and sweeping streaks up the inside of my thumb, and began to feel the little web of skin between each of my fingers. To my amazement, I felt like I was getting pink in all kinds of places.

The door swung open and my mother appeared, hidden behind a large box and a bulging bag of fruit from Waitrose.

"I've brought in your juicer, Helena. Vitamin C is terribly good for the healing process, you know, and you don't get enough. That tiddly little glass of orange they give you at breakfast is just—oh!"

She nearly dropped the juicer when she saw Toby and me. I snatched my hand away immediately, but it was too late.

"Hello!" said Mum, in a very Leslie Phillips voice, delight written all over her face. She strode purposely toward Toby, in a manner not unlike a charging rhinoceros, and he shrank back slightly.

"Eve Nicholls, Helena's mother. And you are?"

Toby stood up manfully and shook her outstretched hand. "Pleased to meet you, Mrs. Nicholls, I'm Toby Middleton."

"Well, I must say, Helena's kept you very quiet. Have you only just heard about her accident? Not that it matters now, anyway, does it? The main thing is that you're here. So, when did you two meet?"

I moaned. This day was getting worse by the minute. "Mum, Toby's not my boyfriend. We met here, the other week, although we knew each other a bit from ages ago. His wife's in Intensive Care in a coma."

Mum opted to cover up her embarrassment with censure. "Oh,

my Lord! So you're the guy whose poor, poor wife is unconscious! How dreadful for her. Well, we mustn't keep you, I'm sure she'll be wondering where you are. They do say that people in comas understand a lot more than we give them credit for, don't they?"

Toby looked at his watch. "Actually, I came a little early to have a chat with Helena, so Kate won't be missing me yet, but I suppose I'd better be getting on. Very nice to meet you, Mrs. Nicholls. I hope we meet again. Bye, Helena. See you tomorrow."

I waved feebly, wondering how soon I could get Mum booked on a flight back to Freehold. Really, enough was enough. Even though her visits were now down to an hour or two each day, her presence seemed to hover around me constantly, like a sort of knitting ectoplasm. It had been quite nice having her there at the beginning, but now she was bored rigid and worried about Dad at home on his own, and I just wanted to get on with my manuscript. We had spent more time together since the accident than in the last fifteen years put together, and the strain was beginning to tell on us both.

Mum began to unpack the juice extractor. "It's too bad," she said thoughtfully. "He seemed so nice, but there he was, taking advantage of you in your vulnerable state, and practically cheating on his poor comatose wife. Men! You watch yourself with that one, Helena."

SUNDAY GIRL

MY FATHER WAS "SOMETHING IMPORTANT IN COMPUTERS," according to my mother, although she, like most other people in 1980, had only the haziest notion of what computers actually did. The company he worked for in Salisbury was owned by a giant U.S. corporation, the top dogs of which had decided to reward him with a huge promotion and a sub-company of his own to run—in Freehold, New Jersey. America.

"I'll have to talk it over with the family," he'd said when he got the news. "It's a very big step."

He broke it to my mother at dinner that night, as she was ladling out the macaroni and cheese.

"No," Mum said, "absolutely not." She slammed the plate down in front of him, and a yellow curl of macaroni detached itself, sliding onto his lap.

I looked up, surprised. I hadn't even been listening to what he'd said, since I was planning in my head what to wear to Melanie Welling's fourteenth birthday party the following night. Melanie was a friend of ours from school, and her uncle was, allegedly, a member of Madness. Even more thrillingly, the word on the lacrosse field was that said uncle would be at the party.

"What?" I said, wondering if Mum would let me wear her Marks & Spencer pale blue eye shadow. It had this really nice iridescence to it. . . .

Dad repeated his news while scraping the macaroni off his trouser leg with his knife.

"NO!" I screamed, all thoughts of makeup and pop stars instantly flying out of the window.

"You don't know what this means to me," he pleaded.

Mum sat down, very suddenly. "Well, I know what it means to me,

George. It means good-bye to all my friends, good-bye to my nice house, good-bye to Salisbury. . . ."

I couldn't say anything further; terror had seized my throat and was holding it closed. I stared hard at the steaming bowl of peas in the center of the table. Macaroni and cheese and peas was my favorite meal, but I was not hungry anymore.

"Eve, Helena, listen. We'll have an even nicer house, and you'll make new friends. And we'll have so much more money, I'm sure we'll be able to afford regular visits back here."

"Forget it, I like this house, these friends. I'm sorry, George. . . ."

And so the debate continued, pleas and retorts, back and forth from one to another. I followed them with my eyes, rooting silently and fearfully for my mother, as if they were playing a tennis match on whose outcome my life depended. The steam from the untouched peas gradually dwindled down to nothing, and they took on a dull glazed appearance. They looked as shocked as I felt.

Eventually my mother's defenses began to crumble. "I do know how hard you've worked for this, George, really I do. How long did you say it would it be for?"

With absolute horror, I watched her edge into capitulation.

"Five years firm, then contract renewable by mutual agreement."

"Weeell, I suppose now is as good a time as any, before Helena starts her O-level courses. And it would be lovely to have a big comfortable house. How much more money did you say you'd get?"

I could almost see the dollar signs in my mother's eyes. It was as good as over. I pushed away my chair and stormed out of the room.

Two weeks later our house was on the market. I was enrolled by telephone in a totally foreign "high" school, whatever that meant. Our airline tickets were purchased. We were leaving in three weeks' time. Sam and I had not been out of each other's sight for more than a couple of hours since the bombshell dropped. We hated the world.

* * *

There were three moving men, all dressed in identical royal blue boilersuits with their company logo on the breast pocket: *Shipley's Ships Safely*. Huge sheets of off-white paper lay around everywhere, and the sound of scrunching and heavy breathing hung in the air as the men wrapped, packed, lifted, carried.

Sam and I drifted despondently from room to room; as soon as the men had cleared enough space, we sat down back-to-back in the middle of the carpet, and remained there until that room had been emptied around us. And so on to the next room. I had to do this, otherwise I wouldn't have believed that we were actually leaving. Up to this point I had not. It had been like a bad dream and I had closed my ears to all talk of real estate, junior and senior high schools, Social Security numbers, work visas. This was what made it real, seeing our possessions wrapped up and carried away, and much as I hated it, part of me realized it was important to accept it.

At first the moving men took our presence as a sign that we were interested in them, and tried to engage us in friendly banter. When they were met with stony silences or abrupt monosyllables, they soon began to mutter about us being in the way. There was a young, jovial Irish one with huge ears, who glanced surreptitiously at Sam's legs more often than he probably should have done; a balding, middle-aged, barrel-chested one who sighed deeply every time he lifted up a box; and an officious gray-haired one with a clipboard, who was obviously the boss. When they went outside for a tea break with their thermos flasks and Dunhill Extras, Sam picked up the clipboard and inspected the list attached to it: an inventory of the Nicholls.

56—Coffee table (SITTING ROOM)
57—Box—assorted ornaments and vase (S. ROOM)
58—Sofa (DITTO)
59—Radio (DITTO)

Peering at this over her shoulder, I lifted the chewed stub of pencil that was dangling from the board by a grubby piece of frayed string, and with a couple of deft pencil strokes I changed the 57 to a 52, the 59 to a 69, and inserted an H between the S and the I of SIT-TING ROOM. Before the men came back, we hastily returned the clipboard to its resting place on top of a crate, sniggering guiltily.

I had been more rebellious of late, with Sam my willing partner, although we hadn't gotten into any serious trouble. My parents were not behaving rationally by taking me away from my home, this place I'd lived my whole life, so why should I?

But even though she seemed to be veering toward a Fattypuff period of lethargy and depression, my mother had been remarkably understanding about our little protestations. She didn't even say "Serves you right" when we stole Dad's razor from the bathroom and I shaved off the bit of hair in front of my left ear. It grew back as a frighteningly bristly sideburn, and I was deeply traumatized. All the same, I felt grateful that she'd never discovered us behind the garage, spluttering and coughing over a bent and creased-up Marlboro cigarette, which we'd finagled from the floor of the Prince of Wales one afternoon.

On moving day, however, Mum gave up trying to get us out from under the men's feet. She was too distracted, stage-managing Dad in getting everything finalized: the gas turned off, the fridge defrosted, the curtains unhooked.

So we sat, watched more boxes go, stayed in the empty space for a while, moved to the next room, sat again. It was so strange seeing all the rooms with no furniture or pictures, like catching a shameful glimpse of somebody's father naked. Walls loomed down on us, blank and shabby-looking, darker squares where paintings had hung.

Once all the rooms were empty, we sat side by side on the stairs.

"Are you sure you don't want to go round to Melanie's house for a bit?" Sam said. "Bridget and Jo were going over this afternoon to look at the program from The Specials concert Mel went to with her brother."

"No thanks," I said crossly. "I've already said good-bye to them. This is hard enough as it is."

"Funny how Melanie's uncle turned out not to be in Madness at all, wasn't it?" said Sam.

"Mmm. Not much of a surprise, though. She's such a fibber. Good fun, but . . ."

I paused, thinking of my other school friends, the ones who Sam would now inevitably get much closer to. I found I didn't wish to talk about them anymore.

"Don't forget about me, will you?" I said abruptly.

My father came down the hallway, carrying golf clubs. "Not getting in the way, I hope, are you, girls? Helena, don't you have things to do?"

"No. My case is all packed. We're not in the way."

"Jolly good, jolly good. Almost time for lunch," he muttered absently. "Now, where did I put my nine iron?"

Sam patted my shoulder, waiting till Dad had gone before answering me. "Don't be daft. How could I possibly forget my best friend?"

We sat in silence again, both of us choked.

"Are you still all right about me keeping the Hel-Sam box?" Sam asked eventually.

"S'pose so. It's a good thing there isn't much in there yet. You'll need the space to keep all my letters."

"But where are you going to put *my* letters to *you*?" Sam wailed, and she suddenly burst into tears. I couldn't comfort her.

Mum called us down for lunch: cheese and pickle sandwiches, Marks & Spencer pork pies, a six-pack of crisps, and orange squash. We had to eat in the garden off paper plates because everything from the kitchen and dining room had been packed up, so Sam and I lolled on a hairy tartan travel rug, sniffling and flicking ants off each other's thighs, while my parents sat on sherbet-striped picnic chairs.

Mum and Dad had linked fingers with each other across the red plastic arms of their chairs and were eating with their free outside hands. Emotions were beginning to run high all round.

"Oh, George," said my mother, surveying her rosebushes, "I'll miss this garden so much."

There was a quiver in her voice, so she took a hasty slurp of squash out of a plastic cup to hide it.

"Our new house will have a lovely garden, too, you'll see. We might even be able to afford someone to come in and mow the lawn," said Dad soothingly, squeezing her hand.

"They don't call them gardens in America. They call them yards," Sam mused thickly.

I was irritated. "Well, that's ridiculous! How can a yard have grass and flowers and stuff? A yard is concrete!"

"Don't yell at me. It's not my fault. I'm just telling you," Sam snapped back.

"I wasn't yelling. I just don't think it makes sense."

"Girls! Simmer down." My mother had recovered her composure. "If you've finished your lunch, throw your plates and cups in the outside bin."

"Can I go over and say good-bye to the Grants, please?"

"Yes, dear, if you've packed. We have to leave in about an hour, so don't be long."

An hour! I couldn't bear it. I trailed miserably down the garden path behind Sam, who was neatly rolling up her paper plate and stuffing it into her cup. I looked around the garden, at the wiry grass creeping up between the paving stones, the apple tree, the little pond. I knew I would miss it as much as my mother would. A sparrow hopped across the lawn in front of me. Did they have sparrows in America? I wondered, already nostalgic.

Sam turned round when she reached the gate. "Come on, hurry up, Augenbrau," she said. "I've got a present for you."

"Here," she said, once we were in her bedroom above the pub. She thrust an album at me: Blondie, *Parallel Lines*.

I took it, speechless for a moment. "Sam—not your Blondie record! That's your favorite!"

"I want you to have it," she said bravely. "I want you to have something of mine that I really, really like, because that makes it a better present."

"Thanks," I said, thinking fast. "I've got something for you, too."

I undid the seed pearl necklace Mum and Dad had given me for my twelfth birthday and put it around Sam's neck.

"This is for you because it looks like the one Debbie Harry is wearing on the record sleeve. If you put it on with your mum's white petticoat, those high-heeled slippers of hers, and a little bandage tied round the middle of your arm, you'll look the spit of her. Well, at least you would if you had blond hair."

Sam was touched and awestruck, by both the gift and the comparison. We were both desperate to have eyes as incredible and cheekbones as pointy as Debbie's.

"Really? Your necklace? Didn't your parents give you that?"

"Yes," I said nobly. "But, like you said, it's the more personal things that make the best presents. Just don't wear it when you come and stay with me in America. Have we got time to listen to the record once more?"

I went over to the stereo and plopped the album onto the turntable. Sam's record player was the coolest I'd ever seen: It played both sides of an LP without you having to get up and turn it over manually. Its needle was on an arm that, when side A finished, skimmed across the surface of the vinyl, turned a laborious and creaky 180-degree angle, and played the B side, upside down.

So we closed an era with *Parallel Lines,* summoning up the emotional reserves to dance around Sam's bedroom for one last time, in a New-Wave, imaginary-microphone kind of rite of passage. But we were just going through the motions. It wasn't any fun.

"Do you really think I look like Blondie?" asked Sam as we pouted halfheartedly in front of the mirror to "Sunday Girl."

"I've told you before, Sam, Blondie's the band, not the singer. And yes, you could pass as her little sister."

I sighed. Much as I, too, wanted to look like Debbie, I knew that in reality I bore a closer resemblance to Velma from Scooby Doo. I wasn't at all sure if I even possessed cheekbones. Sam picked up on my train of thought.

"You know what? If your hair was a bit longer, I think you'd look quite a lot like Kate Bush," she remarked kindly.

Mrs. Grant knocked on the bedroom door. "Helena, your mother's on the telephone. She asked me to tell you to come home straightaway. The taxi's there already."

Sam turned off the record in the middle of "Sunday Girl," and I felt as if all the music in the whole world had stopped, forever. I had a sudden childish desire to run into Sam's wardrobe and hide there among all her clothes, clothes that weren't being ripped off their hangers and crushed into packing cases to be carried halfway round the world. All the blouses that I'd borrowed; all the jeans that I couldn't fit into. Her Olivia Newton-John nightie, which was so staticky that it could power a small generator. The shirt she'd worn when Martin Trubshaw tried to kiss her. The school skirt with the wonky hem that we'd taken up ourselves. The thick bottle-green gym knickers that she'd still have to endure and I wouldn't. I thought I'd even miss those hideous knickers.

I felt myself crumple up from the inside.

Mrs. Grant hugged me, stroking my hair and pinching my cheek gently, as if I were six years old. "Oh, Helena, love! What are we going to do without you? Sam is going to be a right old misery-guts, I bet! Sam, please tell me you won't start moping round here sulking all day, like that brother of yours."

Sam managed a wavery smile and made a face.

"Don't worry, girls, a little ocean between you won't ruin your friendship. It would take a lot more than that. I wouldn't mind betting you'll be back before you know it, Helena. You'll keep in touch, and time will fly by, you'll see."

"Thank you, um, C-C-C-Cynthia." As usual, her name wouldn't come out without a struggle, and I felt foolish and emotional.

Sam took my hand and we all walked back downstairs in silence.

Mrs. Grant gave me a final hug and kiss at the door. "Well, I'd better get back to the bottling up. Mind how you go, sweetheart, and we'll see you soon, okay?"

Mr. Grant flapped his tea towel at me and said, "Look after yourself, love—keep in touch," to which I responded with a tiny smile and a sad little wave.

I couldn't remember ever feeling this bad in my life.

Back at the house, everything was gone. Only our bulging suitcases sat in the hallway, lined up like fat policemen on parade. My mother was leaning exhaustedly against the kitchen counter, peering into an open compact, primping up her hair and powdering her nose.

"Oh, good—there you are, Helena. I think we're almost ready, so you and Sam should say your farewells. The taxi's already here, so make it as quick as you can, dear. Heavens, look at me—I'm worn out! This moving business certainly is tiring." She snapped the compact shut and put it back into her cavernous patent-leather handbag.

Sam and I went upstairs, to the room that had been my bedroom since I was a baby, and would probably be some other girl's bedroom within the next couple of months. We sat down cross-legged in the middle of the floor, and I stared at the faint Blu-Tack marks on the wall where my John Travolta posters had stuck.

The wallpaper in my room was comprised of thousands of tiny air-filled pockets, as though the walls were papered with yellow-painted bubble wrap. I used to deflate these pockets by pressing them with my fingertips—the wall all around where my pillow had been, in the radius of the length of a child's arms, was an inverted sweep of pressed-in paper bubbles, like grass that gets flattened from being picnicked on. I had a sudden urge to pop a few last ones, for old times' sake.

Neither of us could speak for a while. "Don't forget me, either, will you," Sam said eventually.

The hinges of my jaw were aching so painfully from the effort of not crying that I could hardly reply. "Now you're being daft." I had a sudden thought. "Do you think we're too old to cut our thumbs and mingle our blood in a friendship pact or something?"

"Yeah," said Sam, wrinkling up her nose. "Definitely too old. Besides, it would hurt."

I was relieved. I hadn't much liked the idea, either, but it seemed appropriate. "Okay. Well, I'll write to you all the time, and we'll see each other for holidays, and . . ."

My voice cracked, and I couldn't hold back the sobs any longer. This set Sam off again, too, and we wrapped our arms around each other, rocking back and forth in our misery. We were interrupted by my mother's heavy tread on the stairs.

"Oh, you poor dears!" she said when she saw us. "I'm sorry, the taxi's here. We've got to go." She came over and knelt down beside us, putting an arm around each of our shoulders. I breathed in her distinctive smell, lipstick and wool. Sam rested her head against Mum and cried even harder. She let us stay like that for another minute or so, then pulled a pack of paper tissues from her pocket, giving us each one.

"Come on now, have a good blow. This isn't easy for any of us," she said, standing up and pulling us gently to our feet. We blew our noses, wiped the tears off our faces, and traipsed reluctantly out of the house.

Dad was in the front garden smoking a pipe, having finished loading the cases into the boot of the taxi. He came over and gave Sam a hug when we appeared at the door, which prompted fresh floods. The taxi driver, elbow out of the window, drummed his fingers impatiently on the roof of his car as Mum fussed around with keys and passports and plane tickets.

Finally we were all set, and Mum and I climbed into the backseat of the car, Dad in the front. Sam was standing on the bottom bar of the iron front gate, swinging backward and forward, crying.

As the taxi pulled away, I twisted around to look at her out of the window. She raised a forefinger to her face and traced her eyebrow with it. *"You're one helluvan eyebrow, girl!"* she yelled suddenly.

The car turned the corner at the end of our street and she disappeared from view.

My mother looked at me, a puzzled expression on her face. "One hell of a *what*, did she say?"

I wept ceaselessly all the way up the M3, all the way through dinner that night in a hotel near Heathrow Airport, and halfway across the Atlantic the next day.

FRIENDS

TOBY CAME TO SEE ME AGAIN THE NEXT DAY, CARRYING TWO STYRO-foam cups of tea.

"I checked that the coast was clear. Want to come and sit in the garden?" He offered me his forearm.

I was relieved to see him. "God, I thought you might not dare to come back after meeting my mother. I'm really sorry about that, by the way."

"Oh, don't worry, your mother's fine. It's you I'm scared of. Are you coming, then, or what?"

I laughed and then stopped, not entirely sure that he was joking. "Okay. Let me just get my disguise on first."

I donned my dark glasses and a long blond wig that I'd made Mum bring in from home. It was an Abba wig from a fancy dress party Sam and I went to years ago—she'd worn the matching brunette wig. I wondered what had happened to it.

Toby chuckled when he saw me.

"Wow! 'Voulez-Vous'?"

Yes, please, I thought. "How did you know it's from an Abba costume?" I said instead.

"Come on—all straight blond wigs are Abba wigs, aren't they?"

We walked slowly along the corridor and took the lift up to the hospital's little roof garden. It was lovely to see nothing but shrubs and sky, and to feel warm air on my stitches.

"Is your mum always that, um, keen to meet your friends?" Toby asked as we sat down on a wooden bench.

"Basically, yes—the male ones, anyway. She's just desperate to get me hitched. She's already been hopeful that I'll get something together with the physio, the shrink, or the surgeon. It's so embarrassing."

"Don't worry," Toby said. "Mothers will be mothers. So haven't you ever been married?"

I took a slurp of tea. "No. I almost came close to it once—quite recently, actually. But thank God I saw the light. Vinnie was a serial-philandering, commitment-phobic, dishonest asshole."

Toby laughed. "So you're obviously still fond of him, then."

I managed a smile, a rare reaction to the mention of Vinnie's name. But I didn't want Toby to think I was a freak for never having been married. "I know, mad, isn't it. I picked a right dud. Of course, I had loads of, like, casual boyfriends and stuff, when I was in the band—no shortage of offers—but we were on the road for so long, it seemed a bit pointless having long-distance relationships. We just had no time to ourselves. And men did sometimes try and take advantage. I suppose I never really wised up to their little tricks. . . ."

I trailed off awkwardly, but Toby didn't seem to mind my slagging off his gender. I changed the subject. "How long have you been married, then?"

"Five years," Toby replied. "We were together for four years before that, too."

"So Kate wasn't the girl you were with when we met before, after that interview?" I asked cautiously, remembering the silly slapper who'd been all over Justin.

Toby laughed hollowly. "Thank God, no. That was Lorraine. My first nightmare relationship."

"What happened?" I wondered if "first nightmare relationship" meant "first of many nightmares" or "first relationship, which just happened to be a nightmare."

"I bought a flat so we could live together. It was a lot more than I could afford, but she insisted we get it and said she'd pay a third of the mortgage. To cut a long story short, I ended up paying for every-thing because she said she was skint. Next thing, she announced she'd saved up two thousand pounds and was off to New York on holiday without me."

I was appalled. "That's outrageous!"

"Yeah, I suppose it was," said Toby glumly. "Plus it turned out she was having an affair, although by the time I finally kicked her out, I didn't even care. I just wanted rid of her. But it was fine in the end, because I met Kate quite soon afterwards."

I felt a pang in my chest at the mention of his wife. Suddenly I didn't want to hear any more about Toby's love life.

"Toby?"

"Yeah?"

"Do you have many, you know, friends?"

Toby considered the question. A sparrow hopped onto a nearby tub of crocuses and watched us suspiciously.

"Well, not really. It sounds weird, but Ruby's my best friend, and she's two. And Kate, of course. The pair of them have always been enough for me, in the friends department. I have a good mate called Bill, who was my best man, and a couple of university friends I see occasionally. And that's about it—Kate's much more sociable than me. That's why I'm here now, actually; there are two of her art school buddies in with her and it was getting a bit crowded in there."

Nice, I thought. Glad that I could provide a bit of backup entertainment to pass the time. I'd been sort of hoping that he might include me in his list of friends.

"What about you?" Toby asked. "You've got tons of cards in your room. I bet you're really popular."

I snorted. "Oh yeah, and my room's overflowing with visitors—not. Apart from my mother, who doesn't count. What does that tell you?"

Toby looked in my eyes. "It tells me that you and Sam were so close, and you were so tied up with the band from such a young age, that you might not have had the time or the inclination to make any other friends, and now maybe you're regretting it."

I stood up, suddenly annoyed. Bloody Toby and his bloody perfect life (well, I never said I was *rational*). "I don't need the amateur psychology, thanks. I get enough of that from the psychotherapist, and he's a waste of space. Anyway, I'm a bit tired now, so I think I'll get back to my room. Maybe see you around, if you've got the time."

"Ruby'll be here tomorrow, too. I'd like to bring her in, if you don't mind."

I shrugged and walked away, back inside the hospital. As I

pressed the button to summon the lift, a blurry reflection in the metal doors loomed up behind me. Toby had followed me in. He dropped our two unfinished cups of tea into a nearby bin with a soft slosh, reached out his hand, and gently squeezed my fingers.

"See you tomorrow, then," he said, leaning forward and kissing me very tenderly on the lips. I was ashamed at his proximity to my mangled features, but the sweetness of the kiss was too tempting, and like a reflex, I put my hand up behind his head, pulling him closer to me. Everything about him was so inviting, as he roped me in first with the coil of his curls, and then with the warmth of his tongue gently touching mine, coaxing my poor traumatized nerve endings out of retirement. I felt like the stillborn puppy in *101 Dalmatians* being rubbed back to life, poking his tiny nose out of a towel, blinking sleepily at the world.

The kiss went on for a very long time, our bodies being pressed closer and closer together, until Toby affectionately and absently rubbed his nose against my broken one.

"YEEOUCH!" I screeched, leaping away from him, clutching my nose in both hands. My wig got knocked over one ear, and my glasses went flying, exposing the dressing on my left eye socket.

Toby jumped with fright and backed up against the lift doors, palms flat, as if I had pulled a knife on him. Then he recovered himself and rushed over to me, picking up my shades and straightening the wig.

"Helena, God, I'm so sorry! I got so carried away I totally forgot about your poor nose—are you okay?"

I nodded mutely, doubled over, my remaining eye watering with pain. It was true to say that the moment was lost.

The lift eventually rattled up to the top floor, the doors wheezed open, and I staggered in, reeling. Toby followed, white with remorse, incapable of doing anything except pat my shoulder manfully, as if we were business colleagues at a golfing lunch.

We descended in silence to the second floor, where I got out. "Off you go to see your wife, then," was my mumbled parting shot.

But once my nose had stopped hurting, I relived that kiss over and over again, so much so that I clean forgot to do any writing that day.

Jimmy Cliff
SITTING IN LIMBO

WE MOVED INTO OUR NEW AMERICAN HOUSE. IT WAS MADE OF wooden planks, with screen doors, a huge veranda with a swinging love seat, and a mind-boggling selection of numbers in its address. We had a free-standing mailbox instead of a slot in the front door. We had a dishwasher, a garbage disposal, a barbecue, a coffee machine, and a video recorder with a remote control on the end of a long cable. I had never seen any of these things before, not even at the Grants', but I still preferred our old brick-terraced house in Salisbury with its yellow front door.

Mum got her huge "yard," complete with an even bigger set of rosebushes. She quickly introduced herself to everybody on our block, and before long was hosting canasta parties and doing charitable works. Dad—well, I wasn't exactly sure what he did, but he seemed quite happy doing it every weekday and then coming home for a large Gordon's and tonic.

I went to school, and instead of being in the third year at grammar school, I became a grown-up tenth-grader, actually going in a year ahead of my age because of when my birthday fell, and my good reports from the U.K. I did well at school—I had no other distractions, and anyway, everything was so different that I had to give it my full attention. I had never heard of trick-or-treating or show-and-tell, and I had no idea why you shouldn't wear white trousers after Labor Day, who ninety-eight percent of the American presidents had been, what a soda fountain was, or where the Adirondacks were. In my adolescent *weltschmerz* I decided that I didn't really get the *point* of America.

Sept. 17, 1980

Dear Mas Tnarg (Pig Dealer and Donkey Buyer),

Going to school here is still very weird. Everyone has lockers and there are no pegs. We don't play lacrosse or netball; it's all stuff like "track" (running) and tennis and basketball (which is sort of like netball except you can run with the ball).

I don't understand what the girls in my class are talking about most of the time—they are always huddled in corners whispering about boys I don't know, bands I haven't heard of, and TV stars I don't recognize. So mostly I just keep my head down and concentrate on the lessons, which are easy. I'm getting more A's here than I ever did at South Wilts!

So no, I haven't really made any friends yet. It's too hard. I don't have anything in common with any of them, and I think they think I'm a snob because I don't talk to them. They think I'm weird, too, because of my accent and clothes, and because I didn't know what Reeses Pieces are (turns out they're revolting little chocolate things with peanut butter inside—puke).

I miss you so much. I miss your mum and dad, and the pub, and Melanie and Bridge and Jo. I even miss Dylan sometimes . . . but not very often! I bet I'll never get a boyfriend. The boys here all seem to like girls who are cheerleaders. I'm not sure what cheerleaders do, except that there's a lot of rah-rah-rah-ing and shaking big pom-poms and wearing very short skirts.

I want to come home for Christmas, but I don't think Mum and Dad will let me. Mum's gone full-on Fattypuff and hasn't been out for ages. She keeps on at me to "join a club" or "do some sports" (me!?!), but there's no way. I spend enough time at that stupid school every day, why would I want to spend more?

Dad bought a new car. It's called a Lincoln Town Car, but I keep calling it a Lincoln Townhouse, and it gets on his nerves.

Here's another quote for you. Send more back! (Although I don't understand what "Don't say mattress to Mr. Lambert" means—is it from Monty Python?) This is my new favorite: "She came home and sewed on the veranda." I did try to draw you a picture of it, you know, but when I'd finished it looked more like a picture of a woman with a horse trough stuck to her leg, so I decided not to send it.

Anyway, I'm writing this in a "math" class, so I'd better go. Please say thanks to Melanie for her postcard, I'll write back soon. (Don't tell her I was taking the mickey, but this is what her card said: 'Hiya, Helena. How be you these days. Okay yah I hope. Well, life is extremely boring, isn't it—nein? Anyway, I can't even think of anything to say— so until another day—Bye for now, Melanie'!!)

Lots of love,

Helena xxx

P.S. The best thing about living here is yard sales. They're like jumble sales but in people's front gardens (yes, you were right, they are called yards). I bought a brilliant record last month—it's reggae, and it's called *The Harder They Come*, by lots of different bands. I didn't know what it was when I bought it, I just liked the cover, but it's fab. I'll tape it for you. The best track is called "Sitting in Limbo." xx

* ✳ *

I knew I should have made more of an effort to fit in at school, but I felt so resentful. I'd had a social life in Salisbury. Sam and I had other friends; we were just beginning to get invited to the right parties and be noticed by the right people—but now, for me, that was all gone. It gave me a depressing, guilty satisfaction to see my mother's face as I slouched in after school every day, grabbed a drink, and headed straight up to my bedroom to write to Sam and listen to records.

Life seemed gray, endless, boring. Most of the time I felt like a supermarket trolley lying in a ditch, one wheel spinning uselessly round and round. The movie soundtrack *The Harder They Come* was beginning to become an obsession, though. I felt it kept me sane. I played it over and over again, endlessly, particularly the mellow Jimmy Cliff track "Sitting in Limbo," which was the least reggae-ish of the tracks, but the loveliest. It had this gorgeous trickling keyboard sound, which was like water running over stones, I thought perhaps in the River of Babylon.

After listening to that Jimmy Cliff track about four hundred times, the words had imprinted themselves onto my soul, and they bothered me.

"And I know that my faith will lead me on." I, too, was sitting in limbo, but I didn't have anything to lead me on. I began to spend more and more time wondering what it was to have faith. Until one day something happened, and I found out.

Sam and I continued to send each other long, heartrending letters about how we hated our lives apart, and how we were saving up to move to London together and become famous actresses. One school lunch hour, as I was composing one of these missives in the library, a tubby eleventh-grader with frizzy brown hair and hippie sandals came up to me.

"You're Helena, aren't you?" she said.

I nodded, taking in both her cool batik shoulder bag and her rather horrible nylon flared skirt.

"I'm Margie. I live on the next block from you. Your mom talked to mine at the grocery store the other day and told her how lonely you are here."

I blushed and looked at the floor, making a mental note to kill my mother.

"Well, listen, if you'd like to meet some cool kids, some friends and I have a kind of study group every Wednesday. We hang out at my place and listen to Carole King and chat. Why don't you come along next time? Six o'clock at 1114 Connecticut Street. It would be, like, totally rad if you could make it!"

It took me so long to get around the "totally rad" bit that I didn't properly take in the fact that I'd been invited somewhere. Then I was delighted and terrified in equal measures.

That Wednesday after school I spent ages putting on black eyeliner and back-combing my hair into a fashionable bird's nest. I carefully put on my smart black pinstriped jacket (half of a man's suit I'd found in a thrift shop) and black tube skirt, with a turquoise shirt and a long string of white plastic beads knotted around my neck to complete the ensemble. As I dressed, constantly and critically looking at my reflection in the mirror on the back of my bedroom door, I worried nervously about whether there would be either alcohol or boys present at this soiree.

At 6:10—fashionably late—I rang the door chimes of 1114, wishing Sam were with me. I could already hear strains of "It's Too Late" wafting out into the hallway and under the front door, and I took this to be a good sign.

Margie let me in. She took a brief startled look at my panda-eyes. "Oh, wow, you look . . . great! Come on in and meet the gang."

I followed her through to the living room, where seven or eight older kids from school were sitting on the shiny three-piece suite or the violent orange hairball-swirled carpet. Although I had never spoken to any of them before, I knew immediately and with a sinking heart that most of them were very definitely what Sam and I would call prats.

"Hey, everybody, this is Helena. She just moved here from Great Britain! Helena, this is Simon, Randy, Bethany, Mary Ellen, Rich, Sue, and Susie."

"Hello," I said unhappily. I observed them all looking nonplused at my party clothes.

"Have a seat, Helena. We won't bug you with questions about who Prince Charles is dating until later—we're about to start."

I sat down on the edge of a small flip-up chair, with a feeling of dread. My fears were confirmed when suddenly lots of pale green hardback books appeared and Carole King was turned down to an inaudible hum.

"Bethany, why don't you start today?" said Margie.

Bethany flipped open her Bible, for of course that was what it was, and announced dramatically, "Psalm 121!"

I was frozen to my chair with horror and embarrassment, feeling as if the black kohl circles around my eyes were spreading across my face until I was sure I looked like a coal miner in drag. Resentful thoughts spun around in my head as Bethany's strong voice rang on for what seemed like hours. I had changed my mind—Jimmy Cliff could keep his faith, although I bet he'd never had to sit around with nerds like this lot. It seemed to me that a much nicer way to find God would be by hanging out with Jimmy, Toots and the Maytals, and Desmond Dekker. Was Jah the same as Jesus, anyway?

Then Mary Ellen took over. The lilt and cadences of her voice were softer than Bethany's, and her emotive intonation of the

ancient verses somehow made it easier for me to listen. After a
while I began to feel drawn in by it. The words were soothing, justly
measured, and poured as though from a jug of something thick
and comforting. I had a sudden image of my mother stroking the
damp hair back from my flushed forehead when I'd once had flu.

The other kids still seemed dweeby to me, but by the end of that
oddly peaceful evening, I felt as if I "got it," and that particular "it"
was something I might need. After some earnest discussion of the
Psalms' meanings and merits, in which I declined to participate, a
glass of lemonade and side B of "Tapestry," I left, agreeing to come
to their church that Sunday. And feeling I would rather die than
admit to anyone what I'd just done.

I certainly couldn't bring myself to tell my parents. On Sunday
morning I just slipped out of the house, knowing that they probably
wouldn't even realize I'd gone. I had passed the church many times
before without really noticing it—it was one of those modern and
bland-looking redbrick buildings with an abstract swirl of stained
glass above the front doors, and a handkerchief of grass on either
side of the path from the sidewalk.

I skulked around outside for a few minutes, my qualms getting
worse. Two chirpy ladies in loud hats clutching, respectively, a sheaf
of service sheets and a stack of hymnbooks spotted me and
pounced enthusiastically.

"Come in, come in! Welcome to our church. We haven't seen
you before, have we? Well, I'm sure you'll enjoy our lovely service.
My name is Thelma and this is Veronica. What's your name? Please
don't forget to fill out a visitor's slip you'll find at the end of your
pew, and here, let me pin this nice pink ribbon on your lapel so we
all know you're a newcomer!"

I thought I might throw up. There may as well have been a large
neon arrow pointing at my head, flashing the words HEATHEN FOR-
EIGN STRANGER. I wanted to go home, but the ribbon on my jacket
bound me to the place like a prisoner's ID number tattooed on his
arm. It would have seemed churlish to undo the pin, throw down
the ribbon, and just leave. I stood in the entry porch and dithered,
arms full of a churchgoer's paraphernalia, unable to either walk
out or go inside.

At that moment, Mary Ellen and Randy arrived and rescued me. "Helena! Hi! Glad you could make it. Come sit with us."

I smiled, semi-gratefully, and allowed myself to be swept inside and up the aisle to a pew, worryingly close to the front of the church. It was nice not to be the lone outsider anymore, but I still would rather have lurked in a distant corner at the back by the doors, for easy escape.

I stared at my selection of hymnbooks, prayer books, and pamphlets. Mary Ellen and Randy were on their knees next to me, and as I couldn't quite make myself join them, I acted busy by looking up in my hymnbook all the hymns advertised for the service. They were posted on the wall, magnetic numbers stuck onto a nasty white board. This did not take very long, so I watched a jolly girl guitarist strumming gently at the front of the congregation. She wasn't playing "Kumbaya," but she might as well have been.

After a few more minutes the choir—mostly women, large and red-cassocked—and minister wandered in and the service opened with a lusty rendition of "Amazing Grace." So far so good, although it was strange to me that the choir just sat on chairs in front of the congregation instead of being tucked away in choir stalls out of sight. There was no organ, just a tinny upright piano and a couple of guitars. I didn't like the modernity of the whole setup. It seemed to me that a church wasn't a proper church unless it was ancient and had a high altar, a corrugation of stout organ pipes running up the wall, tombstones under the floor, and a lot of processing around with banners and so on. Where I came from the hymns were posted on an old wooden tablet, probably similar in shape to the one Moses had brought down the mountain, big wooden squares with numbers on them slotted into grooves in the tablet. None of this white plastic and Velcro, which, in combination with the pine pews and wooden floors, made for an ambience that seemed too lightweight for any serious spiritual conviction.

The service proceeded not too scarily, the usual prayers and announcements and exhortations. There seemed to be a constant stream of people trailing up the aisle to read biblical chunks from the podium at the front. As their heights were invariably different, they all had to readjust the microphone before they spoke, and every time, the readings would be preceded by squawks of feedback and often a thud or two when the reader's chin or forehead connected heavily with the unwieldy mike stand as they wrestled with it.

The minister himself was mild and unassuming, youngish, a stigmata of acne scars on his cheeks undermining his dubious authority. I thought he looked more like an accountant or a science teacher than a "man of the cloth." He was skinny and appeared rather nervous as he guided his flock through the service.

I was getting slightly bored. We were half an hour in and I didn't feel at all spiritual. I looked around some more, at the tall exposed-brick walls with their trendy woven wall hangings spaced evenly every fifteen feet or so. Actually, these were very pretty—imaginatively designed depictions of harvest festivals, loaves and fishes, Noah's Ark, the Garden of Eden, or simply embroidered announcements like *Jesus Saves!* and *The Light of the World.* The colors were bold and unfaded, and the pictures abstract and artistic enough to be interesting as well as aesthetically appealing—I was sure I'd seen the same tapestries in other churches.

I wondered idly if there was a book of *Church Wall-Hanging Patterns for Beginners* in existence, over which the ladies of the Women's Institute worldwide pored painstakingly. Or maybe you could just buy the finished product by mail order, perhaps by phone: "Hmm, I'll take one *St. Paul on the Road to Damascus* in plum and gold, and"—flipping through the pages—"a *Jesus Walking on the Water*—the turquoise and aquamarine, not the silver. A hundred fifty plus postage and packing? Okay, here's my American Express number. . . ."

A ripple of excitement passed through the congregation and brought my wandering mind back to the service. The minister was introducing today's guest preacher, who was striding up to the podium as he spoke. I didn't catch his name, as I was too busy studying his wide and snappy suit, ruddy face, the oversized Bible he was holding like a shield in front of him, and his thick, plastered-down hair, the exact same pale gray-blond as Kim Novak's eyebrows in *Vertigo* (which I'd seen on television the night before). He fitted much better the picture I had in my mind of an American preacher. He thanked the junior accountant and launched into his sermon in the big booming voice I would have expected, with no need for the troublesome microphone.

Something strange happened to me during his sermon. It was as though he was a wizard who'd cast a spell on me, and I was enthralled and awestruck. He launched into a story about a young boy with churchgoing friends, who scoffed at religion and laughed at their devotion. "I don't have time for this stuff now!" the boy had said. "There's far too much to do—I have to ride my bike and watch TV and build model airplanes. I don't want to be stuck in some boring old church! No, there'll be plenty of time for that later, when I'm grown up. God can wait." But the very next day this boy was run over and killed by a truck when he was out riding his bicycle.

"The Very Next Day," said the preacher, loudly and ominously, staring ferociously at each member of the congregation in turn. He stared at me for so long I nearly fainted. A mulberry blush enveloped me, not just sweeping to the roots of my hair but crawling inside my nostrils and eardrums, too.

"That boy did not have plenty of time. He found out to his cost that you cannot ignore Jesus, you *cannot* turn your back on Him. He loves you, like no human ever could or will—you must not snub Him. God alone knows when your time will come to face Him and repent, but you do not. So you must not be like this foolish boy, you must repent now!"

I was literally on the edge of my seat, freaked out and sweating but absolutely hooked. Randy and Mary Ellen next to me seemed riveted, too, but less anxiously so. I supposed they didn't have anything to worry about. They were well in there already. Fear and exhilaration in combination sent adrenaline coursing through my body. I had never felt like this before. How could I have been so lax, so dumb as to ignore the one who cared about me so deeply, who loved me unconditionally for who I was? I had only one chance to prove myself worthy of His love, and this was it. The preacher's voice got louder and his face redder.

"Jesus *wants* you!" he yelled, pounding the podium with his fist. I imagined myself with a glow surrounding me, holding Jesus' hand and looking into His eyes; He smiles at me sadly but with ineffable love. Suddenly everything else in my little world seemed unimportant—the pain of separation from Sam, what people thought of me, how I hated my body. None of this mattered in the slightest anymore.

"Who has the courage to take this first step? Who will hand their life over to Jesus before it's too late? Who will admit they were wrong? Who among you will change your path to the path leading to heaven? Right here, right now—remember, you don't have the time you thought you did! *This is the most important thing you will ever do. . . .*"

To my amazement my hand shot up into the air, uncontrolled, like a hiccup. I couldn't stop myself. I didn't want to stop. I stood up, glancing briefly back at the sea of faces behind me but not taking them in. I was crying and shaking but proud of myself. Someone appeared from nowhere and guided me out of my pew and up the aisle to the front. The preacher put his hand heavily on the top of my head and said, "Bless you, child," and I felt the tiny click of his chunky signet ring against my scalp, like the first tap of a teaspoon on the shell of a boiled egg.

Then I was led away to a quiet room off to the side. I was dimly aware of others following me, each with his own guide. There was a middle-aged man in a golf sweater, another girl around my age who was also crying, a sheepish-looking teenage boy. We all knelt and prayed together for forgiveness and redemption. I felt like the miserable sinner that I was, but I knew I had been saved. It felt like a very lucky escape. I promised then and there to be a virgin until I got married, that God would be my only love until that time.

The preacher came in and prayed with us. He was sweating heavily and his pale helmet of hair seemed to have had air injected into it from underneath, as it now looked bouffant and alive from his evangelical exertions. He blessed us each again, and gave us a tiny metallic cross pin, which I pinned next to my visitor's pink ribbon. Then we were led back to our seats, accompanied by strains of the guitarist, who had struck up again. It felt like the part in a wedding where the bride and groom and their family go off somewhere to sign the bridal register, and the rest of the congregation sits and whispers to one another while a jowly soprano quavers out a tune to keep everyone from getting bored.

I didn't know what had hit me. I felt overwhelmed, as if there was a new and worthy person inside my body.

Mary Ellen squeezed my arm when I returned. "Welcome, Helena. Congratulations," she said, and Randy whispered, "Praise the Lord," into my other ear. We all stood up to sing the final hymn, a modern happy-clappy number. I was not even embarrassed when everybody put their hands in the air and a few people called out, "Thank yew, Jee-sus!"

The service was over. I shakily filled out the visitor's form at the end of the pew and walked back down the aisle with Randy and Mary Ellen. Strangers congratulated me all the way, smiling and clapping me on the shoulder. I felt proud and self-righteous, and only a tiny bit foolish.

I HEAR THUNDER

WHERE WAS ALL THAT JOY NOW? I WONDERED, DROPPING MY OPEN notebook onto my lap and flopping against the back of my visitor's armchair with exhaustion. My wrist ached and my fingers were cramped into a writer's claw from the effort of so much longhand. I wondered how different my life would have been if I'd remained a Christian. I wouldn't be in this mess, that was for sure. But then, no money or success, either. Ergo no fame. I'd never have survived in the band if I'd kept the church as my priority. I imagined myself instead as a leading light in the Freehold, New Jersey, Baptist Church, organizing youth groups and potluck suppers, married to an earnest young minister with bum-fluff and stiffly creased pants. Three kids, stretch marks, and tons of wrinkles from taking on the cares of the entire parish. No, on reflection, fame had to have been better, even if the fate of my eternal soul was in question.

"Is this a bad time?"

Toby and Ruby hovered in the doorway. I was both embarrassed and delighted to see them, although Ruby looked concerned that I might start shouting again, and Toby had an unreadable, closed expression on his face.

"No, no, come in. I'd just finished the bit I was on. Sorry I was so grumpy yesterday, Toby. It was a bit of a bad day—well, apart from about three minutes of it. . . ."

I blushed at my flirtatious remark, but Toby did not acknowledge it, nor did he ask how my nose was feeling. All the warmth in his face seemed to have been wiped away, like an erased Etch-A-Sketch. Suddenly I felt foolish and ugly, and figured that he was only visiting me because he'd said he would. He was obviously mortified at what had happened the day before outside the lift.

Ruby sidled into the room and insisted that Toby lift her up onto my bed, out of reach of me and my scary face. She was wearing baby Nikes, black sweatpants, and a black sleeveless zip-up jacket.

I decided to act as if nothing had happened. "Wow, Ruby, you look really cool. You have some lovely clothes, you know."

"Tankoo, that's kind," Ruby said condescendingly, sticking her finger into her mouth and smiling graciously. She seemed to have concluded that perhaps I wasn't so bad after all.

Toby sat down next to her on the bed. "Don't worry about yesterday. It's forgotten. So what are you working on?"

He had a bright, false tone that I assumed was his "Pas Devant Les Enfants" voice—or maybe his "Let's pretend we never kissed at all" voice. Then I realized he'd asked me a question. I looked down at the pages of scribble resting open on my knee and hastily closed the notebook.

"I'm, um, writing a book about my life."

Toby acted impressed. "How incredible! And what a fantastically positive thing to do. I bet that's really helping you emotionally, too."

"Mm," I said. "It's certainly, er, focusing my mind. . . . How's Kate?"

Toby's face twisted into another strange expression: half-sheepish, half-pleased.

"Good news," he said. "We've just been with her for an hour, and guess what? Ruby sang her favorite song to her, and she moved her finger! Twice! The doctor says that's a sign that she might finally be coming out of it."

He hugged Ruby and ruffled her curls. "You're such a great girl, aren't you, my angel?"

Ruby beamed and nodded.

I felt a sudden flash of envy for Kate, despite her awful accident. She would wake up and recover with the support and love of these two wonderful people and, doubtless, her life would be further enriched by her dice with death, and she and Toby would be more deeply in love than ever. Toby had, of course, already realized what a hideous mistake he'd made by kissing me, and how much he really adored Kate. Well, bully for them.

I was horrified by my churlish reaction.

"God, Toby, that's great. I'm so pleased for you, honestly. You must be over the moon. And Ruby, aren't you clever, making your mummy better? What did you sing to her?"

Ruby considered for a minute. "I . . . funder."

"Sorry?"

"I . . . *funder.*"

I looked toward Toby for assistance.

"I hear thunder," he translated.

"Oh, right. I don't think I know that one. How does it go?"

"It's the preschool version of 'Frère Jacques.' Will you sing it for Helena, Rubes? It'll help her get all better, too."

Ruby sat up and began to sing tunelessly, with Toby mouthing the words beside her:

> *"I . . . funder, I . . . funder*
> *'Ark, doan you? 'Ark, doan you?*
> *Pipper papper waindops*
> *Pipper papper waindops*
> *I wet froo*
> *THO-ARE-YOU!"*

The song was accompanied by gestures: clapping for the thunder, cupping a hand around her ear for the "Hark, don't you?," finger-twitching for the pitter-patter, plucking at her jacket to indicate that she was wet through, and a final crescendo of pointing. It was really sweet, and if I hadn't been so pissed off with Toby, I could quite easily have welled up with soppy tears.

"Aw, Ruby, that was brilliant. No wonder your mummy is getting all better now. She probably wants to hear it over and over."

Needing no more encouragement, Ruby began again. Toby hastily tried a distraction technique.

"Hey, Ruby, remember that Nurse Grace said she'd found a box of toys for you? Shall we go and see if you can play with them for a bit?"

"Oooh, toys," said Ruby gleefully. "Bye, lady, thee you later!"

"It's *Helena*, Ruby. Say good-bye to Helena."

"Bye, Ellna."

"Bye, Ruby."

"Helena, I'll just go and get her sorted. Grace said she'd take her off my hands for ten minutes—then we can have a proper chat, okay?"

He gave me a meaningful, although still stern, look, and I thought, Right, earwig. It's going to be the "Now my wife's on the mend, I'll see you around" chat.

Nonetheless, once they'd disappeared, I slipped on my silk Liberty dressing gown and quickly ran a comb through my hair. I wanted to be Dumped with Dignity.

But perhaps I was wrong? Perhaps he was just being standoffish so Ruby didn't suspect anything. Perhaps he was coming back for a repeat of yesterday's tryst? I hopped into the bathroom for another swig of mouthwash and to dab some perfume onto my neck. I realized I didn't want to be Dumped at all.

The guilt that had been absent yesterday now pricked at my skin, as abrasive and intrusive as the deodorant I'd just sprayed under my arms. Where was my membership in the sisterhood? Here I was, hoping to seduce an unconscious woman's husband. I felt ashamed of myself.

But not ashamed enough to hope it didn't happen again.

Ten minutes went by and Toby didn't come back. I sat for a further ten minutes, posed in my armchair watching *Time Team* on TV, haughty and abandoned like Miss Haversham. Then I began to get worried, and fed up with watching a lot of loosely woven people getting excited about pot shards. I went out into the corridor and looked up and down—no sign of either of them.

Eventually Catriona appeared. "Oh, sorry, Helena, I forgot to tell you—Toby asked me to send his apologies, but we had to get him back to his wife pronto. She opened her eyes!"

"Great," I said. "That's really great."

HOME AGAIN

THE NEXT YEAR WAS MUCH HAPPIER THAN I HAD IMAGINED IT would be, despite missing Sam terribly.

"Jesus has buttered your paws," said Margie wisely, a couple of months after I'd joined the church.

"I beg your pardon?" I said. I'd also discovered that the more English I sounded, the more popular I became.

"You're like a kitty with a new owner. The Lord has taken you from the pet store of your old existence, brought you to a new home, and buttered your paws. That's what you do with cats to help them settle into a new place. Licking off all the butter helps them relax, so by the time they're done, they feel like they belong there."

"Oh, er, right," I said.

But in a way, it was true. The church had given me a sense of belonging. Although I didn't exactly gel with most of the other God-struck teenagers, having a routine of my own did help ease the sting of reading Sam's letters about boyfriends and parties and rumors of Melanie Welling's famous friends.

I went to church every Sunday, and Bible class each Wednesday. Within weeks I had joined the choir, so choir practice on Thursdays occupied another of my previously empty evenings.

I loved being in the choir. I had a deepish, clear voice and could easily pick up harmonies on the hymns and spirituals, even without the music in front of me. I also loved being in front of the congregation, dressed in an all-encompassing red cassock. It was my first experience of public performance, and I was hooked. It wasn't just the cassock that surrounded me, either. My new faith swirled and eddied about me constantly like an aura; I felt protected by it, elevated, and really, really loved.

At first my fourteen-year-old self wanted to keep it private for fear of ridicule, but as time went on my confidence grew, and I was no longer ashamed of doing lunchtime Bible study with my churchy cronies. I sometimes felt as though I could swing from the rafters proclaiming that Jesus was Lord.

My parents were greatly relieved at the change in me. Their previously homesick and withdrawn daughter had transformed into something approximating a ray of sunshine. In fact, had I not been so happy, I think that they would have found it rather disturbing.

One Sunday I dragged them along to church with me, but they did not enjoy it. When we got home again, I overheard Mum mutter to Dad, "Rather vulgar, don't you think, George?"

I was furious. I burst into the living room, making my mother spill her sherry on the leatherette pouffe. "You're such hypocrites!" I yelled. "You say you believe in God, you drag me to Sunday school all those years, and now when I finally have a faith of my own, you sneer at it! How dare you!"

My father pulled out his handkerchief and tried to mop up the spilled sherry, looking anxious. "Now calm down, Helena, nobody's sneering. Don't shout at your mother."

Mum had the grace to look ashamed. She put her hand on my arm. "Oh, Helena, I'm sorry. I wasn't sneering at you or your faith, really. We're both so pleased that you are so much happier and more settled—we've been so worried about you. It's just, well, you know, your father and I aren't used to people being so . . . vocal in their beliefs. It certainly wasn't like that at St. Thomas's."

I couldn't help grinning. It was true, they had both looked mortified when the congregation's hands started waving in the air during the first hymn. My father hadn't known where to put himself. And in truth I was rather relieved that they had not taken to my church. If there was such a thing as a spiritual style, I felt that my parents would definitely have cramped mine.

"Okay, Mum. Sorry I shouted at you."

Dad, looking relieved that the crisis was over, went out into the garden to practice his golf swing. Mum poured herself another sherry and put her feet up to read a gardening magazine. I went upstairs to listen to my newest favorite record—Carole King's *Tapestry*, ever since that first Bible study meeting—and to try to write to Sam. Normality had resumed.

Although we still corresponded regularly, I'd recently been having trouble finding things to write about. After I first got converted, I wrote her screeds and screeds of babble about how wonderful my life was now, and how she *must* try Jesus, as though He were a new and desirable brand of lipstick. My enthusiasm for my new religion was so overwhelming that I was genuinely surprised when Sam didn't immediately follow suit and get converted, too.

Even from across the Atlantic, I thought I'd managed to suffuse her with the same joy that it gave me. I really wanted her to be as happy as I was. Her replies ignored my pleas entirely, which just made me more insistent, until one day I got a brief note from her, unlike her usual chatty missives.

Dear Helena,

Thanks for your letter. I'm writing this in Home Economics before Miss Parry notices—my cheese and onion pie is in the oven and I'm supposed to be cleaning up. Sorry if this letter's got flour all over it. Have you heard of Hazel O'Connor? She's had a couple of hits here (including a fantastic song called "Will You?") and we went to see her at the City Hall—can you believe it, a proper pop concert in Salisbury! It was absolutely brilliant. Melanie said she read in *Smash Hits* that the saxophone player was blind, but he was wearing a wristwatch onstage, so now we aren't sure.

Uh-oh, Miss P's on the warpath. . . .

(Later. Breaktime.)

It was really funny in PE today, we were playing netball and Marie-Thérèse Higgins got a teeny fly or something on her arm. She flicked it off and said, "Get off me, you nasty little orgasm!" (She meant "organism.") Melanie and Bridget and me all cracked up laughing.

Anyway, this was only meant to be a quick note. Write soon and tell me what you're up to at school. Any nice boys yet? I don't mean to be nasty or anything, but please stop going on about God, it's driving me mad. I'm really happy for you, honest, but horses for courses—I just can't see me getting into all that church stuff.

Lots of love and sloppy kisses,
Sam xxx

* * *

After receiving that note, I didn't go to church for two weeks. I was overcome with a huge, bitter, impotent rage that, because my stupid parents made me move to this stupid country, I now had to derive any enjoyment from life out of a bunch of geeky, earnest people whose idea of a good time was going for a cookout on the New Jersey Shore and singing hymns lustily round a campfire.

Why couldn't I be normal, like Sam, going to pop concerts and reading *Smash Hits* and discussing orgasms with Melanie Welling? I didn't even know what an orgasm was. I inquired, that night at Bible study, only *nobody else knew either,* and some of them were at least sixteen! It wasn't until I asked Mum later, and she went red and told me off, that I realized it was something rude.

But my period of doubting didn't last long. I decided that it was a test from God, and that I should just ignore Sam's reluctance to think about her soul, until such time as I could personally convince her, face-to-face. I certainly didn't want it to spoil our friendship.

So I continued to write to Sam, without the proselytizing, but it wasn't easy. One day, after listening to the whole of side A of *Tapestry,* I sat chewing my pen in the post-LP silence, trying to think of something interesting and non–church related to put in a letter. The remnants of the track "Home Again" chased themselves around my head, and I thought how simple Carole made it sound, just a few chords on a piano, a gentle background guitar, and a clear voice.

I could do that, I thought.

Magically, the melody of "Home Again" faded out and a line from an unwritten song popped into my mind instead. This was followed by another one, so I put the letter aside and wrote them down before I forgot them.

> *Jesus, you talk to me every day;*
> *Jesus, you hear what I have to say.*

I contemplated the crucifix on my desk for a few minutes, Jesus' furled fingers and skewered brass feet.

> *Thank you, Jesus, for being there for me,*
> *Thank you, Jesus, for setting me free.*

I thought this was marvelous. I had an instant fantasy of debuting the finished song, solo, in front of an adoring and appreciative congregation who rose to their feet, cheering when it was over. But I wasn't quite happy with the tune; there seemed to be something missing. I could hear how I wanted it to sound in my head, but singing it wasn't good enough. I decided that it needed accompaniment to do it more justice.

I crept downstairs past my mother, who had nodded off over her magazine, reading glasses askew at the tip of her nose, and into the dining room, where our old piano lived. Closing the door behind me, I slid onto the piano's tapestry stool and lifted up the heavy wooden lid. The old familiar smell of musty ivory and furniture polish filled my nostrils, reminding me of my brief spell as a childhood piano prodigy. I'd lasted less than a year before getting bored at having to do scales all the time.

None of us ever played this piano anymore. I didn't know why my parents had bothered to bring it all the way across the Atlantic. There were faded circles on the little wood squares at either end of the keyboard, where drunken party guests had left their icy glasses of whiskey while hammering out painfully inaccurate renditions of the "Maple Leaf Rag," battle scars that could not be polished off with Pledge.

I played a soft experimental scale. The F key stuck, rendering only a dull *thunk* when pressed. I remembered being responsible for that—actually, that was the day I stopped playing the piano. I was about seven years old, and I'd gotten so frustrated with my pudgy fingers tripping over the notes that I'd banged my finger down hard on each one, as if I was trying to drum the sequence into the piano's stupid brain. It had beaten me at my own game, stubbornly and permanently sticking down a vital note. So to avoid being held responsible for my vandalism, I insisted to my parents that I did not wish to continue with piano lessons, in the hope that they might not notice the damage. And indeed it was probably several years before they did, by which time I was well off the hook.

Using a higher octave to avoid the errant key, I plinked out my tune again, making a few subtle alterations as I went along. Bingo. All the notes fell perfectly into place, and I'd created a catchy and sweet backing track to the melody. I played it over and over again, to make sure I did not forget it, and then went back up to my bedroom to write the rest of the verses. I was thrilled at what I believed to be my creative genius.

That night as I was saying my prayers, I concluded that my song really did need a guitar as well, some cool strumming over the vocals, nothing wishy-washy. I wanted to be a New Wave Christian.

The more I thought about it, the more fixated I became. I had to have a guitar. But how? It was early summer, ages before my birthday. I turned it over to the Lord, trying not to plead too much, but unable to resist bargaining with Him.

"If I had a guitar I would be able to praise Thy glory much better. Not in a hippie-drippy 'Kumbaya' sort of way, but a proper, modern way. The eighties way." I stopped, then added, "Only if it is Thy will."

I went to sleep content that if it was meant to be, it would be. After all, I could see no reason why I should be denied an instrument of praise. I saw myself bringing the entire youth population of Freehold to Jesus' arms, by way of my radical and totally *cool* approach to worship.

* ✳ *

The following weekend I went over to Mary Ellen's house to help her with some schoolwork. She and I had become quite friendly of late. She was a genuine person, not a borderline religious nut, as I couldn't help considering the likes of Margie and some of her friends to be. Mary Ellen was doing a geography project on Scotland and had asked for my assistance—not that I had ever been there, or knew anything about it, but I thought that at least I could tell her how to pronounce Edinburgh and Glasgow correctly.

She lived a few blocks away from me, and as I turned the corner onto her tree-lined road, I noticed a large yard sale on the other side of the street. I still couldn't resist yard sales—they were the closest thing Freehold had to a good old church hall jumble sale— and went over to have a poke around. The house itself was shabby and unkempt, by far the least affluent-looking on the block. Most of the stuff was laid out on the front porch, and surprisingly, the pickings were very rich: cool books, records, some decent-looking granddad shirts, posters. Usually I had to sort through a multitude of used Tupperware and broken kitchen utensils to find anything worth taking home.

A sullen girl of about eighteen sat on the stoop, presumably in charge. I couldn't help noticing what massive feet she had, encased in cheap plastic sandals. She was talking to an older man, who was, I presumed, either a neighbor or another customer.

"Yeah, Scott run away and joined the Marines without tellin' no one. Mama's so mad at him she's sellin' all his gear. She says she don't never wanna see him again."

Wow, I thought, that's harsh. Selling all his things! Poor Scott. Nevertheless, I picked up a battered copy of *Catcher in the Rye* and a stripy shirt.

"How much are these?" I asked.

"Book's five cents, shirt's a quarter," she replied, chewing the ends of her hair. I fumbled in my pocket for the change, paid her, and turned to walk away with my purchases under my arm. Just then the screen door slammed and someone came out onto the porch. I heard a screechy Southern voice.

"Janeane, I'm gettin' rid of this, too. It'll only clutter up the place. Don't see no point in keepin' it."

The daughter sounded shocked. "Mama, you're surely not sellin' Scotty's guitar?"

I wheeled around and stared. Sure enough, the sour-faced owner of the voice had propped a hard black guitar traveling case against the side of the porch. My heart sang.

"Thank you, Jesus, thank you, thank you," I whispered under my breath. I approached the woman, who glared at me. "Er, how much do you want for the guitar?"

"Fifteen bucks," she snapped. Her eyes were small and mean. I was starting to understand why Scott had left home.

Janeane looked even more horrified. "Fifteen bucks? Mama, let me take it downtown to Merchants. They buy used guitars—it's worth more than that!"

"No, Janeane, I jus' want it out my sight. I doan care about the money."

"I'll take it!" I interrupted. "Please could you hold it for me while

I go over to my friend's house and borrow some money? I'll be right back. Mary Ellen Randall, your neighbor, that's my friend, she lives across the street."

The woman nodded, tight lipped, at me, and I felt her eyes boring into my back as I hurried across the road to Mary Ellen's house.

I rang her doorbell and pounded on the door so hard that Mary Ellen stuck her head out of the window.

"Helena—what's the matter?"

"Oh, oh, Mary Ellen, please come quick, there's this guitar but I don't have enough money. I wonder, I mean, please could you . . . ?"

"I'll be right down," she said.

A moment later her blond head loomed behind the frosted glass of the front door, and she opened it, beckoning me inside. I dumped the book and shirt on the Randalls' hall table as Mary Ellen looked on, mystified.

"Okay, what guitar? Where?"

I took a deep breath. "It's across the road, at a yard sale. It's only fifteen dollars but I only have five on me. Do you think you could possibly lend me the other ten until tomorrow? It's just that I've been praying all week for a guitar, and now here it is—I'm sure it's meant to be!"

Mary Ellen nodded sagely. "Sounds like it is. Hold on, I'll get my purse." I could have hugged her.

We walked back across the street. Mary Ellen shuddered slightly when she saw which house.

"That's the Applebaums' place. They moved up from Tennessee a while back. They're a little . . . unusual."

I had the feeling that if she were not so Christian she would have elaborated, and normally I would have asked her to, but at that moment I couldn't have cared less if they'd all had two heads. We approached the porch. The guitar case was still there.

"What kind of condition is it in?" Mary Ellen inquired.

"Er—actually, I haven't looked at it yet," I admitted, feeling a bit foolish.

"Well, you'd better, before you give them any money," she hissed in my ear. Mrs. Applebaum was standing belligerently in front of the door, her hands on her hips.

"Mrs. Applebaum, hi, it's me again, about the guitar—could I have a look at it please?" I asked. She nodded once, and I walked over to the case. Laying it flat on the grass, I popped the stiff metal catches open and pulled the lid up.

"It's *huge*," said Mary Ellen, in awed tones. "Why does it only have four strings?"

Damn! I thought. It's a bass. Now what? This was an unexpected turn of events. I stared at it. It was in fairly good condition; black, with a lovely pearl-effect white scratch plate. I plucked each of the heavy strings with a forefinger, and they all made unpleasant and unmelodic muffled, twanging sounds. How on earth did you get it to play? I wondered. Suddenly I felt terribly disappointed, and nearly closed the case and walked away. But then I thought about my prayers, and how much more than coincidence it had felt when Mrs. Applebaum brought the guitar outside at the precise moment I was there. No, I had prayed for a guitar, and God had sent me a guitar. Everything else I would figure out.

"I'll take it," I said, standing up. Mary Ellen and I pooled our resources, and I paid Janeane. Mrs. Applebaum had vanished into the house, but she reappeared at that point lugging a small black box-thing trailing cables.

"Here," she said, thrusting at me. "I sure don't know what this is, but it goes with the guitar. Take the darn thing."

A practice amp! I offered up another silent prayer. I would not have had the first idea how to go about buying one of those. I collected the stray wires together in a coil and looped them over my forearm.

"Thank you very much, Mrs. Applebaum," I said sincerely, toying with the idea of adding that I hoped Scotty came back soon, but wisely thinking better of it.

"Bye, Mrs. Applebaum," added Mary Ellen, closing the guitar case for me and picking it up. We proceeded back across the road with my strange electrical acquisitions, the start of my future as a bassist.

MY MESSED-UP HEAD

TOBY'S VISITS TO MY ROOM DRAMATICALLY DECREASED IN LENGTH and frequency as Kate began to recover. He did still pop in occasionally, but nothing was said about our kiss, and he avoided the subject of Kate's progress, or any reference to the future. I felt glad in one way and gutted in another.

It would be no good at all for me to go forging complicated relationships with married men at this point in my life, not when I was planning such a huge . . . thing. All my energies had to go into the Plan, and some days I even enjoyed it. I had a secret that no one else knew about.

But on other days I was really sad that I couldn't share it with Toby, and that I could never be part of his future.

One morning, before visiting time, I got dressed. I left my room quite often for little walks, but this was the first time I'd worn proper clothes instead of just pajamas and a dressing gown. It felt like a big deal.

Mum had brought me in a couple of outfits the day before, since I obviously couldn't wear the dress I'd had on at the UKMAs. I didn't know what had happened to that dress—incinerated, I hoped. I shuddered at the thought of the beautiful orange velvet all sticky and matted with blood.

My freshly laundered jeans felt cool and stiff on my still-shaky legs, and I could button them with far more ease than before. Newly ironed jeans usually required a lying-down hip-raiser to make ends meet—wow, if I kept going at this rate, I'd be able to die skinny! Just what I'd always wanted . . .

I put on a big cardigan and a baseball cap and walked slowly out into the corridor. Catriona was writing up some notes at the nurses' station down at the end of the hall.

"Where's Kate Middleton's room?" I asked.

Catriona looked up, surprised.

"You're up and out early, Helena. Dressed, too—good for you. It's a bit early for visiting, though. Kate's still in quite a bad way. She gets tired very easily."

"I don't want to visit her," I said, a bit too sharply. "I mean, not now. I just thought I'd find out where she is in case I decide to go later. While I'm out for a walk. You won't tell her that I might visit, will you?"

Catriona looked at me as if I had a screw loose.

"Turn right, through the double doors, Room 17. She's still in Intensive Care, but we'll be moving her downstairs to a non-ICU room tomorrow, all being well."

I thanked her and shuffled off. I still had this weird floaty feeling whenever I walked anywhere, so I hung on to the wall to prevent myself from weaving about like a drunkard.

The blinds were down in Room 17, to my annoyance. I just wanted a peek at Kate, to see what she looked like. It was a totally unfair thing to do, since I would have so loathed anyone trying that with me, but my curiosity was overpowering. I was sure I'd dislike her—talented, arty, loads of friends, gorgeous husband and daughter. Beautiful, too: Toby had said that her scars wouldn't show, the lucky bitch.

Really, Helena, I thought. You're often not a very nice person, are you?

I loitered casually around in the corridor for a bit, then gave up, intending to go back to my own room to carry on with my writing. I reckoned I was about a quarter of the way through the manuscript. Which meant D day minus three-quarters.

One corridor further down, I heard Nurse Grace's voice floating through an open door:

"Oh, Ruby love, I haven't got any sweeties! Bad for your teeth, anyway, makes them all mossy and soft. Yuck! How about making a nice house out of some of these LEGOs?"

I couldn't resist walking along and peeking into the room. "Hi, Grace. Hi, Ruby,"

Grace looked up, relief at seeing me potato-printed all over her face. She was half-sitting, half-lying on the purple carpet-tiled floor of some kind of visitors' room, with Ruby straddling her, both of them looking squashed in between too many armchairs and coffee tables. They were surrounded by a plastic picnic of bits of LEGO, unfeasibly simplistic dump trucks and locomotives, and a scattering of chunky animal playing cards.

Ruby was in the process of frisking Grace, briskly and efficiently, keeping up a low, growling chant of " 'Weeties, 'weeties, 'weeties." When she spotted me, she released Grace and ran up to me, smiling winsomely.

"You got 'weeties, Ellna!" she announced hopefully.

I laughed. "My disguise obviously isn't as foolproof as I'd thought," I said to Grace, crouching down so I was at eye level with Ruby. "You're a sucker for punishment, Ruby," I told her. "Don't you remember what happened last time I gave you a sweet?"

Ruby considered. "Oh, yeth," she said, cowed. "I done coughing."

She backed away momentarily, worried perhaps that I might jam a gobstopper down her esophagus. Then she brightened again. "How 'bout play Animal Nap, yeah?"

She took my hand and dragged me to the pile of toys on the floor.

"Animal Snap," explained Grace helpfully. "Oh, Helena, you wouldn't do me a huge favor and play with her for a bit, would you? I won't be far away, just outside in the store cupboard. I'm supposed to be doing a stock-take, but I wanted to give Kate and Toby a bit of time on their own."

I began to sweat at the thought that Toby might have caught me hanging around outside Kate's room.

"He's in there now, is he?" I asked, as casually as I could manage.

Grace stood up, brushing a little piece of red LEGO off the knee of her tights and smoothing down her uniform. "Well, he was on his way to her room. He said he had something to do first."

My heart leapt. Perhaps he'd been planning to sneak in to see me first; damn, damn, I wasn't there, my own fault for—

Just then Ruby piped up. "Daddy went to do poo. In *toilet*," she explained carefully. "Then he go thee my mummy."

I was deflated. So much for the romantic notions. But if I hung out with Ruby for a while, then at least I'd probably get to see Toby when he returned, post-dump and post-visit.

"Will you show me how to play Animal Snap, Ruby?" I asked.

"I get cardth," she said enthusiastically.

Grace laughed again. "Thanks, Helena. I'm just next door if you need me. I warn you, though. This may not be the tension-filled, fast-moving game you remember from your childhood, okay?"

She swished out, waving gratefully at me as she went.

"Right," said Ruby bossily. "Eye down."

It took me a few seconds to realize that she wasn't referring to my injured face, but was ordering me to join her where she lay on her tummy on the floor. I thought about the logistics of this—it was a small room, and I'd have had to lie with my legs wedged underneath an armchair, thus risking looking a total prat when Toby came back.

"Tell you what, Ruby. You lie there and I'll sit next to you. Here, shall I deal?"

I sat cross-legged on the dusty carpet, split the pack of animal cards approximately in half, and gave Ruby one of the piles.

"I go firtht." Very slowly, she selected two cards and put them facedown on the carpet. "Your turn," she said.

Discreetly I turned one of Ruby's cards over—a giraffe—before adding a zebra of my own.

Ruby put down a horse, faceup this time. "Horthey."

I turned over a tiger. "Tiger."

The game continued with a tortuous lack of speed, until I placed a pig on the pile, to which Ruby added an identical pig. There was a long pause.

I pointed meaningfully at the twin pigs. "Two pigs, Ruby."

Ruby gazed blankly at them.

I tried again. "Look, Ruby, what do you say when you've got two cards the same?"

Another blank look. Then, "Pigth?" she suggested.

"No. How about 'Sn . . . ,'" I began, waiting for her to catch on.

Nothing.

"Snaaaa . . . ?"

Light finally dawned.

"NAAAAP!" she yelled, as if coming out of delayed shock, and grabbed all the cards. "New game now. Deal prop'ly, Ellna."

I shuffled the pack and did as I was told. Ruby wiggled around on her stomach until she was lying next to me.

"Deal cardth on my botham," she commanded, sticking her backside in the air and looking back at me over her shoulder, in a very sex-kittenish fashion.

I giggled. "On your bottom?"

"Yeth, on my botham."

Feeling perhaps that this was not entirely appropriate behavior, from either of us, but not wanting to risk her wrath, I obliged, dealing Ruby's hand onto the seat of her stripy velour leggings.

Ruby roared with appreciative laughter and rolled around, scattering the cards around her. "More!" she shouted, and I began to laugh, too, flipping the cards one by one on the moving target of her little butt. I felt an unfamiliar stiffness in my chest, and worried for a second that I'd strained something, until I realized that it was just the exertion of laughing out loud after such a long time.

Ruby, encouraged by my response, was becoming more and more overexcited, squirming like an eel in a fishing net, and squealing with joy. I was just beginning to wonder how to go about calming her down a bit, when she flipped over onto her back, spread her legs wide, grabbed her crotch, and yelled, "DEAL THEM ON MY DINKY!"

Of course that had to be the moment that Toby appeared in the doorway. Ruby looked up at him.

"Nice poo, Daddy?"

For a second he and I gazed at each other, and then at Ruby, spread-eagled on the floor surrounded by animal playing cards.

Toby's face was inscrutable. "Yes, thanks, Rubes."

She beamed up at him. "Oh, good *boy*, Daddy!"

That was it. I exploded, belly-laughing until I was worried I'd pop open my skin grafts. To my relief, Toby joined in, and the three of us were united in a magic circle of cartoon zebras and lions and warm, briefly uncomplicated pleasure. Ruby ran over to Toby and he scooped her up into an enormous hug, which somehow seemed to include me, too.

"Grandma's here, darling," he said to her. "She's with Mummy. Let's go and see them."

I began to collect the scattered cards, my spirits already beginning to plummet again.

"Stay there, Helena, would you? I'll just drop Ruby off and nip back, okay?"

"Bye, Ellna, nithe to meet you," said Ruby solemnly, puckering her lips into a fish's mouth and pressing the tenderest little kiss onto my scarred cheek.

Those Middletons and their casual kisses, I thought, trying not to seem too absurdly pleased.

Once they were gone I spent a few minutes slowly tidying up all the toys, and then sat down and flipped through the very poor selection of tatty women's magazines. I was just gazing at a recipe for a radioactive-looking zabaglione and wondering if Toby was actually going to come back at all this time, when I glanced up to find him framed in the doorway, looking at me. I jumped, in my skin and in my heart.

"Didn't see you there."

"Sorry. I did knock."

I pointed at my ear, as if there might be a small OUT OF ORDER sign swinging off it like a novelty earring. "Not loudly enough, obviously." I worried that he'd think I was annoyed, so I continued, "But it doesn't matter. It's good to see you. How's Kate?"

Toby came in and sat next to me, dragging his chair closer so our arms were almost touching. "She's okay. How are you?"

"Okay. You?"

We laughed at the small talk.

"I've missed you," I said without thinking.

"I know what you mean," he replied, tucking a strand of my hair back underneath my cap. "I'm so sorry, Helena, the way that I've been so . . . standoffish with you. I want to see you so badly, but when I do, I feel so guilty about Kate. And of course, I can't let Ruby see the way I feel about you . . . she picks up on everything."

He was looking so tenderly into my face that I didn't even mind when he gently traced the scars on my cheek and eyebrow with his finger.

"Augenbrau," I whispered, thinking of Sam, and how much she would have liked Toby.

"What?"

"Nothing," I said hastily, feeling silly. "God, Toby, what are we doing here? I don't even know if there's something between us, or nothing at all. You say you feel guilty about Kate. Were things bad between you before?"

Toby leaned his head back in his chair in a gesture of desperation. "You have no idea what a complete and utter lowlife I feel when I think about Kate, but I can't change the fact that I fell in love with you the first time we met. It makes me sick to think that I didn't do something about it then, or in the months or even years since then, but you were away on the road, and by the time you came back to the U.K., I'd met Kate. I was afraid to organize another interview or a backstage pass to see you because I knew it would compromise my relationship with her. As it's doing now.

"I do love Kate; she's my wife and the mother of my child. But you . . ." He looked at me with such passion in his eyes that I almost forgave him for having a wife.

"I want to feel every bit of you next to me," he whispered. "Please."

"Except my nose, if you don't mind," I said, grinning.

I stood up and straddled him in his chair, pressing myself against him until as much of our bodies as possible were connected. My stomach felt his stomach, my breasts touched his chest, my arms wrapped themselves around his back. Our lips met, and then our tongues, and finally, with a shiver of electricity we both felt, there was a clash of hard and soft at the heart of us.

That kiss went on even longer than the elevator kiss. It was the strangest and yet the most wonderful thing that had ever happened to me—in a hospital, surrounded by death and pain, me and a married man nearly ripping each other's clothes off. It was utterly surreal. But after crying together and laughing together, it seemed natural that Toby and I were practically making love right there in that chair, surrounded by watchful furniture and out-of-date women's magazines. Perhaps it was the air of heightened emotion that existed in hospitals, the sense that nothing was as it should be, not perspective nor time nor even conscience.

I had no idea how much time elapsed. Just as I thought I was going to explode with lust, there was a sharp accusatory knock at the door. I leapt off Toby as quickly as I could and rolled back into my own chair, puce in the face and aching with passion and exertion. Toby adjusted his trousers and sat up straight, running a hand swiftly through his curly hair as if that would erase all the obvious signs of infidelity.

The door opened after a pause that seemed, even to us, discreetly lengthy. Grace came in and gave us both a very hard stare.

"Kate's mother was just wondering where you'd got to," she said to Toby, disapprovingly. "She wants you to nip out and get some toiletries for Kate."

Toby didn't dare stand up. He cleared his throat noisily. "Right, thanks. I'll be there in a second."

Grace retreated without another word, and Toby and I looked at each other mutely.

"Well, at least it wasn't the mother-in-law," he said with a straight face. I leaned over to kiss him again, but he groaned and pushed me away.

"No, please, don't, Helena, or else I'll never be able to . . . to get myself together," he said, gesturing crotchward.

"Do you think Grace will say anything?" I asked.

Toby shook his head. "It's none of her business. Anyway, I'm sure she wouldn't. She didn't even see anything, so it would only be speculation. For all she knows we might just have been playing an extra-exciting game of Animal Snap."

"That's *Strip* Animal Snap," I said, and we laughed at the idea.

Eventually Toby was able to stand up, unencumbered. He touched my hand lightly. "See you later, then."

"Will I?"

"I hope so."

The door closed quietly behind him, and I was left once more thinking how incongruous it was to feel lustful in a hospital. All my other emotions, however, fit in quite well with the surroundings: confusion, guilt, longing. Grief.

OLIVER'S ARMY

I QUICKLY WORKED OUT HOW TO PLUG THE BASS INTO THE AMP, and what all the knobs and dials did. I also bought a book called *Bass Guitar for Beginners,* but did not pay it much attention because of its marked predilection for the dreaded scales. Instead I figured out my own method of playing, using a lot of chords as if it were a regular six-string guitar, my original choice of instrument. I loved the deep, almost sinister sound that the strings in harmony made. Physically, it was not easy to learn, and for weeks I played wincing with pain as the hard strings cut into my tender fingers. I dipped my fingertips in vinegar every night to try to toughen them up, and thereafter always associated that sharp smell with my early attempts to get to grips with the unwieldy guitar.

The theory, however, came easily to me, and I learned very quickly which notes sounded good with which others. Even though I didn't do formal scales, I could soon perform rhythmical runs up and down the strings. I started playing along to the LPs in my collection, as well as composing more and more religious songs. I was in my element.

Finally, a few months after I started playing, I was allowed to teach the choir one of my songs at our Thursday-evening practice (a better number than my first creation, my songwriting mercifully maturing as rapidly as my guitar skills). We sang it in church that Sunday, with me accompanying on the bass. I didn't get the standing ovation I had envisioned, but I got a healthy round of applause, and a warm glow of pride inside my chest. It was the best moment of my life.

I began taking my bass on the bus with me to school on certain days so I could practice in one of the three music rooms in the basement. They had quite good equipment down there—bigger amps and even some effects pedals. I had told the music teacher, Mr. Penfold, that I was learning to play, and he encouraged me to get involved with the school orchestra. I told him that I wasn't quite ready for that yet, so he offered to give me a spot of coaching when he had a free lunchtime. It was very kind of him, and his occasional input did help me with the more technical and theoretical aspects of playing. The additional lunchtime practices really helped, too.

I became even more of an anomaly at school. Prior to my conversion I had overheard a boy refer to me as "that kinda cool, fat English chick." I was aloof and withdrawn but was not really given a hard time, even about my chubbiness, because of the inherent cool-factor of my accent and charity-shop chic. At the age of fifteen, when the other girls were wearing bright pink blouses, rah-rah skirts, and stilettos, I dressed almost exclusively in black, or in men's secondhand clothes. A few of the football-jock types threw the odd comment in my direction, but I never rose to the bait. I just thought they were all stupid. After I started going to church, and was seen at school associating with the "God-botherers," people decided that I was even weirder, and much less cool than they'd thought. I knew this, but couldn't have cared less now that I was bolstered up by the protective cushion of my beliefs. Yet when word got around that I played bass, the curve on the graph of my acceptability began to climb again.

One day I was sitting on the school bus, my guitar case propped up against the seat next to me, reading an old copy of *Melody Maker* that Sam had sent over to me a while back.

The boy behind me leaned over my shoulder. "Wow, *Melody Maker*. Awesome."

I twisted my head back to look at him. He was cute, with big brown eyes and floppy blond hair. Not many active zits, just the purple shadows of past ones scattering his jawline.

"Yes, my friend in England mails them over to me."

We got into a conversation about the English music scene and ended up talking all the way to school. The boy said he was heavily into Elvis Costello and Ian Dury and the Blockheads. He told me that his name was Justin Becker, he was in the year above me, and he had a band himself. He didn't usually get the bus to school, but his bike was in the shop. He asked me lots of questions: my name, how long I'd been here, if I'd been to any gigs (I hadn't), how long I'd been playing bass for. I answered him methodically, trying to keep cool but feeling, for the first time ever, the rush of adrenaline derived from fancying someone. Not very optimistically, I wondered if he was a Christian.

When the bus dropped us off outside the school gate, Justin said, "Well, nice to meet you, Helena. See you around, I guess. Good luck with the bass."

He was gone before I could reply. I felt a bit let down that he hadn't even invited me to see his band play. I thought about him all day, and at recess I asked Mary Ellen what she knew about him.

"Justin Becker? Oh, he's totally the heartthrob of the twelfth grade. He always has a bunch of girls running after him. I didn't know he had a band. Still, it figures, I guess. I hear he's very arrogant."

I was delighted to have been chatted up by a heartthrob but despondent that he had so many suitors already. I decided not to tell Mary Ellen that I fancied him. I didn't think she would understand.

Except for glimpses from a distance in the hallway, I did not see Justin again for a couple of weeks. After a few days I put him out of my mind, remembering my vow of chastity and my commitments to the church. One lunchtime, however, I was down in the practice room plugging away on the bass when I felt someone's presence. I turned around and saw Justin lolling in the doorframe watching me, chewing on a toothpick and running his fingers affectedly through his thick blond hair.

"Oh, hello!" I squeaked, embarrassed. I had been in a hurry that morning and had not realized until I got to school that I'd only applied mascara and eyeliner to one eye. I kept the naked side of my face turned stiffly away from him in the hope that he would not notice.

"Hi. Hey, you're not bad, you know. What was your name again?"

I was crushed that he'd forgotten. "Helena Nicholls," I said, a little crossly.

"Want to be in my band? My bass player just left."

I couldn't believe what I was hearing. A real live band! Now, that was something I could write and tell Sam about.

"What sort of band is it?" I asked, playing it cool and trying not to appear as though my neck was in a brace.

"Well, you know, it's like, I'm the singer, right? And, well, actually, that's it right now. The guy who played bass left because Coach was gonna kick him off the football team unless he came to more practices. And we nearly got a drummer, but, like, his parents wouldn't let him get any drums. But it's gonna be awesome! There's this other guy, Joe, who might join also, and he plays keyboards. So whaddaya think?"

Sounds pretty lame to me, was what I thought. "What kind of music?" I said instead.

"Well, sorta like Blondie, although with no girl singer, of course, or The Stranglers. We don't have too many songs at the moment, mostly cover versions really. You write?"

I nodded, hoping he wouldn't ask me what sort of songs I wrote. I wasn't sure about this whole thing. *Half-assed* were the words that sprang to mind. However, the idea of being in a band, particularly one that was just Justin and me, was undeniably appealing. I would get to go to his house and everything.

"We could have a rehearsal and see how it goes," I said tentatively.

He smiled and the blood rushed into my cheeks, making me feel dizzy. "Great! How about tomorrow night?"

Luckily that wasn't Bible study or choir practice. "Fine. Where?"

"Seven-twelve Indiana. Say, six o'clock?"

"Okay."

"Okay, see you then." He slouched back round the doorframe out of sight, and I heard his rubber-soled sneakers squelch away on the parquet floor. I took a deep breath, breathing in the strong school smell of adolescents and antiseptic, and swallowed down my excitement. I'd just give it a go. Maybe I could even adapt a couple of my songs so they weren't about God. It would be easy enough to do, and I would love to hear them performed by a real band. I felt faintly traitorous at this thought, but quelled it by reasoning to myself that it was all additional practice for me, practice that would better serve my mission of praising the Lord through my gift of music.

The rehearsal was not a huge success. It was just the two of us, in the Beckers's basement games room, and at first I was so nervous being in Justin's presence that I could not seem to play anything properly. We had a stab at "Oliver's Army," reading the lyrics out of Justin's *Elvis Costello Songbook,* but Justin wasn't very good at playing his guitar—he couldn't get the chords right—the song sounded truly awful without drums, and his mum kept coming down to complain about the noise.

Justin was a total poseur, and sang as if performing in front of thousands instead of a quivering cat and his harassed-looking mother. He did have a wonderful voice, though. After a while he abandoned the guitar and we sang the song in harmony, with just my bass to keep time. It didn't sound too bad, and I began to be a little more cheered. We decided that if we could find a drummer and a keyboard player, we might have something. I told him that next week I would bring in a couple of my songs for us to try. At that point Mrs. Becker reappeared to say that my father had arrived to collect me, so we called it a day. As I packed up my bass and amp, I asked Justin if the band had a name yet.

"Blue Idea," he said firmly, smiling his gorgeous smile at me. "We're gonna be huge. You wait."

I wondered if that "we" included me, but I didn't have the nerve to ask. Instead I said good-bye to Justin and his mother and, much to Dad's irritation, sang the harmony line to "Oliver's Army," loudly, all the way home in the car, my brain filling in the crashing jubilant staccato of the piano chords and Elvis's mellow tenor: "*'And I would rather be anywhere else, tha-an here to-daaay. Woah, oh, oh, ohhh-oh, Woah oh-oh-oh-ohhhhh.'*"

* ✳ *

The following week I went back again. When I arrived, there were two other boys in the basement, drinking Dr. Pepper and horsing around with Justin. I instantly felt even more shy and very out of place, especially since Justin showed no signs of introducing me. I got on with tuning up my bass until finally the shorter of the two, a nerdy-looking character with thick black-rimmed glasses and tufty black hair, came over. "Hi, Helena, I'm David," he said. "That's Joe over there, in case you didn't know."

I waved hesitantly across the room to Joe, who was trying to slam-dunk a foam basketball into a wall-mounted hoop. He was incredibly tall and lanky, with a neck and wrists that seemed to go on forever, and he had heavy metal braces all over his teeth. He waved back at me in a friendly fashion. I vaguely recognized both him and David from school.

After a while I got fed up with waiting for something to happen, and just started to play a bass riff over and over again. Eventually David sat down on a stool behind a shabby-looking three-piece drum kit and picked up the beat, Joe wandered over and started playing some melancholic accompanying chords on a little Casio keyboard he'd brought with him, and Justin managed to add a reggae-style guitar skank over the top of it all. It didn't sound half bad. We bashed away for almost ten minutes until the tune died a natural death and we all petered out, ending it with a cacophony of crashing drums and writhing, frantic guitar chords (luckily Mrs. Becker was out that day). Justin was windmilling his right arm round and round as though he was Pete Townshend onstage at the Rainbow, until I was afraid he might try to smash up his guitar on the three-quarter-sized pool table.

In the ear-ringing silence that followed we all looked at one another, grinning and flushed with the success of our first-ever jam session. Justin and Joe exchanged triumphant high fives and all three boys whooped and yelled with excitement.

* ✳ *

After that we started to play together regularly, quickly learning to belt out versions of our favorite pop and New Wave songs with great conviction. I also taught them the melodies of several songs I had written, substituting the words "my love" for "my Lord" where appropriate. I didn't think anyone guessed that they had ever been anything but simple rock songs about being in love, or finding one's way home. (I'd deleted the line that had originally explained that "home" was in fact "heaven." It worked a treat.)

* ✳ *

May 1, 1982

Dear Tan Smarg (Squirrel Comber and Hedgehog Brusher),

Get this—I'm in a band!! We're called Blue Idea, and it's me and three
boys from school: Justin Becker, David Somerstein, and Joe Jennings.
They're all seniors (like sixth-formers). Justin is really, really gorgeous.
It's his band—I can't believe he's letting me be in it, too. And I've started
writing pop songs, so we might even do them as part of our set!

Oh, guess what—I nearly made such a fool of myself (what's new, I
hear you cry). You know when, ages ago, you used to really like that
awful group Guys n' Dolls? Well, I'd kind of got them mixed up in my
mind with an American band called the New York Dolls—who are
punks! We were round at Justin's rehearsing, and the New York Dolls
came on TV, all leather jackets and outrageous makeup and long hair. I
said to Joe: "Boy, they really had a change of image, didn't they!"

It wasn't till later that I realized my mistake! Luckily Joe had no idea
what I was on about.

I'm so excited, being in a real band! I wish you were here so you
could sing backing vocals or something—wouldn't that be a laugh?
You never know, maybe Blue Idea will come and play Salisbury City
Hall sometime! I'll give you a backstage pass and Melanie will be
totally jealous!!!

Lots of love,

      Helena xx

* ✳ *

Soon band practice took over from choir practice as the high point
of my week. I was still going to church every Sunday without fail,
and to Margie's Bible study class most Wednesdays. But I wasn't that
keen on Margie anyway, and it was not difficult to start skipping a
few of those here and there. Besides, the band missed few opportu-
nities to make jibes at me for being a Bible-thumping dweeb. At
first I rose above it, but as they began to take up more and more of
my time, it was hard not to be influenced by them.

We made our triumphantly awful debut in the living room at one of Justin's mates' parties on a Saturday night, a few months after we'd first practiced. We did all cover versions, as we weren't yet confident enough to perform any of my songs, and we wanted to make sure that our first audience got the crowd-pleasing numbers they obviously wanted. It was terrible, but no one at the party seemed to mind. They danced and cheered, and someone spilled a plastic cup of beer over me and my bass, and a good time was had by all. I didn't get home until one-thirty A.M., sneaking up the stairs on tiptoe so my parents wouldn't hear me. They had not waited up, so I thought I'd gotten away with it, but the next day I received the first in a series of lectures involving the phrases "concentrating on your schoolwork," "not getting in with the wrong crowd," and "what's wrong with just being in the choir?" It was all water off a duck's back to me.

That morning in church I was so tired that I dropped off during the sermon—not an ideal thing to do in my very noticeable spot with the choir, out in front of the congregation. My neighbor had to nudge me awake, and I could see Margie shooting daggers at me from her front-row pew. Since I'd joined the band she had become almost openly antagonistic toward me—in a very *Christian* way, of course. I had no idea why, nor did I care.

In fact I was very happy. I'd gradually become "one of the boys," and after a while, even Justin's smoldering grins ceased to move me. I liked him, but he could be an arrogant little creep. Instead of blushing and simpering in his presence, I started to bully and push him to be more reliable, practice his feeble guitar playing, and cut down on smoking so as to preserve his voice. Eventually, as we learned more and more of my songs, I emerged as the natural leader of the band, and reveled in the responsibility.

I was so relieved not to fancy Justin anymore that I thought for a while I was well and truly back on my spiritual path. But it turned out to be something more insidiously compelling than hormones that ultimately made me stray: the new and heady sensation of raw ambition.

HOME SWEET HOME

IT WAS ANOTHER TWO DAYS BEFORE I SAW TOBY AGAIN. ALL THE hospital emotions stirred up by the last kiss had been quietly simmering, and were just coming to a boil of resentment. Why were we doing this? I knew enough about men to be completely sure that whatever happened, he'd never leave his wife.

I was scribbling away at my manuscript like a mad woman when, out of the blue, he appeared at my door.

"Hello, stranger," I said. "Come in."

"It's only been two days," he replied defensively, but he came in anyway. He did kiss me, but only a peck, and I could tell immediately from the way his eyes slid away from my face that we weren't about to carry on where we'd left off in the visitors' room.

"How's the book going?"

"Good, I think. I'm getting there, slowly."

"So what happens when you finish? Are you trying to find a publisher?"

"Not at the moment, no. I'm sure it won't be a problem, though."

Toby laughed. "No, you're a celebrity. Of course it won't be. Publishers welcome people like you with open arms, don't they?"

"That wasn't what I meant."

"What did you mean, then?"

I sighed and put the notebook back under my pillow. "Nothing."

Toby looked at my legs. "I like your jeans. I thought so the other day, only didn't get a chance to mention it. I mean, it's good to see you in real clothes. Surely you'll be going home soon, won't you? You seem so much better."

I stood up and walked over to the window, peering out between the slats of the blinds at the huge Edwardian guest houses and hotels across the road.

"The doctor's going to let me know when he comes in today. He doesn't want to talk about fitting me with a fake eye until I decide whether or not I really want one. I'm not sure. And I think everything else is okay now, except my ear and a bit of leftover concussion—I still wobble a bit when I walk—so it depends on that."

"So tell me more about your book. Is it about Blue Idea?"

I felt a bit uneasy talking about it, but he seemed genuinely interested, and genuinely not interested in a repeat of what had happened after the Animal Snap game.

"It's about everything. Childhood, Sam, moving to America, being a teenager. The band. I'm just getting to that bit now. I've got some letters somewhere that I'll probably add in later, too, and they'll help me cross-check dates and stuff."

"How do you remember everything without them?"

I felt prickles on my neck. I mustn't give too much away, I thought. "I, um, think of what records I was listening to at the time, and then think back to how I felt."

"Oh yeah, that's how you DJ, isn't it? I've been doing my homework. So you're taking your own requests now, are you? Cool—that would make a great show!"

"Yeah, I suppose it might." I had to bite my lip to prevent myself from blurting out the Plan. Suddenly it was no longer any fun at all, keeping it to myself. With effort, I changed the subject. "Do you have a favorite record, Toby? I'm not putting you on the spot. You don't even have to say why it's your favorite, I'm just curious."

"Phew—bit of an impossible question, that one. There are so many I absolutely adore that I'm not sure if I could narrow it down to one. Lou Reed's 'Perfect Day,' perhaps. Bowie's 'Life on Mars'? 'Another Girl, Another Planet,' just as an example of a perfect pop song. I'd need to think about it more before giving you a definite answer, though."

"Fair enough. I notice you haven't mentioned any of Blue Idea's records."

Toby went red. He was so easy to tease.

"God, Toby, I don't know how you ever managed to be a journalist. You blush far too easily. I'm joking!"

He stuck his finger up at me flirtatiously, and all of a sudden looked so cute that I had a small ballooning urge to leap on top of him.

Then he became serious again.

"So what will you do with yourself once you get home and your mother's gone back to the States?"

"I don't know—celebrate, probably. No, I'll finish the book and then . . . Well, that's it, really."

Toby was obviously remembering my saying I didn't have many friends.

"There'll be someone to look after you, though, won't there?"

I scowled at him. "I won't need looking after! I'm going home because I'm better, aren't I?"

"But I mean, what are your long-term plans?"

He knew I'd lost my job, but I hadn't told him about Geoff's offer of the nighttime show.

"I haven't got any long-term plans, just one short-term one."

As soon as I said it, I thought, What a giveaway. A huge cliff-edge of bitterness had crept into my voice, and I honestly didn't know if I'd manufactured it for Toby's benefit or if it was genuine. The only thing I did know for sure was that one more kiss like the last one and I might not be able to go through with the Plan.

"You will be all right, won't you?" Toby persisted. "I mean, I know you've been a bit depressed and everything. I'm worried about you, that's all."

My indecision and his reversion to "guilt mode" were beginning to annoy me. "Oh, no need to worry. I *am* going to top myself, but not right now, okay? I would hate to give you something else to feel guilty about."

Toby looked at me with what was probably the look he gave Ruby when she drew Magic Marker on the sofa—cross and disappointed.

All of a sudden I made up my mind. I was going to push him further, goad him into leaving, and then I could really just get on with the Plan. He'd had enough traumas lately, and I was sick of him blowing hot and cold with me.

I took a deep breath. "You really think that's what I'm going to do, don't you? You think I'm actually writing a book about my life so that I'll be remembered after I'm dead? Well, if you think you've got it all sussed, then fine. Perhaps you *want* me to do it so you'll be able to tell everyone that you knew me, that you kissed me a couple of times. Would that give you a thrill? Or maybe you'd like to write my obituary for me? Go ahead—the job's vacant."

Emotions flitted across Toby's face: astonishment, hurt, fury. He moved across the room to where I stood by the window and grabbed me by the shoulders, almost shaking me.

"You listen to me, Helena. I'm sorry if I've got it all wrong—I hope to God I have got it all wrong—but you're bang out of order. Don't you even say that as a joke, or even *think* it, you understand? And how could you say I'd actually want you to do something as sick as that—what's the matter with you, anyway? I've told you how I feel and how hard this all is for me! Can't you cut me some slack, for God's sake?"

I felt dangerously out of control. "I'll think and do whatever I bloody well want to! Get off me! How dare you tell me what to do, after you've messed me around the way you have! You come on to me, kiss me; your wife wakes up, you ignore me. We have another kiss, and now you act like nothing's happened! You've treated me like shit, and I want you to get lost and leave me alone—for good. I won't be second best!"

I wrenched his hands from my shoulders.

Toby's arms flopped down to his sides, and he turned his back on me.

"It's not like that," he said, in a voice I'd never heard him use before. "I never meant to mess you around, and I'm sorry. But you know what else I'm sorry about? I'm sorry that you obviously think so little of me. So I'll do what you want and get lost now. Okay?"

He started to walk out of the room, slowly, as if he was waiting for me to stop him. Every stitch of me wanted him to stay, but I didn't move or speak. After the fattest of pregnant pauses, he finally picked up the pace and left.

Operation: Send Toby Away had worked a treat, much better than I could have hoped for.

* * *

The doctor came round later and told me yes, I could go home. Mum booked us a taxi, and I packed up my notebooks and pens, wash-bag and nightclothes. I said good-bye to the nurses and put on my Abba disguise.

Toby didn't come back, and I didn't leave my number or address for him. It would be best that way, I told myself bitterly.

* * *

Being in my own house again was so blissful that I forgot temporarily about the row with Toby. I cried like a virgin bride being lifted across the threshold as I came through the front door—the joy of being reunited with my bed, my coffee mugs, my refrigerator! I was convinced that even my toilet seat was more comfortable than the hospital one.

With Mum staying there in my absence, everything was spookily perfect-looking—house plants all green and perky, drunk on Baby Bio, no dust on the TV screen, kitchen surfaces as swabbed and sterile as the operating theater. The stag beetle in the outside drain and the small spider who'd been living in the fireplace had upped sticks and moved on, obviously in search of a quiet life.

"You put your feet up, honey, and I'll make us a nice cup of tea," she trilled when I came downstairs after a whirlwind tour to reacquaint myself with my home. Then she stopped and clapped her hand over her mouth. "No, wait," she said. "I nearly forgot—there's a very exciting message on the answering machine for you!"

My heart leapt as I approached the flashing red light of the machine. Toby? Maybe he'd tracked down my number after he realized I'd been discharged.

I pressed Play, but the voice I heard was that of a whiny American woman. "Oh, hi there, Helena, here's a blast from the past! It's your old buddy Margie, here in England. I called your mom a few weeks ago and she told me you'd be happy to have me to stay when I was over—I'm here in Man-chester for a conference that finishes on Wednesday. So if that's still okay with you, I'll see you then, around six, yeah? I'm, like, *so* looking forward to catching up with your totally exciting life!"

I flopped into an armchair, unable to stand under the dual weight of disappointment and fury. "Totally fuckin' rad," I muttered under my breath.

Mum appeared in the doorway and took in my livid face. "Isn't that marvelous, honey?" she said nervously. "Your old friend Margie coming to stay! Won't it be a tonic for you to have some girly chats with someone other than your old mum?"

I felt too exhausted and miserable to shout at her. "No, Mum, it is not marvelous. I have not spoken to this woman for about sixteen years. She's a preachy little cow who practically told me I'd rot in hell when Blue Idea got signed. I'm obviously the only wealthy person she knows in London, and she's after some free accommodation. You had no right at all to give out my phone number. And she's coming tonight, my first day home. . . ."

"But I thought you liked Margie!" She was pleating the freshly ironed tea towel in her hands.

I sighed. "I never bloody liked Margie. It was Mary Ellen who was the sweet one out of that church lot. She was quite nice, but the others were a bunch of nuts, and Margie was the worst. What am I going to do?"

Mum came over and knelt by my armchair. She put down her tea towel and stroked the hair away from my scarred forehead, apparently summoning up more reserves of mummyhood than she knew she possessed.

"Okay, here's the deal," she said. "Let her stay tonight because she'll have a problem finding anywhere else now. I'll make sure she leaves again tomorrow—she doesn't know that you've had an accident, so it's quite reasonable to ask her to go. And if you don't want to talk to her this evening, just say you're tired and I'll tell you to go to bed. How's that?"

"All right, then," I said, managing a smile. It was so nice to be taken care of. I had a sudden bottomless pang of remorse at what I was going to have to put her through in a matter of weeks after I'd waved her off at the airport.

"Thanks, Mum."

THERE THERE MY DEAR

BY THE TIME BLUE IDEA FINALLY GOT TO DO BUSINESS WITH A REAL record company, I'd already played out the scene in my head a thousand times. As I sat with the rest of the band in a brand-new restaurant in Greenwich Village, near the offices of Ringside Records, I went over it one more time: "Let's talk money—yes. Now, how does half a million sound to you?" or maybe "You'll have that platinum record before you know it, you mark my words."

Ringside's Director of A&R, Mr. Wallberger, was late, so we sat nervously, saying little and feeling very out of place. The waiting staff hovered around in packs, looking down their noses at us. Eventually a put-out-looking boy detached himself reluctantly from the other waiters and came to plonk menus and iced water down in front of us.

We had come a very long way since the night of our first show, almost a year ago. I could barely even remember it now, although I still had a faint stain on one of my white shirts from the beer some-one had spilled on me. Since then we had practiced, and practiced, and I had written more songs, and we had played in public at every possible opportunity. We'd rocked out to impress our classmates at school dances, got dressed up formally to perform at Justin's cousin's wedding reception, done David's brother's bar mitzvah, and played dozens of dark and sweaty all-ages rock nights at the local bar.

I sipped my iced water, trying to still my overoptimistic imagination by attempting to recall our first five gigs, in order. I failed miserably, but at that precise moment I was so nervous, I was hard-pushed to remember my own address.

Finally the door opened and Mr. Wallberger walked in, accompanied by his A&R manager, a skinny, hippie English guy named Willy

Watts-Davis. Willy had been our introduction to Ringside Records. He had, by chance, heard a set we'd played in Asbury Park: He had driven down to see another Freehold band called Saul, who were headlining at the same venue that night, but was so excited with us that he spent the duration of Saul's set chatting to us out in the parking lot (Justin assured him they were terrible anyway, and that he wasn't missing a thing). Willy had then arranged an opening slot for us at CBGB's in the city the following week so Mr. Wallberger could come and check us out, too. It was an outstanding stroke of luck. We had previously made a cheap demo tape and sent it round to various record companies, but with no response—unsurprisingly, since it sounded absolutely awful.

We'd seen them standing by the bar at the CB's show—not hard to miss, there being only about eight people in the place. Neither of them were a bit how I'd imagined Record Company People to look; I was convinced they all wore sharp Armani suits with just a T-shirt underneath, chunky gold necklaces, loafers and no socks, and sported ludicrously skinny plaits to compensate for bald spots, sniffed continuously, and constantly rushed off to the toilet to do more drugs.

But no, Mr. Wallberger was large and clumsy-looking, thirty-five-ish, with a mop of curly brown hair, too-tight corduroys, and a scruffy button-down shirt. He looked as if he didn't have a penny to his name. Willy had been hovering nervously around behind his boss, patchwork flares flapping around his skeletal ankles. I couldn't see if he had his fingers crossed or not, but I wouldn't have minded taking a bet that he had.

We'd played our hearts out, knowing that this kind of a chance was so slim as to be practically unheard of. When Mr. Wallberger came up to us after the set and invited us to lunch the next day to "talk some business," we were beside ourselves with excitement.

Ringside Records—a real record label! I was sure that Dexys Midnight Runners' first album had been released on Ringside U.K., and they were a fantastic band. A few months earlier, I'd gotten Sam to send us a tape of *Searching for the Young Soul Rebels,* and when it arrived in the post we almost wore it out, committing every single note to memory, and as many of the words as we could pick out.

Justin decided to take Kevin Rowland as his role model, and started sporting woolly hats and quoting from *Taxi Driver*. He wanted us to learn "There There My Dear," thinking that Blue Idea's lack of a horn section would enable us to totally reinterpret the song, but our attempts at a rendition just sounded ridiculous—completely pointless and bald, like a newly shorn sheep. Finally, when Justin tried to get us all to go out for runs together, because he'd read in *NME* that Kevin did the same, we rebelled and chucked out the tape. Consequently it was months before we finally discovered that in fact the record had come out on EMI, not Ringside.

Anyway, the night before our meeting we all stayed in Brooklyn, with Joe's aunt Sandi. The boys slept on her living-room floor, and I got the guest bedroom, but I hadn't been able to sleep for more than a couple of hours with the anticipation. For most of the night I had lain awake whispering, "Please, God, let us get a deal. Please, God, let him want to sign us. Please, God, we're not in it for the money or the fame" (something of a lie).

I wasn't awfully optimistic, though—I saw no particular reason for God to shower his largess upon me at this particular juncture, even if he did overlook the fib. I hadn't been to church for over six weeks, and had left the choir a long time before that. I viewed this lapse as merely a temporary suspension of progress along my spiritual path while sorting out my career, and fervently asked God to understand my position. But somehow I did keep forgetting to say my prayers at night. I *must* go to church this Sunday, I thought, deal or no deal.

So there we all were, hellos and apologies for lateness proffered and accepted. The multitudinous waiting staff cheered up slightly when the big guns arrived; they seemed to be able to detect the presence of a platinum Amex, despite the smokescreen of our collective scruffy appearances.

"Hello, Mr. Wallberger," I said, and shook his hand.

"No, please, no one calls me that. Call me Rob."

I knew immediately that this would be impossible, far worse than having to call Sam's mum Cynthia. It was months before I realized that the music industry really was a first-name-only business.

We all ordered Cokes and designer-type sandwiches, which were just becoming popular in New York—radicchio and Brie, ham with red onion compote, that sort of thing. I could barely swallow because of nerves, and when asked a question, choked on a mouthful of Coke, which spurted fizzily and painfully out of my nose. Justin sniggered and I wanted to cry with embarrassment, but the Ringside Brothers kindly affected not to notice. The bass line to "There There My Dear" thudded persistently and annoyingly through my head, a sort of defense mechanism.

They chatted to us about nothing much for what seemed like far too long: the excessive number of waiters in the place (approximately three per customer), the consequently annoyingly slow service, and the bad attitude of said waiters.

"People are much nicer to you in England," Willy sighed wistfully, and I could tell how homesick he was.

I was plucking up courage to ask him how long he'd lived in New York, and to explain my own British roots, when Mr. Wallberger put down his glass.

"So, like I said, I enjoyed the show," he began casually. "I think there's definitely something there. You're all very green, of course, and the band still lacks quite a bit of cohesion—but once you've done a few weeks on the road, I'm sure that would sharpen up. Your music isn't what's hip at the moment, you're not exactly New Wave, or post-punk either—but I'm willing to take a chance with you and put out your first record. I think it's time for something new, and I think you have the talent. Like I said, I'm willing to take a punt on you guys, see how it goes."

This was not quite the ecstatic welcome I'd hoped for.

"How much will you give us?" said Justin, to the point as usual. I blushed at his directness and folded my napkin up into tiny panicked sections underneath the table. I wished we had a manager. Our naïveté seemed to hover over the table, choking me, like a cloud of exhaust fumes. But a week ago we hadn't needed a manager.

"You'd get an advance to record the album and get you out on the road—all recoupable, of course—we'll have to decide what the amount would be. Enough to cover your expenses, anyway."

"What does 'recoupable' mean?" asked David innocently.

I cringed even more, although I didn't know, either. To his

credit, Mr. Wallberger didn't laugh, or even smirk at us. I think that was what convinced me that this would be a good deal to do.

"Recoupable means that we give you money up front—that's the advance—and then once your record starts selling, we take a percentage of the money from each record sold and use it to pay back the advance. It's like a loan."

David and Justin were horrified. "So how do we make any money, then?" Justin demanded.

"Well, the idea is that we've signed you because you'll sell a helluva lot more records than it takes to recoup the advance. Then we all start making a profit. Sometimes that happens with the first record, sometimes not until the second or third, sometimes never. It's a chance we have to take."

Joe asked, "So what if we don't sell any records, does that mean we owe you all that money?"

This time Mr. Wallberger did laugh, but not in a condescending way. "Oh, no, it's our loss. You see, once you've made a record that we believe will sell, it's our job to sell it. That's why we have marketing and promotions people, someone to take it to radio, someone to get press about the band and the record, someone to make sure it's in the stores, and so on."

I had a mental image of an army of uniformed workers knocking on radio station doors all over the country with big baskets full of our records, saying, "Here, have one of these," but I did not really see what good that would do. I couldn't associate the person in the radio station *having* the record with people going out and actually *buying* it. It was too big a leap of the imagination to picture the record being played on the radio at all. We had a couple of decent stations near us in Freehold, but the reception from our house was terrible, and so I rarely listened at home. I had no concept of college-radio charts or specialty shows playing new bands. It was all a mystery to me, and from the expressions on the others' faces, I knew it was the same for them.

"But you don't have to worry about all that stuff just yet—it's early days. Let us take care of that. All you need to do is think about it for a while. We'll send you a draft contract, you talk it over with each other and your folks, and call me. Here's my card. No obligations. Once we've started the ball rolling, come by the offices and meet the team."

"Yeah, and call me, like, any time if you have any questions," chimed in Willy, who had been nodding in earnest assent during the last twenty minutes, until I was worried that his head might drop off. With every nod a little waft of patchouli drifted across to my side of the table.

I dropped my balled-up napkin surreptitiously onto the floor. A contract! Maybe this thing really was going to happen. I felt excitement rising in my throat like a blush, and "There There My Dear" exploded into a crescendo in my mind, *"Rrrrrobin, let me explain!"*

Willy opened his mouth to say something else, but Justin sneezed suddenly and drowned him out. Willy tried again; Justin sneezed again. And again. And again. Every time Willy tried to speak, Jus sneezed, until Willy lapsed into embarrassed silence. David and Joe smirked, and I alternately examined my fingernails and my surroundings until normal service could be resumed.

"Normal service," it seemed, did not apply to the restaurant. Mr. Wallberger was waving his Amex card indiscreetly in the air, trying to attract a waiter's attention, but they all seemed to have been struck blind. Meanwhile Justin sneezed on and on, pausing only to wipe his streaming eyes with his napkin. Eventually one of the young men sauntered over with our check, and held it out to Mr. Wallberger, who threw his credit card onto the saucer without looking at the amount owed. I tried to imagine my parents doing that, and almost laughed out loud at the thought. I wondered if I would ever be rich enough to not care how much lunch cost.

We said elated good-byes, left the restaurant, and walked over to West Fourth Street to get the subway back to Brooklyn. Justin finally stopped sneezing, and we sang Dexys tunes full blast all the way back to Aunt Sandi's place, substituting the words we weren't sure of with choruses of "la-la-la's." There was a sense of unreality about the whole thing, emphasized by each of us calling out a different song title from *Searching for the Young Soul Rebels* to sing—we couldn't quite believe that we had our own songs to sing from now on, and that people might actually want to hear them.

※

A draft contract was duly dispatched to us. Aunt Sandi had a boyfriend who was an attorney, and he looked it over for us, also showing it to a friend of his in entertainment law. It was deemed to be not a bad deal, for a new, unknown band. We would have to sign options for five records with Ringside, which meant that after each record we made, they could decide if they wanted us to make another one. If not, they could drop us, but we couldn't voluntarily leave Ringside without breaking the contract until the five records were made. It seemed to be a very big commitment on our part, and not very much on Ringside's, but apparently this was standard.

I started to worry that I wouldn't be able to write enough good songs fast enough, but Jus pointed out that if the songs weren't any good, we'd get dropped anyway, in which case I wouldn't have to worry.

"Oh, great, thanks—pressure me, why don't you?" I told him.

Then Aunt Sandi's boyfriend commented that as the songwriter I would get more money than the others, because I'd get publishing royalties as well as artist royalties, which cheered me up no end. Justin looked sulky. After all, I thought, I already have more than fifty songs written, and I've only been at it for a year and a half. Many of them were religious, and I didn't think that Ringside or the band would appreciate them—but that was beside the point.

We would get twenty thousand dollars up front for the first record, out of which we would be required to pay for our studio time and expenses, a producer, equipment purchase or rental, and a van.

"That's a lot of money," said Joe.

"Will there be any left over for me to buy a car with?" David wanted to know.

"It's not our money," I reminded him. "Remember what Mr. Wallberger said—it's an advance. We have to pay it back again later."

"How will we keep track of everything?" I added, as an afterthought.

"You need a manager," said Aunt Sandi's boyfriend firmly. "I'll ask my colleague if he knows anyone good."

That was how Mickey the Manager came into our lives. Mickey looked like he should have been a lifeguard on an L.A. beach. He was very tanned, with a rugged face and a mustache modeled on Magnum P.I. He had a couple of other bands on his roster, one of whom had recently become quite successful, and he was fond of spewing out clichés like "Stick with me, kids, I'm going places." Boys apparently joined bands so they could meet girls (well, that was certainly the reason Joe had joined Blue Idea), and I was sure Mickey had started a management company for the same reason, because he couldn't actually play an instrument or sing. He always had some ditzy little dolly on his arm, picked up from a show the night before. But his womanizing notwithstanding, we all quite liked him. He had a warm heart, under that sharkish exterior, and he did seem to work very hard for us and his other bands. We gave him a lot of healthy shit about how many polyester open-to-the-waist shirts he possessed, and the revolving door through which his girlfriends appeared to pass, but he took it all with good humor.

"Hey, I'm young"—he wasn't. "I'm a mover and a shaker, and I'm gorgeous"—also debatable. "Why would I want to be tied down with a wife and kids?"

Justin had finally met someone who could outdo him in the arrogance stakes.

So within three months of our lunch meeting with Mr. Wall-berger and Willy, the contract was signed, we had a lawyer, a manager, some studio time booked for demoing, and a lot of money in a new bank account that Mickey set up for us, overseen by an accountant also found by Mickey.

We felt like a real band at last. I graduated from high school, the last of the four of us to do so, and told my parents that I was going to defer college for a year to see if my musical career took off.

Everyone in Freehold knew about our deal; the local paper did a small feature about us when we got signed. All our old school friends were beside themselves with envy. The lead singer of Saul punched Justin in the face in the supermarket parking lot, and Margie hissed, "Hell is a very *hot* place, you know," at me from her front porch when I passed her house one day.

My parents professed to be proud of my new enterprise but

couldn't contain their horror that I was not pursuing further education, at least for the foreseeable future. I thought they were
secretly convinced that I would transform overnight into a heroin-
shooting, Mohican-sporting, foul-mouthed menace to society who
would embarrass them in front of their country-club friends. This
was, in a nutshell, how they viewed the protagonists of popular
music—even though I told them that punk was dead.

I phoned Sam to tell her that we'd been signed, and she was hysterical with delight and pride.

"Well," she said when she'd calmed down. "My news is that I got a
Saturday job at Price Rite. I haven't had my O-level results yet, but I
think I did all right—they want me to enroll for four A levels and an
S level. And that swine Mark Symonds dumped me. So I think you
win first prize for interesting news!"

I commiserated with her about Mark, although I had never liked
him. He had acne and was not, in my opinion, good enough for
Sam. When I'd been over to stay with the Grants in Salisbury the
previous Christmas, he and I had fought, subtly but constantly and
viciously, for Sam's attention.

If the truth be known, however, I was also quite jealous that Sam
had a boyfriend and I didn't. I was sixteen and had never even been
out on a date. I was absolutely humbled by this pathetic track
record.

Sam was the only one I confided in about it, and she was very
nice to me.

"Don't worry, Helena, you'll meet someone. Now you've been
signed, I bet you get loads of blokes after you. You're far too good
for those meathead high-school boys, anyway."

That was all very well for her to say, with her long, slim legs and
huge gray eyes.

I still had a massive crush on the doorman of the local club we'd
played at countless times in the past year. He was at least twenty-
one, and enormous, with monstrous biceps bulging out of a lurid
Misfits T-shirt. He always smiled at me, and sometimes commented,
"Yeah, cool set, guys," to us afterward. I felt sure he said this specifi-
cally in my direction, and fantasized that it was only a matter of days
before he asked me out.

Every time we played the club, I spent hours getting ready, trying to look as Gothic as I could—until the night we got onstage and I saw the door open and a beautiful punk girl walk in. She was tiny and elfin, with pink hair, black lace gloves, and purple laddered tights. My doorman immediately locked her in the most passionate embrace I had ever seen. They were like two snails stuck together, and didn't come up for air once throughout our entire opening number. When the song ended, I intentionally sent as much feedback as I could through the speaker, sending the snogging couple, not to mention the rest of the audience, leaping vertically in the air like electrocuted cats.

Oh well, perhaps Sam was right, maybe I *would* get a boyfriend now that we were signed. He would be a musician, too, not just some scummy old bouncer.

I was, however, very impressed at the news of Sam's academic aspirations. "Four A levels and an S level? Jeez, Sam, you'll be busy," I'd said to her.

For a second I stopped thinking about the patent lack of romance in my life, and wondered instead if a patent lack of qualifications would be detrimental to my future ambitions, especially if I planned to move back to England. Sam would end up with examination certificates coming out of her ears, while I wouldn't have an O level to my name.

But no, I decided, I'm going to be famous. I'll concentrate on that, and worry about everything else later.

YOU LOOK SO DIFFERENT

MUM WAS IN THE DOWNSTAIRS LOO WHEN THE DOORBELL RANG at seven o'clock that night.

"Sorry, Helena, you'll have to get that. It's probably Margie," she called through the door. I could hear the embarrassment in her voice at having to be so vulgar as to speak and pee simultaneously.

I plodded up the hall, feeling like the butler from Trumpton, and reluctantly opened the front door.

A hugely fat woman surrounded by an extended family of suitcases stood in the front porch. Only the man-made fibers of her clothes and the wedges of frizzy hair identified her as the Margie I remembered.

Margie, however, had even fewer clues to go on. "Hi!" she said brightly and politely. "Is this the Nicholls residence?"

"It certainly is!" I confirmed, equally brightly, adjusting my eye patch.

"Is Helena home? I'm an old school friend, Margie Westerburg. I believe I'm expected."

I feigned shock and joyful surprise. "Margie! Oh, I'm so sorry, I didn't recognize you. Well, it has been such a long time. Do come in."

Margie looked at me, confused. Even though I was enjoying winding her up, I felt sick with hurt that I was so unrecognizable.

"Helena?" she asked, in a small, shocked voice.

"As I live and breathe," I said heartily. "Excuse me if I don't help you with your herd of bags, I just came out of hospital today."

To my horror, Margie burst into loud, snotty tears. "Oh my Lord, what *happened* to you? Your poor face! And what's the matter with your eye? You look so different, I . . . Oh, sweet Jesus, bless you!"

I turned away from her abruptly and stomped back down the

tiled hallway, just as Mum flushed the toilet and emerged, adjusting her skirt.

I left her to greet Margie and fill her in on all the gory details, and went out into the back garden, where I stared at the birds commuting home across the apricot-streaked sky.

I felt utterly heartbroken. It wasn't just Margie's shock at my appearance, although that was bad enough. It was the comment "You look so different."

* * *

The last time anyone had said that to me was years ago, and it was Sam. I'd brought her to see Blue Idea headline Wembley Stadium, at an all-day concert with lots of bands. It was the first time she'd ever seen me perform in front of a huge crowd like that—her illness had meant she'd missed both our previous big U.K. tours.

It was a sweltering day, and Sam was tired, so while I got ready, she had taken a little nap on the dusty old sofa in my dressing room. She'd woken up just as the makeup lady had finished working miracles on me and I was in all my stage finery.

"Oh, Helena, " Sam had said, staring at me like I'd been beamed down from another planet. There was real awe in her voice. "You look so different!"

"Kinky Afro," I thought now, was the song for that day. Because of my memory of Sam's sheer bliss as we danced around to it, hidden at the side of the stage, during the Happy Mondays' set. I'd never seen her so happy. It was wonderful.

"Are you all right, darling?" asked Mum, who appeared next to me, red in the face from the exertion of shepherding Margie's cases in. "Why don't you come in and fix us all a drink?"

I nodded and came back inside, the whiny guitar intro of "Kinky Afro" coiling up in my head.

"Drink, Margie?" I inquired, opening the sideboard to reveal my standing-room-only collection of the hard stuff. "I've got gin, vodka, Scotch, wine, beer in the fridge—"

"Oh, just a soda, please," Margie interrupted hastily. "I don't touch a drop of alcohol, never have."

Her eyes roved around the room, obviously trying to take in anything other than my offensive face. "You have a lovely home. Have you lived here long?"

"About five years now. Glad you like it."

I poured Margie a tepid Diet Coke and handed it to her, spitefully omitting to add ice. This crime was enough to cause the average American to rush to the airport and jump on the first available plane home, but sadly Margie was made of sterner stuff.

"You Brits sure do like your drinks warm, don't you? I'm kinda used to it now, though."

"Mum? G and T?"

"Yes, please, dear," said my mother. "I'll get the ice." She marched pointedly into the kitchen to find the ice bucket. Traitor, I thought.

Drinks dispensed and chilled, we all sat awkwardly in the living room. Mum and I sat together on one sofa, because Margie's bulk seemed to spread across most of the other one.

"Say, Helena, you *have* lost weight," Margie began. She'd been looking at my thighs, perhaps because it was easier than looking into my eye.

You haven't, you fat cow, I thought, berating myself for being such a bitch.

"Oh, that fell off years ago," I managed airily. "Being on tour was pretty physical work, even though people think you're just sitting around in tour buses all day."

Margie nodded knowingly, as if she went on tour all the time. "It sure was incredible, wasn't it, how you guys got to be so huge?"

I resisted the temptation to say the same went for her. "Yeah, I suppose it was, yeah. It was a pretty interesting few years."

I had no desire to dredge up my life history for Margie. I was saving it for the manuscript. "So, what do you do with yourself these days? You mentioned you were over here for a conference?"

Margie's face lit up. "Oh, yes, it was real fascinating! I'm a rep for a firm that sells evangelical products, and we had our annual sales conference in Man-chester for the first time. It's such a thrill to be in England. I've never been here before! And it was wonderful to meet all the other reps. Such a sense of community!"

"Sorry to be ignorant, but what are evangelical products?" I asked earnestly.

Mum grinned into her G&T, making ice bounce off her teeth as she swallowed.

Margie didn't notice. "Gosh, all sorts of things, really. You know, hymnbooks and chalices and kneelers."

I had a sudden thought. "Hey, you don't sell those big wall-hanging things, do you, like the ones we had in church?"

Margie nodded ecstatically. "Yes, yes, that's right. You remember those? Well, I'm not surprised. They are so beautiful."

I actually managed a smile. "Yeah, they were. You know, I always wondered how churches got ahold of them. Who'd have thought you'd end up selling them?"

Me, for one. It seemed perfectly fitting.

Mum got up from the sofa and began to head for the kitchen. "Are you hungry, Margie? I was going to make a little supper for us all—if you'd like some?"

Margie nodded enthusiastically. "Yes, thank you, Mrs. Nicholls, that would be wonderful."

"Oh, for heaven's sake, Margie, please call me Eve. We're all grown-ups now."

I thought of Cynthia Grant, how she wanted me to call her Cynthia long before Sam and I were grown-ups. I must get in touch with her before the Plan, see her one last time.

Mum vanished off to rustle up a meal, and I realized Margie had asked me something. "Excuse me, Margie, what? I'm still a little deaf in one ear."

"I SAID, ARE YOU IN TOUCH WITH ANYONE ELSE FROM FREEHOLD?"

I rolled my eye. "It's okay, I'm not that deaf. There's no need to shout. No, I'm not in touch with anyone actually, apart from the Blue Idea boys. Mum keeps me up to date with the news—although she hadn't heard anything from you until your call a few weeks ago. You still live there, then? Are you married?"

Margie puffed her chubby cheeks up into two rueful cushions. "Yes, I still live in Freehold. Guess I'll never leave the old place. And no, I'm not married. I was engaged, actually, until last year. But my fiancé left me for someone else."

"I'm sorry to hear that," I said. "That must have been terrible."

"Well, Jesus got me through it. He always does. I hope He's been helping you in your time of trial, too, Helena."

"Yeah," I replied hastily, trying not to add, "Whatever." "So do you know if Mary Ellen Randall still lives locally?"

Margie nodded enthusiastically. "Oh, yes! I see her at church every week. She was so excited when I told her I was coming to visit you. 'Do send Helena my fondest love,' she said. 'I wish I could see her, too. She was such a lovely girl.'"

I was touched. "That's nice. I always liked Mary Ellen. Send her my love, too, won't you? Is she happy?"

Margie looked at me as if I was mad. "She sure is. She has the Lord in her heart, and a wonderful family—two children, cute husband. Great job, too; she coordinates missionary placements in the Third World. Of course she's happy."

Instead of feeling my usual envy, I was pleased that Mary Ellen was happy. She deserved it. For a second, though, I did wish that I'd kept up my faith. It must be wonderful to be content that, whatever life threw at you, you'd be okay as long as you had God, and a supportive community of like-minded people around you.

The telephone rang, and then stopped again. After a couple of minutes, Mum appeared back in the living room, cordless phone in one hand, potato peeler in the other.

"It's for you."

"Who is it?" I hissed at her, annoyed that she had answered it in the first place. Missing a heartbeat, I wondered if she was going to say Toby.

"Cynthia Grant," she replied, in a slightly strained voice.

I stood up and took the receiver, waiting for Mum to get back to spud-bashing, but she continued to loom in front of me, clutching the peeler in a rather defensive manner.

"Hi, Cynthia, it's me," I said into the phone. "I was just thinking about you."

"Helena, love!" said Cynthia, warmly. "How are you feeling? I'm so happy for you, that you're out of hospital—but I feel so guilty for not visiting! Were you thinking that you're going to hate me forever now?"

I laughed. "Of course not. It would be impossible for anyone to hate you, least of all me."

"Well, I rang the hospital—I was going to pop in and see you tomorrow because I'm coming up to London to meet some girlfriends for lunch. But now you're home, I don't think I'm going to have time to come all the way over to Twickenham—I'm so sorry. I wanted to ring anyway, though, to say welcome back."

"Oh, don't worry. It was really sweet of you to think of me. And thanks for the card, too. To be honest, I'm feeling pretty wiped out. *I'm not really up for too many visitors.*"

I raised my voice a tone for the last sentence, but Margie appeared to be comfortably engrossed in a *Marie Claire* she'd found in the magazine rack. Mum, however, was still looming strangely. I made a face at her and she turned abruptly and left the room.

Something occurred to me. "Cynthia—there is one thing. You remember when I came down to Salisbury last time, you asked if I wanted to take that hat box—you know, our, er, Hel-Sam box—and I said no, I couldn't face it yet? Well, I wondered if I could get it picked up by courier. I've started to write a book, and it would really help to have a rummage through it."

"Oh, Helena, of course you can, love. I've been keeping it here for you. What a wonderful idea! You always were a clever girl. Make sure you autograph me a copy, won't you?"

I felt a moment's sadness, for both of us, that I wouldn't be around to do any book signings when the book saw the light of day. "Sure."

"I'll get the box wrapped up and addressed, ready for collection. Mind, it's quite heavy. It'll be ever so expensive to have it couriered. Are you sure you don't want to wait until I can drive up with it? It would have to be next week, though, I—"

I cut her off. "No, no, really, you don't need to do that. I can afford it. And Cynthia?"

"Yes, love?"

"You won't look inside it, will you?"

Old habits died hard.

Cynthia laughed. "Well, I've managed to contain my curiosity for about twenty years, so I think I can probably resist for another few days!"

I laughed, sheepishly, as well. "Sorry—I can't believe I said that! There's nothing very exciting in there anyway, as far as I remember. It's just stuff like our old baby teeth, my second favorite Barbie, Sam's four-leaf clover—you know, things that we thought were a big deal at the time."

"Sam certainly thought that clover was a big deal," Cynthia said, a wistfulness creeping into her voice.

She'd brought up Sam's name! Much as I longed to talk about her, I wasn't sure that I was up to it—I still felt too delicate. And besides, I certainly couldn't cope with doing it in earshot of Margie, marooned on the sofa, and Mum, sulking in the kitchen. Briskly, I headed the encroaching emotional tenor of the conversation off at the pass. "Yes, well, it's mainly the letters I'm interested in. Thanks for doing that for me. I really appreciate it. I have to go now, though. I have a friend from Freehold here, and we're about to have supper."

We said our good-byes fondly, promising to keep in touch. I replaced the phone, got myself a second gin and tonic, and poured Margie another Diet Coke—with ice. When I handed it to her, she put down the *Marie Claire* and, for the first time, looked straight at me.

"You know, Helena, I owe you an apology."

I was taken aback. "You do? What for?"

Margie looked sheepish. "I prayed so hard about this at the time and since, but I know I didn't behave in a very Christian way toward you when we were at school."

"But you were the one who first introduced me to the church."

"No, not that. It's just . . . when you joined Blue Idea and started to go out and play all your rock concerts, I was, well, jealous."

I was flabbergasted. "Really? Why?"

"I'm not sure. I think it was because you could sing and play guitar so well. I always wanted to be in the choir, but I'm, like, totally tone-deaf, and there you were, up doing solos in weeks. And then you got in with the band, stopped coming to church, and got real successful and all. I pretended to myself that I disapproved because you had turned your back on Jesus. I guess that was part of it—but who was I to judge you? Besides, I can't deny that I just felt so envious of you, getting all rich and famous like that. So I'm sorry. I hope you forgive me."

I grinned. What a turn-up. "Of course I forgive you, Margie. You weren't all that horrible to me, anyhow. No worse than a lot of others in Freehold."

Margie smiled back. She seemed genuinely relieved, and I felt a sudden wash of affection for her. It made me remember the kindness and humility of the Freehold Christians that had so touched me as a teenager. They were really nice people, underneath all the dogma and proselytizing.

In the end, Margie's company at dinner turned out to be tolerably pleasant—we sat around my vast kitchen table reminiscing about the few subjects we could claim to have in common. Mum, however, was uncharacteristically quiet throughout the meal. I put it down to her not really knowing the people Margie and I were talking about, but when Margie eventually lumbered off to the spare room to bed, I realized that there was more to it.

"I'll clear up, dear," Mum said, tight-lipped, as I attempted to carry some bowls over to the dishwasher.

"Thanks, Mum. And thanks for cooking, too. It was lovely. Well, for someone who claims to be allergic to dairy, Margie sure managed to put away the ice cream, don't you think?"

Mum didn't answer me. She seemed to have taken it upon herself to rearrange the contents of my freezer.

"Mum? Are you all right?" With horror, I noticed that her shoulders were quaking. "What's the matter? Are you sick?"

Mum shut the freezer door with a controlled *thunk*, and ripping off a piece of kitchen towel from a roll impaled on a wooden holder, she blew her nose and dabbed at the corner of her eyes. Then she picked up the entire kitchen roll holder and brandished it at me. For a minute I thought she was going to throw it, but instead she pointed at its heavy rounded base.

"Are you aware that this isn't an ordinary kitchen roll holder?" she said, in a high-pitched, verging-on-the-hysterical voice I hadn't heard since Thinifer days of yore.

I waited for her to say, *In fact, this kitchen roll holder has special powers! It is Wonder Woman's own kitchen roll holder, and it doubles as a laser gun!* My mother, I thought, has finally flipped.

"No," she continued. "It's also a device for squeezing the water out of cooked cabbage: It is a *cabbage press!*"

"No kidding. Who knew?" I said weakly. "Mum, sit down. What's wrong? Talk to me, please."

Mum replaced the kitchen roll/cabbage press and sat down opposite me. "Helena," she began. "I want you to know that your father and I . . . Well, we've always tried to do our best for you."

"I know," I said. "What's brought this on?"

Her eyes filled up again. My mother hardly ever cried. "Do you still . . . Do you still . . . wish that Cynthia was your mother instead of me?" She looked at me, vulnerability naked in her eyes.

I remembered instantly the occasion to which she was referring. "Mum! Of course not! That was one comment, made in a temper, when I was *nine years old!* Every kid says that kind of stuff to their mother at some stage! Surely you haven't been dwelling on it ever since?"

"Oh, Helena," she sobbed. "I'm so glad to know that. It was just hearing you on the phone to her tonight. You sounded so close . . . and she cares about you very much. But please know that I do, too. I feel so guilty for the way I neglected you—emotionally, I mean— when you were little. I always felt so unwell, you see, and Daddy spent all his time taking care of me. It worked out for us, that you and Sam were such close friends, and that you were happy at the Grants' so much. But I look back and think, What have I done? Especially now, seeing you like this, after what's happened . . . the drugs, and so on. I always worried that something like this would happen, but once the band split up, I thought, No, she'll be okay now. But you aren't."

I put my hand on top of hers on the table. I didn't really know what to say at first. "It's not your fault, Mum. And, apart from that night, I don't do drugs. I never have done. That was a one-off because I was upset about Sam."

It seemed incredible that, in all these years, we'd never had a heart-to-heart like this before. "Why *were* you so sick when I was a kid? You had all those fluctuations and mood swings and stuff. I never knew where I was with you."

"I'm so sorry, I'm really, really sorry. But surely you knew that I had a thyroid problem?"

I gaped at her. "A *thyroid* problem?"

Mum dried her eyes again. "I can't believe you didn't know that, Helena. I thought I told you years ago. I contracted it after you were born: postnatal thyroiditis. In most women it goes away on its own, only mine never did. I kept swinging from hypo to hyper—underactive and overactive. The doctors couldn't keep up with it. They'd give me drugs to boost it when I was underactive, only usually by that time I was heading the other way, which made it twice as bad. It was only when we moved to the States that I finally got the right medication and it settled down. It was dreadful. I just felt permanently dreadful. That's why you're an only child. Neither Daddy nor I could face the risk of it getting worse with another pregnancy."

"Oh," I said. "Wow. I had no idea."

"Well, really, Helena. You must have noticed that something was wrong." Mum felt sufficiently unburdened to continue clearing the table.

"Of course I did. But I didn't know what to think. When I was a bit older I wondered about all kinds of things—you know, an eating disorder. Clinical depression, maybe. Even a drinking problem—except that I know you get a headache after two G and Ts. Anyway, that was why I never asked. I thought it was something . . . sensitive that you wouldn't want to discuss."

I was too ashamed to admit that actually, once I joined the band, it wasn't an issue to which I ever gave much thought, especially after Mum seemed to have recovered. I saw so little of my parents after I left school.

I grinned. "I used to think of your two extremes as Fattypuff and Thinifer."

Mum huffed air through her nose in an approximation of a laugh. "Very appropriate. You used to love that book."

"And now you're just Middleton," I said, thinking of Toby with yearning in my throat.

"Yes, thank goodness," said Mum, putting on the kettle for coffee. "I'm sorry, dear, for that little outburst. It's just that it's so painful, wondering if one . . . did the right thing or not. I think back to you and those boys, off driving around America in a van, unchaperoned, hardly more than children. We let you go, with barely a murmur! It seems such a terribly irresponsible thing for us to have permitted. Anything could have happened to you."

"Yeah, it did—we got rich and famous," I said, gesturing toward the bank of gold, silver, and platinum discs that covered the wall of the utility room (I'd thought it vulgar to have them anywhere more prominent).

"Well, as long as it's brought you happiness, Helena," Mum said.

Happiness? That was a tough one, I thought. I pondered it for a minute.

"I guess it did, at first. I really felt as if I'd found somewhere that I belonged, even more so than with the church."

I didn't want to upset Mum, but since we were being honest . . . "The boys were like a family to me, like brothers. And Mickey was kind of like a dad—not that I wanted him as a replacement for Dad or anything. But you know, just in terms of looking after us on the road, making sure we were fed and paid and all that.

"You guys weren't bad parents. But I was a teenager and I'd been taken away from my home and my friends—especially Sam. I needed something else to fill the gap. And then when we got successful, it was so exciting, and everyone wanted to know me. I felt like finally I could *be* someone. . . . Yes, that made me happy, even if it meant that I had to go without a normal life."

"So do you forgive me?" Mum asked uncomfortably.

Everyone's after redemption tonight, I thought. I got up from the table and hugged her, smelling the chemicals in her hairspray and feeling her stiff hair tickle my forehead, crispy like strands of spun sugar.

"Of course I forgive you," I said, adding silently, *As long as you will one day forgive me, too.*

* * *

Margie and her suitcases departed the next morning, leaving little gifts thoughtfully strewn throughout the house for me to discover over the coming days—an *I Am the Way and the Light* bookmark in the spare room; a poster of Jesus and some small children in the downstairs loo; and a little board book of *Prayers for Toddlers* in the magazine rack.

Mum had been true to her word and explained that this was a difficult time for me, and that as she (Mum) was returning home to Freehold soon, we really wanted to do some quality mother-and-daughter bonding before then.

Neither of us acknowledged, to Margie or to each other, the bonding that had taken place the night before.

GHOSTS

Hi, Music Lovers!

Welcome to the first edition of the Official BLUE IDEA Fanzine!

BLUE IDEA is the hottest, grooviest new band on the planet, and if you haven't heard us on the radio yet, or checked us out in your local flea-pit, then don't worry—you soon will! In fact, catch us while we're still up-and-coming, so you can tell your friends that you saw us on our first ever tour!

I'm Helena, and since I'm the only girl (!), I'll be writing you all a letter every month to tell you a bit about ourselves, and what life on the road is like. I'm sure it's NOT going to be as glamorous as we think it is . . . but we'll soon find out!

First, here are some proper introductions, in our own words:

BLUE IDEA: THE LINEUP

ON LEAD GUITAR AND VOCALS WE HAVE:

JUSTIN TIMOTHY BECKER—"Hi, fans, I'm Justin, but you can call me the Sex God! I'm 18, 5'8 1/2", 143 lbs. I have straight blond hair and brown eyes.

HOBBIES: Watching the Knicks play, track running, listening to records, talking to cute girls.

FAVE BANDS: I like mostly British music: Elvis Costello and the Attractions, Ian Dury and the Blockheads (in fact I wanted to call this band Justin Becker and the Blue Ideas, only the others wouldn't let me!); but I also like Dylan, Tom Petty, and Talking Heads.

FAVE FOODS: Chili dogs, Coke, fries. You know. The usual.

ASPIRATIONS: I WANNA BE FAMOUS!!!"

ON DRUMS WE HAVE:

DAVID J. SOMERSTEIN—"I'm 18, medium height, medium
weight, cool black hair, short-sighted, great
dress sense, awesome rhythm sense. Originally
from Pittsburgh, PA; moved to Freehold as a
senior.

HOBBIES: Drumming is my life (I guess my folks wish they'd
never bought me that kit!). When I'm not playing drums,
I watch movies. My all-time fave is still *The Empire
Strikes Back* (I know, I know). I support the Steelers.
Can't think of anything else real important.

FAVE BANDS: Talking Heads (but I was into them before Justin
was!), The Ramones, U2, R.E.M.

FAVE FOOD: Bananas. I am the ape man.

ASPIRATIONS: To play drums onstage for The Ramones sometime.
Oh, and to be totally rich."

ON KEYBOARDS WE HAVE:

JOSEPH JENNINGS (JOE)—"I'm 18, 6'1", 140 lbs., brown hair,
brown eyes, single and lookin' for lurve!

HOBBIES: Shooting hoops, making out, watching TV.

FAVE BANDS: Blue Idea, of course.

FAVE FOOD: You name it, I'll eat it.

ASPIRATIONS: To marry any of Charlie's Angels. Preferably all
of them."

AND FINALLY, ON BASS AND BACKING VOCALS WE HAVE:

HELENA JANE NICHOLLS—"I'm nearly 17 years old, 5'8", I have
dark brown hair, greenish eyes, and I'm not telling you
my weight! I'm British, but have lived in New Jersey
for three years. I just graduated, a year ahead for
my age.

HOBBIES: Playing bass, writing songs, singing, writing letters
to my best friend Sam in England.

FAVE BANDS: Blondie, The Cure, The Clash.

FAVE FOOD: English fish and chips, chocolate digestive
biscuits.

ASPIRATIONS: I'd like to really make a difference. I want Blue
Idea to be really successful so that I can help promote
world peace through my songs."

Well, that's us. And now for some history, so pay attention, you
guys at the back!

We all met in high school, in Freehold, NJ. Justin, our resi-
dent heartthrob (or so he likes to think), got the band together
and gave us our name. To be honest, we were pretty rubbish at
first (that's an English term for "lame," in case you didn't
know), but like most things in life, if you practice and practice, you eventually get better.

We spent months rehearsing, and yup, a lot of the time it was
totally boring and we thought we'd never get anywhere, but
finally we got our break. A guy from the record company spotted
us at a show at The Stone Pony down in Asbury Park. His name is
Willy Watts-Davis (a Brit like me) and we love him! He hadn't
even come to see us, but had driven down from NYC to check out
the band we opened for (who shall remain nameless . . . Saul).

The rest, hopefully, will be history. We've now been signed
by Ringside Records; they've got an agent to book us on our
first tour, and we'll be in the studio later this fall to record
our first album! So watch this space. . . .

THE TOUR
DAY TWO

The tour began yesterday, early on a hot July morning. It
would've been earlier, only Joe overslept . . . no doubt starting
as he means to go on. Still, as his dad was the one who got us a
great deal on our van, we didn't give him too much of a hard
time.

We love our van. It's metallic blue, and only a little bit
used. We paid for it out of our advance, and it's the first
vehicle any of us have ever owned (even if it is only part-
owned). It has comfortable seats and a radio and everything, and
a ton of space in the back for all our gear.

Let me tell you what we packed:

1. Instruments and equipment (amps, cables, microphones, etc.)
2. Lots of clean socks and underwear
3. Bedclothes, so we can sleep in the van if we have to (shudder)
4. A box of cassette singles of our favorite tune, to sell on the road
5. Publicity photographs—hey, you never know. Someone might want our autographs.
6. Fake ID for me (ONLY JOKING, PARENTS)
7. A ton of blank sheets of paper with "Blue Idea— Mailing List" printed, by yours truly, at the top. For all you future fans to write down your names and addresses so we can send you fun stuff (this 'zine, for starters, hot off the press!).

(You will soon discover that I love writing lists.)

It was sooooo embarrassing—my folks actually came outside and waved good-bye to me when we drove off. My Mum (that's Mum, not Mom, by the way) said that she had to pretend I was off to camp for the summer, otherwise she wouldn't be able to let me go. She can't stand the thought of me and a "bunch of teenage boys gallivanting off unsupervised around the country." She even called the record company (cringe) to try and get them to send someone with us, but it doesn't work like that. (And funnily enough, nobody wanted to come anyway—can't imagine why. . . .) Heh, heh, heh . . . freedom!!!! America is great—I'd never have been allowed to do this in England!

Joe had to swear to his folks that we wouldn't be playing in seedy cowboy bars—he says they thought that every night would be like that scene in *The Blues Brothers*, where they have to play behind a wire screen because everyone is throwing bottles at them. Anyway, we can't play in cowboy bars, seedy or otherwise, because (a) I'm not old enough and (b) we don't play Country 'n' Western.

DAY FIVE

I hoped I'd be able to write this diary every day, but no chance. I'm either too tired or too busy. But I don't care—this is the most fun we've ever had! Being on the road is fantastic! It's incredible to see a new place every single night, especially for a Brit like me, who hasn't been around the States much at all. We were in Washington, D.C., yesterday, and I really liked it. The neighborhood where the venue is was a bit rough, but on the whole it's such a cool place. I hope we get to play there lots more times.

We even did a tiny bit of sightseeing—David had a cousin whose name is on the Vietnam Memorial, so we went to see who could spot it first. (Only we couldn't find it, so David wasn't very happy yesterday.)

But usually there's no time to stop and look at anything historical or notable. Here's what we do on a typical day:

1. Check out of our one, very small, motel room. You'd think I could have my own room, being a girl and all, wouldn't you? But no, I have to put up with these three snoring (and worse!!) all night long. Thankfully we haven't yet had to sleep in the van.

2. Have breakfast, and lots of coffee to wake us up after another late night.

3. Drive, drive, drive, drive . . . and then drive some more.

4. Find the venue, without the driver killing the navigator, or vice versa (we all take turns driving and map-reading).

5. Call Mickey, our manager (this is my job), from a pay phone, to let him know that we're all still alive, and haven't caught scurvy or fleas yet. In the meantime, he's talked to Willie, our product manager at Ringside, and passes on any interview requests or names for the guest list (so far, three of each—but it's early days yet).

6. Unload the van, sound-check, go and eat.

7. Come back, watch everyone arrive, play our set, leave again. We're first on the bill every night, so it's not really surprising that people pretty much stay at

the bar. Willie told us not to mind about this—until
our single's out, no one will have heard of us
anyway, so we should just be looking at these first
few weeks as warm-ups, "for the cohesiveness of the
band."
Anyway, that's all for now, folks! Tune in again for the next
thrilling installment of "Blue Idea on the Road"!
Bye from all of us,
         Helena xxx

* ✳ *

Three months later we made our first album. The studio was in
Manhattan, so we mostly commuted back and forth by train from
Freehold, although occasionally, when we worked late into the
night, we got a cab back to Joe's aunt Sandi's place (where we'd
stayed after our historic first meeting with Ringside) and crashed
there instead.

The weeks we spent recording were a revelation in every way:
from the infinitely superior studio gear we had on loan (my borrowed bass was so easy to play, notes dripped from its neck like
honey off a spoon), to the pressure we felt to finish the record on
schedule, to the huge amounts of pot smoked continually by
everyone—except myself. I thought all drugs were evil.

People from Ringside were always dropping by to see how we
were getting on, although I started to realize that they mostly did so
as an excuse for an afternoon off work and a share of a large joint. I
felt really frustrated and left out when they all spliffed up—people
got so boring when they were stoned, and it made the chances of
our finishing on schedule diminish even further. I just wanted to be
getting on with the task at hand, but if I tried to bully the boys when
they were high, they brushed me away like an annoying little fly,
and settled further down into their exclusive catatonia.

Willy had booked Dean Barnes to produce our record. He was a
well-respected and talented East Coast indie producer, whose mellow manner and quiet good nature belied his absolute perfection-
ism. My only problem with him was that he was the biggest stoner

out of everyone, but Willy assured me that being permanently wasted was pretty much endemic among producers, and not to worry about it.

It was, however, a miracle that we as a band survived the discipline of the studio. Dean would regularly make us repeat a few lines of a song about thirty times in a row, without raising his voice or sounding remotely disappointed in us, until we were all fit to be tied.

"Come on, guys, better. And again."

"Concentrate, David, you're tailing off at the end."

"Justin, you're too pitchy on those high notes. Breathe."

"Nearly there. Keep going. One more time . . ."

Once after Dean had said "one more time" nine times in succession, after we'd already been playing the same song for two days, Justin threw down his guitar and stormed out of the studio, punching and kicking the doorframe in fury on his way out. I sat down in despair, thinking that we would never get the bloody record made—we'd been working for a week already and had finished only three songs. I had no idea that it took so long. I'd believed we would just breeze in there and do the whole lot in a couple of takes, and that would be that. Joe echoed my thoughts.

"I thought we just recorded, then it was Dean's job to fix it afterward," he grumbled.

Dean just looked up from the mixing desk, through the glass that separated him from us, and said over the intercom, "Okay, let's take a break."

Slowly and painfully, however, the album came together. We argued about everything, from artwork to liner notes to sequencing, but with guidance and a lot of hard work from Willy, Dean, and Mickey, somehow the day came when we received a box from Ringside full of pristine shiny vinyl copies of *Switch On* by Blue Idea. Suddenly the hard work seemed worth it, and we all stood around like new parents, grinning stupidly and proudly at one another.

* * *

The tour continued into the spring of 1984, on a considerably larger scale. The album was sent to college radio stations in towns all over the country, the plan being that we should play as many of those towns as possible. We played five shows a week, and by the third week we had moved through Florida and Louisiana, into Texas, and then across to Albuquerque, New Mexico. Our audiences got marginally bigger (about forty-five people had signed our fan-base sheets), but still regularly comprised the afternoon drinkers too inebriated to get off their bar stools and go home when we came onstage; or worse, the frat boys who thought that they were above us.

Some nights they would just stand there, swaying, swigging cross-eyed from their beers, and yelling insults at me.

"Hey! It's *Chubby* Checker on bass!" someone shouted when I wore a checked shirt onstage. "Play some *Fats* Domino!"

"Yeah, anything but this faggy shit!" an answering shout came from across the room. It was occasionally assumed that because Justin was pretty and wore makeup he was gay, although our music was hardly faggy. That particular day I happened to be riddled with PMS and had started to cry then and there. I'd wanted to walk off the stage, but there was nowhere to go except past our tormentors and out into the parking lot, and I was afraid to go and sit in the van on my own.

The comments, and my reaction, had pushed Justin's buttons so far in that they were jammed. He shoved his mike stand over, jumped down into the crowd of approximately fourteen people, and socked one of the offenders hard in the stomach. The rest of us stopped playing and stared aghast as a big fight broke out. Then Joe and David leapt into the fray, which, after several bloody noses and a big black eye (Justin's), was broken up by the barman and the club's owner. We were instantly banned from ever coming back, and Mickey was furious with us.

But thankfully that happened only once. Both Justin and I eventually learned to ignore any derogatory comments that flew up to us onstage, telling ourselves that they were only made out of jealousy.

In the case of the women who insulted me, I think that was true. They had a way, those college girls, of looking me scornfully up and down, then leaning across and saying something in a friend's ear. The friend would look at me with the same expression of disgust, and they would both collapse in peals of sorority laughter. I tried to remember to "love thine enemy," and to "turn the other cheek," and a few times I even tried to go and make friends with them afterward. It was a naive fantasy I had, that maybe I could somehow win them over and become a member of a girly clique like that myself. But it never worked—they'd look at me as if I was something they had found on the bottom of their shoe, and then hustle off to the restrooms, giggling, to apply more lip gloss.

I hated them and their smug catalog outfits and stiff humorless hair.

You won't be laughing when we're famous and earning even more money than your daddy does, I'd think.

Justin, moody though he was, was usually very loyal, too. If he spotted any girls being snotty to me, he would wait until they inevitably approached him after the set, simpering and sidling, then he'd take my arm and say, "Come on, Helena, let's go—don't you think the trash stinks around here?" (Unless, of course, he fancied them, in which case I was on my own.)

David, who was by nature gentlemanly, and Joe, in his own way, looked out for me, too. Despite our incessant bickering, and my occasional yearning for female companionship, I began to feel protected and safe in the company of all three of them. We were in it together. It was like having a new family, and it lessened the sting— if not the guilt—of exchanging my hymn sheet for a fanzine, and my Communion wine for an illegal after-show beer.

* * *

MARCH 1984

Hi, Music Lovers!

I can't believe we're so far into 1984 already—and what a year it's been, even if it's only a quarter done!

BLUE IDEA is back on the road again. (Hence the new issue of *Bluezine*. Do you like the change of title? David thought it sounded better than the boring old *Blue Idea Fanzine*. We all agreed, so *Bluezine* it is!) We're three weeks into our spring tour, but hold on to your hats, there's more: Our first album, *Switch On*, is in a record shop near you!!

We had a fantastic time in the studio; boy, what a learning curve that was! The record was produced by Dean Barnes, who has also worked with the Mai-Tai Micromen and R.E.M. (he coproduced their first release, "Chronic Town," with Mitch Easter).

So if you haven't already done so, haul your butts down to your nearest Music Emporium and treat yourselves . . . you won't be disappointed, we promise!

Also, if you're in a college town, call up your local college radio station. They should have copies of the record by now, so why not request us? Chances are we'll be swinging by there in the near future.

Here are some pictures of us onstage at the Kactus Klub in Albuquerque, at the start of our set. Don't we look miserable? Trouble is, these are the only snaps I have so far, since we all forgot to bring our cameras. It's hard enough to try and remember our instruments, let alone anything else!

(By the way, I HATE that plaid shirt I'm wearing. You won't be seeing that again.)

As you'll see from the tour itinerary, it's been a pretty heavy three weeks, with five shows a week. We're working our way around the country in two giant loops, starting out with the Southeast and Southwestern states. Then a break (PHEW), then back out to do the top half.

Our audiences are getting bigger all the time, and more of you wonderful folk are signing my fan-base lists every night! Keep it up, and tell your friends! We love you all!!

NEWS FLASH FROM FLAGSTAFF, AZ!!

I just phoned the record company and guess what, our album has shot up to NUMBER THREE on the college radio charts! You guys are fantastic, you really have been requesting us. It seems that "This Is Your Blue Idea" is the track that gets the most requests, and so Ringside is going to release it as a single to commercial radio, too!

We can't tell you how exciting this is!

Thank you!

* ✳ *

Come the fall, we were still driving. We were on the second stretch of the tour, and had driven up the Northeast coast for a brief stint in Canada, and a long jaunt across the northern states of the U.S. to do Washington State, Oregon, California, then across the Rockies, Kansas, Ohio, Pennsylvania, and home via New England to New Jersey.

While we were driving through some godforsaken part of the Midwest, which having been summarily christened by Justin was henceforth known as Buttfuck, Ohio, the alternator on the van suddenly went. We knew we were near a town by its prominent landmark—not a church tower or town hall, or even a water tower, but a fifty-foot mast with a large revolving sign on top of it, bearing the words ADULT BOOKS. It was lucky, we supposed, that in addition to the adult books, Buttfuck also offered a garage and a tow truck, but we had to cancel our show that night and stay over while a replacement alternator was installed.

The lugubrious garage owner, whose name was Leland, dropped us off in his pickup at the town's only motel, after taking what must have been a lengthy detour to a farm where, he said, he had to "git his baby boy." A two-hundred-pound acne-ridden youth about our age lumbered out in dungarees and a checked shirt, and sat in the back of the truck with us and as much of our gear as we'd been able to carry. He said nothing, but glared suspiciously at each of us as though he'd like to bash all our heads in with a pitchfork handle. We were very relieved to arrive at the motel, where we booked one room and bad-temperedly resigned ourselves to a night in what was possibly the weirdest place on earth.

"There's only one thing for it," said Justin. "We have to get drunk. All of us, including you, Miss Goody Two-Shoes."

I wasn't having any of it, but at that point I thought it best not to argue. "Whatever," I said, bagging one of the small twin beds. Both beds had yellow nylon bedspreads that looked and smelled like old curry. "Whose turn is it to be on the floor tonight?"

"I'd rather sleep on the floor than share with Joe," said David, hurling himself onto the damp cot under the window.

Joe made smoochy faces at a glowering Justin. "It's you and me, then, honey."

"I'm definitely getting drunk," Justin grumbled. "Let's go. This room stinks."

After a plate of limp pot roast in a deserted diner, which doubled as the town's pharmacy and general store, we found the local bar. It was as empty as the rest of the town, apart from a boot-faced barmaid on the wrong side of thirty with an enormous chest. Justin and Joe cheered up a bit, and I saw money change hands as they very unsubtly placed their bets on her.

"God, they're so juvenile," said David to me. "As if either of them stand a chance with her. And why would they want to? She's awful."

I agreed. On a whim, I also agreed to have a beer from the boys' first pitcher. I'd decided some months ago that I didn't like the taste of beer at all, and fully intended to have just a few sips before moving on to Cokes. But to my surprise, this beer tasted delicious, cold and refreshing, making me want more. Before I knew it, I was on my third glass.

I talked mostly to David, as the other two were doggedly vying for the waitress's attentions, and we decided to start a list of the top ten weirdest things about Buttfuck. It got more and more riotous. After a while, Justin and Joe joined in, and someone decreed that each good suggestion merited a shot of tequila. It was an easy game, and we all managed to have five or six shots. I began to understand exactly why people enjoyed getting drunk so much. Tequila, which I hadn't tried before, turned out to be delicious, too.

"Leland's baby boy!" A shot for Justin.

"That Adult Book pole!" A shot for David.

"The way that no one seems to live here!" Another for Justin.

"The vending machine in the motel lobby—did you see it? It sold driving gloves and jewelry!"

I hadn't been able to get over this, and was very tempted to buy a cheap gold locket to have with the dubious-looking sandwich in the next compartment, just so I could tell people where I'd gotten it from.

"That's a great one—a double for Helena!" cried David, clapping me on the back.

"Uh . . . I saw a license plate on a truck that said *'I'm So Horny I Get Excited at the Crack of Dawn'*—does that count? It was kinda neat; there was a little cartoon guy in the background with his hand down the front of his pants, and the sun coming up," Joe contributed.

I laughed so hard that I didn't notice that there were two more tequilas in front of me in place of the two I'd just downed.

Sometime later I realized I was *very* drunk. Squinting at my watch, I saw that it was past midnight. "Don't you think we should get shome shleep?" I suggested hazily. "We gotta long drive tomorra. . . ."

David stood up, swaying. "Yeah, guess we'd better make a move. I feel kinda wrecked, too. Come on, guys."

Justin looked at Joe and then at the barmaid, who was bending over putting mixers on the bottom shelf.

"I think we'll stay here a while longer, yeah, Joe?" Joe nodded in assent, his eyes glazed with lust.

David and I staggered out of the bar to the sound of Joe telling a very unimpressed barmaid that we were all a famous rock band, and could get her backstage passes to our next gig.

Back at the motel, our room still smelled like damp cumin. It was extremely chilly, but I was too drunk to notice. Uninhibited for once, I yanked off my clothes, stumbled into my pajamas, and collapsed into bed. A few minutes later I heard a small voice from by the window.

"H, I'm cold."

"Put some more clothes on, then," I mumbled groggily.

"I'm already wearing all the ones I have with me. Can't I share with you?"

"No way, David. Go to sleep."

"Oh, purlease, Helena, pleeeeease. I'm frozen. This mattress is all lumpy, too."

"So's mine. Get over it."

"Oh, come on, H, don't be so mean."

Being the only girl meant that, even though we had to share rooms, I always got my own bed. And drunk or not, I would never have let Joe or Justin anywhere near me. I didn't fancy David either, but I was more fond of him than I was of the others; he was much less sex-obsessed than they were, and he changed his underwear more often, too.

"Oh, all right. Just this once."

David rolled off his mattress and into bed with me in one fluid movement. He was still fully dressed, and even had his glasses on. In a moment of inebriated tenderness I pulled them off his nose and put them down by the side of the bed, folding their arms together over the frames. He looked so sweet and vulnerable without them that I couldn't resist giving him a little kiss on the forehead, and pulling his shivering body toward my chest. I must have fallen asleep like that, for a short time later I was awakened by someone prodding me in the thigh.

"Wassamarrer? Are they back yet?" I opened my eyes and looked into David's face. He was gazing at me intently. We were still alone.

"Helena," he whispered. "Have you ever done it before?"

"Done what?" I asked. At that point I realized that David had taken all his clothes off and was lying naked, still in my arms. He was warm now, and smooth. I yelped and scuttled over to the edge of the bed like a sand crab.

"You know what. Have you?" He reached over and stroked my face. I debated jumping out of bed and going to sleep on the floor, but decided I was too drunk and comfortable to move.

"No. Have you?"

"Sure!" he replied indignantly. "I dated Courtney Norman for ages, you knew that."

"Well, I didn't know if you two had done it or not."

"Oh, get real, Helena, of course we did! I can't believe you haven't, though. Is it because of your religion?"

Admitting it wasn't as embarrassing as I'd feared. "Yeah, I guess so. And to be honest, well, I've never had a boyfriend."

David was shocked. "What, never? I've seen guys checking you out at our shows. They think a chick on bass is just about the coolest thing ever. And surely you did before you were in the band?"

"No. Anyhow, I'm not worried about it," I said defensively, although I was secretly delighted that boys checked me out. "I don't want a boyfriend, anyway."

David edged nearer until our noses were touching. "I don't want a girlfriend either," he whispered, kissing my mouth and pushing his tongue inside. It was nice, not as yucky as I'd always imagined. I understood what it meant in books when people's lips were described as velvety.

"So, don't you think it's time to lose your virginity?"

I sat up, too fast. "Certainly not! I'm going to wait until I'm married. And besides, how would we ever face each other afterwards if we did that?"

David laughed and pulled me back down again. "Relax, H, it wouldn't be any big deal. We would just decide right now that we wouldn't mention it again, and it'll just make us better friends. I swear I wouldn't tell Joe and Jus, or anyone. Oh, come on, it's real fun."

"No way, David. Go to sleep or I'm kicking you out of this bed. Besides, I don't want to get pregnant." I felt very mature, talking about taking precautions as though I was actually going to have sex like a normal, healthy teenager with a boyfriend. I didn't for a minute think I would, but the prospect did not seem nearly so scary with sweet old David offering. I was lying down on my back with my legs firmly crossed, and my elbows sticking out so he couldn't get near me.

"Too bad. Oh, well, if you ever change your mind, just holler," he said amiably. A few minutes later I heard gentle snoring, and so I relaxed and fell asleep myself.

Later still I was woken again, this time by an amazing melting sensation coming from between my now–loosely crossed legs, and a familiar prodding against my hip.

"You won't get pregnant, I swear. I have condoms," David said in a low voice.

I was surprised at his persistence, but even more surprised at the feeling of mellow heat that I realized was caused by David's forefinger rubbing me through my pajamas. Actually it was utterly blissful. At that point I pushed aside the memory of my promise of celibacy to God, and the fact that David was not my boyfriend. I didn't even worry about the others bursting in, or David realizing how fat I was. All I could think about was how I felt, and how I wanted more.

I moaned, and David rolled on top of me. He didn't seem to weigh anything at all. He kissed me again and I tasted toothpaste. Not fair! I thought. I haven't cleaned my teeth. The gentle rubbing was replaced by a persistent prodding, but it felt just as good. More satisfying. My pajama bottoms were rolled down over my thighs and I barely noticed until he entered me with one huge, accurate lunge. I waited to feel pain, but there was none. Part of me couldn't believe this was happening, and part of me didn't ever want it to stop.

The next morning I was woken by the splutter and roar of a recalcitrant car engine coming from the motel forecourt. I had a thumping headache and my legs felt very stiff. As I gathered up my clothes and a towel and staggered over to the bathroom, I made out David's and Joe's prone figures crashed out on the next bed, top to tail, with only the curry bedspread draped over them. David had his T-shirt on again. As I passed by, an audible fart emanated from his end of the bedspread, and I shuddered, bolting into the bathroom. The previous night seemed to have happened to someone else, and had I not felt an unfamiliar soreness down below, I might have thought that it was just a story someone told me.

Justin burst in the room just as I emerged, washed and dressed, from the shower. He was in fine form, full of stories about his conquest of the previous night, and insisted we all go en masse to the diner for breakfast so he could brag some more, and taunt poor Joe. Over hangover fodder of pancakes and maple syrup, David and I exchanged small sheepish smiles.

I felt wracked with guilt, but I kept that between me and God. Guilt aside, it was a relief to be able to write to Sam and tell her what had happened, and I was grateful to David for making me feel like a normal person, not someone who was too hideous ever to lose her virginity.

* * *

November 18, 1984

Dear Mar Tangs (Clam Digger and Lobster Trapper),

I did it, I did it, I finally did it! And you'll never guess who with? David!! Yup, geeky little David. What a sly dog. Our van broke down in Buttfuck, Ohio (sorry, Justin's name for a hick town!), so we had to cancel a show and spend the night there. I got drunk, too—don't be too disapproving; it's only rock 'n' roll ("but I like it, la, la, la"). Have you ever had tequila? It's yummy, but it doesn't half give you a terrible hangover. To be honest, I don't really even remember much about It—one minute I was asleep/passed out on the bed, the next, David's all snuggled up with me, and the next, he's . . . you know. The others weren't there—obviously. They were trying to make out with the barmaid.

I think I enjoyed it. It was good and bad, that I did it with David and not some strange boy. Good because I trust him and know him so well, but bad because it's not like we're gonna be an item or anything. We were both drunk. Also, bad because it feels a bit incestuous. Still, at least I am officially No Longer A Virgin. I was getting worried, after you and Martin Trubshaw had that night of passion (what's up with him these days? Is he still blanking you?)—I am a year older than you, after all.

Love from your experienced friend,

H xx

* * *

November 25, 1984

Dear Helena,

Oh my God! Congratulations! Send more details—if you can remember them. Is he, you know, small all over??? And is everything okay now? I mean, isn't it a bit awkward, having a one-night stand with someone you spend all your time with?

Martin "Nadger" Trubshaw is still avoiding me. I think he fancies Mel; she's always telling me she bumped into him, and I haven't bumped into him for weeks. I don't know if I should tell you this, but I heard Mel say to the Nadger's friend (whose name is Chris) that "her" friend Helena is a famous pop star in America, and if he liked, she could get your autograph for him! So you see, she hasn't changed a bit. You'll be pleased to know that whilst I'm inordinately proud of you, and boast about you as often as possible, I wouldn't dream of prostituting your good name (well, your name, you old tart) in that wanton way!

School is quite good at the moment. I'm really enjoying the A-level courses, especially History and English. I've decided that the only men in my life are going to be Urban VIII, Bishop Frederick Nausea, and Oliver Cromwell. Olly's a bit ug, bless him (he really should've had those heinous warts seen to), but we must not forget that he was a Healer of Breaches. Or was that breeches?

"Anthony and Cleo" is great, too. Apart from the death issues, I wish I was Cleopatra. She manages to be a vamp and a romantic heroine at the same time: "O my oblivion is a very Anthony, and I am all forgotten!" I wonder what the Nadger would do if I turned around and said that to him one day? "O my oblivion is a very Martin Trubshaw . . . etc." No, doesn't have quite the same ring to it, does it?

(And there's another funny thing: Why do people "turn around" and say stuff to each other? Usually they're already facing them. It makes no sense.)

French is okay. Here's an insult for you to try out on Joe next time he annoys you: "Joe, tu es un grouillement continu!" It means "You are a seething mass." That'll confuse him.

Anyway, I'm rambling now. Write soon, you exciting, nearly famous person.

Lots of love and kisses,

Sam xxxx

P.S. Handy phrases for you to remember if you're ever on tour in Germany:

1. "Ich habe mein Schtampwappen veloren": I have lost my totem pole.
2. "Mein Beutelmaus hat verstopfung": My wombat is constipated.

* * *

Aside from being the most memorable, that leg of the tour was a lot more rewarding, as our reputation slowly began to precede us. The autumn scenery was absolutely stunning, too. To be confronted with majestic sweeps of red, orange, and yellow on valleys around every corner made the driving infinitely less tedious. I could quite happily stare for hours out of the window at the rich foliage presenting its last colorful stand. The leaves on some of the trees were such a perfect, delicate shade of peach that they made me want to cry. I would search for these particular ones whenever we stopped for gas or lunch, kicking ankle-deep through the carpet at the sides of the road, and if I found any I would put them carefully in the glove compartment of the van, meaning to send them to Sam. I didn't recall ever seeing that peachy tint from English autumn leaves. But after a couple of days their color always faded to a nondescript dull russet, and I ruefully threw them away, along with the myriad McDonald's boxes and Twinkies wrappers that littered the van floor.

We finally made it back to the East Coast. We were driving through Vermont on our way home, engaged in some pointless but vaguely entertaining bickering about whether a girl in my year at high school had suddenly begun to stuff her bra. The mountain vistas were particularly ravishing, but I was driving, and so couldn't allow myself to gaze at the foliage too much.

"She did not! She just discovered those push-up bras. Believe me, women know these things." I was getting interested, despite myself.

Justin snorted. "Excuse me, but I think us men spend more time staring at girls' hooters than you do."

"Generally speaking, I wouldn't count on it," I replied, pulling into the fast lane to overtake an octogenarian couple in an RV, who were rubbernecking at the trees above them.

"Do girls stare at other girls, then?" asked Joe curiously.

"Well, yes, of course. Just out of interest and for comparison purposes. You do the same, don't you? Except that boys have a name for it."

Justin wasn't so keen on this line of questioning. "Since when are you such an expert on men, Miss 'No-Boyfriends' Nicholls?"

I blushed.

Joe joined in the inquisition. "Yeah, Helena—why don't you go out with guys? You haven't dated anyone since we've known you."

He stared at me with mock horror. "You're not . . . you're not . . . one of those lesbians, are you?"

I spluttered with outrage. "No! Of course I'm not! Jeez. What's the matter with you? When have any of us had time to have dates and stuff in the last two years, anyway?"

The boys exchanged glances implying that they'd somehow managed to find the time. Thankfully, David kept quiet in the back of the van. I was worried for a minute that he'd be tempted to chime in with the benefit of his firsthand experience. But he never even had the chance to, because Justin was like a terrier with a toy between his teeth.

"You don't hang out with anyone from school, girls *or* boys, H. I've never seen you put any names on the guest list, except your folks once or twice. Why are you such a loner?"

I misheard him. "I'm not a loser! How dare you call me a loser!"

Justin grinned, making a winding-up motion with his hands.

"For your information, you bunch of mutons, no way am I a lesbian. And I *do* have friends, Mary Ellen Randall and, er, Margie Westerburg, but they just aren't into our sort of music. And my best friend, Sam, is coming to stay with me soon. She lives in England, otherwise I'd be hanging out with her the whole time. Satisfied?"

"Oooh, Sam! She wears the pants in your relationship, does she?" sang Joe from the back.

"Shut up, Joe, shut up, Justin. I'm really sick of hearing your voices. Turn the radio on, can't you?"

Justin smirked maliciously, knowing that yet again they had succeeded in embarrassing me. He did switch it on, though, and after a few minutes of chasing up and down the dial, he stopped twiddling the knob when we heard the final bars of a Jonathan Richman tune.

It faded into something else—a song that we all, in one split second, thought, That sounds familiar, what is it? before we recognized it with screams of joy.

"Turn it up!"

"Oh my God, it's us!"

"Louder!"

"Stop the van!"

Quickly, I pulled over to the side of the road. Cranking the volume up full blast, we opened the windows and let the sound of the first track on our album pour out over the crisp, colorful hillside, accompanied by our voices yodeling along in unison. We were bouncing around with so much excitement that the van shook from side to side, and passing motorists stopped looking at the scenery to wonder what on earth was going on. We'd heard Blue Idea tracks on the radio before, but only when we'd actually been at the station at the time, giving interviews. It was indescribable, the sensation of hearing on the radio, unanticipated, a composition that had come from my own head. As the last note approached, we shushed one another and listened attentively, leaning our heads toward the radio to hear better, even though the speakers were in the doors.

"Shhhh, it's ending."

"Yeah, we know, Joe, we were there, too."

"Shh, see if he says anything!"

There was a moment's pause and we held our breath. Then the DJ came on air. I would have known this was a college station even without him playing our song, because of the sound of his voice. Every college DJ in the country seemed to have the same voice, languid but slightly hesitant, making it sound as if they were smoking reefer while all the records played. Which they probably were.

"Yeah, um, that was a band with a new record out. They're called, ah, Blue Something—wait, I've lost the sleeve—oh, here. Blue Idea, kids, out of Freehold, New Jersey, and that was 'This Is Your Blue Idea,' the first track from their brand-new album, Switch On, *out on Ringside Records. Yeah . . . Actually, they seem, you know, really cool. Check it out. And next up, here's Japan with 'Ghosts.' . . ."*

Every time I hear "Ghosts" now, David Sylvian's autumn voice washes over me like falling leaves, and I see layers of things: peach and red, curried bedspreads, the head-spinning of tequila, hazy sexual pleasure, the purity of unplayed vinyl, and the first thrill of success.

SAM'S TREACHEROUS BLONDE

SOMEBODY WAS LURKING AROUND MY HOUSE. OVER THE YEARS I had of course come across quite a few assorted lurkers, loomers, anoraks, and saddos, but fortunately I'd never had my very own stalker. I'd known plenty of other artists who'd had "privacy-invasion issues," though. Adam Ant once told me that he had someone living in his roof space for months, spying on him through holes drilled in the loft floor—God, how did he not notice? Ever since I heard that, I had examined my bedroom and bathroom ceilings through a magnifying glass. And what about poor Björk, with the nutter who blew his brains out on home video for her? Nightmare.

So, no peepholes in the plasterwork, but an intermittent, undeniable lurky sort of presence, enough to make me feel extremely nervous. A shadow past the side of the dining-room window, as if someone was trying to peek through a gap in my muslin curtains. A fresh footprint in the mud next to the garden path, which couldn't belong to the bin men because they'd been there two days earlier. A dry, bottom-shaped patch on my swinging garden seat, when the rest of the garden was wet.

One night after Mum had returned to New Jersey, I was sitting at my refectory table sorting through boxes and boxes of photographs, fanning them out in cascades around me, wondering how to begin to make sense of them all. It was part of a kind of "get my affairs in order" campaign.

I'd sorted through the Hel-Sam Box of Important Stuff as soon as it had arrived from Cynthia, and pulled out some letters and *Bluezines*, which I intended to copy into the manuscript. The whole correspondence, plus accompanying photographs and press features, etc., was a great source of Blue Idea memorabilia. Might be worth quite a bit after I'm gone, I thought. The rest of the stuff was

more personal, and pretty much as I'd described to Cynthia: a grue-
some collection of baby teeth, Sam's beloved dormouse key ring,
the aforementioned four-leaf clover, my second favorite Barbie
(the top favorite still Missing in Action, last seen at Salisbury Fair in
1977)—oh, and a big Genesis badge, which I won at the same fair.
I'd worn it on my coat lapel for ages, thinking myself quite hip and
unusual to have such a badge. It was only after an older kid at
school asked me if I had all their albums that I discovered Genesis
wasn't just a book of the Bible.

But personal as it all was, I found that these things, though
important, didn't move me as much as, say, hearing two minutes of
a song that reminded me of Sam. This could reduce me to an emotional jelly, as could the sight of her tiny spidery handwriting—but
her key ring was just a key ring, however much she'd prized it.

I looked at all the photographs in front of me. It was odd, looking at a lifetime's worth of little shiny Helenas: teen Helena, tummy
pooched out over the top of tight jeans; Helena in a yellow bikini
ten years later, the same stomach shrunken and bronzed; Helena
scruffy, chewing her cuticles; Helena wealthy and manicured. I
wondered if I scanned all these different images into a computer,
would it come up with the one definitive Helena? And if it could,
what would she be like? Thirty-one years of a digital me, assembled
from the sum of my parts and the snaps of my holidays. I was sure
she would look better than the real thing, this wrinkly, one-eyed,
lonely failure.

The telephone rang.

I let the machine pick up. Unless it was Sam, calling to say hi
from the Other Side, or Toby, I wasn't interested.

But the machine clicked off again without recording a message. I
had a sudden hopeful vision of Toby cradling the receiver between
his neck and his chin, leaving the scent of his aftershave on the
earpiece, a feeling so strong that I got up and dialed 1471. "The
caller's number has been withheld," said the robot inside the
phone, and I was disappointed that I couldn't even smell a trace of
Toby.

Sam was in at least eighty percent of the photographs, always
smiling: Sam in shorts; on a bike; with Cynthia; with me. There was

one of us at about nine, topless, arms round each other's shoulders. Her chest was flat, brown, and smooth; mine lard-white and flabby, the whisper of cotton wool breasts budding. It looked as though Sam was carelessly pinching my pudgy nipple between thumb and forefinger.

The phone rang again. Again the caller declined to speak into the machine.

I put the Cocteau Twins' *Heaven or Las Vegas* on, loud, but it wasn't loud enough to drown out the phone ringing a third time.

I toyed with the idea of hiring a bodyguard. Perhaps that would add another twist to the Plan. The police might think that I'd been kidnapped, or assassinated, if I suddenly disappeared after employing security. No, I thought. Keep it as simple as possible, like Richey from the Manic Street Preachers did. No fuss, bye-bye. Gone.

But in the meantime, I didn't want to be trussed up and knifed to death by a stalker, not before the manuscript was finished.

I picked up a blurry photo of two people kissing, and peered at it for a while until I realized it was Sam and Justin. God, I wished she were here to show it to! What a pity it was out of focus. If it had been sharper, I'd have mailed it to Justin with a note: "You and Sam—remember her now?"

There was a picture of me with Sam and Sam's traveling buddy, Andrea. *Ondrea,* she pronounced it. It was taken in New York right before the two of them set off on their travels, their gap-year round-the-world trip. Even thinking about it now, jealousy twisted like chicken wire in my guts. Andrea looked so smug in the photo. She was tiny and blond and brittle, with big, high *Baywatch* breasts, and I remembered how hard it had been for me to donate a smile to the camera, when this horrible blond interloper was about to take Sam off to the other side of the planet.

It was a funny sort of jealousy, one I'd had to grow up with ever since leaving Salisbury—that Sam was having experiences in which I should be sharing but wasn't. And the Australian trip brought up in me an all-consuming resentment that, now that we were old enough to make our own decisions, Sam had decided to go off without me, to have adventures of which I was no part. I'd tried to explain it to her before she left, but she'd laughed.

"But you're on the road all the time! What's that if it's not an adventure?"

"Well, come on the road with us instead!" I'd replied.

How secretly gleeful I'd felt, then, six weeks later, when Sam had called collect from Australia to ask if she could come and spend the rest of her six months off with me after all, since she and Andrea had fallen out. Blue Idea was about to set off on tour again, but I instantly arranged for Sam to fly to Seattle and meet us there.

When she arrived at our hotel, I'd listened, tutting and head-shaking, to her tale of woe and false friendship. Apparently the trip had gotten off to a great start in Sydney: They'd both gotten wait-ressing jobs, and had rented a flat with a three-month lease. Then one day a beautiful tanned surfer with luminous lime shorts and a washboard belly had sauntered into the café where Sam worked.

Sam had fallen, instantly and passionately, in love, and nearly passed out with excitement when the Sex God (whose name was something ridiculous like Dwayne) had asked her out that night. She raced home after her shift and tarted herself up like she had never tarted before, rabbiting incessantly to Andrea about how wonderful he was, how gorgeous, how sexy, and consequently how nervous she was feeling.

"What if he's late? What if he stands me up? What if I'm left sit-ting there all night like a prat? What will I do?"

Andrea had magnanimously suggested that she go with Sam, just in case Dwayne didn't show up. Once he had, Sam could introduce Andrea and Dwayne, then Andrea would push off, pleading a prior engagement, and leave them to get on with their date.

Only it didn't quite turn out like that. Sam and Andrea arrived at the venue on time, and were twirling on bar stools, sipping daiquiris, when, just as Dwayne walked in, a woman sat down on the stool next to Sam. Before she had the chance to tap the woman on the shoulder and say, "Sorry, this seat's taken," Dwayne had sashayed over and, with a glowing smile and hello to Sam, perched his two walnut-tight buttocks on the stool next to Andrea.

Sam waited and waited for Andrea to leave, but she didn't. Sam kept looking at her watch and saying, "Golly, Andrea, you'd better hurry up, you're going to be late for the cinema," but Andrea just shook her Hollywood hair and said, "Oh, actually, I don't fancy that film tonight after all." Then Sam had waited for Andrea to go to the ladies', so she could casually change seats with her, but Andrea's bladder was evidently extra capacious that night. Instead of including her in the conversation, Andrea gradually and subtly moved her shoulder around so she almost had her back to Sam. Sam had sat miserably sipping her third cloying pink drink and wondering how best to go about cutting off Andrea's breasts.

Eventually Sam got up and said, "Well, I'm off, then. Anyone coming?"

Dwayne and Andrea had looked at the floor and muttered, "Just stay for one more, I think, don't you?"

The next morning when Andrea returned to the flat, wearing the same clothes as the night before and with a red stubble-burn rash around her mouth, Sam was packed and ready to go.

When she asked Andrea, tearfully, how she could have done such a thing to her, Andrea's only defense was, "Well, he was just so gorgeous, and it's been such a long time since a man paid me that much attention. . . ."

Sam was on the next plane to Seattle, and I had a worm of vindication wiggling guiltily in my heart for months afterward.

* * *

I decided not to use the story of Sam's treacherous blonde in my manuscript. It was tempting but not really relevant to my own life. Instead I would just record the facts: Andrea would get a mention, but that was all she merited.

I managed to get most of the photos into some kind of order, chucking away all the overexposed and blurry ones (except the one of Sam and Justin), and filing the others under headings like BAND and SALISBURY and SAM. As an afterthought, I pulled out three of my favorite shots of Sam and put them into the Hel-Sam box, on top of everything else. I wanted them to be the first thing anyone saw when opening the box.

When I was getting ready for bed that night, I thought I heard a heavy dull sound, like a stumble, in the back garden. It must have been quite loud, for my one ear to pick it up. Creeping into the spare room, I watched for a long time through a gap in the curtains but saw nothing except the dusky shapes of trees and silhouettes of shrubs. There was usually a movement-triggered security light on the patio, but the bulb must have blown, for it remained dark.

I wondered again whether to call the police but suddenly felt too tired. Plus, dialing 999 might lead to publicity, and I couldn't risk that, not yet. I'd just have to take my chances with the stalker.

Nonetheless, I double-checked that all the doors and windows were locked, made sure the alarm system was switched on before I went to bed, and slept with a rape siren and a baseball bat under my pillows.

The Jam
TO BE SOMEONE

March 2, 1985

Dear Ram Gnats (Turkey Plucker and Duck Stuffer),

I hate the boys. I HATE THEM I HATE THEM I HATE THEM!!!

I can't stand being on the road a minute longer. Why am I doing this, why? I could be with you in Salisbury, doing A levels, having a laugh with you over all the things you find funny in your English texts, but instead I'm stuck in a van, which STINKS to high heaven, surrounded by hideous mutons.

The books you sent are keeping me sane, though. Oh, I found a quote for you: "The man opened the door and hurriedly threw his eyes down the street." What do you think, good one, eh?! It's from the D. H. Lawrence.

Writing this has already made me feel less like killing the boys. A little bit less . . .

David's not so bad (as he once proved!)—but, man, Joe and Justin are SO JUVENILE. Last night was about the final straw. Bastards. Wait till you hear what they did. We were all stuck in this one tiny dressing room at a venue in Northampton, Massachusetts, running three hours late (we'd gotten stuck in traffic and arrived to find out the club's curfew was midnight, which left us twenty-five minutes to do our set). It was a college crowd, but they'd been waiting for ages, and were chanting and stamping their feet. Troy, our new tour manager (doubles as a roadie), and David got the gear set up in record time, and Joe, Jus, and I were all scrambling over each other to get changed, do our makeup and hair, and get out there before there was a riot. Usually there's a bathroom where I can get changed—I don't mind sharing a motel room with them (if I have to), but I never get undressed in front of them.

I was nagging them like mad to turn round, so I could put my skirt on, and Justin was fed up with me. He goes, "Just do it, Helena, like we care—I'm far too busy here to be looking at you naked."

I begged them, though, and eventually they faced the wall, and I turned around, too, and ripped off my sweatpants and sneakers (my van-driving clothes).

I didn't notice how quiet they'd both gone until I turned back, half into my tights, wobbling all over the place on one leg, and met their eyes in a mirror on the wall they were facing!! I could have died. I burst into tears and they just laughed. Oh, Sam, I was wearing my horrible huge old knickers, and they'd had a perfect view of my massive bum. I hate them.

Anyway, I'm feeling a bit better now. I'm just worried they'll tell David what a massive ass I have, and then he'll feel sick at the thought that he actually went to bed with someone as repulsive as me. Wish I was skinny like you!

Write soon and tell me about Martin, I'm glad he's finally asked you out. Have you "tweaked his deak" or maybe even "pronged his dong" yet?

Oodles of love,

H x

P.S. Further to your enjoyment of *Around the Aardvark in Eighty Days*, might I suggest a few more titles for your reading pleasure?:

80,000 Aardvarks Under the Sea

To Kill an Aardvark

The Aardvark of Casterbridge

The Decline and Fall of the Roman Aardvark

P.P.S. I tried to get Joe to play this game, and the best he could come up with was *101 Aardvarks*—duh. . . . xx

* * *

June 19, 1985

Dear Rusty Harcourt,

(That's your porn star name, in case you ever fancy a change of career: You take the name of your first ever pet, and the name of the first street you ever lived in.)

Thanks for your letter. Your language gets worse every time you write—I must say, you were a better class of girl altogether when you were going to that church all the time!

Only THREE more months till I see you again!

I'm right in the middle of exams. They seem to be going okay so far, although History was a bit of a nightmare. You're so lucky you don't have to do all this studying, you tart, off round America being a rock star. . . . I can't wait to hear you play live. I'm still playing your record like mad, and I make everyone else listen to it, too. It's fabby.

So, my big news is that I am definitely going to take a year off before law school. There's a girl called Andrea Parsons who's started a Saturday job at Russell & Bromley with me (did I tell you I wasn't working at Price Rite anymore?), and she's saving up to backpack around Australia. She's asked if I'd like to come with her! I'm so excited. I've always wanted to go to Australia. So what I thought is, I'll still come and stay with you for a month first, then Andrea can fly out and meet me in New York.

Right, this was just a quick one, got to get back to the revision.

Lots of love and kisses,

"Hammy Chestnut"

xxx

P.S. You know that Squeeze song about Maid Marian and William Tell—"Pulling Mussels from the Shell"? It was on the radio the other day, and the Nadger said to me: "You know, I've always wondered what exactly that means—'Pulling Muscles Off a Shelf.' It doesn't make sense!" I couldn't stop laughing.

* ✳ *

August 25, 1985

Dear Gas Mnart (Monkey Shaver and Sheep Dipper),

First, CONGRATULATIONS!!! You little brainbox—there's just no call for anyone to have such a disgusting amount of grade A's. What a creep. I'm not sure I can be friends with you anymore. Don't take a year out—get into that law school and hurry up and qualify, so you can become Blue Idea's lawyer. Wouldn't that be great?

Second, sorry I haven't written for so long. I've been saving it all up for this letter, so make sure you're sitting comfortably!

I can't wait to see you! I wish you were coming for more than a month. In fact, I wish you were spending the whole year with me instead of swanning off to Oz with Andrea Parsons, whoever she may be, but that's your choice! Just remember, backpacks are really heavy, Australia is full of those horrible black widow spiders that bite your bum when you go to the dunny, and there are fifteen-foot crocodiles who'll rip your foot off as soon as look at you. Don't say I didn't warn you.

I'm sorry that I probably won't have much time to show you the sights in NYC (although the interior of our tour bus is a complete sight after a few days, and so is Joe in the mornings—would that do?), but at least once we're on the road, you'll get to see some of the bars and diners of America.

Can you believe it, Blue Idea's been on the road for two years! I was so shocked when David told us that yesterday. I suppose I hadn't realized that we'd been touring for so long. So much has changed, and a ton of it has been really gradual—it's sneaked up on us. Like, we're headlining more and more shows, in bigger, packed-out venues. I feel so sorry for the poor bands who are first on our bill; they look so despondent, hammering valiantly away to an empty room. It seems like yesterday since that was us.

We still have a little table at the back of the venue where people can sign our fan-base sheets—that's worked out really well. I remember, from the first tour, feeling really stupid when I'd have to collect all those blank pieces of paper at the end of a show, thinking that nobody would ever sign them. These days Troy leaves out about eight sheets a night, and they're all filled up—about thirty names and addresses per sheet! He sticks them in the mail to Ringside, and half the time they're all beer-stained and illegible. I really pity the poor minions who get the job of typing them all onto our master mailing list. Still, at least we know who to send the fanzine to!

Have I sent you the famous *Bluezine* lately? What an exquisite work of art it is! (Joke.) I really hate writing it these days, I never have time, and I can never think of anything new to say, apart from droning on about chart positions and new singles, etc. I think I'm too hung up on the idea of trying to make it "a good read." Justin teases me about it. "It's not supposed to be *Catcher in the Rye*," he said last time, when I wanted to put in a story about that weird fan we had (you know, the one who kept sending David his toenail clippings).

It has gotten easier, though, touring. I'm much less self-conscious onstage these days, since "This Is Your B.I." was a hit (and I think losing my virginity has also definitely helped!!). It was a real turning point. Suddenly it was like people were starting to respect us, and not just lust after Justin.

The best thing was when kids in the audience stopped yelling insults at me—in fact, these days they quite often make suggestive remarks, or compliments, even. I love it. Some guy shouted "Lovely tits!" from the crowd last week, so I have to assume that he was talking to me! Actually, I've lost quite a lot of weight. I'll never be as slim as you, but I'm down to an American 8 (English 12), and my hips and cheeks and other assorted bits are much less wobbly. Touring is surprisingly hard work, considering how much sitting around on the bus we have to do.

Did I tell you that the second single, "Conditions of Love," is in the *Billboard* Top Ten? Number four, currently, up from seven last week. We've been on a bunch of regional TV shows, in the places we're touring, and girls are recognizing Justin in the street quite often. We even made a video for it! (I'll try and get you a copy.) I had this letter the other day from a thirteen-year-old girl in Michigan who said she wished she could meet me because I'm "really cool." Isn't that hilarious? I wish twenty-year-old boys would write to me and tell me that. . . .

God, I wish I had a boyfriend. You're so lucky to have the Nadger, even if he does get song lyrics wrong (well, at least he didn't think that the first line of "You're the One That I Want" by John T. and Olivia Neutron-Bomb went: "I got shoes / They're made of plywood," which Joe claims he thought were the words, although I can't believe that even Joe is that dumb).

For a while I wondered if David was going to make another move— I don't fancy him, and I know it's a bad idea, with us all being on the road the whole time, but I do have some nice—if a bit vague—memories of that sex. You'd been telling me for ages how lovely sex is, but I never quite understood—you don't, until it happens to you, do you?

Anyway, I'm wasting my time with David. He's got a big crush on the sister of some friend of his. And none of us have time for lurve at the moment. *Love and a Door* (hopefully not "that difficult second album") is coming out in a month's time.

Write soon, and I'll SEE YOU NEXT MONTH!!! CAN'T WAIT!!!

Oodles of love,

   H x

* ✳ *

We arrived in Manhattan for our New York show on a chilly late-September afternoon. I was on pins because I'd told Sam I'd meet her at the venue at four, and it was twenty past by the time we got there. Justin and Joe were taking bets among themselves about who'd cop off with her first—the idea of a Woman on tour with us was almost too exciting for them to stand, especially since I'd built Sam up as something resembling an English Charlie's Angel.

"Get lost," I said to them. "She's far too good for any of you. She likes real men."

Justin groaned lasciviously. "And she'll be in the van with us for four whole weeks. She'll give in to the Becker charm eventually, I just know it!"

I snorted with derision. "In the van? You must be kidding! We're renting a car, and we'll be in a different hotel room, so you've got no chance."

"Oh, goody—a choice of two hotel rooms to screw her in," said Joe, halfheartedly joining in to wind me up. He'd been as quick as

Jus to place his bet, but we all knew that when Justin decided he wanted something, he usually got it. I was beginning to wish I hadn't raved about Sam's attributes quite so enthusiastically.

When I burst through the door of the club, Sam was sitting alone at the bar, stirring a swizzle stick around a glass of cranberry juice. Her face lit up when she saw me, and she jumped off her bar stool.

"*Sourcil! Ma chérie!* I've been looking at all these posters with you on them, I can't believe that you're so famous!"

She waved an arm at the wall of our tour posters next to her and then hugged me. "My famous friend—who'd have thought it? And look at you, you're so glamorous, too! You *have* lost masses of weight."

"Thanks—well, you look as cool as ever. I have to warn you, the boys are gagging to meet you. Justin will definitely try to get off with you, and so will Joe, if Justin's not around, so just keep your eyes open and your legs crossed, okay?"

Sam laughed. "I don't know—Justin looks pretty cute to me."

"But what about the Nadger?"

"Oh, he's history. He wanted to know if it was all right for him to go out with other girls, seeing as I was going to be away for such a long time! The cheek of him! He's just had an ingrowing toenail operated on, too, and he's got to wear this really horrible sandal thing everywhere. So I thought, Hmm, schoolboy with ingrowing toenail problems, or up-and-coming gorgeous American pop stars? Tough choice, but the Nadger had to go."

I made a face at her. "Well, I hope that's not the only reason you're here, to try and seduce my fellow band members!"

Sam hugged me again. "Of course not, you old tart. God, I've missed you so much."

* * *

With trepidation, I introduced Sam to the rest of the band, none of whom seemed to be remotely disappointed by meeting her in person. She was very casual with them, shaking hands and saying "pleased to meet you," without even raising a blush. I envied her insouciance.

After we'd finished loading in and sound-checking, we parked the van in a nearby lot and went out for something to eat. The boys and Mickey steered us toward a noodle bar on Avenue A, so they could ogle the gorgeous Indonesian waitresses, but at the last minute I whisked Sam off to a pizza place a few doors down. I wanted to have her to myself, for a gossip and a leisurely Hawaiian pizza, without having testosterone dripping like stringy cheese over our plates.

By the time we got back, it was around nine-thirty P.M. The first band, Loud Licks, had finished, and our support band, Kabuo, were setting up. A smattering of people sat at side tables drinking and chatting, and Loud Licks fans were drifting away from the stage toward the bar. They were a local band with quite a healthy fan base, but this didn't look like a very good turnout for them. I hoped their set had gone okay—the challenge of being first on the bill was still fresh in my mind.

There was no "backstage" as such, which was ludicrous in a venue of that size. Instead Sam and I were directed to a door at the opposite end of the venue to the stage, which led down a narrow flight of stairs and through a passageway with crates and crates of beer stacked on either side, to a tiny boiler room.

This was, laughably, our dressing room. Its ceiling was less than seven feet high and was covered with ancient hissing and banging pipes. The temperature in there must have been ninety-five degrees or more. A door off the back of it led to a small bathroom, into which I disappeared with relief to get ready, dragging Sam with me. The others, with the exception of Joe and Mickey (who were doubtless at the bar trying to meet girls), were all sitting round a small table whose centerpiece was a black plastic basin full of bottles of beer in rapidly melting ice.

Troy, our new tour manager/roadie, was there, as was Dean, our producer. Dean lived in New York and always came to our shows when we were in town. He, Justin, and David were smoking a joint and discussing Joe's sartorial shortcomings as we emerged from the bathroom and sat down with them.

I glanced at Sam, who was staring open-mouthed at the sight of the enormous joint. I could tell she was shocked, even though she immediately pulled herself together again, not wanting to appear uncool.

"He's gotta lose that hair," said Dean. "Does he think he's in a glam rock band or what? Not that that's any excuse, he just needs to get over it. And as for that hideous black and tan suede bomber jacket thing . . . Dave, have a word with him, will you?"

David looked down over his shades at him. "No way, Dean, that is absolutely not my department. You talk to him, you're the producer."

"Like it has anything to do with me? . . . Ah, here's Helena and Sam. You're the women, you do it."

"Don't be so sexist," I said. "And anyway, I don't think Joe's hair is all that bad."

"Actually, I think it's quite attractive," said Sam demurely, fluttering her eyelashes at David and Justin. Justin looked horrified at the thought that Joe might be a rival.

I never realized Sam could be such a flirt.

In between his turn at puffs of the joint, Justin was chewing the skin around his fingernails, chewing and picking at it until three of his fingers had sudden bright spots of crimson welling on them.

"Oh, for God's sake, Jus," I said, noticing. "We're on in half an hour. Stop it."

Sam handed him a Kleenex, which he wove around his fingers and held clamped in his fist, and they exchanged a smoldering gaze.

I caught the look and began to feel kind of at sea. I didn't know whether I should warn Sam off Justin or not. But my dilemma was temporarily forgotten as I started to get a familiar cramping in my stomach, heralding my pre-show need for the toilet, and I had to focus all my energy into not giving in to it. Once I started I couldn't stop, but I knew if I just held out till I was onstage, then the feeling would pass. Besides, there was no way I was going to disappear back into that not-very-private bathroom with the others sniggering outside.

Joe came back into the room, in a bad mood because Mickey was copping off with Ringside's press assistant.

"Give me a hit," he said, grabbing the joint from Justin and inhaling deeply.

"You look nice tonight," Justin remarked to me sweetly, transferring his bloody tissue to the other hand so he could suck his fingers instead. "That color suits you."

I was pleased. I had on a new purple silk shirt with a long black skirt and a purple and black drifty shawl over the top, and I felt hot, in more than just temperature terms. It occurred to me with amusement how many teenage girls would give their eyeteeth to have Justin say that to them. We had a joke among ourselves: "What's thirty yards long, has no pubes, and goes, 'Aaaah!'?" The answer being, of course, the front row of a Blue Idea concert. Maybe it wouldn't be such a bad thing for him and Sam to have a fling. It would be a great story for her to take home.

Being in that sweltering room became like a Zen thing after the first few minutes. It was unbearable, but pleasant at the same time. You just had to rise above it. The pipes occasionally spat out a trickle of steaming hot water, and we nervously estimated their age and contemplated the consequences should one of them actually burst. On the wall by my head were scrawled the words, "Thanks for everything to Mary, Michael and Michael from us in Duran Duran," with the autographs of Simon Le Bon and Nick Rhodes underneath. Sam was impressed.

"Duran Duran! I love that band. I can't imagine them all holed up in this little sweatbox, too—I bet they weren't too pleased."

Justin said loftily, "Oh, well, Duran Duran aren't very big over here. We're way better known."

Dean and Troy shook their heads in disbelief.

"Music, that's what we need," Joe announced, pulling a tape out of his sports bag and sticking it into our worn-out portable cassette player.

David, Justin, and I groaned. We were sick to the back teeth of all the tapes we'd taken on tour with us, and I didn't think I could stand listening to Billy Idol one more time.

"No, no, guys, listen," Joe said proudly. "I've got a new one, specially for the Brits among us!" He pushed the Play button, and the tape clicked on in the middle of a song.

Sam recognized the album first.

"Oh, brilliant! The Jam—*All Mod Cons*. But that's hardly new!"

Joe and Justin exchanged admiring looks. A girl with long legs and big breasts who knew about music? Even better.

"I meant new to us. Listen, darling, they're playing our tune," Joe hammed to Sam, pursing his lips and pretending to strum along. "God, I wish we'd had real Mods over here. They're so damn cool." "I don't know this song," I said. "What is it?"

Justin reached over and cranked the volume up to the top, and the harsh chords of "To Be Someone" filled up the room. It seemed to suck out what little oxygen there was left, and made us all sweat even more.

David jumped up out of his chair. "It's about fame!" he shouted over the music.

Justin leaped up, too. "And money, and chicks! It's our fucking song!"

Joe joined them, and they all began to play air guitar, stoned and exhilarated. Sam and I watched and laughed as Justin, Joe, David, Troy, and Dean bellowed out whichever of the words they could remember.

"*'No more swimming in a guitar-shaped pool!'*" yodeled Joe.

"*'No more reporters at my beck and call!'*" retorted Dean.

"*'AND DIDN'T WE HAVE A NICE TIME! AND WASN'T IT SUCH A FIIIII-NE TIME! TO BE SOMEONE MUST BE A WONDERFUL THI-IN-ING.'*"

I looked at Sam's face, shiny with sweat and delight. No wonder they all wanted to sleep with her, I thought. She's even more gorgeous in the flesh than I'd made her out to be.

This thought made me wonder, for a split second, if maybe I was a lesbian. After all, I loved Sam more than anyone else in the world. But then I imagined myself kissing her, tongues and everything, and felt so queasy that I knew I couldn't be.

The track finished and Sam spoke up. "Well, I hate to be a killjoy, but are you sure you want to make that your song? It's about has-beens—it's all in the past. *'No more taxis, now we have to walk'?*"

The boys looked sheepish. They obviously hadn't ever thought about the lyrics that closely.

Sam and I rolled our eyes at this apparently prevalent male short-coming. "*'Pulling muscles off a shelf,'*" we chorused, and fell about laughing.

"What?" said David, looking askance at us.

"Nothing," I said. "Don't guys ever listen to the words of a record properly, or are you all too hung up on who engineered it, what studio it was recorded in, and what sort of strings they used on their guitars?"

"Sure we do," said Dean hotly. "It just depends how much of a fan you are, that's all. The more attention you pay to the lyrics, the more you like the band."

"Well, then, how come none of you realized what that Jam song is really about?" Sam asked.

"We *kind* of knew!" Justin said defensively. "We just mean that it can be our song in forty years' time, don't we, guys? When we've spent all our millions on gambling and loose women."

The others nodded gravely and Justin went into the bathroom, as if to indicate that the discussion was closed. Dean rolled another joint and lit up, and we continued to listen to the album at a lower volume.

A young black-haired girl in a miniskirt appeared in the doorway, looked us up and down, and disappeared again in disgust, not realizing how unlucky the timing of her Justin-hunt was. She obviously thought the rest of us looked too frumpy and stoned to be worth her attention.

Even though the press was all over us as the latest "big thing," the teen magazines were still capitalizing on Justin's "dream boat" looks, which meant that the rest of us hadn't really got a look-in yet (the promo shot for our first album featured Jus in prominent and sharp focus, with David, Joe, and I lurking blurrily in the background). I was secretly happy with this state of affairs and was dreading the inevitable individual interviews and photo shoots that I knew would be imminent once the press ran out of ways to describe Justin's eyelashes.

"Want to come upstairs for a bit of fresh air, Sammy?" I asked. She nodded, and we headed out of the room, away from The Jam and the fog of sweat and spliff.

A welcome blast of air-conditioned air struck us when I opened the door back into the now-packed club, so we stood there for a while, flapping the collars of our shirts and turning our hot faces up to catch the artificial breeze.

Once we'd cooled down a bit, we managed to find a tiny space at the bar, where we stood nose-to-nose in the crush, drinking water from plastic cups and trying to catch up on almost three years' worth of gossip.

Fifteen minutes later Joe came to find me, carrying my bass. "Come on, we're up."

With a nervous swallow of the rest of my icy water, and a quick hug to Sam, I turned and followed Joe through the crowd to the stage. Across the room I noticed that Justin and David were making better progress. Justin was holding his guitar in front of him like a battering ram, separating the ranks like a hot knife through butter. People were cheering, and reaching out to touch him as he passed. I had a shiver of recognition that this was just the start of it, and that very soon there was no way we would be able to push through a crowd like this without getting torn to pieces. It was a sobering thought, but once we climbed the steps at the side of the stage and took our places, it didn't matter anymore.

The cheering intensified as Justin struck up the intro chords of the first number, and from that point the set flashed past, seemingly in seconds. The four of us were in harmony, literally, emotionally, almost spiritually. I felt the strange blissful connection with the others, the same as I got when I used to go to church—a feeling of true belonging.

When I was onstage, I never focused on my surroundings too closely. Small details caught my attention for a second and then flitted away again: the way Justin's ears got pink and transparent when backlit by a red stage light, the way the girl in the front row recoiled in pain when her boyfriend shouted too loudly into her ear, how silly Joe's guitar-playing stance was—he always put his feet in Fourth Position in ballet.

I tried never to look right into the audience's faces when I was singing. Justin stared hard at them, trying to intimidate them, but I found that very off-putting. Instead I became an expert at the sweeping glance that roved over thousands of eyebrows, foreheads, and hairlines, but never directly into the eyes.

I also loved to chart the progress of one individual through the crowd. I would pick someone distinctive—usually a tall man with a punk hairdo or a hat—and glance discreetly over at him every now and again to see if he'd moved or not. Almost always he would end up in an entirely different spot from where he started. Sometimes he pushed his way to the front, elbowing and ducking and weaving, eliciting scowls from those who'd been waiting patiently for hours to get that close. More often, though, the person was just borne sideways, organically carried across by the ebb and flow of moving bodies packed together. That night, though, I just kept my eyes on Sam, and the Cheshire cat grin of pride splitting her face told me that I'd finally made it.

The show went really, really well. When we finally left the stage, glowing with triumph, I grabbed Sam's hand and heaved her through the crowd with me to the exit, wanting her to share the moment. I could see Mickey and Willy at the side, grinning maniacally at each other. Then they, too, started shoving toward the back, paralleling our own progress but getting there much faster (they didn't have the congratulatory slaps on the shoulder or attempted kisses and hugs to deal with en route).

Unable to bear the sweatbox any longer, we all went out to a nearby bar to celebrate the successful night. Mr. Wallberger (Rob, finally, to his face) had arrived in time to catch the last few numbers, and obliged us by putting his much-vaunted credit card behind the bar so the drinks could flow freely. Besides us four, along with Sam, Mickey, Willy, Troy, Rob, and Dean, there was a small crowd in attendance that included several Ringside promotions people; our product manager, Tom; a couple of journalists and radio program directors; Aunt Sandi and her latest boyfriend; and a few of the boys' old school friends who had driven up from Freehold for the show.

Sam, predictably, snogged Justin in a corner, and then crashed out from jet lag and excitement. Mickey carried on what he'd started with the press assistant, and David got off with a young Chinese fan. Only Joe and I failed to score—but I didn't care, since I hadn't been trying. My spirits, like my knickers, remained undampened. It was a great impromptu party, and I felt on top of the world, successful, happy, replete.

I danced over to Joe, standing hopefully by the door of the

ladies' restroom. "*To be someone must be a wonderful thing,*'" I sang joyfully in his ear.

He grinned and clinked his beer bottle against mine in a triumphant toast. "It's a *damn* wonderful thing, baby!" he crowed back at me.

MARY ELLEN APPLEBAUM

IT WAS EIGHT-THIRTY A.M. I'D BEEN WRITING FOR TWO SOLID DAYS, including since three o'clock that morning, and I was exhausted. I was starved for fresh air, my limbs felt numb, my back was stiff from being hunched over my computer (not only was I writing new stuff, but I'd also been transcribing the notebooks I filled in hospital), and my eye was red, watery, and aching. Above all, I was furiously angry.

Rather irrationally, the object of my rage was my eighteen-year-old self. I remembered, with crystal clarity, the elation fizzing up inside me after that New York show with Sam: Joe and I clinking bottles and congratulating ourselves. That night, in that sweaty venue, I had it all, and didn't realize. I was beautiful, and didn't notice; healthy, and didn't appreciate it; talented, and took it for granted.

I couldn't imagine ever feeling that happy again.

There was a strange silence in the house. At first I welcomed it, since it indicated that my stalker had gone to the garden center, or on a day trip to Hastings, or whatever it was that stalkers did in their spare time. Then I realized that it was the prolonged absence of the sound of my own voice. Since Mum had returned to New Jersey five days earlier, I had not spoken once. She had left several messages, beginning with a sarky "Thank you for checking that I landed safely," working up to a stroppy "For heaven's sake, Helena, pick up the telephone," but I'd ignored them all. I decided to talk to her only when she started sounding actively panicked.

Now that I was alone, I no longer even had to pretend to be coping. Plus the more time passed, the harder it got to cope. The adrenaline of mere survival had finally dissolved altogether, dissipating into the air around me like the smell of my mother's hairspray. Only a teeth-gritting determination to finish the manuscript prevented me from giving up completely.

I knew I should try to snap out of it, but I didn't have the energy to do anything further than glance at the psychotherapist's phone number, which my mother had left on a Post-it note, stuck prominantly to the top of my computer.

I had refused to see Dr. Bedford again after leaving hospital, much to Mum's chagrin. I was all in favor of the *concept* of therapy— I'd just found it too damn difficult, and, in my case, irrelevant. After a few bedside talk sessions, I decided that it was a waste of time for me to concentrate on any kind of long-term recovery.

I peeled off the Post-it and flicked it into the corner of the room, where it lay forgotten behind my dusty bass.

I didn't need therapy, but I did need a rest, so I decamped to my TV room and lay down on the squashy leather sofa. Remote in one hand and can of Coke in the other, I embarked on a marathon of daytime television. I started with the breakfast programs and post-breakfast chat shows, the tame English versions of *Jerry Springer* and *Ricki Lake.* Instead of "My Son Is Having Sex with My Mother," the subjects were "Am I Doing Too Much Gardening?" and "Help! I've Got a Crush on My Dental Hygienist."

Then I moved on to the children's programs. Teletubbies. Noddy. Someone called Kipper the Dog and his friend Tiger. Lurid, unlikely representations of humanity in all shapes and sizes. What did toddlers make of those fake beings, those Day-Glo–padded mutant creatures who talked baby talk and danced? I wondered. Did it make them believe that they might see Dipsy or Laa-Laa strolling down the high street, doing a spot of shopping?

I thought of Ruby, little proud Ruby with her twangy curls and fake fur coat, her inexhaustible capacity for cuteness and her sad eyes. I wondered how she was and then realized this probably depended on how her parents were.

Through a lunchtime quiz show, I daydreamed about Toby. How he had gotten me through those weeks in hospital simply by treating me like a normal, whole, appealing person. God, that was more than most men ever did when I was whole and relatively appealing. Suddenly I missed him. Why, with his wife unconscious down the corridor, had he kissed me and flirted with me, and then gone cold?

I supposed, over the one o'clock news, that there were a few possible reasons. He could be some kind of groupie, clinging on to an idea of Helena Nicholls from a long time ago—perhaps he'd collected my records, masturbated to my poster, featured me in his own private porn movie. Then again, maybe he'd just been trying to prove something to his wife. Happily married people whose spouses were in a coma didn't, on balance, start affairs with other patients in the same hospital.

Or he really was in love with me.

I dismissed all of the above. The groupie scenario because Toby was about my age, and unless he'd been a fan in the early days, he would have been a bit old for all that adolescent fantasy stuff. Besides, he'd never come across as starstruck, or even particularly as a fan. The "proving something to Kate" theory was also unlikely, because it was a nasty thing to do, and Toby wasn't a nasty person. Plus he'd obviously felt guilty about it. Which left the last option: Toby in love with me. Well, this was also unlikely, despite his professing that he'd fallen for me at first sight. He'd only kissed me twice, and had not tried to contact me since our argument in hospital.

Hang on, though, I thought to myself over another can of Coke and the weather forecast; how did I know he hadn't tried to get in touch? I toyed with the idea of calling the hospital to see if he might have asked Grace or Catriona for my telephone number, but then decided against it. I realized that since I'd put the fear of God into the nursing staff about guarding my privacy, they were unlikely to have handed out my home number to the first person who requested it.

In the sudden vain hope that the postman might just have brought a passionate epistle from Toby, I hauled myself off the sofa, swaddled my head in a huge woolly scarf (despite the temperature being a sunny seventy-two), and ventured outside for the first time in five days to inspect the contents of the mailbox by the front gate.

Seven takeaway menus representing the cuisine of four continents, three free property newspapers, a plethora of leaflets advertising the services of local handymen and gardeners, five assorted envelopes from banks and credit-card companies, and one flimsy blue airmail letter with American stamps on it were jammed into the box. The return address on the airmal letter was smudged and illegible, but it was postmarked Freehold, so I suspected a sugary note from one of my mother's bridge friends. Nothing at all that might conceivably be from Toby.

Just as well, I thought as I trudged back into the house again, heading TV-wards. It was good that he hadn't gotten in touch, however much I missed him. I had to look at the big picture, the limited future. The reason I'd picked a fight with Toby in hospital still stood: What was the point of pursuing a new friendship, let alone a relationship? I wasn't going to be around after the show.

Ensconced on the sofa, in the indentation left by my morning's viewing, I ripped open the American letter and extracted two tissue-thin wisps of writing paper and a photograph of two strange children (as in unfamiliar children—although all children look pretty strange to me, with the exception of Ruby, who is gorgeous).

* * *

June 1998

Dear Helena,

I know it's been years and years since we last talked, but I always wished you well, and followed your progress as much as I could in the papers. I felt so proud that we were once friends. I had a feeling that great things would happen in your life. You always had that air about you. I remember when you first came to our Bible study meeting, you were kind of heavy, and so shy and nervous—but at the same time you still had this sort of inner confidence. I don't know what it was, but I remember watching it grow and grow, once you joined the choir and started writing songs. You just got more and more beautiful, inside and out. It was a lovely thing to see. I guess it was a kind of power, that you could do anything you wanted.

Margie said you'd been feeling kind of down since your accident, which is understandable. I thought it may perhaps make you feel a little better to know that an old friend is thinking of you. I don't want to preach or anything, but please try not to let this ruin your life. You still have so much to offer in so many ways. Jesus will take care of you, if you let Him.

* * *

Mary Ellen Randall! Well, well. I snorted with derision at the notion that I still had so much to offer. Thanks, hon, I feel so much better now.

I couldn't summon up the energy to read on, and instead turned back to the TV. An old Ealing Studios matinee had just begun on Channel 4, and I watched a violent but very gentlemanly murder take place in a frightfully well-coiffed lady's front parlor, but somehow my attention kept drifting back to Mary Ellen's loopy writing.

* * *

I don't know if it's of any interest at all to you, but I run a program here in Freehold that organizes missionary trips to Africa. Don't be misled by the name "missionary"—they aren't colonial dictators, trying to brainwash the natives into their way of thinking. These days they are more like volunteers who go to remote villages to live with the locals to help them with basic health and education issues. Some of the people who go out there aren't overly Christian, although obviously it helps if you believe in God! It depends more on the type of person than how religious they are.

Anyways, I just wondered if you were looking for a change, or a break of some kind? It might appeal, and I'm sure you'd be great at it. I'm always looking for good new people who don't have too many ties at home (Margie said you weren't married, but she didn't know if you were in a relationship or not). If you are interested, let me know and I'd be happy to send you some literature. But please don't think that I'm trying to coerce you into anything. What's that expression: A change is as good as a rest? Well, the work sure isn't particularly restful most of the time, but I have known other folk who've gone out there after a big personal tragedy, and they certainly say it helped.

* * *

A missionary! Me! If the idea hadn't been so preposterous, I'd have found it hilarious. Idly, I wondered how the well-coiffed Ealing lady, who by now had been taken hostage by the murderer, managed to go to the toilet, since she'd been held in her parlor for over twelve hours. This reminded me of my own need for a wee, so I peeled myself off the sofa and staggered into the downstairs loo, still clutching the letter. I sat on the loo and read on.

Also enclosed is a snapshot of my family: my husband, Scott (he's a PT instructor); Scotty Jr., who's six, and Cathey, four. My little angels!

I do hope you don't mind me writing to you—Margie gave me your address. I know I could have gotten it from your mom when she still lived in Freehold, but, truth is, once you got real famous I just thought that you'd be too busy to want to hear from me, or else that you might think I was only sucking up because you were so big and successful!

It would be real nice to hear back from you, even if you think the missionary idea is dumb. . . . Next time you visit your folks (I hear their new house is beautiful), please do take a drive over to Freehold and visit us, I would love to see you again.

> Take care and God bless,
> Your friend,
> Mary Ellen Applebaum

P.S. Oh yes! I nearly forgot: I don't know if you knew this, but I married my neighbor Scott, after he got back from the Marines. He always brags to folk that he got your career started when you bought his bass guitar! I feel kind of silly, almost, telling you—do you remember we used to think his family was so weird? (Well, his mom kind of was, but she died ten years ago. Not an easy woman to get along with, may she rest in peace!) Scotty's sister Janeane turned out real well, though. Sells real estate in town. x

* * *

Even in the depths of my doldrums, I couldn't resist a chuckle at the memory of the absent Scott and his Clampitt-esque family. Life was certainly full of surprises.

I flushed the toilet and trailed back into the TV room to reinstate myself in front of the box. There were now a lot of 1950s cars driving slowly around Piccadilly Circus, with pedestrians in hats and long overcoats striding past the statue of Eros. One of them looked like Toby, or perhaps Toby's grandfather as a young man. I tried to get back into the plot but, annoyingly, my mind kept wandering back to the letter.

After a couple of years of living in America, I'd ceased to notice the Yankness of the place, but as soon as I left, it jumped out at me like a cowboy from behind a saloon door. My first thought after reading Mary Ellen's letter was, How *American*. Everything about it: her hoopy American cursive, her name, her phrasing, her Scotty Jr. The photograph gave out the same message: Scotty Jr. in a baseball mitt and cap. Cathey in Kmart frills, with real ringlets. Scott in the background tending to a barbecue, on a deck. The fact that it made me cringe slightly indicated to me that America was another country I'd never really belonged in. It was merely a place going past outside the tour bus windows, or expectant faces in stadiums, or airport concourses and baggage carousels.

I sighed. It was nice to hear from Mary Ellen nonetheless. I reread the letter, paying more attention to the part about missionaries: "Some of the people . . . aren't overly Christian . . . I'm sure you'd be great at it." What did she know? She hadn't seen me since I was sixteen. I wasn't sure if I even still believed in God.

For a few moments, I wondered whether it *could* be an alternative. If I couldn't face going through with the Plan, perhaps I could "disappear" from public view for a few years and become a missionary?

Immediately, however, I foresaw a few logistical problems. One, I hated hot climates. Two, I'd been known to throw a wobbly if my hotel suite didn't have a spa bath and chilled champagne waiting for me. The notion of actually living somewhere without flushing toilets, air-conditioning, shopping by phone, or chocolate Hobnobs was too horrific to contemplate. I thought that I really would rather be dead. Three, I had extremely sensitive, and succulent, skin. A mosquito in a room full of three hundred people would always make a beeline right for me, sampling at least twenty-seven different parts of my body before declaring itself sated. Whenever we toured in hot, humid climates, I used to walk around practically shrouded in mosquito nets.

I remembered doing an MTV interview in the Dominican Republic, during the rainy season. I had bought a new, natural mosquito repellent made from tea tree oil and citronella, and had smeared it on every exposed inch of skin I could reach. It hadn't smelled too bad in the tube, but somehow it reacted with the heat of my body, and within minutes of my leaving the hotel room, people were behaving as if I had appalling body odor. The interviewer, a beautiful, haughty Cherokee Indian girl, had moved gradually further and further away from me, and eventually began to snigger so hard that the interview had to be suspended. I found out later that Justin had whispered to her beforehand that, although I had good fashion sense, I had the most hideous taste in perfume, and insisted on wearing the cheapest, most disgusting brands, which I thought were divine. . . .

Which led on to four: I was the most squeamish person in the world. It wouldn't just be mosquitoes, would it? There were all manner of creepy crawlies: scorpions, hornets, blood-sucking flies and poisonous spiders . . . urgh. And as for crapping in holes and having to kill my own food—forget it.

It obviously wasn't such a good idea after all. My squeamishness also meant that the actual suicide was, technically speaking, going to be a bit of a dilemma. I knew there was no way I'd be able to blow my brains out, which was a shame really, since that would have the biggest impact, thus creating the maximum of publicity for the manuscript, and the best prospects for my future place in rock history.

Slitting my wrists would be too messy, as well. There were no bathtubs or showers at New World. So that left pills and booze. The best way to go, I supposed, if not the most dramatic. I'd just have to lock myself into my studio and do it.

God, this was all such hard work. It was tempting just to stay in my house for the rest of my life. The TV could be my friend. I'd be safe. I could get everything I needed delivered via the phone and Internet.

But then I realized I'd never be remembered. Nobody would hear my story, or Sam's. I felt I owed it to Sam for people to read about our friendship and how brave she had been.

It would have to be the original Plan, then. I'd treat today as a day off before knuckling back down to the manuscript tomorrow. Settling into the sofa again, I channel-hopped until alighting on *Can't Cook, Won't Cook,* grateful to Ainsley Harriott for reminding me that life really wasn't worth living. . . .

SHIPBUILDING

Two years later Blue Idea played New York again, this time at the Academy on Forty-seventh Street. It was five times the size of the venue Sam had seen us at, and there was no question of us hanging out at the bar before the show, or of having to load our own gear into the van. We had two roadies to do that for us now, and Troy, rather unnecessarily, had a walkie-talkie to coordinate them. There were fans hanging around the stage door after the gig, and a limo to take us to and from the hotel.

I hadn't seen Sam for ages, apart from a long weekend we'd had in Paris together the year before, which I'd organized as a birthday treat for her. She was well into her law degree in London, working in the holidays, too, so the days of her being able to accompany us on tour were long gone.

She had returned home after her abortive round-the-world trip not speaking to Justin because he'd given her crabs, but otherwise having had a fantastic time, she assured me. After four months of her continuous company (except when she was off shagging Justin somewhere—a casual but apparently mutually satisfying relationship), I missed her even more than when we'd first moved to New Jersey, but I was too busy to indulge the hollow ache of her absence. Four days in two years felt unbearably meager to both of us, but we coped with it by speaking weekly on the phone.

The Academy show went pretty well, although I couldn't really remember it that clearly. With a few exceptions, our gigs had all blurred together over time.

Aunt Sandi had come to the gig and partied with us afterward. On a drunken whim, and to her delight, we invited ourselves back to her place to crash that night. It was a lot less comfortable than our suites at the Royalton, but we felt quite sentimental about

Sandi's apartment, the epicenter of the action when we were first signed. Plus the appeal of hotel accommodation, however smart, wore very thin after a few weeks of a tour.

I remembered waking up, staring at the orange flowery wallpaper of the spare room, and feeling rather queasy. It had probably been way past four by the time we'd finished at the party Ringside had thrown for us after the gig, and the limo had driven us over the vast glittering peaks of the Brooklyn Bridge. In the end, Sandi had had to accommodate only Joe, David, and me, since Justin had left with a pretty student he'd met at the party; he was such a cliché— on average he went through two groupies per month.

At first I'd kept this fact from Sam, in case it upset her, but she was remarkably nonchalant about their whole dalliance. "He's cute, it passed the time. We were never planning to keep in touch or anything," she said. I was surprised at her attitude—I'd always assumed that she'd take these things much more seriously. It was a part of her life I didn't really know that much about.

I got up and got dressed, sandpaper on the inside of my eyelids, feeling like I'd woken with a squid on my face. Stepping over the prone sleeping figures of Joe and David in the living room on my way to the kitchen, I glanced at the incongruous Superman clock on Aunt Sandi's kitchen wall and noticed with horror that it was already 12:45.

Simon, Ringside's radio promotions guy, had impressed upon us that we needed to be at the office by three P.M. for a couple of radio phoner interviews in the Ringside conference room. Our third album, *Spin Shiny,* had just come out, and the promotions machine was at full throttle.

I made coffee and took it in to the others to herald the start of their long, drawn-out waking process, which was accompanied as usual by much moaning and groaning. Eventually we were all up, showered, and in a chauffeur-driven car that would drop us at the office only a little past three. I was desperately hoping Justin had not forgotten the commitment, and to my surprise and relief he was already there when we arrived, lounging on Ringside's visitors' sofa looking peaky.

He grinned weakly but proudly at me and shoved his hand in my face as if he expected me to kiss it. "Look, see, bet you thought I'd forget!"

He had R'SIDE 3 PM in faint but thick, wavering blue letters on the back of his hand.

"Very good, Jus, well done, we're all impressed," I told him, not entirely sarcastically.

Tom and Simon ushered us into the conference room, plying us with more coffee and welcome bagels, as we had had neither the time nor the stomach for a proper breakfast, let alone lunch. They conferenced Joe and Justin in with the first radio station, and myself and David with the second. After a few minutes we switched round and talked to the other station.

When we were finished, Tom had us sign some posters and CDs to give away as prizes in competitions, or as incentives for record store clerks. We were working away at the conference-room table when I had a sudden thought.

"Oh, my God—what's the date today?"

Being on tour for so long seemed to have confounded our time clocks. None of us had a clue what city we were in half the time, let alone what day it was.

"It's August twenty-eighth," said David. "Why?"

"Shit, it's not, is it?" I wailed as the door opened and Willy came in with a fresh supply of posters.

"Hi, guys. Tom's on the phone, so he asked me to bring you these. What's the matter, Helena?" he asked, looking at my stricken face.

"Oh, nothing . . . It's just that I've missed someone's birthday, that's all."

It was Cynthia Grant's birthday, and I always sent her a card. I had thought about it the week before but had promptly forgotten again.

Willy put down the posters, and they fanned out in a graceful arc across the shiny surface of the meeting-room table. "Do you want to call them?"

"Really? But it's long distance." I felt faintly cheeky at the thought of running up Ringside's phone bill, until I remembered that they were about to move to new, much more palatial offices, the upgrade funded in no small part by the sales of our records. They could stand me the price of a phone call to England, and hopefully I'd be able to chat to Sam, too.

"It's no problem, honestly. You can use the phone in my office if you like."

He lowered his voice conspiratorially. "I'm always on the phone to my mates in London—but don't tell Rob."

"Well, thanks. I'd love to."

I stood up, calculating that it would be only nine-thirty in Salisbury, and the Grants should be around on a weeknight. Cynthia might be working, but would more likely be having a few birthday rum and Cokes in the saloon bar with her girlfriends, and Sam would probably be there, too. I knew that she was working in a Salisbury solicitor's office during her summer break. Either way, I didn't think it would be a problem. There was a phone at the bottom of the stairs where they kept the boxes of crisps, and I knew that it could easily be heard from the bar.

Willy led me over to what he had laughingly called his "office" but which was in reality a desk in an odd corner cranny of the open-plan but terribly cramped label workspace. I had to climb over several boxes of Blue Idea T-shirts and a huge and perilously unstable pile of records to get to his chair. A Big Star album was blaring from speakers in the center of the room, and I wondered how I'd ever be able to hear anything. There was a stack of black-and-white eight-by-tens of us on Willy's desk, and I turned the top one facedown so I wouldn't have to look at my monochrome face looming up at me while I talked.

With the receiver clamped hard against my ear to try to block out the noise, I dialed the Grants' number. It rang for ages.

Eventually an unfamiliar woman's voice answered, and I put my finger into my free ear. "Prince of Wales, hello?" she said faintly.

"Hello, can I speak to Cynthia Grant please?" I asked.

There was a pause. "I'm sorry, she's—not around at the moment."

"Well, could I speak to Sam instead, then?"

A longer pause. I heard the sound of a hand being put over the receiver and a muffled question in the background. Then a kind of scuffling noise. The woman, whom I assumed must be a new barmaid, came back on the line.

"Who is it?"

"It's Helena," I said, starting to feel worried. Something did not seem right.

"Hold on a minute please."

The receiver clunked down, and I visualized it resting on top of a box of Worcester sauce crisps. The Big Star record, thankfully, came to a sudden scratching halt. Then Mrs. Grant came on the line.

"Helena, love, how are you?" She sounded terribly tired, not the festive person I'd expected at all.

"Happy birthday to you!" I chirped enthusiastically, as usual avoiding having to call her Cynthia. "How's things? Are you having a nice day? I'm really sorry I forgot to send you a card, but our new album is—"

She cut off my apology abruptly, a terrible catch in her voice. "Oh, Helena, I . . ."

"What is it, what's the matter? Are you ill? Has something happened to the pub?"

I felt fear begin to swoop down over my head like the corners of a black veil.

"No, worse—Helena, I'm really sorry—it's our Sammy."

The veil enveloped me completely and I thought I was going to faint. Mrs. Grant sounded completely devastated. She's dead, I thought. Oh God, Sam is dead. Then she spoke again, as if from the bottom of a well. "She's in hospital."

A sensation like gravity's pull assailed me, a strange mixture of relief and terror. Relief that she wasn't dead, terror because this obviously was not an inflamed appendix or troublesome tonsils.

"What's happened—has she been in an accident?" I managed to stammer. I could hear Mrs. Grant struggling for breath, or for strength, at the other end of the phone.

"Helena, I don't know how to tell you this. . . . She wasn't feeling well, so she had some tests. . . . They've found out that she's got leukemia. Acute myeloid leukemia, it's called. She's already started the treatment."

The wall in front of me rocked violently, and I had to grip on to the edge of Willy's desk. My mind went completely blank for a second, and then out of a gray cloud emerged some tiny animated images, like frames of an old home movie: Sam and me as children cycling home from school on our little kiddie bikes, hers turquoise, mine pale pink.

"Helena, are you all right?" I heard in the distance. "Don't worry, love. The doctors say she should be okay. There's lots of things they can do for it these days. We only found out yesterday, and she's started the chemotherapy right away. . . ." Mrs. Grant's voice broke, but she rallied herself. "And it should be fine, she should be fine. Really. Try not to worry. Say something—are you still there?"

Sam had had a little white plastic basket tied to the handlebars of her bike. It had pale blue ribbons that streamed out behind the fake wicker when she pedaled, and I had coveted it without shame. In the silence I could faintly hear the pub's jukebox playing Robert Wyatt's "Shipbuilding," and a man's deep, distant laugh. I swallowed hard.

"I'm here. But how is she? Is she in pain? Has she been ill for a long time?"

"Mike and I have just come back from the hospital now. She's feeling dreadfully sick, but otherwise she's not in actual pain. They've got her heavily sedated. We have to wait and see how she responds to the treatment."

I think we may have talked for a little longer, but my mind had whirled off into a realm of grief somewhere else, and I couldn't remember any more of the conversation. For some reason, I couldn't get the image of that little white basket and the doleful lyrics of "Shipbuilding" out of my head. With every atom in my body I wished fiercely that I could be where Sam was, and not in that stupid, filthy office full of strangers. I sat at Willy's desk for a long time, gazing dry-eyed at the wall, not having any idea what to do next.

A hand touched my shoulder. It was David. "We're done, Helena. Are you ready to go?"

As I stood up, my stomach suddenly heaved and seemed to flip over. Aware of David, Justin, Joe, Willy, and half the Ringside label staff staring at me with incredulity and concern, I careered out of the room, just about managing to grab a nearby office rubbish bin on the way, and was copiously sick.

David came and rescued me from the women's bathroom. Throwing up had also induced a flood of tears, so he tidied me up, clucking and crooning over me, listening to my sobbed-out story while wiping my face with a scratchy paper towel and stroking my hair clumsily. I allowed myself to be led out of the office and into a waiting limo, and taken back to Aunt Sandi's apartment. I didn't want to go back to the impersonal, empty hotel room.

When Sandi got home from work, she and the boys talked in hushed voices in the next room, then she came in and gave me a sleeping pill and a cup of hot chocolate. Fortunately there was no show that night, and I fell into a deep, exhausted sleep of grief and disbelieving.

NOT SUCH A COINCIDENCE

HOW DID PEOPLE WHO LOST LIFELONG SPOUSES HANDLE THE PAIN?
Sam had "only" been a friend, not a lover or partner, but I couldn't
cope with knowing that I'd never see her again. As I sat at the
kitchen table staring glumly into the middle distance, something
inside my stomach snarled at me, loudly enough to be heard above
the moaning of my depression and the dolorous bass of "Shipbuilding." After a moment's consideration I realized, with some surprise,
that it was hunger.

Suddenly I knew that I had to get out of the house and get some
food. I was absolutely, overwhelmingly ravenous. If I stayed indoors
for even one minute longer, I would start gnawing the kitchen
counters.

Mum had stocked up for me before she went home, but now the
freezer was empty except for half a packet of broad beans. I was
down to chocolate spread and capers in the cupboard, and my fruit
bowl contained four shriveled grapes and a fossilized lime. I'd been
living on noodle soup for the past four days, and I was craving fresh
juice, hot bread, colorful salads.

I usually got Sainsburys to home-deliver my groceries, but such
was my frame of mind that I hadn't been able to face the hassle of
trying to order over the telephone, let alone exchange small talk
with a delivery man. My snap decision to get in the car and go there
myself was probably borne from a combination of physical need
and mental exhaustion—I needed food, quickly, and I needed to
do something to take my mind off my terrible sense of loss.

My daring plan to venture into the outside world filled me with a
sudden sense of wild recklessness. Donning shades and a floppy
sun hat, I picked up the car keys and left the house, glancing con-

stantly around me as I locked up and got in the car. Still no sign of the stalker, thank God.

I drove to Sainsburys with the roof open and a fresh summer wind flapping the brim of my sun hat, congratulating myself on my positive decision, and beginning to feel a tiny bit less miserable. It was fantastic to be back behind the wheel of my car after so long.

Everything was going much better than expected—until I reached the supermarket. I hadn't realized it was Saturday. The car park was full to capacity, and row upon row of hot metal chassis glinted at me, taunting me with the knowledge that each car equaled one or more people banging up and down the aisles inside. If I went in, I'd be face-to-face with them all. There would be no security men or velvet ropes or limos to keep us apart, not even the soundproofed cocoon of a DJ's studio and the coziness of headphones. Just me and the great, ordinary unwashed.

I drove right around the perimeter of the car park and straight out onto the road again, just about managing to avoid a huge wobbly line of pushed-together trolleys being coraled into a pen by two bored employees.

Change of plan. I *could* go home and phone Home Shopping, but then I'd have to wait for them to deliver, and I was too hungry. I took a detour past my favorite deli, but in the three months since I'd last been there, the windows had been whitewashed and the door locked. CLOSED DOWN DUE TO DEATH, read a shakily lettered sign in the window. I know how that feels, I thought, and carried on into Richmond.

There was a Tesco Metro in the town center—still a supermarket, but a smaller, less intimidating one. I'd be in and out much more quickly, I reasoned, hunger forcing me to try again. Eventually I found a parking space by the river and made my way back toward Tesco's, realizing with rising panic that there were probably even more people jostling around on the sunny town center pavements than there had been in Sainsburys. My legs were already beginning to quiver with the unaccustomed effort of walking, and I was so tense that my jaw and nose were aching. I felt a pang of longing for

my mother, wishing that she would materialize at my side and prof-
fer a plump elbow for me to hang on to.

But I made it. As soon as I got through the door of Tesco's, I
grabbed a carton of cherry-flavored milk from the shelf and
chugged it straight down. This gave me the energy to continue, and
in five minutes flat I was queuing, blissfully unnoticed, at the checkout with a basket full of prepackaged salad, milk, bread, croissants,
a bag full of individually wrapped cheeses, bananas, oranges, and
the empty carton. I promised myself that I'd order all other
nonessentials by phone when I got home.

The checkout girl barely even glanced at me as I paid. Too pre-
occupied with trying to hike her bra strap back onto her skinny
shoulder, she shortchanged me, but I was too eager to escape
unrecognized to point it out to her.

Flushed with success, I even dared to sidle into HMV on my way
back to the car, where I purchased a copy of The Jam's *All Mod Cons*
on CD. I'd only ever owned it on vinyl, and I needed to start thinking
about collecting CDs together for the show. This would be a start.

By now I was really beginning to feel unwell. My legs still felt wobbly,
and the hunger and the cherry milk had collided in my stomach to
form a queasy compromise. I needed a sit-down, and possibly a
croissant. I took a right turn down toward the river, and my car, but
instead of emerging in a quiet side street, I came out in a large riverside area next to Richmond Bridge. This, too, was crowded with people.

The Richmond riverfront in summer had a definite beach-
resort, Club 18–30 feel to it: sweaty people queued at ice-cream van
windows, clutching their plastic cups of European lager in one
hand and their small change in the other. The bars were packed,
there were boats for hire, and half-stripped bodies lay sprawled on
the grassy terraced area above the river. An extremely high tide was
just receding, water still lapping over the edge of the bank, a wash
of dark cooling the hot pavement. A few lads were standing in this
puddle, shoes off, trousers rolled up, glugging their pints and looking around self-consciously to see who was watching them. A dog
leaped into the river, scaring away a scattering of ducks and making
a group of implausibly tanned girls scream as the splash sent drops
of murky Thames water into their vodka and limes.

I was about to turn in the direction of my mislaid car when I felt another hot stab of panic. I was in the middle of this huge crowd of strangers, vulnerable, exhausted, and sick, and my only protection against recognition was shades and a sun hat. I raised a hand to my head to check that both were still in place.

Deep breath, I thought. These people are your listeners and—some of the older ones—your fans. Just sit down and have a rest. No one will bother you.

Finding a space on the patchy town-center grass, I brushed away a few fag ends and a rusty bottle top, and lowered myself gingerly. It felt nice, actually. The sun was warm on my thighs, and scratchy stems tickled the backs of my legs. I rolled up the tops of my shorts, scoffed a croissant, and tried to relax.

Not wanting to appear unoccupied, I delved into my bag for my new CD and began to wrestle with the shrink wrap. As usual, the sticky top-spine bearing band name and album title didn't peel off in one go, but broke away in irritating little slivers, behaving in the way that Sellotape does when you're tired. I jabbed at it with my thumbnail and eventually managed to unwrap it.

I opened the jewel case and extracted the booklet, reading snatches of lyrics while trying to recover my energy and courage. A couple near me in matching Stussy T-shirts and denim shorts suddenly nudged each other, jerked their eyebrows in my direction, and laughed.

I froze with horror, as color flamed across my cheeks. Ramming the CD back into my bag, I stood up, brushing grass off the seat of my shorts, and moved away through the throng to find somewhere else to sit.

"Check her out," I heard another man say to his companion, and he pointed at me, sniggering.

Why, oh why, hadn't I worn a wig as well? Obviously hat and shades were nowhere near enough. I was still recognizable as me, but because I was no longer beautiful, all my musical achievements had ebbed muddily away in people's memories. It was a cruel realization, to discover how quickly disfigurement could transform me from a respected rock star into a laughingstock. I had no idea that people could be so mean.

My queasiness had escalated into a full-blown green wave of nausea, and I blundered toward the nearest pub to try to find a quiet loo in which to puke. A bottleneck of drinkers were jostling one another in front of the doorway, however, and I couldn't get in. As I stood, jiggling desperately from foot to foot, I realized what the problem was.

A man was holding everyone up, planted firmly in the narrow entrance to the pub, and clutching a pint in each hand.

"Come on, mate, get a move on," someone shouted at him from behind.

"Oh, for God's sake, someone get him out," yelled a woman next to me, waving her lipstick-printed empty glass. "I'm dying of thirst here!"

Eventually a large burly person in an unbecoming sports vest and rugby shorts gave the man a shove, and he flew out of the porch, spilling his pints and apologizing profusely to the doorframe as his shoulder connected with it en route.

Suddenly we were face-to-face. The man looked exactly like Toby, if Toby's body had been occupied by somebody else, someone loose and miserable.

I stared incredulously for a moment longer. It *was* Toby.

Lager dripped off his hands and wrists, dampening down the whorls of blond hair on his arms. I looked down and saw his legs in combat shorts, warm with fuzzy golden hair, and it gave me a tiny thrill, as if I was seeing him naked for the first time. I had an urge to hang on to one of those knees as if it was the only thing that would anchor me down. I suddenly felt like crying, realizing how much I'd missed him.

Then I noticed that the legs were swaying, and it sunk in that Toby was absolutely, horrendously, and disgustingly drunk.

He looked at me without focusing, looked away, and then did a slow-motion double take. I waited for his face to light up, to say hello. Instead he grinned vaguely, as if something had amused him.

My hand shot out and grabbed his soggy arm. "Toby? What are you doing here? This is such a coincidence!"

He stared at me as directly as he could and burst out laughing. "Helena, ohGodit'syou! YouhavenoideahowmuchIwannedtoseeyou," he slurred, handing me one of his half-empty pints and stretching his free hand toward my face. I waited to feel his warm palm cup my cheek, but instead I felt him peel something off each side of my chin.

"Why'veyougotthesestucktoyourface?" he asked, squinting at the two little strips of CD top-spine that had somehow adhered to either side of my mouth, like goaty whiskers.

I groaned. For fuck's sake. *That* was why people had been staring at me and tittering.

Without waiting for an answer, Toby gave me an enthusiastic hug. He smelled of stale beer and sweat, faint aftershave, garlic. A very different smell from the one I remembered as his.

"Listen," he said. "Bitpissedatmoment. Reallywannaseeya, though. Missedcha, man, somuch."

He hugged me again, nearly toppling us both, sending lager cascading down the front of my favorite dry-clean-only Betsey Johnson top.

I pulled away. "What's going on, Toby? What are you doing here?" I wanted to add, "Drunk, in the middle of the afternoon."

Just then a man appeared at his shoulder. He was thin and balding, but with great big dark eyes and chimney-brush eyelashes, like a little boy's. He didn't seem to be quite as drunk as Toby.

"Where's my pint?" he said to Toby, glancing at me. The lack of interest in his gaze was a refreshing relief.

Toby pointed at the glass in my hand. "She'sholdingitforyou," he said.

She? I was beginning to feel a tense, choking sensation in my gut, driving out the previous nausea and filling it with something much more painful: disappointment.

"I'm Helena," I said pompously, handing him his pint. Since half of it had been spilled, it looked as if I'd had several hefty swigs out of the glass, but I decided it was beneath me to try to justify myself.

"Loveofmylife," said Toby dreamily, and put his arm around my shoulders. I shrugged him off crossly.

The man's eyelashes stood at attention. "I'm Toby's friend Bill," he said. "It's a pleasure to meet you. I've heard so much about you."

Tight-lipped, I shook his hand. "Listen, I should really get going. I was just passing through."

Bill touched my elbow briefly and bent to whisper in my ear—my good ear, fortunately.

"Ignore him—he's not himself. I expect you know he's never usually like this, drunk and stuff. It's just that—"

Toby caught the word *drunk* and shoved his head in between ours. "Noneedtomakeexcuses," he said. And then with supreme concentration he managed to separate his words: "*I'm not as thunk as drinkle peep I am,* you know."

He roared with laughter and then sank into a miserable silence, morosely sucking the beer off each of his arms in turn. "Sorry, Ellna," he said eventually, sounding like Ruby in disgrace.

I badly wanted to ask how Ruby was doing but didn't think I'd get a comprehensible reply.

"I'll call you, okay?" he added, obviously making a colossal effort to hold it all together.

"You don't have my number," I said.

"C'n I have it?"

I hesitated. I wasn't sure that I wanted to see him again. Toby's imploring look suddenly turned to one of horror, and his face went a nasty shade of mustard. "Aaargh," he said, putting a hand over his mouth and shoving his pint back into my hand once more. "Gonnabesick." And he dashed unsteadily off into the pub.

There was a sound of popping in my head, as all my romantic bubbles burst.

"Give him a chance," muttered Bill again. "He really needs to talk to you."

I was about to say, *He's married, what is there to talk about?*, when I had a terrible thought. "Um, Kate . . . Kate hasn't *died*, has she?"

Bill almost grinned, but not quite. "No. But Toby's left her. As soon as she came out of hospital, she told him that she was having an affair. He and Ruby have gone to stay with his sister Lulu."

I didn't know what to say. I stared toward the dark interior of the pub, hoping that Toby would be able to feel my shock and sympathy vibes. My first thought was that he must have really loved Kate, for him to get so rip-roaringly inebriated.

"Poor Toby. Poor *Ruby,*" I said.

Bill put a hand on my forearm again, and my skin crawled with the effort of not shaking it off. I hated it when strangers touched me. "Helena, listen," he said. "It's not as much of a coincidence as you think, bumping into us here. We've been down here four days in a row, looking for you. Toby's been on this bender, see, and he insisted on coming here because he knew you lived in the area. I told him it wasn't such a good idea, but he wouldn't listen—I mean, you don't want to see him in this state, do you?"

I shook my head. "Who's looking after Ruby?"

"Lulu, and Toby's mum. She's been staying there, too. They've been brilliant, but I think they are starting to draw the line at baby-sitting just so Toby can go out and get hammered. But at least he's found you."

I was getting even more irritated. Bill made it sound as if I were a lost puppy, or some mislaid car keys. I was tired and unwell and wanted to go home.

"I'm sorry," I said stiffly. "I don't give out my phone number. Why don't you give me Toby's address, and if I get the chance, I'll contact him?"

Bill produced a Biro but couldn't find any paper, so I handed him the receipt for *All Mod Cons* and watched as he scribbled down an address and telephone number.

"Please call him. He'd kill me if he knew I was telling you, but he's really mad about you. He's in shock about Kate, of course, but they both knew it wasn't working out long before her accident." Bill's eyelashes were practically begging me, and even though my head was pounding, I smiled.

"You're a good friend to him, aren't you?"

"Mmm. Well, speaking of which, better go and check he's okay." He handed me the receipt and, with a brief wave, vanished into the throng before I could say anything else.

I was still clutching Toby's drink, so I walked over and left it next to the pub wall. As I set off toward my car, the dog who'd jumped into the water reappeared and stuck his damp nose into the abandoned pint, sucking greedily at it. I heard the splintering crack of breaking glass and the dog's whine as his owner smacked him away from the beery shards, but I didn't look back.

Once I was in the car, I glanced at Toby's address. For a split second my heart did a tiny tap dance, but then I screwed the receipt into a tiny ball, dropped it to the floor by my feet, and drove home.

DEEP BLUE DREAM

OCTOBER 1, 1987

*I don't really have the time to keep a diary, but Cynthia said I should
try, after I told her on the phone the other day that everything was such
a blur. She said, "Do it so you can remember the tour later on."*

*I don't think I want to remember it, though. This tour is a complete
nightmare, I can't stand it. I just want to be with Sam. What sort of
pathetic friend must she think I am, that I just carry on like normal,
while she's lying there so sick? If I could talk to her for more than two
minutes at a time, then I'd be able to persuade her to let me come over.
But she's not too sick for a spot of the old emotional blackmail. She
says she'll never speak to me again if I quit the band or leave the tour.
I know she's bluffing. Of course she'd still speak to me, but I also
know that she'd never forgive herself if I chucked in the band because
of her.*

*I suppose she's right. Wait till the tour's done and then I can go
straight over to Salisbury and stay with the Grants. It'll be easier all
round when Sam's first round of chemo is finished. She's too ill to even
talk to me on the phone most days, and Cynthia says she can't face any
visitors. At least if I wait awhile, she'll be able to appreciate my company
more.*

*BUT I FEEL SO GUILTY! I think B.I.'s success makes it worse, too.
Spin Shiny's been number one for four weeks now, but frankly, I
couldn't care less. It's only success. And money, I guess—although come
to think of it, we haven't seen very much of that. I'd have thought we'd
be getting far more royalties than we actually do. . . . Oh, who knows.
Who cares.*

Boston, NYC, Philly, and D.C. this week.

* * *

October 9, 1987

We were on Saturday Night Live *and* The Tonight Show *last week. It was kind of funny. The whole time we were playing, all I could think of was whether the hospital lights hurt Sam's eyes the way the studio lights hurt mine. Dumb, really. It's this awful dream I keep having: Sam's lying helpless, strapped to a table in a great big empty operating theater, with one huge white light glaring right in her face, while all that poison is getting pumped into her body, killing all her cells and not just the leukemia ones in her bone marrow. I wish there was an easier way to make her better.*

Shit, crying again. My eyelids are permanently like two great big puffy water wings—the makeup lady on The Tonight Show *nearly had a fit. Cucumber slices just don't do it for me anymore.*

Still, let's look on the bright side. I've lost tons more weight.

New Orleans, Austin, Dallas. A bunch more places, too, but I can't remember where and I don't have the itinerary at hand.

* * *

October 18, 1987

I'm crossing off the cities on my tour schedule, one by one, after each gig, like a prisoner counting the days to freedom on his cell wall. Half the time I don't even know where the hell we are. Why am I wasting time writing this when I should be finishing writing to Sam?

Well, at least if I try and get at least some of the terror and pain and guilt out of my system in this diary, then hopefully it'll be easier to find something lighthearted to tell her in my letters. Blathering on to her about the band, even though she always says she wants to hear it, makes me feel awful. Here am I, banging on about our success, when she's fighting for her life.

Surprise, surprise: crying . . . again. Change the record, Helena.

Success is definitely going to Justin's head. He's started taking cocaine—how predictable. Joe has, too, but thankfully David's got more sense. I have to admit that I tried it, a tiny bit, and yes, it was pretty nice. I felt great. But somewhere, from the depths of my being, however tempting it is to get completely out of it and forget about Sam, I haven't repeated the experience. I only tried a weeny little amount, a line as thin as a piece of cotton, practically, but Justin's already on great big thick ones. He can handle it, but I don't dare. The last thing Sam needs is me becoming a drug addict! I remember when she came to New York that time, she was horrified when the boys spliffed up. I have to keep focused on her recovery; it's the least I can do, when I'm stuck on a different continent from her.

David and I have had a few whispered conversations about whether or not to confront J&J about the coke (I didn't dare mention to him that I'd tried it, too). But we decided ultimately that, unless they seem to be getting way out of control, it would just cause more trouble than it's worth. So David's gone for a spot of damage limitation instead. He figured out who they were buying it off, and apparently it's Gavin the roadie's girlfriend, Trish. Then he took Trish aside and told her, totally politely, that she was NEVER to tell Jus or Joe that she had any more than a gram at a time to sell them, and that if she did, he would personally see to it that she went to jail! I hope he knows what he's doing—Gavin's built like a brick outhouse. But I think David's so brave.

I wish David and I fancied each other. He'll make someone a lovely husband. And he's been so supportive of me in the past few weeks. He didn't even gang up on me with the others when we had that row. Okay, so he didn't exactly take my side either, but it can't have been easy for him: It was after I cried onstage in Chicago last week.

I don't know what happened—I'm usually pretty good at holding it together when we're playing. When my eyes fill up, I just turn round and fiddle with the amp or my bass cable, or something. (It's a weird feeling, looking at stage lights through teary eyes. They all swirl together, like gasoline in a puddle. I've never dropped acid, but it makes me think that it might be like that.) Anyhow, last week we were in the middle of "Love and a Door" and I got an image of Sam's hair falling out, and her face getting all sucked-in and gray. Suddenly I just felt so fucking furious. I wanted to scream at God, "How could you let this happen? Sam is a beautiful person, and she's never done anything to deserve this! It is not fair!" And it wasn't just like my eyes filled up, it was as if my whole body filled up. I couldn't blink it away that time, not a chance. I actually thought that I was going to explode. It was all I could do to not throw my bass into the crowd. I wanted to hurt them for being so trivial as to care about stupid us and our stupid, dumb songs, when there were so much more important things to care about.

I unplugged my bass and walked offstage, mid-song. I saw David's face from behind the drum kit; his jaw just dropped. I didn't stop to see what Justin's and Joe's reactions were, but after the show they had such a go at me. It was awful. I was crying and crying and they just kept shouting about "professionalism" and "commitment." Then Joe even yelled at me for not being pleased about our success! If it hadn't been for Sam, and for David intervening, I would have quit then and there. Even Mickey told me to "try and pull myself together" on the phone. He said that Justin had complained about me. Well, to hell with the lot of 'em. Those are all my songs they're playing every night, so they can hardly fire me, can they?

* * *

November 9, 1987
Fantastic news!! Sam's come through her first round of chemo, and it's been successful! I knew she could do it! Please, God, I know I don't talk to you much these days apart from complaining, but please carry on making her better. Please. She's fighting so hard. Help her get through the next round, too, if she has to do it again.

Oh, and Spin Shiny's *gone platinum. That's pretty cool, too.*

I'm completely exhausted.

Atlanta, Athens, Tampa, Miami. I like playing in Athens; I'm glad I had some good news before going onstage there. It was the first show I've enjoyed in ages.

Plus I'm getting on better with the boys now, too. It was pretty shaky there for a while, after the row. But we all went out for margaritas after the Miami show, and it was fun. Although I was pissed off when Joe said, "Careful, Helena, you just smiled. You don't want to make it a habit—your face might shatter." He's so juvenile.

God, I'm so tired. . . .

* * *

March 31, 1988
Having a few problems with the folks at the moment. I don't know why Mum gets so upset when I don't come home in between tours—it's not as if she pays me any attention when I am there. But apparently I'd told them that I might be down in February, when we got back from

those dates in Canada, and of course I just flew straight over to England to see Sam. I've tried to make Mum understand that Sam needs me, that it's still one step forward, two steps backward, and I can't risk not being there. Especially not to go and be paraded in front of Mum's friends and their spotty teenage sons gurning at me and asking for autographs.

Last time I went to Freehold, I hardly even saw Dad much. He was working, and then he was off on the golf course the rest of the time. If I wasn't getting so famous, I think they'd forget that they even have a daughter.

They're a complete mystery to me, those two, a "totally self-contained unit" of coupledom. I don't know why they bothered to have a child—maybe they didn't, and I was a mistake. It's so weird being around them: They complain, laugh, cry, cook, shop, live for each other alone, within the exclusive confines of their relationship. Dad's always so protective of Mum since she had that eating disorder, or whatever it was, when I was a kid—but she seems fine now, and he's still just as clucky over her. Well, I guess they always were a couple with a child, not a family. I suppose that was why they encouraged my friendship with Sam so much—it gave them more time for each other.

Still, I don't resent them. Not really. I probably wouldn't be in the band if it weren't for them. And it's not as if they haven't given me a lot of love and encouragement, too, in their own way. They'd better just understand that Sam always comes first, that's all.

* * *

Salisbury
June 20, 1988

Dearest Sam,

I can't believe that I'm here and you don't want to see me. I can't begin to understand how ill you feel, but I know how hard it's been for you to have to go through radiotherapy as well as the chemo.

Your mum says you're too frightened to see anybody. Oh Sam, if you only knew how heartbroken I am that you're so afraid. Please, please don't be scared; we're all here for you. I hope this doesn't sound too trite, but I really believe that angels are watching over you, too.

I wish there was something I could do to help you—you know I'd go through this for you, if I could.

I'm in the U.K. for ten days, so I can come down again at any time. We're opening for Simply Red on their tour. No pressure, of course, but I would love to see you while I'm here, even just for a few minutes.

Listen to the enclosed tape. It's the soundtrack from *The Big Blue*, and it's all about struggle and achievement and bliss. I've been learning to meditate, and this is the best music to do it to. Listen to it and imagine yourself well again. If it works for you, visualize yourself floating weightless in a warm, clear sea, full of light. Imagine that you're made of light. Please listen to it over and over again. Even if you don't have the energy to meditate, I'm sure it will help you to feel more relaxed.

All my love,

      Helena xxx

P.S. I've written a song for you; hopefully it'll be on the next album. It's called "Over This." As soon as we've recorded it in the studio, I'll send you a tape. x

* ✳ *

BLUEZINE

SUMMER 1988

Hi Fans,

What do you think of the impressive, new-look, glossy BLUEZINE? Do send in your comments for the band.

At the moment they're still out on the road, but they want to let you all know how much they appreciate you coming out to see them in your hundreds of thousands, and for keeping *Spin Shiny* on the charts for so long.

They were in the U.K. for ten days in June, opening for Simply Red (see page 3 for photograph of Justin and Mick Hucknall meeting Princess Diana), and this fall they're off on another big world tour—THE BLUE CEILING TOUR. Check out the attached dates, and see page 4 for a fabulous chance to win a pair of tickets to their show in Tokyo; flights, accommodation, and backstage passes included!

Blue Idea has leased a new, top-of-the-line tour bus, which you may have spotted outside a venue—it's the size of a barn and therefore pretty hard to miss. It even has its own recording studio inside, so not only is the band traveling in way more comfort, they've also been whiling away those long hours on the road by recording demoes for their new album! The title will be *Painting the Ceiling,* and it's scheduled for release in October.

The lucky winners of the competition in the last issue of *Bluezine* were Julie Weatherley and Charlotte-Emma Moore, from Lawrence, KS (both aged sixteen). Well done, guys! They joined the band on the road for a day, and wrote the following note describing their experiences:

We are Blue Idea's biggest fans in the world, and we couldn't believe it when we won! The band treated us real good, they even sent a black stretch limousine to meet us at the Chicago airport and take us to the bus! The bus was so neat, it had everything on there. Ovens and showers and beds and recording gear and everything. We had an awesome time, it was the coolest thing that ever happened to us, ever. Everyone in the band was real nice, Justin is a beautiful person, and David gave us some drumsticks, and Joe gave us the shirt he wore in the video for "Conditions of Love"! Helena had real bad hay fever, her eyes were streaming the whole time, so we gave her some shades to wear onstage that night, and she wore them! The concert was unbelievable. It was the second time we'd seen the band (but the first time without our folks being there).

Thank you, Blue Idea, WE LOVE YA!!!

Love from Charlotte-Emma and Julie xxooxx

The band wants to thank all of you who've sent them gifts while they've been on the road. They're promising to write up a letter to send out to all fan club members, but please be patient, there's a whole bunch of you fans out there!

Finally, here's a personal note from each of the guys, and what they've all been listening to on the road this summer:

JUSTIN: "Hey! Thanks so much for all the soft toys, people, but please stop sending them—I have so many on my bunk in the bus that there's no room for me to sleep! Seriously, we're gonna have to start giving a few away to charity soon. Appreciate it, though. Catch you later." (*Lovesexy* by Prince)

JOE: "Did you hear the one about the guy who visited his doctor, naked except for some Saran Wrap around his waist? He said, 'Doctor, doctor, am I going crazy?' and the doctor goes, 'Yes, I can clearly see your nuts.' Geddit?" (*Tougher than Leather* by Run DMC)

DAVID: "Oh well, at least Joe didn't tell you one of his drummer jokes. Thanks for coming out to see us, everyone. We love ya, too." (*Tracy Chapman* by Tracy Chapman—buy this album, it's awesome)

HELENA: "Another summer, another tour. The sands of time slip on by, folks, so take my advice and make the most of everything in your life. Tell your family and friends you love 'em as often as you get the chance." (Soundtrack to the movie *The Big Blue*)

Love from us to you,
        Justin, Joe, David, and Helena xxxx

* * *

Review in Q Magazine, November 1988
Painting the Ceiling
Blue Idea
Ringside RNG 2075
★★★★

Presumably there is something about Freehold, New Jersey, that drives the youth of the town to need to escape. Perhaps the high school forces each pupil to study the social insights of the self-appointed "Boss" of blue-collar rock—if so, no wonder this quartet left town on tour when the youngest of their number was just sixteen.

They started out as darlings of the American college scene in 1983, purveyors of bubbly post-post-punk, and since then have gone from strength to strength, learning how to adapt to the times in the way that only those in the highest echelons of the rock world—R.E.M. and U2—have managed.

Despite the rather facile and dated title (*Blancmange,* circa 1982, anyone?), British-born songwriter Helena Nicholls has pulled off the not-inconsiderable feat of creating a complete change of direction, without losing the lively intensity hallmarking Blue Idea's earlier material. Rumor has it that Nicholls is going through some unspecified "personal difficulties," but if that's the case, they've certainly taken her writing up to another level. The songs have a much more wistful air to them than the boisterous energy of the band's three previous albums: The subdued loveliness of "Over This," for example, forces an unconscious overly emotional response that seems at odds with the adrenaline-filled passion of their hallmark sound; "Take Me Away" manages to be effortlessly breezy and grin-inducing, but with heavy overtones of bleeding-heart vulnerability (*"If you're easily pleased, you'll be happy with me")*; and "Pop Artie," "National Health," and "Royal Flush" are all vogueishly attractive pop songs, but with a detached and stylish coolness to them.

Vocalist and lead guitarist Justin Becker is still as engaging as ever—surprisingly, this more mellow delivery seems to suit him— while keyboard player Joe Jennings and drummer David Somerstein are able to turn their hands equally expertly to anything from a polka to a punk anthem. Fine songs, fine musicianship. Beautiful artwork by Russell Mills.

There isn't a weak track on this mature, complex album. *Painting the Ceiling* will turn Blue Idea from interesting intercontinental journeymen into heavyweight contenders.

* * *

Auckland
November 27, 1988

Dear Sam,

Thanks for your letter—that's wonderful news, about Dylan being compatible (would it be churlish of me to suggest that this is about the only time in his life he's ever been compatible with anyone, apart from that fiancé of his!).

Will I be able to visit you during the transplant? It looks as if we'll have a few days off after we've toured Japan, and I could fly back for a quickie visit then. I did ask your mum this question on the phone the other day, but she thought that you might have to be in isolation, my poor baby. Another six weeks in hospital—God, you must be so fed up with it all. Well, if I'm not allowed to see you this time, I'll be over for Christmas.

Hang in there. I think it's fantastic that the doctors are saying you're now strong enough to go through with the operation. I have a very positive feeling about this. You can do it. This'll be the end of this whole nightmare; I know it will.

Good old big brother. I was just kidding before—I knew Dylan would come into his own one day. Will he have to take a lot of time off work to donate the bone marrow, or is it a quick in-and-out-of-hospital job? (Does he actually do any work in that pub, anyway? I have this vision of him being "mine host," drinking the profits, and only getting up from the bar stool for a couple of leisurely games of darts. . . . Although now, of course, that he's giving you his bone marrow, I am his number one biggest fan. I'll even marry him, if it all goes horribly wrong with Fiona. As long as he promises not to give me any more Chinese burns, of course.)

I'm so happy that you're still playing *The Big Blue* so much. It feels like a kind of spiritual lifeline between us, don't you think? ("Pretentious, moi?")

I realized something profound this morning, Sammy. I woke up in this posh Auckland hotel, and the first thing I saw was a huge half-opened pile of fan mail on the table in my room—as much of it addressed to me as to Justin or Blue Idea. It blew my mind, the idea that all those strangers had taken the time to sit down and write to me, another stranger, to try and make me a part of their lives. Or for them to become a part of mine. And seeing that big stack of letters brought something home to me, in a way that all our increasingly luxurious hotel rooms, the flights on the Concorde, and screaming fans hadn't—in all the horror of you being so ill, it seemed to have somehow passed me by. But suddenly it really sank in. I'm twenty-two years old, Sam; our new album is number one on both sides of the Atlantic, and I'm really, really famous. But you know what else? I'd give it all up in a heartbeat, if it would make you better.

All my love,

H xxx

P.S. I'm glad you like "Over This"—Ringside is going to release it as a single next year, in the U.K. as well as over here.

FAME

FAME HARDLY EVER LASTS, THOUGH, NOT UNLESS YOU REALLY WORK
at it. You have to water it and feed it and pamper it, plumping up its
own brittle ego in the hope that it will reward you with its continued existence. That was what the Plan was for, so I could stay
famous, without the hassle. I thought I was still famous as a DJ, but
it seemed people forgot so quickly.

After all, fame was all I had left. It was my anchor, the thing that
reminded me of who I was and what I'd achieved. Perhaps other
people had friends whose faces lit up with pleasure to see them,
and that was their reminder. But now that Sam was gone, I could
only get that from my fans. There was no one else, not now that I'd
decided Toby was out of the picture—I simply couldn't run the risk
of getting hurt by anyone, ever again. I felt like Blanche DuBois,
depending on the kindness of strangers.

* ✳ *

For the second time in the month since I'd been home, I was going
out. Not publicly, as such, after the riverfront disaster, just into
town for a meeting with my agent, Ron. I could have insisted he
come round to me, but once again I was filled with the desire to feel
the thrum of London's streets, to see office girls out on their lunch
hour buying their Pret A Manger avocado wraps and their Boots
reinforced-gusset tights; to watch faceless motorcycle couriers give
taxis the finger, and prowling traffic wardens tap into their handheld ticket machines. As long as I could observe it all from the
safety of my car, I'd be fine. I was people-hungry, and I missed my
listeners, living their ordinary lives with their secret hearts.

Not that they were my listeners anymore.

I'd scheduled our meeting for ten A.M., to coincide with the late rush-hour traffic. I actually felt well enough to want to pretend that I was a Normal Person, commuting into town for a Normal Job; plus, it afforded me another opportunity to drive my car. I hadn't yet bothered to inform the DVLA about my mislaid eye, as the doctor had told me I was required to, but since I was never, never going to touch cocaine again, driving, and drinking (separately, as opposed to drinking and driving), were about my only remaining pleasures.

Taking no chances this time, I put on my smallest eye patch, my darkest shades, and the Abba wig. Then I tied a cotton bandanna around my fake hair—the "belt and braces" approach to anonymity.

With a mixture of trepidation and exhilaration, I left the house. As I was opening the garage door I found five cigarette butts, clustered together by the corner of the garage, and my heart sank. There was only one person I knew who smoked Gauloises. I had discovered the identity of my lurker.

I decided not to even think about it until after my meeting with Ron.

After a careful lookout for paparazzi loitering in cars on the road outside, I backed my neutral metallic-blue 5-series BMW out of the gate and pulled away toward the A316 and Central London. I felt very lucky that the papers didn't seem to have discovered where I lived—I'd been sure that I'd be fending them off night and day, as they tried to worm confessions of drug addictions and God knew what else, but all had been surprisingly quiet.

I was thankful that I'd always been almost paranoically circumspect about my home and possessions, even if it had had the corollary of turning me into something of a recluse. I could have afforded a much flashier car, for example, and a mansion in the country, but after the band broke up, and the trial, I had vowed that I'd make every effort to keep my public and private personas completely separate.

Very few people knew where I lived, and most of those who did believed that I was someone else. I had no close neighbors (my house looked out over the Thames, and was on a secluded plot with only four other houses in the immediate vicinity), all work-related inquiries went directly to Ron, and I'd never thrown parties.

When I first moved in I'd entertained a notion of myself having intimate little soirees, impressing all my yet-to-be-made friends with my skill in the kitchen, but since I never actually got around to making any of those friends, the dinners remained uncooked.

Consequently the only people who knew where I lived were Mum and Dad; Mrs. Grant and Sam (who, of course, had practically been a lodger); Justin, Joe, and David, who'd all visited on separate occasions; Vinnie; and Ron (although he'd never been to the house). I had a sweet Serbian cleaner who couldn't speak English, and everyone else who visited had come to give me some kind of private lesson in something spiritual, esoteric, or fitness-related (Pilates, yoga, tai chi, etc.), and I told all of them my name was Dora. None of them ever let on if they recognized me. The locals knew me as Dora, too, although since almost all of them were elderly millionaires, I doubted that they had ever even heard of Blue Idea.

I drove slowly over Twickenham Bridge, crawling along in a fog of exhaust with hundreds of other anonymous commuters, reveling in my proximity to the outside world. I loved to watch people singing in their cars, their silent yodeling through the windscreen, and the way they picked their noses or pulled faces in the mirror as if convinced no one else could see in.

Feeling extra-brave, I switched on the car radio—tuned to New World, naturally. I hadn't listened to my show since that brief snippet in hospital, and to my surprise, Ralph Porter wasn't on air. Rather, it was Millie Myers, a twenty-five-year-old pneumatic "It" girl ("It," in my opinion, being an acronym for Intensely Thick). Of course, I shouldn't have been surprised; she'd had her eye on my slot ever since she arrived at New World a year ago, doing the afternoon show. Consequently she'd constituted the hard-core base of the Anti-Helena Brigade.

I had never had any time for her and her frothy, silly-girly style of broadcasting; I thought it was too frivolous for words. Why on earth did she think London gave a shit about the tragic fact that her Jimmy Choos gave her blisters, or that she'd lost her sodding pashmina? I wondered if she was doing a request show, too. Bet she'd only play a listener's record if they could verify at least one celebrity shag, or prove that they'd spent over £500 on one item of clothing.

News, travel, ads. Millie gushing over some execrable TV program from the night before. Meatloaf, back-to-back with a Steps record. Oh, please. Still, I supposed that Millie had to let the computer pick her records if she wasn't doing a request show. Geoff probably didn't give her as much freedom as I'd had.

Nonetheless, Geoff Hadleigh was a sucker for cleavage and some spindly legs in a miniskirt. I bet he loved Millie—although it was the listeners whose opinions really counted. I was fully expecting to find several sacks of fan mail at Ron's office, demanding to know when I'd be back on air. He wouldn't have forwarded them, since I'd told him I was away recuperating in the U.S.

"And that, darlings, was the fab-ulous Steps, who you recently voted seventeenth best band ever in our New World poll, between dinosaurs like Led Zeppelin and Fleetwood Mac. Well-deserved success for a happening new band! And next up, we've got, um, Lucy and Meg from Bounds Green! Hi, are you there, girls?"

A ripple of crackly tittering filled the airwaves. I accelerated with irritation through an amber traffic light at a pedestrian crossing.

"Hiya, Millie!" they chorused eventually.

"So what are you two up to this morning?" Millie asked unimaginatively. DJing by numbers.

More tittering.

"Oh, you know, just getting ready for school an' stuff."

Yawn, I thought. After a couple more tedious minutes of chat about which school, which teacher, which subjects, Millie finally got around to asking them why they were calling.

"Well, like, we just wanted to say, we think your show is really, really wicked, and the music you play is deadly. All our mates used to listen to Radio One before school, right, you know, when that other one was on New World, Helena Whatserface, but since you've been doing the show, our whole French group listens to you, and we all think you're totally happenin'."

Millie laughed, a tinkly, frosted-pink, Met Bar kind of laugh.

"Hey, thanks, girls! That's soooo nice of you to say so! Can I play you both a record this morning?"

"Yeah, Millie, can you play us 'Over This' by Kitsch 'N Sync?"

"No problemos—consider it done! This one's for Lucy and Meg: the fantastic Kitsch 'N Sync, hottest band around, with a really, really amazing new single, 'Over This.' I believe it's an old song, but they've certainly made it a hit this time—number one for the second week running!"

I turned sharply off the road into a petrol station and screeched to a halt beside the car vacuum. Surely not. . . . But instead of my tender bass and the mellow Hammond Joe had spread like treacle on top of the intro, I heard the same notes tortured out of a synth. A naff five-part-harmony vocal "choo-choo chooooo" sound preceded the start of the verse.

It got worse. My lyrics were delivered in the hideous faux-R&B style of some teenage pretty boy who probably thought Ronan Keating was a pop legend; completely devoid of any real emotion, more concerned with how complicated he could make it sound.

Banging the radio's Off button with my fist, I put my head down on the steering wheel and wept. With the humiliation of fifteen-year-olds liking Millie Myers better than me. With the shock of hearing my precious tribute to Sam's strength and courage reduced to such soulless crap. With the fury of that daft bimbo not even *knowing* that it was my song: Sam's song.

Everything that I'd felt when the record was released—all that joy and relief and optimism—was erased, like a chalk masterpiece on a rain-washed sidewalk.

Tears poured down one side of my face. I sat lost in memory until there was a loud beep behind me. Blearily I lifted my head and saw in the side mirror a man gesticulating at me from his Ford Escort. He was parked right up next to my rear bumper.

"Is yer gonna use the soddin' hoover or wha'?" he demanded, leaning out of his window.

Giving him the finger, I put my car in gear and shot back onto the road, but I could drive only a few hundred yards before I had to stop again. One blurred eye, a deaf ear, and a head full of grief did not make for entirely safe driving conditions.

This time I pulled up outside an antique shop, which had a large amount of very un-antique anemic pine piled up on the pavement outside it. My head throbbed as I stared unseeing at spikes of blond chair leg and smooth Swedish tabletops, some inverted for ease of stacking.

There were so many bitter and sad thoughts crowding my head that it took me a few minutes to begin to articulate them to myself. When I finally stopped crying I managed to think up a small furious list. I could either:

1. Call Ringside Publishing to find out who gave permission for Kitsch 'N Crap to use my song, then have them fired.
2. If they hadn't gotten permission, sue Kitsch 'N Crap for using my song without clearing it first.
3. Phone Millie right now, to point out that actually Blue Idea's version of "Over This" had been number one for three weeks in 1989, and raised a million pounds for leukemia charities (how could she not know that?).
4. *Finish the manuscript and do the show.* No more assing about, no missionary trips to Zaire, no question of a copout. I had to go through with it—if not actually on air, then in the studio.

It was the only way I could be sure that the Millies of this world didn't get remembered where I was forgotten. Life sucked, and now more than ever I wanted out.

The Cure

LOVESONG

I SAT DOWN ON A WINDOW LEDGE IN THE VIP AREA TO WATCH THE Cure's set through the thick plate glass, my knees drawn up to my chin, giddy with the combined bliss of having played a fantastic show *and* being back in England. On a practical level it was also nice to get my feet off the sticky floor—at every step my soles had stuck to the filthy beer-soaked carpet tiles with tiny uncomfortable squelching sounds. And this was meant to be the "luxurious" hospitality area! We were in a long, narrow room that faced the stage, directly underneath the balcony. Not enhanced by the dingy lighting, everything around was black—walls, curtains, carpet—presumably in an attempt to render cleaning less necessary.

Justin was loving it. Every time he moved out of the relative safety of his vantage point next to me on the window seat, he would be surrounded by a group of gossip-hungry journalists, competition winners seeking autographs, or plain old groupies who had somehow inveigled a backstage pass, and he happily chatted away to all and sundry, reveling in the attention. I, on the other hand, had the black curtain practically wrapped around my head to avoid being quizzed, despite the resultant reek of stale cigarette smoke that enveloped me.

Our set had gone extremely well, and I was content; I just wasn't in the mood to socialize with strangers. Besides, I liked to watch The Cure's show too, even though the sound was muffled from up here. Blue Idea and The Cure were alternating between the middle and the headline spot every night on this tour, and it was their turn to go on last. I preferred it that way—more of a chance to get a relatively early night. I loved to slip back to the hotel, as soon as I could escape, to the peace of a crisp white pillow, some top-class British

television, and a usually futile attempt to get through on the phone
to the new man in my life, Patrick.

Patrick was a film actor. He'd recently played the lead in a
medium-sized Hollywood movie called *Time Waits for No Man,* and
since then had been inundated with offers, of different sorts, from
film directors and nubile young waitresses. We'd met after he
hosted a charity gig in San Francisco that Blue Idea headlined, and
had spent a thrilling week together, licking Ghiradelli chocolate off
each other's navels in my hotel room, or walking hand in hand over
the Golden Gate Bridge at dawn, when the paparazzi weren't
around to see us.

That had since been followed by the odd night of passion here
and there, when we were in the same country, but I sensed without
asking that Patrick saw it as a casual thing, and I felt somewhat hesitant about calling him my boyfriend. It was quite depressing,
really—after the first thrill, it no longer seemed that different from
any of the other flings I'd had on the road. Patrick was handsome
and funny and successful, but I still felt like an accessory, or some
kind of trophy.

I wished Sam was there. She'd nearly puked with envy when I
told her about Patrick and me, and I'd been trying to think of a way
to engineer a meeting between them for weeks. But it was hard
enough to pin Patrick down at all, let alone get him and Sam both
on the same continent at the same time.

Unbelievably, Sam hadn't heard us play live since that time in
New York, almost four years before, and she'd never heard me sing
her song to her. But although the bone marrow transplant had
been a success and her life was no longer under threat, she had
been suffering from a condition called graft-versus-host disease,
where her body had begun to reject the new bone marrow. She'd
been trying all sorts of different treatments to combat it, but they
all seemed to have horrific side effects, and consequently she still
felt awful most of the time. She was definitely too delicate to
endure a hot, smoky venue.

She kept telling me that all she had to do to hear it was turn on
the radio, though, and her song still seemed to be blasting out. She

couldn't get over the fact that a song about her had been at number one, let alone that it was still on the charts a year later.

I told her that next time hopefully we'd be playing a huge outdoor gig, and she would have no excuse not to come to that show. The success of "Over This" ensured that we were big enough in the U.K. already. In the meantime I had to be content with talking to her for hours on the phone every day I was in the U.K., with just one swift trip to Salisbury on our only free weekend.

Sam, although still feeling poorly, looked so much better than when I'd last seen her the year before—then she had been all chubby from the steroids she was taking, and following the chemotherapy, her hair had grown back in stringy patches. But this year there was a definite improvement. She was back to her old slim self, albeit much thinner than she should have been, and with a wheezy chest. She had an attractive fuzz of really short hair that made her look trendy and boyish. I'd cried with relief to see the improvement in both her spirits and her health: Some of her old verve had returned, and she was full of plans to get back to university as soon as she could, and catch up on all the work she had missed.

I became aware that I was panting slightly from the heat. Even the air seemed to be sweating—I'd forgotten, until I walked in, that English venues never had air-conditioning. I pressed my cool champagne glass against my hot cheek. Condensation on the black shiny walls had made most of the taped-up posters announcing the release of our new record hang disconsolately down at at least one corner, and I could see the harassed-looking junior product manager from the record company running around trying to make them stick up again.

The Cure struck up the opening sequence of their current single, "Lovesong," and the audience went wild, dancing frenziedly, seeming not to care that it wasn't the most uptempo of numbers. It was all about people expressing their appreciation with the movement of their bodies, an extension of applause. I could see flying drops of sweat caught silver in the spotlight that swept across the crowd's heads, as they waved their arms and jumped up and down.

I heard Justin announce, "Back in a minute, guys," prompting a synchronicity of heads turning to gaze after his retreating back. Deprived of his company, the groupies drifted instead toward me.

"That was a fabulous show, Helena."

"Your voice sounded great."

"Please could you sign this for my little sister?"

The question was from a boy of about fourteen; he was wearing his laminate proudly over his Blue Idea T-shirt, and a big badge stating, I WON THE RADIO ONE BLUE IDEA COMPETITION!. I smiled at him and took the sticky Biro he thrust at me, scribbling my name and three large X'ed kisses on the front of the poster he was holding. The others, I saw, had already signed it, too. "Wow, thanks," he breathed reverentially. "Now I've got you all."

The other two people who had spoken to me did not expect an answer. They were trying to be ultra-cool and had already drifted away, probably rehearsing how they would say to their friends, "Yeah, of course, when I was talking to Helena from Blue Idea backstage after their show . . ." Their sort would never deign to ask for an autograph. They usually either worked for the record company in some minor capacity, or they had a friend who was a crew member who'd somehow managed to get them on the guest list. They always adopted an aloof and slightly superior attitude to us, a sort of "Just because you're famous, you needn't think that I'm going to fall all over myself to be nice to you" look. Not that we ever did think that. But they always managed to get a piece of me somehow—a carefully posed snapshot taken of them by a friend which just *happened* to have me looming in the background; a seemingly casual request for a light, or use of a pen, some trivial thing, or just a throwaway comment in my direction.

I really didn't mind when true fans came up and introduced themselves, or plucked up the courage to tell me how much they liked the band, or the record, or my bass playing, or whatever. At the risk of sounding corny, the light and passion in their eyes was what kept me going, what made it all worthwhile. I needed it. It was just those shallow, self-important industry liggers and their hangers-on I had a hard time dealing with.

The wife of the president of Ringside Records hove into sight, and I leaned forward to try and avoid her by swinging the damp curtains of my hair across my face. Focusing intently on an ugly bar ashtray next to me on the window ledge, I began to push it around in a circle by its heavy glass corners, the layer of old cigarette ash black and condensed in the bottom. Luckily Justin returned at that moment, and we both pressed our noses against the warm glass window, pretending to be engrossed in watching the band. He did not like this woman either. He said she once propositioned him in the back of a limo, plying him with Cristal and cocaine, then leaning seductively toward him until her famous breasts were almost completely adrift from their flimsy silk mooring. He told me that he wasn't having any of it, but he didn't sound entirely convincing.

"Has she gone yet?" he muttered as she teetered by in high heels and the latest Dolce & Gabbana miniskirt.

I looked sideways through my hair, which by now reeked of smoke. "Yes, you're safe—if you want to be."

"Phew!" He knocked back the contents of another glass of champagne.

Holly, Ringside U.K.'s cheerful press officer, rushed up to us, puffing and sweaty.

"Hello, Jolly Holly," said Jus.

"Hello, you two. Gosh, it's hot out there. Are you ready for your interview? David and Joe and Toby the journalist are waiting for you in the dressing room—hurry up!"

I'd forgotten we had an interview with *Melody Maker*, and Justin must have also, even though he normally loved giving interviews. But we'd done so many on this tour that we were all heartily sick of the same old questions. One particularly naff feature was for a glossy women's magazine with the headline HELENA—SHOOTIN' FROM THE HIP!, which had me parading around in cowboy clothes, complete with chaps and fringes, and brandishing a cap gun. Sam told me she'd laughed like a drain when she saw it.

Holly chivvied us along through the maze of narrow backstage corridors until we reached our dressing room, which was so cool and comfortable, in comparison to the dingy melee we'd just left, that I wondered why I had ever let Jus persuade me to go up there in the first place. Much as I loved The Cure, it wasn't as if I hadn't seen them a million times already. David and Joe obviously had more sense, and were lounging on an outsized sofa looking relaxed and refreshed, Joe puffing on a joint and David slugging a beer.

"This is Toby from *Melody Maker*," Holly said, introducing us to a sweet-faced youthful guy in jeans and a checked shirt, with blond curly hair and huge red-framed glasses. He had such a gorgeous smile that I was prepared to forgo summoning the fashion police to have him arrested for the awful specs (it being a good year after they'd become a must in the wardrobe of every journalist and architect).

Toby shook my hand firmly and, still smiling broadly, looked me steadily in the eyes. I liked him right away. In fact, I *really* liked him. It was as if something zinged between us, a flash of connection acknowledging our mutual attraction. It hit me in the stomach, an unfamiliar hourglass-shaped feeling of quick suction.

He got on with the interview in a very businesslike manner, individually asking us interesting and well-researched questions, and proffering a handheld cassette player for our replies. After a while it seemed that he was asking me a lot more questions than the others—than Justin even, who began to fidget restlessly.

I talked about the tour, and the new record, and the usual question of what it was like being the only girl on the bus with the others as well as the all-male crew, and all the time Toby was looking at me with his friendly, crinkled-up eyes, and nodding enthusiastically so that his curls boinged around his head like an animated halo. I did have a weakness for men with curly hair. . . .

"So how do you feel about your younger fans emulating your trademark style?" Toby asked seriously.

"What trademark style *is* that—singing flat and spending hours in front of the mirror?" asked Justin derisively. I punched his arm hard enough for him to squawk.

"Well, there are several girls outside wearing long coat-jackets over straight-legged trousers, and big shawly scarves," Toby explained.

I was as surprised as Justin, and very flattered.

"Oh, that's not emulating a style," said Justin. "That's because they obviously have as little taste as Helena."

I knew Justin was jealous of the attention Toby was giving me, but I was embarrassed by his put-downs nonetheless, and blushed scarlet.

Joe slapped Justin upside the head, and David told him to shut up. Holly looked anxious, worried that a fight was about to break out, but Justin put his arms around me.

"Only joking, honeypie. We all know you're gorgeous and totally fashionable, really."

Toby acted as if nothing had happened. "Having done quite a bit of research on Blue Idea for this interview, I noticed that girls who join your fan club can actually send away for a 'Helena scarf.' Didn't you notice how many of them were being waved in the audience when Helena was singing 'Over This'? And Helena, if I might say so, you shouldn't look so surprised that young girls are choosing to look like you. You are, after all, a very well-respected songwriter, not to mention an extremely attractive woman."

"Wa-ay hey!" sniggered Jus lewdly, an English expression he had picked up from our Yorkshire bus driver. I felt my face grow hot again, but this time with pleasure and gratitude. Toby sounded as though he really meant it.

"Thanks," I said, coyly. Even David and Joe tittered that time.

Toby mercifully took another tack. "Now, 'Over This' is your first chart-topper, and obviously a huge success, not to mention the first charity record by a single band ever to get to number one. Did all the proceeds go to help fund research into leukemia? David?"

David said, "Well, it's our first number one in England, but the third in America. Our first number one at home, 'This Is Your Blue Idea,' only got to number twenty here. You'd better ask Helena about the charity thing. I'm not really sure of the details."

"Yes, yes, of course, *third* U.S. number one, yes, I did know that. I meant in the U.K." Toby looked flustered, as if he was afraid we'd despise him for a potential error in research.

"So, Helena, can you tell me the story behind this song? It's about a friend of yours, isn't it? Is that why you sing it instead of Justin?"

"Yes. It's about my best friend, Sam. I wrote it when she was really sick with leukemia, and at first, whenever Justin used to sing it, it made me cry. So we thought if I sang it instead it would give me something to concentrate on, and I wouldn't start crying. And it did work, sort of."

"So, Sam, did she . . . er . . . I mean, is she . . . ?" Toby looked sympathetic and embarrassed at the same time.

"The leukemia's in remission, thanks, but she still hasn't properly recovered. She got a bone marrow transplant from her brother about a year ago, although since then she's had all sorts of problems as a result. Anyway, I'd offered to donate the song to the Leukemia Trust, and a couple of months back they called and suggested that we release it ourselves and give them the proceeds. I don't think they thought we'd agree to it, but we talked about it for a long time with our manager and Ringside, and decided that it was the least we could do. I'm just real happy that she survived it."

Toby smiled at me again, as if he was really happy she had, too. I had the sudden thought that Sam would approve of him.

"It turned out pretty well all round, then, didn't it! Well, I think that's about everything I wanted to know. Thanks, all of you, you've been great. Congratulations on the number one, and best of luck with the new album. It's absolutely brilliant. It hasn't been off the office turntable since we got it. When will you next be in the U.K.?"

We all concluded that we didn't know, but hoped it would be soon, depending on how the record went, and then after we'd all shaken hands with him again, Holly ushered Toby out into the corridor. As she opened the door, a pretty but ditzy-looking red-haired girl grabbed Toby's elbow and whispered something in his ear. He turned reluctantly back into the room, the girl still hanging on to his arm.

"Er, this is Lorraine, my girlfriend. She was really hoping to get to meet you all."

Lorraine, however, had eyes only for Justin. She rushed up to him, practically elbowing me out of the way, and started gushing about how wonderful he was, and how she was actually a singer, too, and that she had several songs down on four-track, etc., etc. Justin recovered his lost good humor and, steering her over to the empty side of the room, gave her a beer and settled down to enjoy a good, wholesome ego-bolstering.

Suddenly I felt deflated. For some reason, the words "Lorraine, my girlfriend" had put a damper on the whole evening. Awkwardly, I turned round to Toby. "Well, I think I'll go back to the hotel now. I'm kind of tired. It was very nice meeting you. Please come and say hello next time we play in London."

He looked at me with what I interpreted as the ghost of a resigned expression, his eyebrows raised in an almost apologetic way, and then there was that smile again.

"Yes," he said. "I'm sure we will definitely meet again."

* * *

A couple of weeks later when the tour had finished and I was temporarily imprisoned chez parents back in Freehold, Holly sent me a package via the U.S. press officer, with the *Melody Maker* interview clipped on to the top of a pile of press cuttings and reviews. The headline for the feature was BLUE IDEA . . . AND THEIR GREEN-EYED DEAR, and the whole article glowed with praise for my talent, humility, and striking beauty (all Toby's words, not mine!). Holly's sardonic note read, "Hmm, he didn't fancy you much or anything, did he!"

I hadn't had a chance to tell Sam about the interview yet, so I mailed her a copy of the clipping and the note. She phoned me when she got it, laughing. "Well? Was he as nice looking as the divine Patrick, then?"

"What do you mean? I just wanted you to see your name in print, that's all. . . ."

"Oh, yeah, pull the other one! Come *on*. Like the woman said, he wasn't interested in you just because you've got a record out!"

"Yes he was, actually. Interested in the record *and* nice looking, in a very cute sort of way. But he has a girlfriend, and I have a boyfriend."

"Oh, well, it's probably not serious—his girlfriend, I mean. I'm sure you can get rid of her."

"Sam! The man lives three thousand miles away! Get a grip! She was awful, though. And she fancied Justin, so you never know. . . ."

"There you are, then!" Sam said triumphantly, and we both laughed. She sounded as though she was just talking to me from around the corner. "How are things with Patrick, anyway? Have you spoken to him since you got back?"

"He hasn't returned my last three calls."

"Oh, no," said Sam. "Are you upset?"

I considered. "Not really. The sex is nice, but it's just so hard to maintain a relationship when we're on the road. He's filming now, and can't jump on a plane every time he wants to see me. I did think I'd get to see him when we got back, but there's no chance now. We're off to Japan on Monday. It was fun at first, but I can't see how it's going to last."

"Oh, Helena. Poor you. But I hope you're going to settle down someday. I want to be godmother to your kids, remember."

"Jeez, give us a chance, Sam! I'm only a year older than you, not ten years older. Twenty-three is far too young to think about babies."

Sam was silent for a minute. "Not if you can't have them, it isn't."

I could have cut my tongue out. Poor Sam had been told that she wouldn't be able to conceive, after all her treatments. It was one more cross that she bore without complaint—in fact, so uncomplainingly that I had been selfish enough to temporarily forget the fact.

"I'm so sorry, Sammy. I don't know what to say."

She sighed, a long, weary sound that traveled slowly along the wire connecting us. I imagined that sigh, deep down underneath the ocean, and wished I could make it stay there forever, trapped, with all the rest of Sam's ailments and worries.

That night I lay uncomfortably on a bed that, although it was in my old bedroom in my parents' house, felt as strange and unwelcoming as a hotel bed. I must buy myself an apartment, I thought. Surely I could afford one by now. Mum and Dad were always pleased to see me—for about fifteen minutes, after which duration they resumed whatever "leisure activity" (golf, canasta, bridge, gardening, etc.) they'd been involved in before I arrived. Apart from the home-cooked meals, I hated going back to Freehold in between tours.

I thought of Sam's poor shriveled-up ovaries, her indefatigable courage, and her constant small triumphs over adversity. I thought of my own life, how exciting it must seem to everyone else, but how exhausting and pressured it really was. I thought briefly of delicious Patrick, his plucked eyebrows and exfoliated cheeks, manicured nails and color-coded socks, and of how many thousands of women would kill to sit in bed with him and eat a bag of postcoital Cheez Doodles, as I had. But I felt nothing except a desire to sleep.

So I got up, retrieved my Sony Walkman, and slotted in a Cure tape. Climbing back into bed and snuggling up into the pillows, I lay there listening to "Lovesong," a song I wasn't remotely sick of, even after hearing it on tour every night.

But I was not thinking about all the arenas and academies, the theaters and ballrooms, the clubs and festivals. As I finally drifted off to sleep, I was dreaming of a journalist named Toby, and the way his eyes had held me, and the nice things he'd written about me.

YOU AIN'T MS. NICHOLLS

I WAS IN A COMPLETE STATE BY THE TIME I FINALLY ARRIVED AT THE private carpark at the back of the building in which Ron's office was housed. Hearing "Over This" murdered by some spotty adolescents had upset me, far more than listening to Millie Myers's listeners diss me. I felt as though I'd been driving drunk, emotions were whirling around inside the car, and I missed Sam so badly that I wanted to slam my head down on the steering wheel.

I pulled up to the automatic barrier and collected myself together enough to talk to Cecil, the large black carpark attendant. If I had been less distraught, I'd have been delighted to see him. We always had a chat whenever I came for a meeting with Ron. He was such a genuine, sweet man, and would always tell me about his kids' triumphs and his wife's gallstones.

"Hi, Cecil, long time no see," I managed through the open window.

Cecil loomed out from the doorway of his dinky little booth. He frowned and scratched his head. "Who you here to see, ma'am?"

I glared at him. "Ron, of course! Who else do I come and see? He's expecting me. Do I park in the usual place?"

The barrier remained resolutely down.

"Sign the visitors' book first, please, ma'am."

Cecil passed the book through the window, and the proximity of his huge, creased brown hands made me want to grab them, hold on to them for dear life to protect me from feeling this way. He was still looking at me, trying to place me.

Suddenly it clicked. Of course he didn't recognize me! I whipped off the bandanna and the wig, and shook out my short brown hair.

"Sorry, Cecil, what was I thinking? No wonder you didn't recognize me. It's me, Helena Nicholls."

But Cecil's frown merely deepened. I scrawled my name with irritation in the book and handed it back to him.

"You ain't Ms. Nicholls," he said slowly. The buttons on his uniform blinked suspiciously at me in the sunlight.

I didn't think the day could get any worse. "Of course I'm Ms. Frigging Nicholls! Look at me! Listen to my voice! If I wasn't, how would I know that your kids are named Cheryl and Simon, and that you've worked here for eighteen years? Don't you even remember my car, for God's sake? I had an accident, okay? My face looks different. I broke my nose and my jaw. I've lost an eye. I'm scarred. Call Ron, right now, if you don't believe me."

I burst into tears.

Cecil looked mortified. He reached his big sausagey fingers through the window and stroked my sleeve tentatively. "Ms. Nicholls, I'm really, really sorry, ma'am. I see it's you now. You don't look all that different, honest. It's my eyes, they ain't what they used to be, and it's been a while since you was last in. Please forgive my rudeness. I'm so sorry to hear you had an accident. Ron never told me."

He retreated into his booth and the barrier shot up at speed. I drove in without another word and had to sit in the car for a full ten minutes until I'd stopped crying again. Whenever I glanced up into the rearview mirror, I could see Cecil staring at me, anguished, from the safety of his Wendy house.

The irony of the situation did not strike me until later. For the past twelve years I'd been trying to make myself inconspicuous, unrecognizable, but now that people really didn't recognize me, I was devastated. So much for the kindness of strangers, I thought. That only worked if the strangers actually remembered who you were. First they had to recognize you.

* ✳ *

"Helena, darling! How *are* you? Great to see you again! Feeling all right? Bet you were glad to get out of that hospital, weren't you? What's it like being home again? Coffee? Cindy, can we have two coffees in here, please?"

Ron, ever the PR man, bombarded me with questions so as to avoid commenting on my appearance, which was by now even less appealing due to all the crying. I'd gone into the ladies' to try to repair my makeup, but the sight of my reflection threatened to start the tears off again, so I'd left it blotchy.

Still, Ron himself was no oil painting. He used to work as a director of promotions for a major record label, but I had a theory he'd been sacked for wearing golfing sweaters and slacks. He was the only gay guy I'd ever met who had absolutely no fashion sense.

"Yeah, yeah, fine, thanks." I moved across Ron's office to the window so I could stand with my back to him. "So what's new, then? Any suggestions as to what to do for an out-of-work DJ?"

Ron laughed nervously. "You aren't out of work, darling. Geoff offered you another job, didn't he?"

I leaned my forehead against the cool glass of the window, only the prospect of more stitches preventing me from head-butting it. I tried to keep my voice measured and calm.

"I don't consider the graveyard shift a proper job, Ron. It's humiliating. Plus I won't be able to do my request show at that time. I just wondered if anything else had come up. Before I . . . the accident, didn't you tell me that you had something really hot in the pipeline for me? You were getting more details, you were going to let me know. What about that? Is it still available?"

There was a silence, broken when Cindy, Ron's PA, brought two mugs of coffee in.

"Well?"

Ron swiveled awkwardly in his chair, making it squeak uncomfortably. "Uh, Helena, well, no, that turned out to be a blind alley. . . ."

"What was it, then? An offer from another station? Was it Radio One?"

Another silence. Ron tore a day off his Dilbert desk calendar.

Something about the sound made me turn round, puzzled. I stared at him. "Do that again for a second?"

"What?"

"Tear a page off that thing."

Ron gaped up at me as if I'd asked him to take his trousers down. "I can't—I'm up to date now. I can't tear off today until tomorrow. Or at least not until the end of the day. It's Tuesday today."

I couldn't believe that I entrusted my career to such an idiot. But nonetheless, his voice sounded different, too.

"Please, just tear off another one. You can Sellotape it back on again afterwards."

Ron was obviously thinking that my concussion was worse than I'd let on. I gave up waiting for him and, reaching over his desk, ripped Tuesday off myself.

The little jagged sound it made was *in stereo!*

"Oh my God, Ron, my right ear's just started working again! I can hear properly! I can't believe it!"

Misery temporarily on hold, I jumped across the room and hugged Ron round his pudgy middle-aged neck. For a second I felt so exhilarated that for the first time I seriously imagined abandoning the Plan.

"This is fantastic! It means I can work again as a DJ! Maybe Radio One would hire me after all—no problem with driving my own desk now, and—"

Ron interrupted me, disengaging himself from my arms. "Er, Helena, I thought your hearing returned ages ago—didn't you already tell Hadleigh that it had? He wouldn't have even given you a nighttime slot if it wasn't back to normal."

Crushed, I realized this was true. "Oh. Yes. Well, I lied. But now it really is better, so maybe that will help find me something else? You were about to tell me what the other job was."

Ron looked crossly at his Dilbert calendar. "Look at that—you've made it Wednesday now, when it's still only Tuesday."

"Ron!"

He sighed and took a slurp of coffee. "Sorry, darling, but it ain't happening now. You were up for a presenter on a new celebrity chat show Channel Five is scheduling. Lisa I'Anson got the gig. . . ."

I sat down opposite Ron and let my head sink onto his desk with despair.

TV! I'd been about to start a career in TV, something every prime-time DJ dreamed of. . . . And now I was disfigured. As with deaf DJs, you didn't see too many ugly TV presenters.

"And you don't have any other other job lined up for me?" I asked in a small muffled voice, my breath dampening the shiny surface of Ron's mahogany desk.

I didn't have to look up to know that he was shaking his head.

My emotions couldn't stand the pace—they'd been up and down all day. It looked as if we were back on course for the Plan again. I stood up.

"Ron, listen. I just wanted to say, in case I don't get the chance again, thanks for everything, you know. You've been a really great agent, and—"

Ron leapt up, too, cupping his hands to his chin in a big queeny gesture of horror. "You're *firing* me? I don't believe it! After everything I've done—"

"Ron, for God's sake, I'm not firing you! I'm certainly not looking for another agent, I just . . . Well, you never know what might happen. It's always good to tell people how you feel. And I want you to have this as a gesture of my appreciation."

On the spur of the moment I pulled off the plain silver ring I wore on my forefinger. It had been given to me by a fan in Singapore, and I was very fond of it, but I suddenly thought, What did I need with it now?

Ron looked overcome. "And you're sure you aren't firing me?"

He tried to cram the ring onto his little finger, but it only reached as far as the first joint.

"Sure. It's just a present to say thanks for maintaining my privacy, you know, keeping the press off my back when I was in hospital and stuff."

"Well, thank you, darling, that's ever so sweet of you. I don't know what to say. . . . I'll put it on a chain round my neck. Mwah, mwah."

He kissed me on both cheeks and I tried not to flinch.

"If there's nothing else on the job front, I'll get going. Got a busy day ahead of me, you know, doing . . . stuff. I really just came in to get my post and catch up."

"Ah yes, your post! I'll tell Cindy to fetch it." Ron rushed to the office door.

"Cindy! Could you bring in Helena's mail, please!"

I waited for Cindy to arrive with a huge sack, like Father Christmas. She was gone long enough—perhaps there was more than I thought, and she'd gone to get a forklift to carry it.

While we were waiting, I remembered what else I'd been intending to ask him.

"Hey, Ron, you might know this. A bunch of brats have covered 'Over This'—Kitsch 'N Sync. Apparently it's number one—"

"Oh, I love that record! Of course it's number one. Congratulations! That'll be a nice little earner for you. I think they've done a really great job, don't you?"

I glowered at him. "No, I do not. 'Over This' is a very important song to me, and I certainly would never give permission for it to be slaughtered by a posse of prepubescent morons. I want you to call Ringside Publishing for me and find out who was responsible for letting them—"

Ron was shaking his head again.

"What?"

"Helena, I can't call the publishers. There's no point. They don't need the publishers' permission to do a cover version of a song, because it's an interpretation. You only have to get permission if you sample it. You ought to be pleased—it's more money for you."

I thought of Sam's face and wanted to weep again.

Just then Cindy appeared back in the office clutching a faintly paunchy A4 brown envelope. She handed it to me.

"There you go, Helena. Sorry I didn't bring it straight in, but I was desperate for a pee."

I blinked at her, which in my one-eyed state must have looked like a wink. I hoped furiously that she didn't think I was coming on to her.

"Is that it?" I was genuinely surprised.

Cindy nodded, blushing and not meeting my eye. I took the envelope and peered inside to see about ten unopened letters.

"There must be some mistake—where's the rest?" The words fell out before I could stop myself.

Cindy and Ron exchanged looks, and Cindy edged tactfully back out of the room. Ron assumed his best long-suffering expression. "No, sweetie, I'm afraid that really is it. Don't take it personally. Being a DJ isn't the same as being in a band, you know. People don't get so attached. I'm sure you got heaps of letters when you were in Blue Idea, but that's because kids really loved your music, wasn't it? They don't bother to write to DJs on the whole: DJs are just part of their life like their mates, or bus drivers, or whoever. I bet Chris Evans and Zoë Ball don't get that many letters."

I bet they did, but it wasn't worth arguing about.

"You did an awesome job, Helena," Ron plowed on. "You know how far you bumped up New World's ratings—but trends change so fast in radio. That confessional thing is a bit, well, over now. We all just have to move on."

"Oh, don't worry, Ron. I'm going to be moving on, all right." I laughed bitterly.

"So you are going to take that nighttime slot, then?"

I looked at him for a long time, thinking how little I cared about never seeing him again. "Yeah. I'll give it a whirl. Let's just see what happens, shall we?"

Happy Mondays
KINKY AFRO

Two years later I was back in London for another show, although it didn't feel that long. We'd been around the world twice, and had number-one hits in eighteen different countries. I was older, more tired, much richer, and utterly ecstatic because Sam was with me.

"It's going to be really hot today, I heard it on the radio this morning. It's boiling already, and it's only eleven-thirty," she said when she came to meet me in my hotel room. She was wearing baggy denim cutoffs and an antique sleeveless lace top that buttoned up the back.

"I love your top," I said, fixing her a cold drink from the minibar.

"Gee thanks, *hon*," she said, trying to imitate my American accent. "I swear, Helena, you sound more like a Yank every time I talk to you. I'm afraid if this continues we will no longer be able to maintain our friendship. . . ." She grinned, and pushed past me into the room to inspect everything.

"This is incredible! This room is bigger than my whole flat! You didn't stay in such a posh hotel last time, did you?"

"Not quite, but almost. Onwards and upwards, you know."

"That was my school motto. What was yours?" Sam looked out the window at the spectacular view of Hyde Park.

"Oh, I dunno. No, wait, I remember. It was 'The Fighting Bucks,' or as Justin called it, 'The Biting—'"

Sam cut me off. "I can imagine, thank you, Helena. Moving swiftly on . . ."

I laughed. "Okay. Well, speaking of your flat, how's the decorating coming on?"

The Grants had sold the license to the pub and bought a house on the outskirts of Salisbury with a basement granny flat for Sam so that she could have her independence but be near the family, too. Mr. Grant had gotten a job as a brewery sales rep, but before he started, he was decorating Sam's flat from top to bottom.

Sam still wasn't very well—the legacy of the graft-versus-host disease (exhaustion, miserable skin problems, and a nasty asthmatic-type wheeze) still persisted—but it hadn't stopped her from continuing to study for her law degree, part-time and by correspondence. I could not fathom how she had the strength of character and determination to do it, when every ounce of her energy was at a premium.

"Great," she said, taking the cellophane off my huge complimentary fruit basket to get to the grapes. "I can't believe I've got the whole place to myself—and I can still take my washing upstairs to Mum! Mum loves not having to work in the bar. She's always off having these really long lunches with her mates, and she's taken up aerobics, and done a tie-dying course. She wants to tie-dye my curtains, but I've told her to forget it."

"I would have thought she knew how to tie-dye already, without needing a course," I commented, zipping my stage clothes carefully into their plastic carrier and hooking its coat-hanger top over the bathroom door.

"Oh, she did. It was like a refresher course. Actually, I think it was really just an excuse for her to get together with a load of other old hippies-turned-housewives."

Sam's voice got a bit echoey as she disappeared into the bathroom to riffle through the freebies by the sink. "Can I have this shampoo? I love Molton Brown! Are you going to steal the bathrobe?"

The phone rang. It was the front desk to tell me that my car had arrived.

"Yes, take it—the shampoo, not the bathrobe! And you can have that little shoe-polishing thing, too, if you like. Are you ready? The car's here."

I ran around collecting everything I needed for the gig: vanity case, a bottle of mineral water from the minibar, my toothbrush and toothpaste. Sam was emptying half the contents of the fruit basket into her backpack.

I thrust the suit carrier into her arms. "Here, you carry this. I'll take your backpack—it'll be heavy with all that stolen fruit in it."

She made a face at me, then grinned. "Wembley, here we come!" she said as we set off down to the marble-and-glass lobby.

I handed in my key and pushed through the heavy revolving doors, Sam being swept along in the next segment behind me. The roasting sunshine hit us as we emerged from the air-conditioning onto the sticky tarmac of the hotel's driveway. It felt more like Arizona in high summer than London.

A huge black stretch limousine was purring in front of us, both the passenger door and the driver door opening simultaneously as we approached. Mickey leaned out and beckoned us into the backseat, and the driver came round and put our things into the boot with a courteous stiff-faced nod and a muttered "Good morning, ladies" in our direction. A doorman leapt forward and needlessly held the already-open passenger door. At the same time, five Japanese girls rushed up, squealing, with Blue Idea records for me to sign. They snapped a volley of shots of me with their Nikons, laughing and nodding at one another ecstatically as I scribbled my name for them. Sam's mouth was hanging open at the size of the car and the spectacle of me signing autographs, and I had to prod her in the back to make her get in as I waved good-bye to the fans.

Once inside, I was grateful to feel cool air on my cheeks again. Sam and I sat facing the driver, and Mickey made his way across the carpeted floor to sit opposite us. The car was so long and low that he had to walk with a movement like a hunker in motion, which made him look like a chimp loping through the forest.

"Sam, this is our manager, Mickey. Mickey, this is my friend Sam, who 'Over This' is about."

"Ah, the famous Sam! We meet at last—I'm honored. I would shake your hand but you're too far away." Instead he blew her a smarmy kiss and inclined his head in a little bow.

Sam smiled graciously at him. "Actually, we have met before. When Blue Idea played New York, about six years ago. But I'm not surprised you don't remember me—you were otherwise occupied that night."

Mickey laughed uneasily as the car glided away from the hotel and swung out into the London traffic. There were many shows to which Sam's comment might have applied.

"We're meeting the boys at seven, aren't we?" I asked Mickey, making sure I had my facts straight. We had been out there the previous day for rehearsal and soundcheck, and as we were headlining, technically none of us needed to be at the venue until the evening. But Sam had wanted to watch the entire day-long concert, and Mickey said he had some "business" to attend to there—hence our early departure. I didn't mind going early. I was looking forward to a day out with Sam.

We stopped at a red light and laughed at the pedestrians gazing curiously at the car, trying to make out who was behind the black tinted windows.

"It's funny how people always stare at limos, even though they know they can't see anything inside," Mickey said, making a rude face at a Chinese boy who almost had his nose pressed up against the glass.

"They're just wishing that for once they could be the one inside being driven around in luxury, and not having to go down the market and get fish for dinner, or deliver the newspapers, or go to their dreary Saturday jobs. I think it's envy as much as curiosity, and who can blame them?" Sam was looking with sympathy at the crowds of harassed shoppers.

We drove on, until the shopping streets turned to residential ones, and a few scrappy trees began to dot roads outside dusty rows of semis. Not many had front gardens, and those that did had mostly been paved over to make off-street parking. Everything seemed much smaller than its American counterpart; cars, houses, birds, even the people appeared hunched and melted-looking. The sun had bleached every sparse blade of grass to an almost colorless shade of bile.

"Where are we, anyway?" I asked.

Sam and Mickey both shrugged.

"Don't ask me." Mickey reached over his shoulder to slide back the glass partition separating us from the driver. "Where are we, bud?"

"Willesden Green, sir," came the faint reply from under the driver's peaked cap. "Shocking roadworks on the A41, so we're much better off going through town."

There seemed to be shocking roadworks everywhere. The sound of pneumatic drills hung in the air, and orange traffic cones and big yellow diggers were strewn around countless junctions. Sweating road menders toiled away, their upper bodies as bronzed as if they had been lying on a Caribbean beach for a fortnight.

The white twin towers of Wembley Stadium eventually hove into sight. The driver whisked us through various security gates, following handwritten signs tied to fences that read ARTIST ENTRANCE THIS WAY.

Sam squeezed my hand. "I'm so excited!" she said, her eyes out on stalks as she looked at the other limos lining up in front of and behind us. "Isn't that Kylie Minogue over there?"

Mickey dug in his bag and produced our laminates in a tangle of black shiny cord strings, which he separated and put over our heads as though awarding us medals. They had swirly red and yellow patterns on their shiny plastic, with thick black letters over the top saying RADIO ONE'S BIG DAY OUT: ACCESS ALL AREAS. Mine also said ARTIST at the bottom.

"Right," he said. "Let's go find the dressing rooms and you girls can dump your stuff. Then I'll see you back there at seven."

He consulted a Xeroxed map and motioned for us to follow him. As we climbed out of the limo, the heat once again filled my eyes, nose, and mouth. I dreaded to think how hot the stage would be after baking in the sun all afternoon. Sam and I set off behind Mickey, me carrying Sam's backpack and her with my suit. After a few yards, however, Sam was lagging behind.

"What's the matter?" I asked, anxiously. "Aren't you feeling well?"

"No, I feel fine," she said, a little crossly. "It's just this plastic stuff, it keeps wrapping itself around my legs. It's making my shins sweat."

She was trying to hold the suit protector by its coat-hanger handle aloft and away from her body, as though it were a lead with a snappy dog on the end. Sure enough, the thin plastic casing was drifting back as she walked and insidiously tangling itself around her. I laughed.

"Why don't you just fold it in half and put it over your arm?"

"Well, because then I have to hold all that sweaty plastic, and that's even worse."

"Shall I take it?"

"No, I can manage. I just need to twist it out of my way, that's all."

Mickey turned round to see where we'd gotten to, almost bumping into a huge black man wearing a PVC bib-type garment emblazoned with the word SECURITY. The man glared at him.

"Come on, girls, hurry it along here!" he chivvied, glaring slightly nervously back at the security guard. We trotted after him again.

"I didn't think shins *could* sweat," I mused aloud to Sam.

"I bet they bloody can in this weather. Let's see, shall we? Shin check!" she barked in a military fashion. We bent down, giggling, and rubbed our respective bare shins. Sure enough, there was a thin film of condensation on our skin.

Grumbling at our childishness, Mickey managed to lead us to my dressing room, whereupon he promptly disappeared in the opposite direction to try to locate the production manager, muttering worriedly about stage plots. Once inside, I relieved Sam of the troublesome suit cover by hanging it on a metal rail between the mirror and the wall. Sam gazed around.

"It's even got a star on the door!" she said in an awed voice.

"Come on," I said. "I'll show you the stage."

We dumped our bags and headed off again, both keen to get back outside. The glaring sunshine and rocketing temperatures were still preferable to the strip lights and dingy corridors of the interior.

I opened a door marked TO STAGE, and we followed a passageway round a couple of corners until we saw daylight. Emerging as though from the bowels of the earth, we came out, blinking like moles. All we could see was blue sky and what seemed like miles and miles of scaffolding with heavy black material covering parts of it.

"Blimey, it's *enormous*," said Sam, sounding faint. "Just look at all those people!"

The stadium loomed hugely all around us—towering banks of seats as far as the eye could see, and the massive central area, still filling up with bobbing heads. A dull roar from the crowd could be heard over the throb of the music from the towering stacks of speakers on either side of the stage.

The sound desk in the middle looked like a little boat on a big lake. It had all looked very different yesterday when the seats were empty; blank, and less intimidating. The expectation from the wait-ing audience was hanging in the air like heat haze, mingling with the smell of hot dogs and the slight acrid scent of sweat. I sniffed the air and got an additional inexplicable whiff of fresh raspberries.

We were right at the back of the stage, in itself an area about the size of four tennis courts. Technicians, sound men, lighting men, stage managers, and promoters, all with their laminates flapping as they ran, were milling around frantically. People were marking out lines on the floor with duct tape. There were men swinging from lighting rigs; men popping up from trapdoors in the stage like rab-bits from a magician's hat; men tapping microphones and fuzzily intoning "Testing, testing, one-two-three"; men screwing together drum kits and tuning up guitars. One minute thumbs-up signs were being proffered; the next, obscenities were ringing out. Everyone, without exception, was sweating like Nixon. The first band of the six on the day's bill was about to come onstage.

"I feel as if I've just walked into a beehive," said Sam, staring at all the activity before her. "I'm certainly sticky enough." She fanned the neck of her shirt and wiped her forehead. Then she looked more serious. "How can you stand the thought that there will be seventy *thousand* pairs of eyes looking at you this evening?"

I wished she hadn't asked. This was almost twice the size of any gig we'd ever played before, and up to this point I had chosen not to consider this bowel-loosening statistic. The whole daylong show was also being broadcast live to the nation on Radio One, but I didn't remind Sam of this.

"Um—I'll be okay once we start playing," I said nervously.

Sam suddenly threw her arms around me.

"This is incredible!" she said. "I am so proud of you! I can't believe I'm here, and you're here, and you're doing this unbeliev-able thing!" She had tears in her eyes.

"I'm just glad you're here to see me do it," I said, hugging her back.

We found an out-of-the-way space at the side of the stage, and perched on top of a huge square flight case: Sam nearest the audi-ence, me (trying to be inconspicuous) lurking out of sight behind her, watching the excited crowd preparing for their day's entertainment. I fanned my hot face with a tabloid newspaper I found next to me, and thought about how all those people had come to be there. Maybe they had heard the show announced on the radio, and they had been excited at the thought of three or four of their favorite bands playing at the same gig. Perhaps all their favorite bands were playing. They'd have mustered up a group of friends, or told their partners to mark it in their diaries, and then gotten their credit cards out to phone the ticket hotline; or maybe they had sent away for tickets in the post.

Either way, their tickets would have arrived a week or so later, plopping onto the doormat in an anonymous envelope, with that exciting, shiny new-paper smell. They'd have put them somewhere safe—a drawer, or stuck to the fridge door with a magnet in the shape of a London bus—and told all their other unluckier friends that they were going to the Big Show. Finally, the day had arrived, and they had climbed onto trains at dawn, or filled up their cars with petrol and packed lunches, or boarded chartered coaches.

And now here they were, many at Wembley for the first time, smelling what I was smelling, staking out their spots on the covered-over football pitch, wondering if it was better to go further back where it was cooler, and where they could sit down without being stepped on, or to go for it—right up to the front, elbowing their way to a prime viewing position close enough to see the little hidden nuances of performance that the huge video screens never picked up. I imagined the real fans who had been queuing outside for hours and hours, bursting through the turnstiles and running, running across the pitch at Wembley to be the first to the security barrier at the front. They would risk losing their places if they had to go to the loo or to get something to eat—perhaps they just didn't go all day, and their enjoyment of the show would be marred by the pressure of a bursting bladder.

"They look so excited, don't they?" said Sam from her perch. "Look at that girl down there in the front, with the Blue Idea baseball cap on. She's jumping up and down already, and nothing's happening yet!"

I looked at my watch. "Well, it must be about to—it's two o'clock."

As I spoke, music abruptly ceased thumping from the speakers, and a lone figure in a sparkly gray suit ran onto the stage. A massive cheer went up.

"That's Jeremy Jackson, the comedian," I said. "He's emceeing the show."

"I know," Sam replied. "Everyone knows who he is."

Actually, I'd never heard of Jeremy Jackson before that week, but Sam assured me he was very famous in the U.K. He welcomed everybody, made a few lame jokes, and read off a list the coming attractions for the day. Every time he moved, his suit twinkled and glittered in the sunlight. After each band he mentioned the crowd cheered, louder and louder until he said, ". . . and of course, closing the show tonight: your favorites, the amazing, phenomenal, spectacular . . . BLUE IDEA!!!" and everyone went absolutely wild. Their arms were raised, waving and punching the air, and the sound of whistling and screaming was deafening. I felt a cold but excited shiver from the bottom of my stomach, and Sam leaned across and squeezed my knee with both her hands.

We stayed in our spot at the side of the stage for most of the day, as Sam was absolutely riveted by seeing the best bands of the moment from such close quarters, only leaving it between sets to get more water, eat, or pee. Occasionally other musicians came up to introduce themselves to me, and I made sure they all shook hands with Sam, too. The guys in the Happy Mondays were surprisingly sweet, and autographed a photo for her to keep.

It was a great day. Over the previous couple of years I had become so jaded and sick of these self-congratulatory, bombastic events, which I believed served only to boost egos and extract hard-won money from starstruck children. Sam's genuine and whole-hearted excitement put me back in touch with what it should be about: the spirit of the occasion. She always seemed to show me the positive in an experience.

The next time I looked at my watch, it was 6:45 P.M., and the stadium was still steaming with heat and excitement. The Happy Mondays, who were the penultimate band, were about to take the stage, but Sam and I were starting to wilt.

"If we're this hot, just think what it must be like in the crowd!" she said, feebly puffing air onto her face from the corners of her mouth. "I'm feeling a bit tired. Is there somewhere I could go and rest for a while? I want to make sure I'm on form for your set."

She was beginning to look very pale. I felt concerned for her.

"Well, I need to have a shower and get changed, and the guys will be here shortly. Why don't we go down to the dressing room, and you can have a lie-down on the sofa while I get ready?"

Sam nodded, and we climbed off the flight case to make our way backstage. As we got through the door a massive cheer rose from the crowd, and we heard the opening strains of "Step On" strike up.

Sam looked torn. "Oh, I *love* this song! I really need to lie down, though . . . but I really want to see them! Specially after they were so nice to me. . . . Oh, what shall I do?"

"Go and lie down," I said firmly. "They'll be on for at least an hour. Have a rest and then we'll go back up and catch the end of their set."

Sam capitulated, but walked very slowly with one ear cocked toward the ever-fainter sounds from the stage.

We got back to the dressing rooms, where in the one adjoining mine—an identical harshly lit, un-air-conditioned cell—I found Justin, Joe, and David smoking and playing poker. I stuck my head around the door while Sam lurked in the hall behind me, partly from shyness but more to avoid the effects of the cigarette smoke.

"Hi! You're early," I said to them, impressed.

"Yeah, we've been here ages—what kept you?" asked Joe, flapping the collar of his shirt in the direction of a fan in the corner, which was halfheartedly moving air around.

"Guys, you remember Sam, don't you?" I pointed proudly at her. She waved from the doorway and blew Justin a provocative kiss. "I'm not bringing her in because you're smoking out the place. But she'll be around later. We're going next door so I can get ready."

I caught a momentary flash of shock in Justin's eyes as he clocked the difference in Sam's appearance, how much older and gaunter she'd become, and I found myself willing him to still fancy her. But nonetheless he rushed over and pecked her on the cheek enthusiastically. "Hi! Fantastic to see you again!"

Totally unprompted by me, he added, "Hey, you know, we're all real glad that you're better now. Helena was so upset, and we all, like, thought of you and stuff."

Joe and David mumbled agreement. I felt like a proud mother at a nativity play.

"Thanks," said Sam, uncharacteristically shy all of a sudden. "See you later."

"They've gone all kind of designer-y and smart," she commented to me as we entered my dressing room.

"Yeah, well, no more jeans and T-shirts for us worldwide superstars," I said, going to stand in front of my own floor fan, which someone had kindly turned on in advance. Sam flopped down onto a big velveteen couch in the corner, putting her feet up on the cushionless arm.

"I'd never have believed that Joe could look so much like a model. Justin looks the same, though. Has he got a girlfriend at the moment?"

"Why do you ask? Fancy another dose of crabs, do you?"

Sam shuddered and giggled. "Ugh, no thanks. But you know, I like to keep my options open."

"Well, the answer is, yes he has. She's a model, six-foot-two, looks like Cindy Crawford, and is very possessive. She's arriving any minute from a fashion shoot in Paris, so you'd better not encourage Justin or else the feathers'll be flying."

Sam closed her eyes. "Don't worry, I'm far too knackered to flirt. She can keep him. Nice to see them all again, though."

"Yeah, they obviously thought the same about you. Have a bit of a kip—I'm going to risk this dodgy-looking shower in here. See you later."

"Mmm," said Sam, with one arm thrown over her eyes. She looked out for the count.

She was fast asleep when I emerged from the bathroom fifteen minutes later, having washed and dried my hair, and done some energetic singing in the shower to get my voice warmed up. The makeup lady was coming round at 7:15 P.M., so I did not touch my face. Normally I preferred to do my own makeup, but given the excessive heat, I thought I'd better defer to her professional expertise on this occasion. I did not want my mascara sliding down my face after the first number.

I zipped my suit out of its plastic sheath, examining it for wrinkles, but it had been hanging all day and was fine. I slid the black nubby raw silk jacket on over my bra—too hot to wear a shirt as well. The fabric was shot through with a subtle gold thread that picked up the light and shone faintly when I moved my arms to do up the big gold buttons. I worked each foot through the tight legs of the pedal-pusher-style trousers until they were liberated and I could straighten to do up the zip. I had been wearing this style of outfit for two years now—a old Hispanic lady in Manhattan made them individually for me.

The genesis of the idea had come when I'd started wearing big long shirts over tube skirts, back in the early, chubby days. I wanted something that covered up my hips and thighs, but shirts somehow were not smart enough for the image I wanted to convey, so one night I had worn a long jacket with its buttons done up, over some thick black leggings. I felt instantly transformed—my trunk was hidden underneath its length, yet I could expose the respectable part of my long legs (from mid-thigh down). From there I'd graduated to trouser suits with frock-coat jackets, and even after I got slim enough to wear miniskirts, I still loved my suits. I could look chic but not girly, smart but not secretarial.

I made it my mission to find as many funky and unusual fabrics as possible, and whenever we toured in exotic places like the Far East, I would disappear to the local markets for hours (probably a throwback to my days spent happily rummaging around jumble sales), returning joyously with a bolt of thick bronze satin, or ten yards of sari material. Annie Lennox had said more than once in interviews how much she admired my dress sense.

It was the first time I'd worn this particular suit, and even I had to admit I looked pretty hot. I had recently had a gold streak put in the front of my short chestnut hair, which I had dried and gelled back into a kind of high rockabilly quiff, and the outfit was completed by a pair of sparkly gold crepe-soled brothelcreepers. It didn't seem to matter that we weren't even remotely a rockabilly band.

There was a soft knock at the door. I opened it to admit the makeup lady, Glenda, with her big zip-up bag of tricks. I pointed at Sam, comatose on the sofa, and put my finger against my lips.

"I don't want to wake her just yet," I whispered, motioning Glenda over toward the spotlit mirror. She sat me down and got to work in silence, painting and lining with a rock-steady hand; puffing and brushing my face with an assortment of tiny little sponge-tipped sticks and twirly brushes; applying metallic brown-gold shades of eye shadow and lipstick to match the rest of my outfit. The only sounds in the room were Glenda's concentrated breathing, the whirr of the fan, and Sam snoring softly in the background.

Just as Glenda had finished and was packing up her bag, Sam woke to the sight of me in my finery standing before her. She rubbed her eyes and stared at me with disbelief.

"Ta-daaa!" I said, spreading my arms and grinning. "Whaddaya think?"

Sam sat up. "Oh my God," she said incredulously. "You look so different! It's absolutely amazing! Helena, you look *so beautiful!*"

"Oh, please," I said, pretending to be offended. "Could you try and sound a little less surprised?" But I was glowing with pleasure as I picked an imaginary speck of fluff off the sleeve of my suit.

"Bye now," said Glenda, who was also looking rather pleased with herself. "I'm off next door to sort out those boys of yours."

"Good luck! Tell them I hope they're ready in ten minutes."

"Good luck to you. Break a leg. I can't wait to see your set. You lot are great. I've got all your records." She blushed and edged out of the room, closing the door behind her.

"Right," I said to Sam. "Are you set? Feeling better? You look a bit less pale."

"Yes, I feel much better. I'll just have a glass of water and a pee, and then can we go back up to the stage?"

"Sure—I'll tell the guys to meet us up there. Are you hungry?"

"No, I'm much too nervous for you! I'll take some of that fruit up for later, though."

Sam went into the toilet and I went next door, where Glenda was trying to put eyeliner on Justin while he smoked a cigarette.

"Oh, for God's sake, Justin, can't you stub that out for two minutes?" I said as Glenda coughed pointedly. "Poor Glenda doesn't want to breathe in your disgusting smoke. Or better still, give it to me and I'll smoke it."

I was beginning to feel very nervous by now, and decided that a few puffs would calm me down a bit. I snatched the cigarette from his dangling hand and inhaled deeply, hoping to finish it before Sam returned.

"We're going to catch the end of the Happy Mondays. See you by the monitor desk in ten minutes, okay?"

Justin nodded with his eyes closed, making Glenda paint a black line on his cheek by mistake. As I left the room she was tutting and scrubbing at his face with a cleanser-covered cotton wool ball. I stubbed out the cigarette as Sam emerged from my dressing room.

"Let's go," I said, leading the way back upstairs.

We came back outside to a tumult of cheers and shouts of "More!" Shaun Ryder and the others were running back to their mikes and picking up their instruments again, bowing and dancing and grinning wildly at one another. As the introduction to "Kinky Afro" thudded out around the stadium, the crowd erupted. Everyone, including Sam and me, began to dance on the spot, the infectious rhythm making it impossible not to. I saw color in Sam's cheeks for the first time in years. She looked ecstatic.

When the song ended the Happy Mondays sauntered offstage for the last time, waving at the audience and shoving one another with manic delight. They grinned at Sam on their way past, and she turned to me, clapping enthusiastically, thrilled.

A lull followed; the calm before the storm, it seemed to me. Once the crowd's screams for the Happy Mondays had died down, a small tumult brewed among them, as they realized this was their last chance before the end of the show to buy beer or queue for the loo without missing our set. The music came back on over the speakers, and all the techs scurried onto the stage to do our line check. I wondered whether I had time to go back down to the dressing room for a final pee myself, but decided it would only make me more nervous. Instead I stayed, watching the crowd and chatting with Sam to David and Joe.

The boys had appeared next to us looking very dapper, Joe in a baggy cream suit and Panama hat, David in smart black trousers and an open-neck patterned silk shirt.

"You look great, H," said David affectionately, squeezing my arm. "Nervous?"

"So do you, both of you. Yup, nervous," I replied. We hung out in a state of limbo for the next fifteen minutes or so, gathering our respective strengths. I was beginning to get very anxious about where Justin had gotten to.

Jeremy Jackson reappeared in front of the audience to a howl of applause. We knew that the cheers that arose were not for him but because his appearance heralded our own imminent arrival, and that made me more nervous. Jeremy made a gesture with his hands for everyone to quiet down.

"Here's a small joke for you, ladies and gentlemen, in honor of the nationality of tonight's headlining artists." Renewed screams from the crowd. "If you're an American in the kitchen, what are you in the bathroom?" Various unintelligible and derisive yells from the audience. Jeremy adjusted his tie smugly. "You're a-peein', ladies and gentlemen!" He gave a low bow. A collective groan arose.

I leaned over to Sam, affronted. "Who's he calling American, then? I'm not a bloody American!"

She replied, "Maybe he meant that you're the European."

"Charming," I sniffed, no more mollified.

Jeremy made a couple more limp quips and concluded with a very big buildup for us: "And any minute now, the moment you've all been waiting for . . . your favorites and mine . . . BLOOOOO IDEEEEAA!!" More hysterical screams, and then another groan as the music came back on again.

"Must be a technical hitch somewhere," I muttered to Sam, feeling pretty hysterical myself.

Justin sauntered up to where we stood, a fresh cigarette between his lips, accompanied by his drop-dead-gorgeous Amazonian girl-friend. He looked incredibly sexy in a chocolate-brown pinstriped gangster suit.

"I'm friggin' boiling in here," he grumbled. "What are we opening with?"

The rest of us raised our eyes to heaven. "'Lotus Flower,'" we chorused.

"Oh yeah, sorry, it just went right out of my head."

I checked nervously that the set lists were all taped to the floor by our mike stands. They were. Mickey rushed up to us, sweating profusely.

"Everyone all right?" he asked, sounding by far the most nervous of all of us. "Sorry I didn't see much of you earlier, you know, bit of business to take care of." He looked very shifty and distracted. I wondered if there was a fresh-faced groupie somewhere downstairs who was at this moment tucking in her shirt and hoping she wasn't pregnant.

Five more endless minutes passed in anxious chitchat and last-minute activity from the crew, until one by one they left the stage and we got the thumbs-up. The crowd's excitement was hitting me in waves; I could feel it running through my veins and into all my nerve endings. All our gear was set up and ready by our mike stands. David pulled a pair of drumsticks out of the back pocket of his trousers and twirled them around in the fingers of his right hand. I went over and hugged Sam hard.

"Good luck," she whispered in my ear, hugging me back.

Justin stubbed out one cigarette and lit another, wedging it firmly in the corner of his mouth. The music stopped, stage lights came on despite the still-bright evening, and the loudest cheer I'd heard all day rose up all around us. In the split second before we ran onstage, I analyzed the sound, thinking how strange it was, how it seemed to have nothing to do with all the thousands of people whose eyes were about to be fixed on us. I would not watch sports on television for the simple reason that I could not bear the constant background baying of the crowds, but this did not bother me.

Oh, well, I thought, taking a last deep breath and tensing all my muscles as we launched ourselves toward the center of the stage, I suppose it's different when they're screaming for you.

A FAMILIAR HAND

IT REALLY WAS GOOD TO HAVE MY HEARING BACK TO NORMAL again. As I drove despondently home from Ron's office, I tried to remind myself to at least be thankful for small mercies. But it seemed a bit pointless, really, like everything else in my life. The option of a glass eye, the ability to hear pins drop, one-off kisses from sweet guys and lisped songs about stormy weather—what was any of that to me now? I could bear all of it, all the bad stuff, if only I still had Sam to help me. But I didn't, and I couldn't.

The tide was high as I drove down the gravel road to my house, water lapping over the top of the rushes and reeds on the bank. It was almost up to the riverside footpath, washing up detritus from a careless consumer society, cans and plastic and yesterday's news. I knew that by the next day when the water had receded, I'd be left with all those scraps of litter, plus the faint smell of sewage and lots of mud outside my front gate. It was the least pleasant part of living near the river. Oh, well, I wouldn't be going out tomorrow, so I wouldn't have to see it.

I pointed the remote control at my electric gate, and it heaved slowly open to let me through. As it clanged behind me, I thought once more how nice it would be to never leave the house again.

Pulling off the wig and glasses, I felt my body relax slightly as I climbed out of the car clutching the meager brown envelope from Ron. I was looking forward to holing up inside for another long stint of wallowing in solitude.

As I headed for the front porch, a small but familiar sound filtered in through my newly responsive ears. It was emanating from the bushes—a series of crunchy little clicks, ensuring that my terrible day was made even worse. I knew what that noise was, I'd been dreading it for long enough.

Cursing myself for removing my disguise prematurely, I dithered for a split second: Should I run inside, or stay and fight? Then all the rage and grief and disappointment from the day boiled up inside of me, and there was no contest—whoever was out there wasn't going to get away with it this time.

With a huge painful bellow, I charged toward the bushes. There was an alarmed rustle, and the glint of a camera lens being hastily retracted. As I crashed through the scratchy greenery, I saw a skinny back spin around and try to head for the gate, but his camera strap had become entangled with a branch and he lost valuable seconds trying to extract it. The delay enabled me to get close enough to grab the strap, and to see the hand of the photographer pull at the camera itself. He was wearing a black balaclava, but once I'd seen his hand, my suspicions were confirmed. I didn't need to see his face.

The bitten nails, the shape of the ovals of wrinkles at his thumb joint, the nicotine stain on his middle finger from so many Gauloises—this was a hand that had given me a thousand orgasms, belonging to a person who had given me a thousand more sleepless nights.

"COME HERE, VINNIE, YOU EVIL LITTLE SHIT!" I roared at the top of my voice, as we engaged in an unseemly tug-of-war in the shrubbery. "I'M GOING TO KILL YOU!"

With one last terrified wrench, Vinnie hauled the camera strap out of my grasp and legged it across the lawn, over the gate in one smooth leap, and away down the riverside path.

I ran after him, still screaming like a fishwife. "HOW DARE YOU! YOU WON'T GET AWAY WITH THIS! YOU BASTARD!"

But he was out of sight by the time I got to the end of my drive.

For the fourth or fifth time it occurred to me that the day really couldn't get any worse. Turning back to the house, I stooped like an old lady to pick up the letters and cards that had spilled out of the A4 envelope I had dropped after giving chase. They made a pathetic little bundle, scribbled messages of . . . what? Most likely they were from people whose records I had played, making them feel important for two minutes of their lives.

Suddenly I didn't care what they had to say. I walked round to the dustbin next to the garage, lifted the heavy metal lid, and dumped the whole lot in, unopened, with the smell of rotting vegetables and stale take-aways. Slamming the lid down on the only feedback from my career as a DJ was a symbolic gesture, I knew.

It didn't make me feel any better, though.

Randy Newman
I'LL BE HOME

THAT WEMBLEY SHOW WAS THE LAST TIME BLUE IDEA EVER PLAYED in England. A year later it was all over. Two years later I was still recovering.

It was a letter from Sam that finally spurred me into a decision. I had my whole life ahead of me and an exceptionally large bank balance at my disposal, but all I'd done for sixteen months was mope around rural New Jersey as though in extended shock.

I had been required to stay in the area for the duration of Mickey's trial, because the prosecution needed me to give evidence, so I'd holed up at my parents' new place, an architect-designed house in the countryside, ten miles outside of Freehold. I'd paid for most of it myself, so I figured that justified my extended residency there. My name was on the lease of a blandly luxurious apartment in Manhattan, too, but I'd moved out because the paparazzi knew the address.

I hadn't even seen Sam since the band broke up. I was happy that she had a life of her own again, but I hated that I currently wasn't part of it. She had eventually finished her law degree and was back in London starting her one-year postgraduate LSF course at Store Street. She was still frail, but well enough to move into a hall of residence.

We wrote to each other regularly—it was too problematic to try to get through to her on the pay phone in her digs—and she always asked me when I was coming over, preferably to live. But then she'd launch off into a description of her latest boyfriend, or what dinner party she'd been to, or what all her college friends were up to, and I would be assailed by such a feeling of alienation from this life that could have been mine. A normal existence! It felt as foreign to me

now as a Martian existence. The only place I felt safe was within the
whitewashed walls of my parents' dream home.

Then I'd gotten this letter. I had noticed that Sam's handwriting
was getting worse, but I had put it down to the probable hurry with
which she scrawled my letters, eager to get out and about with her
new friends.

I'm writing this, . . .

I deciphered with difficulty,

> . . . with my nose about an inch away from the paper. It gives me
> hideous backache, but the only alternative is to pile textbooks up
> to eye level in front of me and rest the letter on top of them. That
> method is fine for reading, but gives me cramps in my arms
> when I try and write that way. Even with Coke-bottle glasses my
> sight has gotten so bad—that bloody radiotherapy just com-
> pletely screwed it up. Lectures are a nightmare. I'm having opera-
> tions for cataracts in the next few weeks, and although I'm
> nervous, that should fix it. I don't think it'll be too bad—they just
> zap them with lasers, one at a time. I can't wait to "see" you
> again. I miss you. Come and live in London! It would be so great.
> We can go to Salisbury in the holidays, it'll be like the old days.
> I've been listening to Randy Newman's *Little Criminals* a lot
> recently, and the track "I'll Be Home" really makes me think of
> you. It's so sad, and it makes me miss you so much. I just want
> you to be home, too . . .

I put the letter down, my mouth agape with shock. I thought
only old people got cataracts. Sam was still by far the most important person in my life, and if something as serious as that was going
on without my being aware of it, then something was very wrong
with me. Why hadn't she told me before?

I asked my mother that question when I found her in the kitchen
taking a bubbling roast out of the oven. I got myself a glass of wine
from the fridge.

"Would you like one, Mum?"

She was bending over the cooker with her oven gloves and apron
on, her hair disarrayed from the steam.

"No thanks, Helena. Is that your second glass already? We haven't even sat down to dinner yet."

I ignored her. "Sam is having an operation for cataracts."

"Cataracts? Oh, dear, that's terrible! I didn't know young people got cataracts."

"Neither did I. It was those leukemia treatments she had."

Mum tutted in a shocked manner, and stuck a long roasting fork into the center of the meat to see if it was done, sending a thin plume of steam up toward the ceiling.

"Why do you think she didn't tell me? She's having the operation next week and I didn't even know she *had* problems with her eyes. She normally tells me everything."

Mum turned the oven down to a *Warm* setting and put the joint back in while she strained the vegetables.

"She probably thought you had enough problems of your own, dear."

"None as big as practical blindness, though!" I replied vehemently. But now that I thought about it, it was possible that I had maybe moaned rather excessively in my letters about how miserable life had been recently. In a flash I made the decision. I downed the rest of my glass of wine in one gulp. "I'm moving to London!" I announced.

My mother looked relieved. She had done a lot of laundry for me in the past year. I had bought her a brand-new washer-dryer, but still, laundry was laundry. She untied her apron and sat down next to me at the kitchen table, putting her hand over mine.

"I think that's a great idea, Helena. You're only twenty-seven; you should be out having a social life and making new friends, not cooped up here all day like a hermit. You miss Sam, and besides, I think it's time for you to move on. I wish London wasn't so far away, but I truly think that you would be happier back in England near Sam."

I smiled at her. Whether she was trying to get me out from under her feet or not, I appreciated the good intentions behind her words.

Dad came home and I told him my plan over dinner. He, too, agreed that it was probably for the best.

"When will you leave?" he asked, spearing a forkful of meat and roast potato and trying not to sound too enthusiastic.

"As soon as possible. I'm going to start sorting through my stuff after dinner," I announced firmly, placing knife and fork together on my empty plate.

The lethargy that had plagued me for months suddenly dispersed, and I felt adrenaline course back through my veins for the first time in ages.

When we all finished eating, my parents retired to the living room, Mum to call one of her bridge friends, and Dad to smoke his pipe and read *The New York Times*. I went down to the basement, where I had stored three big boxes of band-related memorabilia. I had not been in there for a year, as I had been trying to forget the band had ever existed. Leaning against the wall, in between Dad's golf clubs and the brand-new mountain bikes I'd bought us all but we'd never ridden, was the battered guitar case containing my old, cheap secondhand bass, the one on which I'd learned to play.

I laid it down on the dusty carpeted floor, and with difficulty popped open the rusty clasps. I remembered how wonderful I had thought it the first time I'd set eyes on it at the Applebaums' yard sale, how desperately I had wanted to have it. I hadn't even known it was a bass guitar then! All I had known was that it had been, literally, the answer to my prayers.

I still felt guilty at the memory of the pure desire that had fueled my original acquisition of the instrument. To serve the Lord, if I was not mistaken, I thought ruefully, remembering my teenage fervor. In the grand scheme of things that guitar and I had done very little serving of the Lord, and a great deal of serving myself, the band, the record company, and Mickey's bank balance. The Lord certainly gave me more than I bargained for. Perhaps this was His way of punishing me for transforming my religious ambitions into secular ones.

I lifted the guitar by its neck out of the cheap velvet-lined case. It emerged stiffly, like a corpse from a coffin. The pearly scratch plate I'd thought so pretty looked warped and yellowed with age, and the enamel of the guitar's body was scraped and battered-looking. Everything about it was cheap and shoddy. I recalled how difficult learning to play it had been, and how I had been able to persevere only because I really believed it had been a gift from God. I put it back in the case and moved it to a space on the far wall of the garage, which was the start of my "to trash" pile.

Before getting stuck in, I ran upstairs and got my own CD of *Little Criminals,* and my Discman. Putting the headphones in my ears, I came back down to the basement and played track nine over and over again as I attacked the big sealed boxes, ripping off the brown tape holding the top flaps closed. It gave me strength, to think of Sam all those miles away listening to the same music for the same reason. "I'll Be Home" was such a simple, moving song. I wished that I'd written it instead of Randy Newman. Blue Idea should at least have done it as a cover—we could have done a great version of it.

When I'd moved out of the New York apartment, I had just stuffed everything in these boxes, and a lot of the posters and album sleeves were creased or torn. I toyed with the idea of chucking everything out, but couldn't quite bring myself to do it, so instead I selected one of every item in the box: a copy of each of our records, a press shot from each album, one copy of each *Bluezine,* programs from a couple of the bigger gigs we'd played. I picked up the program from the Radio One show at Wembley and something fell out. It was a photograph of Sam and me onstage, taken during Blue Idea's set that day and sent to me afterward in a kind gesture by Holly in Ringside's press office. I was very pleased to see it. At the time I had intended to make a copy of it for Sam, but had forgotten that I'd put it in the program to keep it flat, and later assumed it to be lost.

Everyone said that Wembley show was the best we'd ever played. It certainly felt that way. To me it represented what I perceived to be the very highest pinnacle of our success and my own personal sense of achievement, despite the fact that Blue Idea was just as hot for most of the following year.

The proudest part of all was when I sang "Over This," turning away from the audience and beaming at Sam in the wings through-out the entire song. Out of the corner of my eye I noticed the front rows of the audience trying to follow my gaze to see who or what I was looking at. When the final note from Joe's Hammond hung in the charged summer air, there was a moment of pure silence, and then an overwhelming storm of cheering and applause, which felt as if it would knock me off my feet with its warmth.

I ran forward to where Sam stood clapping, grabbed her wrist, and pulled her back onto the stage with me. "Sam Grant," I'd said to the audience. "My best friend." We'd hugged in front of all those thousands of people, and, strangers though they were, it felt as though they supported and understood us, too. Sam told me afterward that it was the best moment of her whole life, bar none.

I put the photo aside to send to Sam that very day. I could make a copy of it later, I thought, and borrow it back from her. Continuing to sort through the three big boxes, I found several gold and platinum discs, more photos, laminates, press interview schedules, masses of copies of *Bluezine,* and newspapers that had run features on us. I systematically junked most of it.

At the top of the third box was a copy of *Rolling Stone,* not the one with us on the cover, but an issue from a few months after that. I looked at the date: May 1992. I flipped it open and found the huge feature with the headline screaming out at me: BLUE IDEA BREAKS UP! They'd printed a photo that I absolutely hated—us leaning over a freeway bridge somewhere, shot from below, all concrete and steely gray skies. We all looked incredibly pissed off, I appeared to have an enormous double chin, and even Justin looked moronic. There were lengthy quotes from the four of us. I picked out a random paragraph and read:

"It really just seems the right time to move on. I've been writing a lot more songs lately, and making a solo record is a new and exciting direction for me. Blue Idea has come to the end of its natural life. We've been getting stagnant. I wish the others all the best of luck, and strongly encourage them to continue without me, if that's what they want to do. I hope we will stay friends."

Justin's smug words brought back some of the anger I had felt at the time. Writing songs, my ass! He had churned out a few trite little numbers that we sometimes did live, or used for B sides, but none of which Ringside or the rest of us wanted on any of the albums. His fans were in for a bit of a shock, in my opinion. Justin's ego had been inflated to the point that he really thought he alone was the key factor in Blue Idea, and this was what I couldn't stand. He might have been the good-looking one, but my songs and David's and Joe's excellent musicianship had been equally important.

The truth was, I had secretly been quite relieved when Justin dropped his bombshell. I was furious with him for making the decision for us, but we were all so tired. We had been on tour, whether in the U.S. or around the world, on and off for the best part of ten years, and when we weren't on the road we were in the studio. I couldn't remember when I'd last had more than two straight months off. It had gotten to the point where I simply didn't have the energy or the inspiration to write any new songs. I felt completely drained. We had no private lives—we couldn't even walk down the street without getting mobbed. Everyone knew who I was, but I had no real friends except Sam and the band. I'd had no time to make any.

To carry on without Justin hadn't even been an issue; David, Joe, and I had not given it a serious thought. We did not want to become one of those sad once-huge bands who struggle on with the old name, but without the frontman who helped make that name.

"Let's quit while we're ahead," David had said, and I'd agreed heartily. "We're rich enough," Joe added.

But it turned out that we weren't nearly as rich as we'd thought. As soon as Mickey heard the news about us disbanding, he became impossible to contact. After trying to get ahold of him in every way we knew—including sneaking down to his office in disguise (to no avail, it was locked and empty)—I eventually phoned our accountant directly to find out what state our finances were in. I had never spoken to him before, as Mickey had handled our money from the start. He, too, had sounded shifty.

"I just operated on Mickey's instructions," he'd said. "I paid you what he told me to pay you."

We had got artist royalty checks quarterly through Mickey, usually for a lot less than we'd expected, but he told us that a lot of the money needed to be funneled back into Ringside's coffers to front tours, or to pay off producers' percentages, or for a variety of other plausible-sounding reasons. We saw no reason to doubt him, as heeding his advice from the outset never seemed to have done us any harm before.

There was something I found very suspicious in the accountant's defensive tone of voice. With the agreement of the boys, I ordered an audit of our accounts by an independent accountancy firm, and it became apparent that both the accountant and Mickey had been stitching us up like kippers for years. We instantly informed the IRS, who contacted the police, and a warrant was issued for their arrests.

They found Mickey in Key West, clad in a pineapple-patterned shirt, sipping lurid cocktails with umbrellas in them and flashing wads of cash around, like the cliché he always had been. He was brought back to New York for trial, and after a long, drawn-out court case, both he and the accountant were put behind bars for two years.

The trial had been a media circus, and during the days I was required to give evidence, I'd been practically blinded by the flash-bulbs in my face as soon as I set foot outside the courtroom. The whole experience had been a trauma of epic proportions—daily reports on the local news, gossip plastered in all the worldwide press, masses of really unflattering shots of me trying to put my hands over my face or scowling at reporters. Once it was all over I just wanted to be somewhere safe, completely out of the public eye, where I could lick my wounds in peace. I really started to understand what Princess Diana went through.

I pulled a photograph out of the box of us with Mickey and one of his bimbos, and ripped it up in disgust. Financially I was extremely well-off, because of my publishing royalties, but I felt really sorry for Joe and David, who hardly had any money to show for their hard work and dedication. Justin hadn't come out of it any better, but he'd gotten a massive advance for his solo album, so he would not struggle to get by. But the worst thing was that we had really trusted Mickey, and the sting of betrayal hurt more than the feeling of being made fools of before the world's media.

I finished my sorting, having compressed the contents of the three boxes into one half-filled one. My hands were black with dirt, but I felt a cathartic satisfaction from my efforts. I carried the box upstairs to my bedroom, washed my hands and face, and got on the phone to my travel agent. If I booked a flight to England in a week's time, I could be around for Sam's operations and convalescence.

Then I took the photo of Sam and me at Wembley, clipped it to a piece of writing paper, wrote, "Dear Sam, I'll Be Home—next week!!," put it in an envelope, and sent it to Sam's address, by courier service.

* ❋ *

It didn't take me long to find a place in London. I had no need of a mortgage, as I was paying outright for it, so it was really just a question of knowing where and what.

"How about Richmond?" said Sam when she'd recovered from the shock of my arrival. "Handy for Salisbury. Close enough to town, really beautiful, and not full of poseurs like Notting Hill. I'm going to move there when I finish my LSF."

She'd had one eye lasered and was waiting till that healed to get the other one done. She said it hadn't been painful, more uncomfortable really, and she felt like a prat with an eye patch. It made her look a bit like a cocker spaniel.

"People will think I was faking it when they see me next month with the patch on the *opposite* eye," she grumbled.

So the Richmond area it was. I went to an estate agent, told him how much I wanted to pay, and that I wanted somewhere as anonymous as possible, which wasn't too built up. The agent's name was Adrian and he looked like a Labrador puppy in a cheap suit, all clumsy and panting and overenthusiastic, chubby and sandy-haired. I hated the way that all his colleagues nudged one another and stopped talking when I walked into the office, but Adrian did sell me the perfect house, albeit reluctantly. I'd spotted it in the property paper and pointed it out to him, but he hadn't wanted to even show it to me at first.

"You won't like it, Ms. Nicholls," he'd said. "I'm sure you need something much more . . . upmarket. We have some lovely modern houses on Richmond Hill that are in your price bracket."

"I want to see this one."

"It's not in Richmond. More Twickenham way, really."

"It's by the river, isn't it? That's even better."

"It needs an awful lot of work done on it—there was an old lady living there for forty years. She didn't have any central heating."

"That's okay. I told you I don't mind spending money on a place, especially one this cheap. Is it big?"

"Oh, indeed it is. Six very spacious bedrooms, an extremely sizable kitchen, three huge reception rooms, big garden, and two bathrooms."

"Do you know what the neighbors are like?"

"The nearest neighbors are a fairly elderly couple, I believe. There are four other similar houses in the road, but they are all quite far apart. All the others have been extensively renovated—it's a very affluent and secluded little road, directly opposite the Thames."

"Perfect. Can we go and see it?"

The mention of the elderly couple next door made me even more convinced, as they were unlikely to phone their friends up and say, "You'll never guess who just moved in!" Or, as my neighbors in Manhattan had done, invite people round to hang out in the hallways in the hope of catching a glimpse of me coming back from a jog.

So Adrian and I went to see it. We had to drive there in his car, a low-slung Capri-type affair out of which I had to haul myself inelegantly when we arrived. To my complete embarrassment there was a Blue Idea CD case visible on the floor by my feet. I discreetly kicked it out of sight underneath the passenger seat and felt thankful that at least he hadn't tried to play it in my presence.

Adrian drove down a little gravel road, more a lane really, running alongside the river, before pulling into a driveway. We surveyed the property gloomily. It was a great Victorian pile, with curlicues of paint peeling away from every windowsill, and a scruffy front door with a cracked pane of frosted glass at eye level. Weeds sprouted enthusiastically from the gravel drive, and the house had a blank, unloved look of despair.

Adrian let us into the damp, chilly hall with keys that he fished from the depths of his satchel-type briefcase. He'd changed his tune, and was chatting inanely the whole time about what a great investment a house in that area was. I followed him into a malodorous but enormous living room and gazed around at the swirly walls, blotchy balding carpet, and dead houseplants.

Adrian had slung his satchel over his shoulder, and with every step he took, the strap made a loud and insistent squeaking noise, as though there was a small furry animal held prisoner within. I was beginning to wish I'd listened to him when he had told me I wouldn't like the place.

Then we walked down the hall to a twenty-five-by-twenty-foot sunny kitchen, and my doubts began to be dispelled. Despite the terrible sagging wallpaper, dripping taps, and dark, cracked linoleum, I could see that the place had immense potential.

All the rooms were indeed huge and high-ceilinged, with original cornices and skirting boards, which I hoped were not rotten. Both bathrooms sported titanic freestanding claw-footed baths, and there was a plethora of wonderful original fireplaces tiled in every kind of rich color with marble surrounds.

We returned to my favorite room, the kitchen.

"It's worse than I remembered," Adrian commented sheepishly, looking with disdain at the black-encrusted gas oven in the corner. "Of course, you'd have to get a new kitchen fitted. A new everything fitted, really—although the extremely low asking price does, naturally, reflect that fact."

"It's a great space," I said enthusiastically. "I love all the original features, too. In fact, I think I could really like it."

Adrian cheered up. I went off and explored all the rooms again, trying hard to look at the space itself and not the damp, musty carpets and dark walls. My biggest concern was that there might be something structurally wrong with the place—my father's advice on surveys, dodgy roofs, and dry rot was still ringing in my ears. I looked out of the window and was relieved to see that there were no huge trees close enough to cause any obvious subsidence, and decided that pending the results of a full structural survey, I wanted it.

I informed Adrian, and he nodded vigorously in assent, causing the little creature in his bag to agree hysterically.

The survey duly showed up that the property was basically sound, if rather damp, and I was overjoyed. I wrote Adrian a massive check; then engaged builders and decorators to install central heating, do damp courses, fit a new kitchen, lay new carpets, and generally transform the place from attic to cellar. It took four months, during which time I "commuted" between a small hotel in Chiswick, the Grants' house in Salisbury, and Sam's hall of residence.

Sam recovered well from both her eyes being zapped, and said she felt a million times better now that she was able to see properly again. She took me to Habitat to pick out my new wallpaper and to look at furniture and curtain fabric, but we soon realized that as I needed everything, from beds to bottle openers, it would probably be best just to stick with one big department store.

So, early one morning about a week before the workmen were finished, I donned dark glasses, opened an account at Selfridges, and Sam and I did a total blitz on the place.

"It's like those game shows where you win two hours to go round a shop and fill up your trolley with as much as you can," said Sam, looking overwhelmed at the task ahead of us. "Where do we start?"

"Bathrooms—that's easiest," I said firmly. "Let's break ourselves in gently."

I had told the store how much I intended to buy, so they gave me carte blanche to go around with a clipboard marking item numbers and prices down for purchases that they would deliver to me later. I had a feeling that they suspected Sam and I of choosing items for a wedding list for our lesbian marriage, and when I told her this, she kissed me extravagantly on the cheek and declaimed, "Please say we can have hers-and-hers bathrobes, oh please!"

After buying a shower rail (circular), a clear shower curtain with gold stars on it, a wrought-iron-effect toilet roll holder and towel rack, four matching sets of honey-colored towels, screw-in iron hooks with dolphin noses, bath mats and toilet-rug things (neither

of us knew what the little horseshoe-shaped carpets were called),
two toilet brushes, soap dishes and toothbrush holder, we were
both exhausted and had to go and have a cup of tea.

Duly revived, we set off again. I felt like an ant in a giant's doll-
house, scurrying around the massively ornate halls and high-
ceilinged rooms, and wondering if at any moment the whole shop
front would open on its hinges and a gigantic hand would reach in
and move the fittings around on a whim.

After choosing four different double beds and a single, five wardrobes, three chests of drawers, bedside tables, curtains, eight rugs,
and a magnificent walnut sideboard from Selfridges's antiques
department, our heads were reeling. Sam had to go back to the
bedding department and take a small nap on one of the mattresses.

"It's all right," she said haughtily to the blue-rinsed sales assistant
who kept coming over to check on her, obviously thinking she had
been testing the bed for longer than was acceptable, "we're buying
it." Her head plopped back again onto the crackly plastic-covered
pillow, and she closed her eyes.

"Are you okay, Sam?" I asked, beginning to worry that I'd tired
her out completely. "Do you want to go home?"

"Home?" She opened one eye and squinted at me. "No way. We
still have the kitchen, dining room, and living room to do! Tell you
what, though. I can live without the appliance department. Can you
buy that stuff over the phone instead?"

So we battled on, amazed at how many *things* were needed to fur-
nish a home from scratch. For the first time ever I enjoyed the fact
that I was able to spend money in this carefree fashion. I had
bought presents for my parents and the Grants before, but I had
never really needed anything other than the essentials for myself,
having been on tour so much. It was fun.

A week later I stood in my brand-newly refurbished house, reveling in its transformation. The smell of fresh paint and new carpets
filled my nostrils, a welcome change from the previous musty odor.
I walked slowly down the hallway, marveling at the slickness and
dazzling white of the freshly glossed skirting boards and door
frames, trailing my fingers across the lush yellow wallpaper. I felt
very grown up and proud of myself. The air around me was very still

and somehow charged, as though a small indoor thunderstorm might blow up at any moment, and it occurred to me that this might just be my own excitement.

The place was still empty, apart from the few possessions I had brought with me from Freehold (two cases of clothes, my bass, some pedals, a practice amp, a few CDs, boom box, and the stuff I'd cleared out of the garage), plus a little television set Mrs. Grant had insisted on giving me. The Selfridges delivery vans were due at any time, but for the moment I was enjoying being completely alone in this wonderful new space.

Carrying my boom box and *Little Criminals,* I went upstairs to the master bedroom. I put the CD on, programmed track nine, cranked the volume up loud, and lay down, stretching my arms and legs out on the bare chestnut floorboards, a big smile on my face.

"I'll Be Home" flowed over me and through me and around my house, cleansing us, clearing out the old energies like burning sage, creating a fresh start.

I was home. I wanted to fill this huge empty shell with my new life, with what I would soon see as the essence of me. I would make new friends who would come over and say, "Oh, this place is really you," and I would be relieved and thankful, because from that starting point maybe I would be able to figure out who "I" really was.

I was twenty-seven and, despite all my money, had never owned a car, lived permanently away from my parents (the Manhattan apartment was just a temporary change of scenery), or had any real financial independence. I'd never even had a serious boyfriend.

I felt as if my life was just beginning, and I was convinced that everything would be smooth sailing from then on.

My new brass door-knocker banged resoundingly, and I clattered down the stripped wooden staircase to open the front door. It heralded the start of a long procession of large square yellow boxes and pieces of furniture coming into the house, carried by four bulky and sweat-ringed delivery men. They cursed when trying to get something cumbersome around the corner leading to the second floor, and then they'd remember that they worked for Selfridges and were not allowed to swear on the job, so they would bite their lips and exhale sharply instead. One of the mattress bases and two of the bigger wardrobes proved particularly onerous, but they struggled manfully on. I had not expected there to be quite so many boxes—I wondered how on earth I was going to get rid of them once I'd emptied them. The place would be up to the ceiling in packaging.

I wished Sam were there, not only for a bit of assistance with the unpacking, but so we could have had a reminisce about my last major house-moving experience, with the Shipleys Ships Safely guys. Thirteen years ago. Wow, what a lot could happen in thirteen years, I thought idly, watching two beautiful Chinese vases being carried into the dining room. Those vases alone were probably worth more than the entire houseful of furniture that had been shipped off to Freehold that day, even allowing for inflation.

But Sam had her exams coming up, and pleaded infirmity and overwork.

"I'll help you with the fun part, spending the money, but count me out of the boring unpacking bit," she'd said airily when we last met. I couldn't blame her, but I wished she could have just been there for moral support.

Several hours later the men had eventually cleared the huge Selfridges lorry. They puffed up the garden path for the last time, carrying, respectively, a standard lamp, an ironing board, a very large potted plant, and a boxed microwave oven. I signed the delivery note, and was so excited at the thought of unwrapping all my new possessions that I did not even mind when the youngest of the men asked if I would sign an autograph for his twelve-year-old daughter.

Once they had left, I tied a silk scarf determinedly around my head in the style of a 1940s munitions worker and attacked the boxes frenziedly. Sure enough, within minutes I was wading through a sea of white paper and crinkly cellophane wrapping, big boxes, and the smaller boxes in which the household items were packaged—saucepans, an iron, lightbulbs, some silk flowers, a laundry drying rack, four telephones, and an answering machine. I tried to be more organized about the procedure, breaking each big box down flat after unpacking it, and leaning the sheets of folded cardboard against the kitchen fireplace.

Everything was so . . . new. I felt as though I was furnishing a model house, and that I would never be able to sully these beautiful shining implements by doing anything so base as actually using them.

I braced my back to lift a very heavy canteen of silver-plated cutlery out of a box. Furniture aside, this had been one of the more expensive purchases. Sam had nearly fainted when she saw the price tag. "Are you *planning* to have ten people round to dinner?" she'd asked sarcastically.

"I might—you never know," I had replied. I felt as though anything was possible. I made sure I bought a long enough oak refectory table to seat my eight other—so far imaginary—friends. I really liked the image of me entertaining: cooking in my own kitchen, bunches of dried herbs hanging from the ceiling, a pot of pasta and sauce bubbling fragrantly on the stove, everyone lolling around the table chatting, windows steamed up from the warmth of the room's mutual companionship.

Yes.

I lifted the wooden lid of the canteen and admired the chunky reflective knives, forks, and spoons within. The box was lined with soft green baize, and each piece of cutlery was neatly trapped between a deep ridge at the bottom and a little green flap at the top.

I had forgotten nothing, from food processors and *cafetieres* to teapots and egg timers. Each found its own natural place in my pristine Smallbone kitchen, and gradually all the cupboards and surfaces began to chatter with the noise of tin rubbing shoulders with copper, china rattling next to glass. I felt as though my soul was filling up at the same pace as the kitchen cabinets. I trashed rectangular bits of card, with holes or pieces of nylon string at the top and bottom, that had backed slatted spoons or chopsticks or skewers, and ripped open sanitary plastic casings that had served the dual purpose of hanging the implement on the display rack, while also preventing the germ-laden breath of the customer from miring its virgin purity. I thought that I, too, had been hanging like this for years, behind a plastic sheath, pawed and gaped at, untouchable on my own display stand. But now I had torn the plastic bubble from my existence. I was no longer on display, or for sale.

* * *

After a few weeks the square shop-creases on all my sheets fell out, I figured out how to program my VCR, I stopped making fresh orange juice every day just for an excuse to use my new juicer, and I burned through the first set of candles I'd bought. I remembered not only everything that I'd purchased, but also where I kept it all. The curtains were hung, the rugs laid, pictures and photographs arranged on walls and over fireplaces. By spring, flowers had bloomed in the garden. Music filled the rooms of the house—I always had a CD in the stereo, or the radio on.

Sam passed her exams and moved in temporarily. We danced and sang together, clowning around, laughing, tipsy and sober, night or morning. My house became a home.

CYNTHIA

AFTER THE VINNIE INCIDENT, I DIDN'T EVEN BOTHER TO LICK MY wounds. I just let them bleed freely all over the house. There were framed photographs of Sam in every room, and I trailed in and out looking at each one in turn. She became the personification of my grief, a symbol of everything I'd lost. When I thought about it, it made me feel guilty. Sorry, Sam, I told her repeatedly. Forgive me. I'm sure you've got enough of your own stuff to think about up there, but please just help me out this one last time.

I began to wonder if I was losing my grip on reality. I didn't eat properly, sleep, or bathe. I just roamed the house, stared at Sam's image, or when I was completely worn out, lay on the sofa and stared at the television. I never played music anymore—it either irritated or upset me. The silence inside my home, whenever the television was off, was deep, dark, and endless, a kind of oblivion. It was how I wanted the inside of my head to feel.

The only concrete action I managed was to phone up my local newsagent and arrange to have every tabloid delivered daily to my door. I didn't want to see Vinnie's photos of me splashed over the front page, but equally I couldn't bear not knowing. Plus I wouldn't be able to sue anybody if I didn't see the evidence. I wasn't sure whether I felt up to being litigious, but I wanted to have the option.

When the papers arrived each morning, in a big bundle that the paperboy flung resentfully over the gate, I got my only fresh air and exercise for the day. Heavily disguised, I trotted out to meet them and then lugged them back to my front porch, where I sat down on the mosaic-tiled floor and cut the string holding them together with a pair of scissors I kept by the doormat. I didn't even bother to take them inside the house.

I flicked rapidly through each paper, from cover to sports pages, looking only at the images, before chucking it aside. I saw inky breasts in all shapes, sizes, and colors, but no photos of me. Within five days my porch was almost full of newspapers, but I didn't have the energy to take them outside and throw them away.

After a week of doing this and nothing else, the monotony was broken by a message on my answering machine: "Hello, Helena, sweetheart, it's me, Cynthia. I just wanted to know how you're getting on. Actually, I'm coming up to London tomorrow to do some shopping, and thought I might call in on my way home if that's all right? It's been a while—I hope you got the hat box all right. I'd love to see you. I'll be there at about five o'clock, okay? See you then, then. Bye."

I noticed that she hadn't even considered that I might be out, or away.

Ugh, a visitor. Of course, I adored Cynthia, but I didn't want to see anybody at all. Plus I'd fired my cleaner in a fit of pique three weeks earlier, and the house was a tip. Oh, who cared. Cynthia could come over and cluck over my face, we'd sit and have tea and not talk about Sam. If it made her happy, fine.

* * *

I came out to meet Cynthia when she arrived the next day, teetering up the drive, getting mud stuck to her pointy heels. She hugged me and chatted on about whether the car would be all right by the river—the tide didn't rise that fast, did it? And she'd locked her shopping in the boot because you never could tell; someone might put a brick through the window when they saw lots of Liberty bags on the seat. . . .

I wondered how she could act so normal. The last thing I felt like doing was shopping for clothes at Liberty. She even had a fresh perm.

Cynthia held me at arm's length and scrutinized me. "You're in a bit of a state, aren't you, love?"

"Well, losing an eye after colliding face first with broken glass tends to have that effect." It seemed tactless to bring up the loss of my best friend, too.

We climbed into the house together, over all the piles of newspaper.

"I didn't mean your appearance. Actually, your face isn't nearly as bad as I'd imagined. I thought you'd look completely different, but you're almost the same old lovely Helena. Bit pale, but still you."

"What are you talking about? I'm hideous!"

I led her sulkily down the hall, our footsteps chasing dust balls out of their hiding places by the skirting board.

"Good grief, Helena, don't be so ridiculous, love! Of course you aren't hideous! You can hardly see the scars on your cheek, you've just got that tiny patch covering your eye, you'd never know anything had happened to your jaw. Okay, your nose is a little bit bumpy, but unless you really look hard, you wouldn't notice. Honestly, I'd say you've recovered brilliantly!"

I felt like saying, "Don't fob me off, I'm not a kid anymore," but out of respect for her I refrained.

"Tea?" I offered, putting the kettle on.

Cynthia glanced around my scummy kitchen. "Yes, please. Tell you what, while you make it I'll have a little clean-up, okay? And you can fill me in on what's been going on."

"Nothing's been going on."

Cynthia took off her coat and began to squirt washing-up liquid into the sink.

"Well, for a start, what's with all the newspapers in the porch?"

I sighed. "My ex, Vinnie. Do you remember him?"

"We never met, but I remember Sam telling me about him. She wasn't his biggest fan. Have you got any rubber gloves?"

Cynthia had already mentioned Sam's name! I felt an odd little thrill, as if she'd just passed me a joint to smoke. I unearthed some unopened gloves from the utility room and handed them to her.

"Yeah, I know. She couldn't stand him. When we were dating I didn't think he was all bad. A bit of a sponger, maybe, but he did come to the hospital with me when Sam . . . But now, of course, he's proved me completely wrong."

"What happened?" Cynthia attacked the dishes with gusto.

I blew air in an exhausted puff out of my mouth, suddenly finding it hard to talk. "Hardly anyone knows I live here—not the press, anyhow. There was someone prowling round here for days, but I didn't know it was Vinnie until about a week ago. I came home from a meeting and he was hiding in the bushes taking photographs of me. I know he's going to sell them to the papers, because he's always skint—more so now we've split up and he hasn't got me paying for everything anymore. Plus the press haven't managed to get hold of me yet, not since the accident. He's bound to make a fortune out of me."

I unhooked two mugs from the Welsh dresser and found some tea bags in the battered tin near the kettle.

Cynthia seemed appalled. "My God, Helena, the man's a monster! How could anyone do something like that! Especially since he must know what you're going through. Treacherous bastard, if I could get my hands on him, I'd—" She waved her soapy yellow gauntlets in the air, causing bubbles to fly across the room, and I couldn't help a small grin. I'd never heard her swear before.

"Can't you stop him? Get an injunction or something? It's not that I think the photos would be terrible. Like I said, your face doesn't look bad—it's just the idea of him profiting from your misery! It's awful!"

She sounded exactly like Sam, leaping to my defense. I didn't know whether this made me happy, sad, or just even more confused.

"There's nothing I can do. If someone prints a picture, then maybe I'll be able to sue for invasion of privacy. It's just really depressing. We parted on bad terms and he probably wants to get back at me. And you know what the worst thing is? Even his damn camera was paid for with my money."

Cynthia came over from the sink and put a wet forearm around my shoulder. "Poor old you," she said, with so much warmth that I began to crumble.

I shook her off. "No, please don't be nice to me or I'll cry. I'm fine, really. How are you? It must be just as hard for you."

Cynthia snapped off the gloves and sat down at the table. "Let's have that tea."

I managed to make two cups of tea without sloshing too much over the side, and carried Cynthia's over to her, remembering to touch the table with my free hand first so I could see where to put the cup. Having one eye meant that my depth perception was all shot to hell, and several mugs had already gone crashing to the floor because I hadn't checked first. Then I went back for my own tea.

"I'm okay, in answer to your question. As okay as you could ever be a few months after losing your only daughter . . ."

Now she was openly talking about Sam. I envied her; she had obviously turned some corner in her acceptance of Sam's death. The tremble in her voice was still there, though.

"It's terribly hard, Helena, you know. We all loved her so much. I miss her every minute of the day—I'm sure you do, too. And Mike's taken it dreadfully hard. He just mooches around the house all day, won't do anything. Doesn't even want to play golf."

I couldn't speak at all by then. I wondered if I'd actually preferred it when Sam's name never came up.

"But let me tell you something amazing, Helena. You read that book Sam once lent me, you know, *Testimony of Light*? So you do believe in life after death and reincarnation and so on, don't you?"

Cynthia took a few sips of her tea. She had an odd expression on her face: grief, sheepishness, and a look that willed me to agree with her.

I nodded warily, not sure that I would be able to handle whatever was coming.

Even though Sam hadn't known she was going to die, in the months leading up to her death we had talked quite a lot about the concept of the afterlife. At first she wasn't at all sure about it, and the nebulous belief system I had built from my teenage dabblings with Christianity was fine with heaven, but pretty much precluded such esoteric ideas as reincarnation. But then we'd both read *Testimony of Light,* and it had changed our way of thinking.

It was written in the sixties, allegedly by the spirit of a deceased ex-nun, communicating via automatic writing through her lifelong friend, who "physically" wrote the book. It was a completely plausible-sounding and wonderfully reassuring description of the afterlife. In heaven there were beds and gardens and artists' palettes and canvases. There was beautiful music, rolling hills, clothing, and telepathic conversation. You were reborn into this place with a spiritual body (which was like a perfect, ethereal version of your last human body), to review your life's lessons and bide your time until you either incarnated into a new body if you needed to learn more earthly lessons, or moved on up through the spheres of Light toward God and perfection. I was so glad Sam had read it.

I wondered if Cynthia was going to tell me that Sam had been in touch in a similar way, and already felt myself getting jealous. If Sam got in touch with anyone, there'd be trouble if it wasn't me. . . .

"Well, you see, the reason I mention it is this—you know my friend Amanda who runs the Three Feathers?"

I nodded.

"Well, she's into these, you know, spiritualist meetings. After Sam died she kept asking me to come along and try it out, but for the first few months I couldn't face it. I thought it would be far too upsetting. Mike was against the idea, too."

"But you went to one?"

Cynthia nodded, twisting her wedding ring around her finger. "A few days ago."

I leaned forward. *"What happened?"*

"It was incredible, Helena, I couldn't believe it. There was this enormous woman on a stage, sort of swaying around, and then suddenly she says, in a great big deep voice, 'I have a message from someone who left us recently after a long illness.'"

I was skeptical. "Why didn't she know Sam's name, then?"

"I don't know. It wasn't her speaking, anyway, apparently. Someone from the Other Side was communicating through her, and that was why her voice was all gruff. Although if you ask me, it sounded a lot like her real voice."

"What did she say next?"

"'She says she wants to talk to her mother.' I look around at everyone, but nobody else moves. Amanda nudges me, but I can't say anything. So Amanda says, 'Is it Sam?' and points at me."

My eye opened wide, and goose bumps rattled down my back. "And it was?"

Cynthia nodded, tears already beginning to leach out over her cheeks. She got up, tore herself a square of kitchen roll, and sat back down again. Involuntarily, I reached out and gripped her hand as if we were watching a horror movie together. I waited for her to continue.

"The medium says, 'Sam wants you to know she is very happy here.'"

That was more than enough to start me off, too. Cynthia squeezed my hand back.

"Wait, that's not all. Then she says, 'But she's telling me she's worried about . . . Oh, I can't catch the name. Someone beginning with the letter *H*—do you know who that could be?' I said, 'Helena?' and the woman nods. 'Tell Helena I love her,' she says."

I was sobbing by now, all restraint gone, in Cynthia's arms. I still felt almost furious that Sam hadn't come and talked to me herself, if she could. This was like a tantalizing glimpse of something denied me. I was delighted that Sam was happy, after all her suffering, and that she was still existing somewhere else—but until I wound things up here, and did the show, somewhere else was simply too far away.

Cynthia stroked my hair and kissed the top of my head, her arms wrapped tightly around me, holding me in the fierce protective way she used to hold Sam, the same way I always witnessed with such jealousy when I was a little girl.

"You let it all out, sweetheart, it'll do you good."

"But I miss her so much," I howled into her chest, barely able to form the words.

"I know you do, darling, I know. So do I. It's okay to say that, it's okay."

I cried so much, tears pouring out of my right eye, that I had an image of my body shriveling up from dehydration on the right side only, like a bath pillow with a hole in it.

Eventually Cynthia pried me away from the temporary security of her cleavage, and wiped the tears gently off my face with her thumb. She got up and handed me a new sheet of kitchen roll so I could blow my nose.

"Helena, love, you shouldn't have to go through this on your own. Promise me something?"

I looked at her mutely. I wasn't in a position to start making promises to anyone.

"Promise me that you'll talk to me in future, whenever you feel like this. You're like another daughter to me, you always have been, and I want you to know that I'm there for you if you need me, okay? I'm so sorry if I've upset you by telling you all this, sweetheart, about the medium and everything. I just wanted you to see that Sam's happy now, and that's helped me so much. I hoped it would help you, too."

Our mugs of tea had turned cold and treacly on the table in front of us. Refilling the kettle and making a fresh brew provided me with a moment to try and reknit my unraveled edges together. I couldn't promise Cynthia anything, but I did manage to thank her. After we'd drunk the fresh tea, and the teary blotches on both our faces had subsided, she hugged me again and picked her coat off the back of her chair.

"Best be off now. Hopefully the rush hour will have died down a bit. Remember what I said, won't you? You're a very special person, Helena. Look after yourself, please—for Sam's sake as well as yours. It will get easier."

I walked with her to the front door and, resting one knee on a slippery stack of *Sun*s and *Daily Mirror*s in the porch, watched her pick her way back down the drive again. She turned at the gate and waved, and I waved back, catching a glimpse of Sam's expression in her profile.

In a way, what she'd said about Sam had helped, but it also strengthened my resolve. I had nearly finished the manuscript. I was ready to do the show. I wanted to be happy, too—I wanted to be in the same place as Sam, as soon as possible.

I double-bolted the front door and stood in my silent hallway, alone.

SAFE FROM HARM

LIFE IN TWICKENHAM MOVED SMOOTHLY ALONG, COUNTED OFF from month to month by the flow of rugby traffic to the stadium, and the highs and lows of the tide along the river opposite my front gate. Whenever I wasn't in Salisbury with Sam, I tended to stay inside on Saturdays and Sundays, as there were so many more people around to spot me and snigger behind their hands at the novelty of sighting someone famous.

Sam lived in my house with me for the first year, before moving out to rent her own flat in Mortlake, nearer the legal firm where she was doing her Articles. She also acquired a new and flashy boyfriend, Timothy, whom I believed prompted her defection. Mortlake was quite nearby, and she did still come and stay, but it was obvious she preferred the carnal pleasures Timothy had to offer over another night watching TV round at my place. I was hurt that she hadn't stayed permanently with me, but she claimed that it would have been "too easy." I did understand, I supposed. After all the time she'd spent living in her parents' basement, she wanted to taste complete independence.

Occasionally I went out with them and their old college friends, but I always felt uncomfortable. Her friends never said anything directly, of course, but they made such an effort to be "normal" around me that the evenings were invariably terribly strained and awkward in their forced jollity. Sam told me that I was paranoid, and imagining things, but I had a lot of experience in that type of situation. I knew that they could not get out of their minds the fact that they were having a drink with someone who was as widely recognized as a member of the royal family.

I couldn't understand why, but it also seemed to bug Sam that I was happy just staying home and tinkering around with my bass.

"Why don't you get out more, meet more people? You could get a job," she suggested several times, until I snapped at her.

"I had a job I liked, and I made enough money that I don't need to work anymore. I've just taken early retirement, okay?"

"But aren't you bored?" she'd say incredulously.

The truth was that, yes, I was beginning to get a little bit bored. I had undoubtedly needed a really long break after the stress of years on the road, and then the trauma of the breakup and the publicity of the trial, but enough was enough. I needed to do something with my time.

I thought about setting up a music publishing company for my newer songs, but somehow I never got round to it. Besides, all my existing songs were in the firm grasp of Ringside Publishing, who were understandably unwilling to relinquish their ten percent, and there wasn't much point in having my own company without my old material, too. Then I thought about music management, but decided that it would be too much like hard work. I even toyed with the idea of becoming some kind of upmarket chef—since buying my ten-piece dinner service and cutlery canteen, I had whiled away many a day teaching myself to cook exotic dishes in preparation for the big dinner party—but that one got nixed on the grounds that I was far too famous to go into catering (this was before the cult of the celebrity chef had invaded our TV screens).

After that, I was stuck for ideas. But then Vinnie came into my life, and suddenly I was no longer bored.

I met him on a winter Saturday in my small but exclusive local deli, the only place I deigned to visit personally to do my shopping. I never went to the goldfish-bowl supermarket, preferring the privacy of ordering my groceries by phone and having them delivered. But the deli was lovely, and I couldn't resist the occasional browse. I'd never been recognized in there, and it felt safe.

So when Vinnie came up and earnestly quizzed me in a strange but sexy accent on how to cook fennel, having, he said, spotted it in my basket, I thought that he had a sweet, ingenuous smile, and explained at length my favorite fennel recipe.

All the time we were talking Vinnie showed no signs of knowing who I was, which endeared me to him still further. We chatted for about ten minutes near the sun-dried tomatoes and porcini mush-rooms, and then amicably moved toward the till together. I was flushed with exhilaration when, once we had both paid and packed our stuff in brown bags, he invited me to go for a drink with him.

Sitting in a nearby pub drinking pints of dry cider, our respective bags propped up on the velveteen-covered benches next to us, I couldn't believe myself. A pub! Pints of cider! It was an old-fellas' pub, gnarled hands cradling creamy Guinnesses; nobody asked for my autograph or even looked askance at me. I got such a huge buzz out of the normality of the whole situation that I even deigned to remove my shades.

After establishing the origins of each other's strange accents—mine mid-Atlantic, his half-Zimbabwean—I discovered that he had lived briefly in Florida, and we got embroiled in a slightly bizarre discussion about the cultural differences between Britain and the USA. This turned into a debate on the comparative merits of English and American supermarkets—although I had to pretend that I knew more about Sainsburys than was strictly true.

"Don't you just love Sainsburys! There are some good supermarkets in the U.S., too, but they're pretty few and far between. The towns around where I grew up in New Jersey just had these terrible poxy places where you had to check the sell-by dates on everything, and the cashiers were so dumb that tomatoes were about the only produce they could identify."

Vinnie giggled, a weird, high-pitched, girly giggle, obviously thinking I was exaggerating.

"No, really, I'm serious. They were so ignorant that they'd hold up a mango and ask what it was. You'd say, 'Oh, those big peaches, ten for a dollar,' and they'd just ring it up at ten cents when actually they were a dollar seventy-five each, or whatever. Once my mother was buying broccoli and the girl picked it up and said, no joke, 'Is this cabbage?'"

Vinnie laughed and laughed, rather excessively, I realized in retrospect, and I felt witty and entertaining, a girl who could make strangers laugh without them knowing I was worth millions.

After the second pint, Vinnie said, "What are you doing tonight? Can I see you again?"

I was thrilled. "What do you want to do?" I asked, with genuine innocence.

Vinnie looked seductively into my eyes and my spine suddenly seemed to dissolve.

"I mean, where do you want to go?"

Vinnie just kept gazing at me, until he leaned forward and gently brushed my lips with his.

"How about your place?" he said casually. I hesitated. I never let strangers come to my house, but Vinnie wasn't a stranger, and I had a feeling he was going to become something much more important. Besides, here was someone besides Sam I could try out my cooking skills on.

"Shall I cook you dinner, then?"

Vinnie grinned triumphantly and thrust a sticky beer mat and a Biro at me.

"Great. I'll be there at seven. Write down your address for me, would you?"

* * *

When I got home half an hour later, slightly drunk from too much Dry Blackthorn, I dumped my upmarket groceries on the kitchen table and immediately tried phoning Sam. Timothy picked up the telephone.

"Hi, it's Helena. Is Sam home, please?"

Timothy answered in the guarded, slightly disapproving tone he always adopted with me. "Sorry, Helena, she's having a nap at the moment."

"Is she okay?" I'd thought Sam had stopped having afternoon naps months ago.

"Yeah, I think so. She's just feeling a bit under the weather at the moment."

"Oh. Right. Could you just let her know that I rang, and that I'll give her a buzz tomorrow?"

"Okay. Bye, then."

I hung up, concerned for two minutes until thoughts of Vinnie swarmed back into my head. It was three-thirty; he'd be here at seven. Three and a half hours to prepare.

First, what was I going to cook? I had a quick flip through a couple of cookery books, and decided on *Casarecce* with Ricotta, Basil, and Arugula—quick, hearty, and quite posh. We could have that, with some fennel in orange sauce as a starter. Bit of an odd choice, but with some hot bread it would be okay, and after all, it was the fennel that had got us talking. The whole thing would only take fifteen minutes, and I had all the ingredients.

Next I ran myself a hot bath with lavender bubble bath and put Massive Attack's *Blue Lines* on the stereo. The bath was my favorite place to listen to music since I'd had extra speakers wired through and wall-mounted in there. After drawing the blinds and lighting a couple of candles in the bathroom, I climbed slowly into the steaming bathtub, one toe at a time because the water felt as though it was scalding my chilled feet. As I gradually immersed myself, body acclimatizing to the temperature change, I relaxed and listened to *Blue Lines* in a tipsy, euphoric state. I lay motionless as the bubbles died around me, only my face, breasts, and knees like icebergs breaking the surface of the fizzy water.

When I raised my hand, steam flew from my outstretched fingers in the flickering candlelight, and I felt like a witch. I wondered if I'd put a spell on Vinnie, if he was as excited as I about the forthcoming evening. Already I couldn't quite remember his face, other than a sly sexy smile and his crinkly green eyes. He was whippet-thin, medium height. Sinewy. A little tremor of lust juddered through me as I visualized him naked, disturbing the tiny uniform bubble-remnants outlining my body.

I could not quite recall the last time I'd had sex. It must have been at least three years ago, because Blue Idea had still been together. I had a vague memory of an unsatisfactory liaison with a marketing director from Ringside's Mexican company, after a promotions dinner and too much tequila. . . . Best forgotten about, like most of my dalliances.

All being well, I estimated that Vinnie would become about the seventh notch on my bedpost. I made a brief tally in my head, to check. First had been my one-night stand with David. Then there'd been a particularly persistent French fan named Claude, who followed us across the Alps in his 2CV when we were on tour in France and Switzerland. After one show, drunk, I had conceded to let him into my hotel room. He had smelled of pesto sauce and body odor, but that was all I could remember about that night or any of the other nights of that particular tour.

Next there was a highly public but very short-lived relationship with the lead singer of a West Coast grunge band, who ceremoniously dumped me for a soap star after only four weeks. I'd been totally humiliated, having made the cardinal mistake of believing myself to be in love, and telling the papers so.

Then there was the lovely Patrick, who, much to her chagrin, Sam never got to meet. He never did return my calls, and eventually I just gave up trying, writing him off as another disaster.

The others I couldn't even identify, apart from the Mexican marketing director. I was ashamed of myself, but they were just groupie shags, one way or another, and they always left me with the belief that men only wanted me for what I was, rather than who I was. I think a few of them probably had wanted to see me again, but when I sobered up I invariably gave them the kiss-off, in no uncertain terms.

After Grunge Boy and Patrick, I decided that I couldn't take the risk of a relationship—it would never have lasted, with the amount of touring we did.

But I wasn't on the road anymore. . . .

I decided that it was of paramount importance for me not to repeat the mistakes I'd made in the past, if I wanted this one to last. No drunken sex, certainly no sex on the first date, and definitely no being sweet-talked into bed. If Vinnie wanted me, he could have me on a grown-up, mature, relationship level, taking things one step at a time.

Of course, I wasn't saying that I wanted to get married and have kids, not yet, anyhow, but I was ready to make more of a commitment to somebody now. I had the time, the energy, the inclination. Mmm, regular sex, I thought as my fingers slipped quietly beneath the surface of the now-lukewarm water, in search of submerged pleasures.

Ten minutes later, I roused myself and washed my hair thoroughly, sluicing off shampoo and conditioner in alternate hot and cold rinses, which made my scalp tingle and my hair feel soft like wet silk. I shaved my legs and armpits—well, you never knew, even if sex was off the agenda, I might let him fondle my calves, if he was lucky—and climbed out of the now-tepid bath. I dried myself, then slathered Issey Miyake body lotion over every inch of my skin. I wrapped my head in a neat hand-towel turban, baby-powdered everywhere that didn't require body lotion, and donned the toweling bathrobe that hung on the dolphin peg behind the door.

Planning to start my makeup, I wiped the steam off the bathroom mirror with my sleeve, but the warm moist air immediately put another, thinner layer of fog on the cleared surface, so instead I went into the bedroom and blow-dried my hair until it sat in a sleek, smooth chestnut bob around my face.

So far so good. I decided to get dressed before doing my face, in order to match my makeup with my outfit, so I slipped out of my dressing gown and deliberated for a long time in front of my open wardrobe.

The phone rang. My heart leapt at the thought that it might be Vinnie, ringing to cancel, but when I picked it up, it was only Sam.

"Hi, what's up?" she asked.

I walked with the cordless phone over to the full-length freestanding mirror in my bedroom and stood naked in front of it. "I've got a date, that's what's up," I said proudly.

There was a screech from the other end. "Who with?"

I surveyed my body, trying to see it through someone else's eyes. Large but perky breasts, tight stomach. Hips and thighs a tiny bit bigger than I'd have liked, but still a safe size twelve. I thanked God that I hadn't stayed chubby. It was so difficult to be in the world's spotlight if you were carrying even a few extra pounds.

"He's called Vinnie, I met him in a shop, he's originally from Rhodesia, Zimbabwe, whatever. He's coming round for dinner."

There was a slight pause.

"You met him in a shop? What shop? What does he do?"

"The deli. He doesn't work there or anything. We just got talking and then went for a drink to the pub. He's a mature student, does art and design. Oh, Sam, he's so hot. All thin and trendy, with a really sexy way of talking. Confident. I like that in a man."

"And does he . . . I mean, did he . . . know who you are?"

"That's the best bit—I really don't think he did. He didn't say anything, anyway. Isn't that neat? He just fancied me for my own sake."

Sam sounded thoughtful. "Yeah—that's great. Just be careful, okay, Helena? Don't get carried away. I'm not sure how I feel about him coming to your house, though. He could be anyone. Do you want me and Timothy to come over for moral support? We're not doing anything tonight."

I laughed. "No way! I don't want you gate-crashing my romantic dinner, thanks very much! But I appreciate your concern. I'll call you first thing in the morning and tell you how it goes."

"You'd better."

"Anyway, gotta go, Sam. I have to start cooking. Thanks for ringing. Lots of love."

"Good luck. Lots of love to you, too, Helena. Let's meet up tomorrow, okay? You can give me all the gory details over lunch."

"Okay. Deal. Bye."

"Bye."

It was only after we'd hung up that I realized I'd forgotten to ask how she was feeling.

I got dressed, finally deciding on my Agent Provocateur underwear underneath a low-key but very sexy Ghost dress. The steam had dissipated from the bathroom mirror when I returned, so I leaned against the sink and got to work on my face. Foundation, blusher, golden-brown eye shadow, black eyeliner and mascara, and finally a tawny-gold–colored lipstick. A generous squirt of perfume completed the transformation.

I flung my wet towel over the shower-curtain rail and picked the sodden bath mat up off the floor, feeling new, polished, and as ready as I'd ever be. It was six-twenty.

* * *

By six-thirty, I was in the kitchen chopping fennel and mashing garlic. There was a bang at the door at around six-forty, just as I'd put the fennel into boiling water and weighed out four ounces of pine kernels.

"It's Vinnie," he said, through the stained-glass panel in the front door.

"Oh, hello," I replied from the hall, completely overcome with panic. Thank God I'd put my makeup on before beginning to cook.

"Well, are you going to let me in, then?" he called, mock-impatient, through the letterbox.

I opened the door.

"You're early," I said nervously.

Vinnie looked me up and down appraisingly. "You look totally gorgeous," he said. "Great house, too. Do you live here alone?"

I nodded, blushing at the compliment. He looked exactly the same as he had earlier, right down to the large brown paper bag he held in his arms. A five o'clock shadow gave away the fact that he probably hadn't spent hours in the bath, and the same clothes indicated the unlikelihood of him agonizing in front of an open wardrobe. Still, that was guys for you.

Vinnie stomped down the hall into the kitchen as if he'd been there a hundred times before, plonked the bag down on the table, and unpacked it. It turned out to contain not his groceries from earlier, but a medium-sized bottle of gin, a large plastic bottle of tonic, two lemons, a packet of Gauloises, and a family-sized pack of tortilla chips.

"Thought we could get started with a few G and Ts," he said airily. "Where do you keep your glasses?"

Somewhat surprised, I got two tumblers out of the cupboard. "How do you know that I like gin?" I asked.

"Oh, most people like gin. You do, don't you?"

"Well, kind of, but . . ."

"There you are, then."

He sloshed a large measure into each glass, topped it up with tonic, and helped himself to ice from the freezer. I stood and watched, mouth agape, as he deftly chopped up lemons, found a bowl to pour the tortilla chips into, opened his packet of cigarettes, and without asking my permission, lit one from the gas ring on the hob.

"Make yourself at home," I said sarcastically.

"Cheers," he replied through a cloud of evil-smelling smoke, handing me a glass. "Your good health. Now, shall we adjourn to somewhere more comfortable before dinner? That looks done," he added, turning off the gas underneath the bubbling fennel. "Why don't you just strain it, and then you can finish the cooking later?"

"I'm surprised you don't want to strain it. You've done everything else," I said, fetching a colander. Again the sarcasm seemed lost on Vinnie.

"Oh, no—you're in charge."

Somehow I found his assertiveness very attractive. He was so different from any other man I'd ever met, and I wondered if it could be because he wasn't the slightest bit in awe of me. I showed him back down the hall into the sitting room and offered him a choice of sofas. But he leapt over to the stereo and pounced on the Massive Attack CD case I'd left out from earlier.

"Hey, I love this. It's amazing. Is it in the machine? Great, let's listen to this."

He pressed Play and the opening bars of "Safe from Harm" chugged out around the room again. "Fantastic album, this. Much better than the follow-up—although that was pretty great, too."

"Bit of an expert, then, are you?" I inquired. If he was that much of an expert on music, surely he'd have known who I was.

"Well, I know a lot about most things," he replied shamelessly, grinning at me.

The first G&Ts slid down very easily, and Vinnie insisted on dashing off to the kitchen to replenish our glasses himself.

"I just love this house," he kept saying to me.

During the second drink, I learned that Vinnie shared a place in Richmond with an Asian girl from a course he was taking; that he was twenty-seven; that he used to be a graphic designer but he'd gone back to college because he wanted to be an artist instead; and that, like me, he was an only child. He didn't ask me anything about myself, not even what I did for a living, for which I was grateful.

By the time he'd rushed off to fix us a third gin, I was feeling very drunk. On the verge of being too pissed to either cook or want to eat, I decided that I'd better get back to my pasta and my orange sauce. Unsteadily, I followed him back into the kitchen.

Vinnie had his back to me. He was hunched over the little portable TV that lived on the end of the kitchen work surface, concentrating on something hidden by his shoulder. I wondered what he was doing—at first I thought he was writing, using the top of the television to lean on.

I studied the part of his profile visible to me: pale skin, one or two not-unattractive pockmarks, lovely cheekbones. Light from a halogen spotlight above him glinted off the lenses of his round tortoiseshell-rimmed glasses and filtered through his stubble. He was actually not as good-looking as I remembered him from the pub—his appeal came more from his sexual confidence than his physical attributes. He had wiry hair, which defied gravity and stood straight up, like Kramer's from *Seinfeld*, and I could smell his aftershave from where I was leaning against the doorframe. At least he'd bothered to put aftershave on, even if he had skipped the actual shaving part.

I stood watching his thin back curved over in its black-and-white stripy T-shirt, and for a second I felt an overwhelming attraction to him.

Then I realized exactly what he was doing, and attraction turned to fury. He was chopping out two neat lines of cocaine—with my credit card, on top of my TV. I couldn't believe it. All Sam's words of warning came flooding back.

"What the hell do you think you're playing at?" I said, outraged at his lack of manners and his presumption.

Cynthia Grant gave me that TV, I thought. She'd be horrified. It was an old, nasty little twelve-inch, encased in grimy white plastic, with a bunny-eared aerial that sat shakily on its top. She'd wanted me to have it when I first bought the house—it had been her own "kitchen telly," but she said she had nearly sliced the tips of her fingers off by trying to watch soap operas and prepare meals at the same time, so please would I take it away? I'd laughed and said, "So I can slice my own fingers off?" but it had been in my kitchen ever since.

Vinnie had moved the bunny aerial down onto the worktop so as to have more room to maneuver. The cocaine he was expertly chopping out hardly showed up at all on the white surface, but this did not make it any more acceptable.

"How dare you do that in my house!" I spluttered. "Get out, now!"

Vinnie looked a picture of contrition.

"Oh, God, I'm so, so sorry. I had no idea you'd object. You just seem like such a cool person, I was sure you'd be into a little livener now and again. You know, special occasion and all that. I'm bang out of order, I know. If it upsets you, I'll leave, now."

He immediately swept the cocaine back into its white paper package, folded it safely into the corners, and put it back in his jeans pocket, before standing up to face me. He was hitching up his baggy jeans by the belt loops and shuffling from foot to foot like a guilty schoolboy, and I suddenly had the urge to put my arms around his hard waist. In my heels, I was about two inches taller than him, so he had to look up into my face.

"You don't have to go. But I warn you, though, I won't sleep with you," I blurted, feeling foolish.

"Who said anything about sex?" he asked innocently, touching my breast lightly.

"Get off. And don't even think about getting that stuff out again, do you hear me? I don't do drugs, not even spliff, and I won't have them in my house."

"Awww. You're such a spoilsport. You'll have another G and T, though, won't you, eh?" he said hopefully, turning back to his more legal supplies.

I couldn't believe his nerve. It was extraordinary, but it just made me fancy him even more. I watched him clumping around in his heavy Doc Martens, whistling, opening and closing cupboards, crashing ice cubes from a tray, chopping more lemons, the *hiss* and *fizz* of the tonic bottle being unscrewed again.

I felt as if suddenly there had been a tilt, and it was I who had come to visit him in his house. It left me standing aimlessly, like an uncomfortable stranger amid my own familiarity, waiting for an invitation to be seated.

Vinnie flourished two more huge gin and tonics and a bowl of chips, and ushered me out of the kitchen back into the sitting room.

"I really think I should start dinner now," I said weakly, wondering if perhaps this was all a bizarre dream.

"I don't know about you," Vinnie said, "but I'm actually not all that hungry now. We're having such a laugh. What do you say we just keep drinking for a bit?"

As if under some spell—to think that I'd believed I could put a spell on him!—I found myself saying, "OK, well, if you don't want to eat . . . I'm not very hungry now either."

"Cheers," he said, handing me my drink. We clinked glasses, and he smiled slowly, almost sheepishly. Later, after I got to know him better, I found out that it was the smile that meant, "Come on, play the game, I know you know what this is about."

We gazed at each other for a long time, too long for there to be any doubt about what we both wanted. I must not sleep with him, not yet, I thought. But I was transfixed by the sexy curve of his lips, and the way his eyes held mine in a blatantly flirtatious way. I found myself wondering what his kisses would be like.

Vinnie got up to rifle through my record collection, running a commentary on its contents as he did so. "How can you admit to having a Bruce Springsteen CD? American jingoistic crap!" "Incredible! You're the only person I know who has the Unknown Cases record!"

He put on a CD, listened to one track, took it off again, put on another. In between tracks he moved from sofa to armchair to the floor by my feet, where he briefly pleated the fringes of the rug, before hopping back up to the sofa, talking talking talking all the time, and chain-smoking.

"Get your shoes off the sofa," I said when I could get a word in edgeways. "Why are you so bloody hyperactive?"

His familiarity with me was causing me to behave in an equally familiar way toward him. I didn't recognize myself.

"Can't help it. Must be my natural high spirits. Speaking of which," he said, bouncing up from the sofa like Tigger in monochrome, "another drink?"

If he hadn't sworn he wasn't, I'd have said he was definitely high.

Once more he disappeared into the kitchen, grinning, without waiting for my answer.

Somehow the drinks got topped up more and more often without me noticing. The chips were reduced to a few greasy crumbs at the bottom of the bowl. It was only eight-thirty, and all ideas of dinner had gone out of the window.

Vinnie finally put *Blue Lines* on again, the third time I'd heard it that day. He turned the volume up full blast and pulled me out of my chair to dance, still talking nonstop: politics, music, architecture. Irrespective of his knowledge or lack of knowledge of a subject, it transpired that he always had to be right. He was goading me as we danced, trying to woo me into one of the interminable debates that came to characterize our relationship (besides the sex, that is).

"I can't dance, talk, and drink at the same time," I said. His smell and his weird accent pulled at me like a magnet. I will not sleep with him, I told myself. We were getting closer and closer together, laughing as we danced drunkenly around. I wanted him.

"Whoops," I thought—or maybe I said it aloud. "You'd better go and get me another drink."

I was drunk enough by then that I kept on dancing even when he was out of the room. All my familiar possessions—pictures, books, chairs—took on a different and jiggly appearance, as though they were my new dance partners. Vinnie came back with two half-filled glasses. "That's the end of the gin," he said, laughing.

"You're joking!"

I stopped dancing and suddenly felt exhausted. "We've drunk the whole bottle?"

"Yup. Come on, let's send it out in style. Down in one!" We clinked glasses again, swigging the remainder of the gin. The room started to spin and I had to hold on to Vinnie's arm to keep steady. Massive Attack ended but we still swayed together, closer and closer until our heads touched. A hair from one of his wiry curls detached itself and found its way scratchily under my eyelid. I felt his erection press hard up against my thigh and I shivered with excitement. As I blinked the hair out of my eye, I ran my fingers lightly over his bare arm, feeling the contours of his little moles and goose bumps, squeezing a rough elephant's trunk of loose skin at his elbow. My other hand traced the knob of his spine.

He told me that he broke his back, parachuting, during a youthful stint in the army. "I was lucky," he said. "The person who jumped out of the plane after me was killed—his parachute didn't open at all."

I couldn't imagine him being in the army; I bet he'd been useless—a sort of opinionated, bossy, male equivalent of Private Benjamin. I laughed at the thought and Vinnie kissed me. His tongue felt nice, firm and insistent, not skinny like the rest of him.

"Whoops," I whispered again as we went blurrily upstairs to my bedroom, shedding garments en route.

I sobered up briefly in the middle of the sex, our limbs a flailing tangle on the bed. The undersheet had twisted itself sweatily off, exposing the little stitched peaks and valleys of mattress beneath it. My body was loving it while my mind yelled furiously at me to stop—but by that time, stopping was out of the question.

Afterward we both had to go and throw up in the toilet to rid ourselves of the lingering alcohol, and I felt that I was vomiting out more than just the gin. I was puking caution, good sense, discretion. I cleaned my teeth and stared at my face in the mirror; there were two bright red spots on my cheeks that could have been from sex or gin, but might also have been from shame.

When I got back to the bedroom, Vinnie rolled contentedly onto his back, as at home in my bed as he was in the rest of my house. He grinned at me.

"Do you realize we've just had an entire night's events crammed into about three hours?" he said. "We've talked, danced, drunk a whole bottle of gin, shagged, puked, slept—and it's only ten o'clock."

He gave me a triumphant peck on the cheek and curled up to dream a victor's dreams.

I looked at him, small and vulnerable without his glasses or his clothes; astonished at the evening's events. It couldn't have been me who'd just done that, surely: gotten drunk and had sex with a stranger. Thankfully it had been wonderful, but I had a nagging feeling that I'd had absolutely no choice in the matter. I wondered whether I should kick him out, or perhaps go and sleep in one of the spare rooms, but he looked all warm and soft and inviting, so I climbed back into bed with him instead.

He turned over with his back to me, so I was spooning him, and muttered sleepily, "You know, I'm a huge fan of yours."

But by then it was too late.

THE DELECTABLE SANDIE

AFTER DAYS AND DAYS WHEN I'D BEEN UNABLE TO DO ANY writing at all, Cynthia's visit spurred me back into it. Suddenly I found that I was actually getting close to finishing the manuscript. I estimated two more weeks of working several hours daily, and I'd be ready to do the show. Not, of course, that I'd actually be reading the magnum opus on air—how could I, in a two-hour show?—but it had to be complete, for me to leave behind as the explanation for my choice of music.

It was time to start thinking seriously about collecting the music. I wanted to be sure that I brought every single CD with me into the studio, just in case New World's library couldn't produce a copy. I wanted to leave nothing to chance.

As I conducted a detailed rummage through my CD collection, I wondered who the producer for the two A.M. show would be. I supposed it was too much to hope that it would still be Chrissie, my last breakfast-show producer. She was very professional, and, I'd thought, a lovely person, too—she'd been the only one to visit me more than once in hospital, although she hadn't rung me since. She had probably gone on to much better things by now.

It would probably be better if I had someone awful, anyway. Some thick-skinned dim novice, who wouldn't get upset when the press asked, "How could you not have known what state Helena was in?" and "Didn't you think she was acting strangely?" Someone who could bask in his fifteen minutes of fame, as the last person to see me alive.

I made a tidy tower of CDs next to the fireplace, containing the majority of tracks I had planned for the show. I'd already bought *All Mod Cons,* which I realized must still be in my car somewhere, a painful reminder of that sunny, hungry, sick day when I bumped into Toby. I couldn't help wondering how he was, and if I would be able to find his sister's address, which was also on the floor of the car. I decided I'd look for it when I went out to retrieve the Jam CD.

A few of the other CDs I'd need were also missing: My copy of *Tapestry* by Carole King was nowhere to be found (I suspected Vinnie had half-inched it), and I realized that I had never owned *The Sandie Shaw Supplement,* "Wichita Lineman," or any Happy Mondays records.

I rang round all the Richmond record shops to see what they had in stock and managed to reserve copies of *Pills 'n' Thrills & Bellyaches, Tapestry,* and *20 Greatest Hits of Country Music.* Only the Sandie Shaw was missing now. But after ten minutes on the Internet, it was ordered, delivery time one to two weeks. Better not take any longer, I thought.

Even though I needed the album on CD, the original vinyl version, source of so much friction between Mum and Dad, would have done if all else failed. I decided to phone Dad to see if he still had it, as a backup in case the CD didn't arrive in time. The record somehow felt like a bond between us.

Dad nearly fainted with surprise when he picked up the telephone to hear my voice.

"Hi, Dad, it's me."

"Helena, my honeypie! How the heck are you!"

I gritted my teeth with annoyance at his Southern twang. God knew where he'd picked it up from—my mother had managed to cling to her Home Counties vowels as if her life depended on them. An American accent was fair enough, after more than twenty years living in the country, but did he really need to sound as if he was just about to go out roping steer?

I was very fond of my father, but in an abstract way, the way one feels about having nicely manicured fingernails. He was a bit of a nonperson to me, really, a pipe-smoking appendage to my mother. In fact, the only time I could actually remember seeing him without her being there was in the early days of the band, when he had reluctantly come to one of our gigs (Mum had refused point-blank to come with him, as she was sure that she would hate it, although she did grace us with her presence once or twice after we'd begun to get successful). Dad had stood at the side, flattened against the wall away from all the moshing high-school kids, sucking on his pipe and looking so uncomfortable that anyone would think that I had been performing a striptease onstage. Justin and Joe had spotted him and, mid-set, began a lugubrious rendition of a *Sesame Street* song: *"One of us is not like the other ones. . . ."* I'd been mortified.

"I'm fine, Dad. In fact I'm going back to work soon."

"Aw, that's just fan-tastic! I'm real happy to hear that, honey. Me and your mom's been so darn worried."

I shuddered.

"We wish you'd just come on out here and visit awhile, Helena. Why, it must be over two years since I last saw you!"

This was how all our conversations went.

"But Dad, you're always off on your cruises at Christmas, and you know how busy I . . . used to be with the radio show. You have to be there every day. You can't just go on vacation whenever you fancy it, you know that. I wasn't really well enough to come over before, and now I'm starting a new show. There's nothing stopping *you* visiting *me,* is there?"

Dad hemmed and hawed. "Well, honey, it's kind of hard this side, too, what with work, and me being chairman of the Country Club Society Committee. . . . Anyways, to what do we owe the honor of your call? Want to talk to your mother?"

"No, actually, Dad, I wanted to ask you something. I'm, um, getting some records together for my first show back on air, and I really want to play a Sandie Shaw track. You used to have it on vinyl, I remember it from when I was a kid. The album was called *The Sandie Shaw Supplement.*"

Dad laughed. "Oh my, I *loved* that record! As I recall, it featured the delectable Sandie spray-painted gold—lots of hair and a teeny chain bikini. Your mother disapproved."

"Yeah, that's the one. I've ordered it off the Net, but I'm worried it won't arrive in time for my show. Do you still have it?"

There was a pause while he considered.

"You know what? I believe I might do. I sure haven't seen it for donkey's years, though. I'll have a scout round for you. I remember your mother tried to throw it away, but I'm sure I rescued it and hid it in my study."

Dad's study in New Jersey was exactly the same as his study in Salisbury had been: whole mountain ranges of paperwork, yellowing newspapers, golf books, and an assortment of pipes, jumbled together in one huge fire hazard. It was hard enough to spot Dad when he was in there, let alone one thin vinyl record. I didn't hold out much hope of getting a copy anytime this decade.

"Oh well, don't worry, Dad. If it turns up let me know. Is Mum there?"

"No, honey, she's out playing canasta. I'll tell her you called."

"Okay—well, that's all, then. Thanks anyway. "

"Good to talk to you, sweetheart. We don't do it enough. You take care of yourself, mind."

I was going to have to hang up pronto, because a marble seemed to have gotten stuck in my throat. "Yeah, thanks. Bye, Dad. I love you."

"Excuse me?"

Dad must have thought he'd misheard.

"I love you, Dad. Bye."

"Love you, too, angel," he said in a bemused voice.

I put the phone down and cried for ten minutes.

NOTHING COMPARES 2 U

ARE YOU REALLY A FAN OF BLUE IDEA?" I ASKED VINNIE AFTER OUR first night together.

"Oh, man—yeah! *Painting the Ceiling* is one of my favorite ever records. I can sing all the words to it."

"Go on, then," I challenged him.

For a split second, when he thought I was serious, the look on his face was priceless. He later told me that was the moment he fell in love with me, although it was another ten months before he actually said it in so many words.

* * *

The already-subdued lights in the restaurant dimmed further, and a beaming young waiter emerged, bearing a beautifully decorated cake in the shape of a champagne bottle, five tiny flickering candles atop it.

Sam leaned over to me as everyone began to sing.

"Vinnie organized the cake for you," she said, squeezing my hand.

I threw my arms around Vinnie's neck and kissed his cheek repeatedly, breathing in his distinctive Vinnie scent of aftershave and Gauloises.

"Oh, Vin, baby! It's wonderful! Thank you so, so much!"

"You're welcome, angel," he replied, a faintly puzzled expression on his face.

As the final "Hap-py Birth-day to yooouuuuuu!" faded away, the other diners in the restaurant applauded politely, and Sam, Timothy, David, David's wife, Joe, Vinnie, and I all clinked glasses in a noisy and protracted toast to celebrate my thirtieth birthday.

I stood up, fingering the beautiful bracelet Sam had given me earlier, and smiling from ear to ear.

"This is so fantastic," I said. "It's the best birthday I've ever had. I've got my wonderful best friend here, my gorgeous and considerate boyfriend, old friends David and Joe, and, er, new friends, too! I just feel totally . . . great!"

They all cheered. Vinnie delved into his backpack under the table and brought out a thin, flat tinfoil package (from my kitchen—I'd caught him replacing the Bacofoil in the kitchen drawer earlier). He handed it to me, and it was so light that at first I thought there was nothing inside.

"Careful how you unwrap it," he said. "It's fragile."

I gingerly undid the foil corners and opened the present to reveal a piece of wire twisted painstakingly into the wavy fingers, trouser creases, and joint bends of a realistic little wiggly man.

"Oh, Vinnie," I said. "It's lovely! Thank you so much."

I showed it around the table, and everybody duly admired it. Only Sam had a slight frown furrowing her forehead. But Vinnie constantly gave me homemade presents, etchings and sculptures he'd done at college—a cute clay dinosaur with a rose in its snout, a hand-enameled mirror—and I loved them. After years of receiving vacuously expensive corporate gifts as tokens of gratitude for making Ringside rich—cashmere dressing gowns, vintage wines, state-of-the-art audio equipment, and so on—Vinnie's little trinkets touched me deeply.

Vinnie clicked his fingers to order another bottle of champagne. After further toasts to the future happiness of David and his new wife, Cherry; Peter Gabriel, for kindly coinciding his world tour with my birthday (the reason Joe and David were in town as they were now employed as members of Gabriel's touring band); absent friends (Justin was making his second solo album in a studio in the Bahamas); and Vinnie for generally being wonderful, we ordered a third bottle, and I cut the cake.

As we tucked in and Joe regaled us with tales of how sick-makingly in love David and Cherry were, Sam noticed that a table of older diners across the restaurant were looking askance at us.

"Do you think we're being too loud?" she asked worriedly, when she could get a word in edgeways.

"Nah," said Joe, in mid-flow of a story about what the newlyweds had been discovered doing underneath the stage at Earls Court, much to Cherry's embarrassment. "They probably just recognize us."

At that moment one of their group, a middle-aged woman with overplucked eyebrows and a tight Jaeger banana-colored suit, came up to our table and tapped me on the shoulder.

"Hi," I said brightly to her. "Would you like an autograph?"

She looked at me for a minute, as if I was being facetious. "No," she said. "Thank you. The thing is, you see, it's my husband's birthday today, too, his fiftieth, and *that*"—she pointed at the crumbs and slabs of icing, which was all that remained of the champagne cake—"was his cake."

"What do you mean?" I asked indignantly. "My boyfriend brought it. Maybe yours was the same. Why don't you ask the waiter?"

The headwaiter materialized immediately beside the woman. I felt, rather than saw, Vinnie squirming in his seat beside me.

"No, madame," the waiter intoned sonorously. "We were only in possession of one birthday cake. Unfortunately, my junior waiter was not aware that there were *two* birthday parties taking place, and so when the signal was given for the cake to be brought out, he brought the cake to your table, when, in fact, it was intended for the other party."

Everybody fell about laughing, and then looked at Vinnie.

"Hey, this isn't my fault!" he protested.

"Well, where's the cake you brought, then?" Sam demanded.

Vinnie lit a Gauloise and managed to blow smoke into the faces of both the headwaiter and the cakeless woman.

"Thing is," he said, "when I said I'd organized it, what I meant was that I'd asked matey-boy over there"—he pointed at the greeter by the door, who suddenly became very engrossed in his reservations book—"if he could sort us out with a piece of apple pie or something with a candle in it, you know—something to bring out for Helena so we could all sing. I was well chuffed when the other waiter appeared with this great cake. I thought, Wow, what a cool restaurant. . . ."

We all slapped our hands against our foreheads, Homer Simpson style, and a chorus of "Doh"s arose.

"Well, how was I to know that someone else was having a birthday?" Vinnie said to the headwaiter. "You should have been better organized, mate. It's not our fault if you bring out a cake to the wrong people. Here, let's see what we can do."

He leapt up and went round all our plates, collecting the chunks of discarded icing that had originally formed the label of the champagne bottle. After piecing them together on a side plate like a sugary jigsaw, he stuck a candle on top, lit it with his cigarette lighter, and, with a flourish, bounded across the room to present the cakeless candle to the birthday boy.

By this time the entire restaurant had ground to a standstill. Vinnie spread his arms wide, Gauloise still in his mouth. "Come on, everybody!" he shouted, and led all the diners in another round of "Happy Birthday," sung lustily by him, ourselves, and the fiftieth-birthday party, grudgingly by everyone else (who were beginning to look at one another with "We're not coming here again" expressions), and not at all by the birthday boy's wife, who was furious.

I put my head in my hands and groaned, although I couldn't help laughing.

David leaned over the table. "Quite a guy you got there, H," he said affectionately. "I'm glad you've met someone you like so much. He sure seems crazy about you, too, I hope it works out. You never were that lucky in love before, were you?"

"No—it's about time, isn't it? I'm pleased you've found your soulmate, too."

I grinned at him and Cherry, clasping hands with each other across the debris of scrunched up napkins and misappropriated cake crumbs.

"Thanks, Helena. I'm sorry we didn't invite you to our wedding, but like I said, we just slipped away to Barbados on the quiet. You should try it—married life is awesome!"

"Maybe we will, some day," I said. "You guys are certainly a good advertisement for it."

Eventually the fuss was smoothed over. The headwaiter, a muscle twitching violently in his cheek, was forced to offer the fiftieth-birthday party desserts on the house, and several free bottles of champagne, and I thought it was probably time to ask for our table's bill.

"It's my birthday, I'm treating everybody," I said when Sam and David began to protest.

I paid up, and Vinnie courteously helped me into my coat.

"There you go, old lady," he said, kissing my cheek. "Have you had a good time, despite the, er, unfortunate incident?"

I nodded. "Fantastic, thanks. And even if you didn't get it together to actually *bring* a cake, thanks for organizing someone else's for me. It'll be a great story to tell our grandchildren, don't you think?"

"Mmm," said Vinnie, tilting my head back for a huge, passionate birthday kiss, and wrapping his arms tightly around my waist.

"I love you, Vin," I said when I came up for air.

"Love you, too, Helena," he replied, for the first time ever.

I grinned and hugged him triumphantly. "You staying over tonight?"

Vinnie looked at his watch, a Rolex I'd given him for his birthday two months earlier. "Can't, angel. I really have to get back and work on that project I'm in the middle of."

"But it's my birthday!"

Vinnie kissed me again. "Sorry. See you tomorrow, okay, baby?"

Sam looked hard at me. "He doesn't stay round at your place much, does he?"

Two weeks later, we found out why.

* * *

Sam and I had gone to Richmond Park on a warm September day, for a picnic. I'd thought of asking Vinnie to join us, but then I remembered him telling me that he'd been enlisted to help his friend Ivan lay a patio that afternoon, but would see me that night at seven to accompany me to a rare function: a dinner party I'd been invited to at Ron's house.

I'd secretly been relieved that Vinnie was busy. Even though I was looking forward to the dinner party, I was feeling quite stressed about the prospect of meeting lots of strangers, and I just wanted a chilled-out afternoon in the sun. Sam and Vinnie would only have sniped at each other—they had never gotten on all that well, and it was getting worse. Sam made snide comments about his new Paul Smith suit, his penchant for meals at tiny, very exclusive restaurants, and his sudden urgent need for expensive equipment for his art course: computers, scanners, cameras, VCRs, and the like. All paid for by me.

"It's my money," I'd say defensively to Sam. "I like spending it on Vinnie."

I could tell she didn't want to make too much of an issue out of it, in case I thought she was jealous that I wasn't spending it on her. I didn't think that at all. In fact I was touched by her concern; I just thought it was entirely misguided.

So that day it was a joy, as well as a relief, to have Sam all to myself. Since my birthday she'd been feeling a bit low and unwell, and I was terrified that her ill health might presage the return of her leukemia.

"It's definitely not that," she insisted as she unpacked the picnic hamper. "I promise you, Helena, it isn't. I've been working too hard, that's all, and my lungs are playing up from the graft-versus-host. Plus it's so depressing being dumped for 'not being enough fun.'"

Timothy had recently decided that he did not require a girl-friend who went to bed exhausted at nine o'clock practically every night, and Sam had taken it badly.

"Timothy's just a shallow loser, if that's all he cares about," I said as I put a compilation tape into the boom box I'd brought with us. I was about as fond of Timothy as Sam was of Vinnie. I'd only tolerated him at my birthday party because Sam wanted him there.

I spread out an Indian throw under a tree in a secluded part of the park, away from all the families biking down the yellow gravel paths, and the hesitant children on horseback. Our nearest neighbors were a couple snogging near the next cluster of trees, about fifty feet away, and a father flying a kite with his young son on our other side.

"I'm sorry, though, Sam, I know how much he meant to you. I'll throttle him if I ever see him again, for putting you through all this. Here, have a sarnie—I made your favorites, look, peanut butter and pickle."

Sam reclined on a cushion, halfheartedly toying with her sandwich, as we spent an intense hour analyzing in excruciating detail every single word and gesture of Timothy's, trying to deconstruct the whys and wherefores of rejection.

"Do you know," Sam said afterward, "I really feel like going away for a bit, somewhere really relaxing. I'm owed some holiday. Fancy coming to Greece with me for a week? Santorini's meant to be amazing. We could get one of those last-minute deals."

I was delighted, until I thought of the prospect of being without Vinnie for that long. "Hmm . . . maybe once Vinnie's term starts again," I said, opening a bottle of wine and pouring us each a glass.

Sam tutted irritably. She wasn't used to me not jumping at the chance of having her company. With a start, I realized that I wasn't used to it either.

"Oh, come on, Helena. Please. It wouldn't be the same without you, and we haven't been on holiday for ages. Hey," she added, turning up the volume as Sinead O'Connor began to sing "Nothing Compares 2 U." "I love this song. What is this tape?"

"Just a compilation I made. Brilliant, isn't it? I'll let you know about Santorini. I must say, I've always fancied it myself, too."

I lay down on my back beside Sam, and we watched the clouds float across the sky as the music drifted over us.

"This sky reminds me of a poem I wrote once, when I started writing song lyrics. You know, when I was going through that religious phase."

"Can you remember it?"

"Um, hang on, let me think. . . ."

I paused for a while, trying to recall the words. Sam sniggered and pointed over to the lovers by the trees.

"Look at them—talk about hot 'n' heavy. They'll have completely ripped off each other's clothes in a minute."

The couple was indeed horizontal, him on top of her, bumping and grinding and rolling around. I was temporarily distracted from my poem, remembering the similar behavior Vinnie and I had indulged in the previous night.

Sam sighed. "I'll probably never have sex again. Life sucks. So, quick, tell me your poem before I get consumed with depression."

I cleared my throat dramatically. "Okay, here goes: 'Christians kiss with their eyes closed, he said with a sigh / Rolling over to watch heavy clouds drag by. / I smiled, and opened one eye.'"

Sam grinned. "I prefer your later stuff," she said.

She sat up and helped herself to some broccoli quiche. Suddenly she froze, napkin in hand, and her triangle of quiche fell into her lap.

"Bloody hell, I don't believe it," she said, staring into the middle distance.

"What?"

"Oh," she said, collecting herself and picking up crumbs of pastry. "Nothing . . . I just thought of something I forgot to do."

I sat up, too. Her tone didn't fool me for a minute.

"What?"

Sam shook her head. "I'm sure it's nothing, but . . . for a minute I thought that was Vinnie over there."

I laughed and looked over at the almost-copulating couple. They were sitting up now, rearranging their clothes, still kissing. The girl looked Asian, with beautiful long, silky black hair. The guy had his back to us.

"No, of course it's not!" I said. "He's about the same build, though, I can see how you thought it was."

Then they stood up, folded their travel rug, and began to walk hand in hand toward us, presumably on their way to the car park.

Within ten paces, I saw that it was indeed Vinnie.

My peanut-butter sandwich stuck to the roof of my mouth, and my head whirled with disbelief and panic.

"It can't be," I whispered thickly. "There must be some mistake. Perhaps he has an evil twin."

"Has he?" asked Sam hopefully, her hand grasping my arm.

"No."

They were getting closer and closer, their heads leaned together, laughing and tickling each other in a nauseatingly lovey-dovey manner. I felt sick. I picked up our half-full wine bottle.

"What are you going to do?" Sam looked alarmed.

At that moment, Vinnie glanced over and spotted me. Without breaking his stride, he wheeled around at a ninety-degree angle and steered the Asian girl away from us, toward the opposite end of the distant car park. He didn't look back, although I sensed a definite tenseness in the way he held the hairy travel rug under his arm.

I took a deep swig of the Pinot Grigio.

"Oh, Helena. I'm so sorry. Are you all right? You've gone really white."

Sam hugged me hard, partly, I thought, to prevent me from leaping up and bottling Vinnie from behind.

"Men, eh?" she continued, with feeling. "Can't live with 'em, can't shoot 'em." She looked anxiously at me. I was still silent. "He's a bastard. Better you found out now than later. Is that the girl he shares a house with?"

I said nothing, but tears welled in my eyes.

"Speak to me, Helena, please." Sam shook me gently.

I looked at her and took a long, deep breath. "When can we go to Santorini, then?"

"As soon as we book somewhere to stay?"

"Fine."

* * *

I had been sure that was the last I'd see of Vinnie, and I was heartbroken. I intended to phone Ron and pull out of the dinner party that night, but Sam nagged me until I agreed to go anyway. She said, rightly, that Ron was new in my life (I'd recently hired him with a vague idea of getting some of my old songs remixed by hot new producers, although nothing had come of it thus far), so it wouldn't do to let him know how antisocial I really was.

Plus I might meet a new man there (not that I wanted one). Plus, I so rarely went to these sorts of functions. Plus, I was a professional. Plus, it would be good to have something to take my mind off Vinnie. Etc., etc. I eventually caved in. I had bought a new dress to wear, the cab was booked, I'd even been looking forward to it, albeit with trepidation.

Sam stayed long enough to zip up my dress and do my hair for me, before she drove back to her flat for another night in watching

ER and wondering who Timothy was out having fun with. She'd been gone about five minutes, and I was just putting on my lip liner, when there was a hammering at the front door.

Assuming she'd forgotten something, I ran down the stairs and flung open the door, lip pencil in hand.

Of course, it was Vinnie, standing there all spruced up and clean-shaven, clutching a bottle of wine.

I was flabbergasted. I stood there, open-mouthed, as he grinned jauntily at me.

"Don't forget to color in the rest," he said, gesturing toward my outlined lips. "Right, what time are we off?"

I hung on to the doorframe, blinking in disbelief and fury. "You have got to be fucking joking."

Vinnie had the gall to look surprised.

"Is it canceled? What are you all dressed up for, then?"

I was approaching meltdown. "How *dare* you!" I spoke through gritted teeth. "I can't believe your nerve, I really can't. You were all over some whore in Richmond Park this afternoon. How could you think that I'd ever want to clap eyes on you again, after seeing that? Just get lost, and don't bother coming back."

Vinnie slapped the side of his head as if he had forgotten that he'd snogged someone else in front of me only hours earlier.

"Oh! You mean Miyuki! Man, we weren't all over each other. We're just housemates, you know, old friends." He paused. "You saw us walking through the park together, didn't you? Hey, you should have called out. I'd have introduced you!"

Miraculously, I stayed relatively calm; i.e., I didn't actually kill him. "No, Vinnie, I didn't 'just' see you walking through the park. I saw you lying on top of her, dry-humping away like a terrier in heat. I saw you suck the face off her. I saw you whisper sweet nothings in her ear. And now I learn that you live with her, too! Please don't insult me by telling me you're just friends. God, it's so obvious now. No wonder you never liked to be seen out with me; no wonder you said you were 'embarrassed' by what a mess your house is."

Vinnie grinned. "Listen, it's fine. She doesn't mind if I see other women, honestly. She's cool."

That really was the final straw. To my utter disgust and humiliation, I burst into tears.

"I MIND!" I bawled.

I was about to slam the door in his face and retire to bed with a bottle of vodka, when a black cab bumped along the path outside the front gate, tooting at me. There was no way I was going to let Vinnie see he'd ruined my evening as well as my life.

Mustering up what vestiges of dignity I could, I snuffled, "Excuse me, I have a dinner party to attend," and shot back in the house to grab my makeup and handbag. Ron lived in Highgate, so I had a good long cab ride ahead of me in which to apply enough slap to disguise the fact that I'd been crying.

I locked the front door behind me, ignoring the fact that Vinnie was still standing outside the porch behind me.

"Have a nice life, asshole," I hiccuped as I barged past him, grabbing the bottle of wine from his arms on the way.

It was only once I was barreling safely around the North Circular, having just about managed to repair the damage to my face, that I looked at the bottle I'd purloined from Vinnie. It was Blue Nun.

I left it in the taxi.

* * *

It must have been a remnant of the discipline I'd learned in Blue Idea, the same consummate professionalism that had gotten me through a grueling national tour knowing that Sam was lying in a hospital bed, but I was *great* that night. Vinnie's betrayal at least had one positive effect: It swept aside all my qualms about meeting new people.

From the moment I sat down at the snowy linen and sparkling crystal–set table in Ron's house (which was ultramodern, architect-designed, and overlooked the cemetery; it had a very public-toiletesque exterior, but was beautiful inside), I was in top form, caring about nothing, allowing my wineglass to be filled repeatedly. I didn't even feel too ashamed for not having brought a bottle myself—I told Ron I'd left it in the taxi. He waved away my apology with a flourish of his napkin.

I knew I was a hit, and I loved it. Suddenly I wondered why on earth I didn't get out more, why I had wasted yet another year for the sake of Vinnie's infrequent attentions.

The other guests were Clint, Ron's young boyfriend, who wrote screenplays and was an absolute sweetheart, and a couple named Maggie and Gus—she worked for Reuters and he was deputy program director for a London radio station called New World, which I never listened to. I apologized profusely for Vinnie's absence, and told them he had caught a nasty stomach bug from eating some dodgy shellfish, and had not been off the toilet for the past five hours. Wishful thinking.

Gus and Ron had been at university together. "Isn't she fabulous? Didn't I tell you she was awesome?" Ron kept saying to Gus about me, and Gus kept nodding, until Maggie looked quite annoyed and stabbed her fork into her *champignons farcies* with enough force to make Gus desist.

Over the course of the evening, in answer to their questions, I told them all about Blue Idea: what it had been like, how we got our first deal, how it felt to be in front of a crowd of thousands and thousands, what I missed about it, what I'd loathed about it. How I managed to remember it all so well.

I told them that I could remember most of the key events of my life through the songs that had been in the background, the "soundtrack to my life"; not Blue Idea songs, because so much work and sweat and tedium went into the perfecting of each of them, but other people's songs, the ones that struck me deep down, in a way I knew I'd never forget.

"I have a theory, right?" I said, elbows on the table, on my second glass of Beaume de Venise. "If I were a DJ, I would play the only records that had done that for other people, because if you think about it, it's rarely the completely crappy songs that people remember and weep over for years to come. My theory is: Say something totally momentous happens to you when you're listening to the radio—for example, you open a letter saying you've won a million pounds. If the particular record being played at that moment is, say, 'Agadoo,' then you just forget that you even had the radio switched on. But if it's something brilliant, maybe, 'Life on Mars,' then forever afterwards you associate that song with winning the money, and get all nostalgic when you hear it."

Ron joined in with Gus on the enthusiastic nods, and handed round the after-dinner mints.

I was on a roll. "So I reckon if you got people to ring in with the songs that meant something to them, then you'd have a fair chance of getting a decent show. Of course, you'd have a few morons saying that they lost their virginity to 'The Birdie Song,' or whatever but anyone who has that as their favorite song probably isn't articulate enough to ring into a radio station and request it. Because that's the other thing. . . ."

I quickly checked that everyone's eyes weren't completely glazed over, but they were all still agog.

"It wouldn't be enough to just make a request; I'd make them explain why the record meant so much to them. In detail. Right down to what color underwear they were wearing that night. If they couldn't remember exactly what was going on, then I wouldn't believe the record could be that important to them.

"Take today," I plunged on recklessly. "I was in the park, having a picnic with my best friend, Sam, when we saw"—at the last minute my sense of circumspection thankfully returned—"her boyfriend, kissing another woman."

Tuts and sighs rippled around the table.

"We were playing a tape at the time, a song that Sam hadn't heard for ages, and that she'd just told me she really loved."

"Which one?" interrupted Clint curiously.

"Sinead O'Connor, 'Nothing Compares 2 U,'" I said impatiently, wanting to get on with the story.

Clint swooned theatrically. "Oh, I just love that record, too. Her face on the video! Makes me want to cry just thinking about it."

"Yeah, yeah. So, anyway, I reckon that if Sam hadn't liked the song, she wouldn't even have known we'd been listening to music at the time. But since she did, I'd put money on the fact that forever more, when . . . Sam thinks of her lousy, two-timing *dickhead* of a boyfriend"—(I may have thumped the table at that point)—"she'll think of that song, and watching clouds, and eating quiche, and how prickly the grass felt, and she'll feel really, really sad and hurt and betrayed."

I was about to have to leave the room to go and splash cold water on my face, when Gus spoke. "How would you fancy a job on New World, as a DJ on the evening session?"

The salty tension that had been building inside the bridge of my nose suddenly disappeared.

"Pardon?" I asked, clutching the tablecloth. Now they were all nodding, like it was catching, and beaming moronically at me.

"We've got a slot opening up soon. I think you'd be perfect for it."

"But I don't know how to DJ," I burbled.

"Don't worry. You'll learn. We'll train you up before you start. The main thing is, your music knowledge is great, your name is already well-known, and you've got a great new idea for a show."

I was astounded. "I have?"

"Yes, definitely. A kind of confessional request show? I think it would be terrific. What do you say?"

After three seconds thinking about it, I finally joined in with the nodding. "Okay. Why not?"

THINKING ABOUT GOD AND TOBY

I LAY IN BED LATE ONE HUMID NIGHT, UNCOMFORTABLE ON A creased-up fusty sheet which I hadn't bothered to change for weeks, drowsy from the pill I had to take to make me sleep. I had taken off my eye patch and was tracing the stitched-up socket where my eye once was. The skin had healed, but it was twisted and velvety, like a stick-on scar, and the absence of my eyeball made the space feel concave and hollow. I marveled at how even I had kind of managed to become accustomed to being one-eyed: Like anything else, it was a process of adjustment. It was a bit like having contact lenses, really; you eventually just got used to fiddling about with sterilizing fluids and screw-top containers, intermittently blurred vision, and the ever-present fear of a lens popping out at an inopportune moment. Not that anything could pop out of that sealed-up space now, but the rigmarole of adjusting eye patches and being vigilant about not bumping into lampposts was vaguely comparable. Having to pay attention to one's vision instead of taking it for granted.

Even if I was getting used to it, though, it didn't prevent me from loathing and detesting the fact that my eye was gone. I wished fancifully that it would just *come back*, the way my mislaid hearing had. But it never would, and neither would Sam. Or Toby. It surprised me that I was still thinking about him, after the beery debacle, but I was—albeit with a lot more reservations and a lot fewer expectations.

It was two A.M., and despite the pill, I still couldn't get to sleep. I wondered if I ought to say a prayer, to ask for some sort of spiritual guidance and healing. What with my hour of need being at hand, and all.

But I couldn't do it. It somehow didn't seem to work anymore. It wasn't that I ever stopped believing in God; He just didn't seem to be around very much.

Perhaps I'd gotten too confused over the years. I had briefly dabbled in so many different esoteric and spiritual practices that the easy faith I'd gobbled up in high school had been usurped by something more . . . well, *cool*. It wasn't cool to think of God as a white-beardy man peering anxiously down at us from His cloud. God was a spark of pure light. God was an essence. God was all around us. God was inside me. God was an energy. I'd had so many different people tell me what God was, or wasn't, that I no longer knew what to think.

I wanted to ask Him to help me, only I didn't know to whom to address my inquiry. Angels didn't seem somehow senior enough, and Jesus seemed too busy. It was a dilemma. But, apropos the Plan, I didn't think God would kick me out if I suddenly turned up on the Other Side prematurely. Whether He was big or small, cloudy or solid, I was sure He would understand. That idea about suicides being eternally damned was a medieval concept; I'd read that somewhere. Besides, Blue Idea had given tons of cash to charity, surely that would stand me in good stead. . . . I might have a bit of extra karma to work off, like calories after Christmas, but it would be a small price to pay to see Sam again, and to not feel this emptiness anymore.

It was quite funny, really. I could still recite all twenty-six lines of the Creed, faultlessly. I knew how to chant Nam-myoho-renge-kyo until my voice turned into white noise. I could do the Yang Style Tai Chi Long Form and the yogic Sun Salutation. I'd wrapped myself in white robes and meditated in silence for hours, and been put in touch with my angels (right before they took early retirement, apparently).

The only thing I still didn't know how to do was to get anybody, or anything, to help me cope with what I was currently going through. When I thought about religion, I felt like a tourist trying to buy a 50p pencil sharpener in the Harrods sale while being shoved to the back of the queue by diplomats' wives waving Platinum Amex cards. Overlooked and invisible. I was in the right shop, but all the shop assistants were busy swiping credit cards, or else were standing about examining their fingernails and ignoring me.

I supposed I should have gone back to that therapist, the one who visited me in hospital—but therapy wasn't what I wanted. It was too rational, somehow, and I was afraid that I'd end up getting talked out of the Plan. End up calm but forgotten. No, no, that would be no good.

After I finally got to sleep, I dreamed about Salisbury Cathedral, and about Toby and Ruby. They were adjudicating a Great Continental Quilt Bob-Sleigh Race between two teams: me and Sam versus Vinnie and Sam's ex, Timothy. The event was being held in the cathedral close, on the long stretch of smooth gray path outside the west front.

Toby sat on a big throne in the cathedral doorway, wearing a bishop's miter, and Ruby sat on his right-hand side in a fetching sparkly crown. As we raced past them, I relived the feeling of thrilled fear I always got when Sam and I used to play there as kids: that all the stone saints and gargoyles looking down from their ledges and drains and corners could actually come tumbling off on top of me; that the whole towering stone facade could topple down and crush me at will. It was as much a sensation of respect as of fear, the power of the building pouring into and through me.

Sam and I beat Vinnie and Timothy to the finish line.

"Well done, you're the winners!" Ruby said graciously to us. "Here's your prizes. You"—pointing a magic wand at Sam—"get six mini-packets of M and Ms, and you"—pointing at me—"get a lifetime supply of being my mummy."

I was delighted.

I woke up freezing cold, with my duvet on the floor and a fresh pack of memories of the cathedral shuffling themselves around inside my head, sharp as knives, summoned by the dream. As I wrapped myself up in the chilly quilt, I turned the cards over in my head before me, one by one. I was surprised at how many there were. Even at eight or nine years old, Sam and I used to love going on guided tours up the cathedral tower, retracing the steps that the drunken shepherd must have taken before he made his maiden flight.

Memories of walking outside along the cathedral roof's base, knowing that its waterproof lead coverings heated up in summer and became soft to the touch of our small fingers, as though the roofs were all lagged with giant slabs of gray toffee.

Memories of looking up the tower, from the inside now, and seeing the crisscrossing scaffolding of thick oak rafters, jumbled together, the veins and supporting arteries of the spire, getting closer and tighter toward the top, a giant pyramidal bird's nest of twigs the thickness of a man's torso.

Memories of climbing from ground level up and up the tiny winding steps carved into the thickness of the walls, round and round until we felt dizzy, with vertigo and the joys of a secret hidden place.

Memories of daylight filtering into the narrow stairwells from arrow-slit windows, throwing weak dusty stripes of light on our faces.

That's odd, I thought. All those memories, and no accompanying song anywhere, not even the vague low chants of the cathedral choir singing matins. It felt like watching television with the sound turned down.

*✳ *

The other effect of my dream was that I couldn't stop thinking about Toby. If his friend Bill had been telling the truth, that Toby really was mad about me, then I owed it to him to see him just once more. I had retrieved from my car the receipt with his sister's address scrawled on it, and put it for safe keeping into the Hel-Sam box. The receipt was still scrunched into a ball about the size of a hazlenut—I was putting off unwrapping it until every other part of the Plan was ready.

Although I didn't know them very well, Toby and Ruby were going to be the hardest people to leave behind, because they represented the only part of my life that might possibly look to the future.

Ann Peebles

I CAN'T STAND THE RAIN

OUR TRIP TO SANTORINI ENDED UP BEING POSTPONED UNTIL THE following spring, not only because of my new career as a DJ, but also because Sam started feeling iller and iller. Within five months she'd had to leave her job and move back to the basement flat in Salisbury again. She got a part-time position in a local solicitors' office, but even that was a strain. Every time I talked to her she sounded more wheezy and exhausted. She qualified for a disabled parking sticker, started popping an array of Day-Glo tablets, and had to embark on a program of physiotherapy to try to clear her malfunctioning lungs.

I was worried sick. If it hadn't been for the job, I would have moved to Salisbury to be with her, but by that time I'd been promoted to the breakfast show, and had to get up at five o'clock every morning as it was. Commuting, even in my new 5-series BMW, would have been a nightmare. Instead I sped down to see her as often as I could on weekends, taking her tapes of my best shows from the previous week and entertaining her with stories of who I'd met, how the New World ratings were going up, what songs I had played and for whom.

* * *

I did believe that I had dumped Vinnie for good, but somehow, when he turned up on my doorstep again a few weeks later, wheedling me with stolen roses and come-to-bed eyes, telling me that I was the only one he'd ever really loved—well, I just couldn't resist him. I made it clear that I'd never trust him again, but strangely that didn't seem to worry him in the slightest.

He had moved out of the house with Miyuki ("Been thrown out, more likely," Sam said) and was staying with another "friend" until he "found his feet" ("Tell him that they're on the ends of his legs," suggested Sam wheezily). I immediately realised that he was angling to move in with me, and to my boundless relief, I stayed strong enough to refuse permission. If it hadn't been for the memory of him and Miyuki rolling around in the park, Vinnie would have had his misplaced feet planted firmly underneath my table—at least that was something for which to be thankful. We contented ourselves with frequent sex and no questions asked. When I thought too deeply about it, it broke my heart, but I was too busy with New World and Sam to allow myself to take it too seriously.

* * *

By spring of the following year, I felt established enough at New World to risk taking a week off. I had spotted nine HELENA LET ME TELL LONDON MY SONG bumper stickers on my way home from the show that morning, plus I'd just had a very complimentary review in the media section of *The Independent*. Sam wasn't getting better, but she was no worse either, and we both really needed some sun and a change of scenery.

"Come on, then," I said to her on the phone. "Pack your bikini, we're off on vacation. I'll drive down and collect you on Wednesday morning. Be ready by ten."

At ten-thirty the following Wednesday, Sam and I were heading back up to Heathrow Airport to catch an afternoon flight to Santorini. My car was full of things to maximize Sam's comfort: cushions to support her bony ass on the plane; a borrowed hospital wheelchair to help conserve her limited energy; enough medication to start a small pharmacy; her own feather pillows. I wondered how she had suddenly managed to turn into an invalid, and it made my throat swell with sorrow.

It was a beautiful April day, and we decided to take the scenic route to the airport. Being on tour, all those years of bleak American highways, always made me so thirsty for the English countryside. I drank in every bright yellow acre of rape, the green of the patchwork fields, the arches of tree branches overhanging the smooth arrow-straight roads.

Sam was uncharacteristically quiet for most of the drive. At one point she switched on the radio, tuning it to Radio One just as the DJ announced, *"Next up, that classic song that stormed the charts six years ago—seems like only yesterday—the fabulous Blue Idea, with 'Take Me Away'. . ."* I laughed and cringed a little as the synth intro started up, joined by my bass and then Justin's high-pitched voice, as familiar as my own skin.

"Turn it off, turn it off!" I cried. "Radio One is banned from this car!"

Sam refused. "Don't be a spoilsport! You know New World doesn't reach out to the sticks." She cracked a smile for the first time that day. "It's funny, but I still get such a thrill when I hear you on the radio or see you on TV—even after all these years, I still want to yell out to everyone, 'Hey, that's my best friend!'"

And even after all those years, I was still pleased.

After a couple of miles speeding along a deserted Roman road, littered with the tiny corpses of squirrel, pheasant, and rabbit, the Blue Idea song finished and was replaced by a dreary interview with a techno band. I clicked off the radio again and slid my Ann Peebles CD into the CD player, to listen to the title track: "I Can't Stand the Rain." I was humbled by how far superior that song was to ours: her creamy vocals, the pounding rhythm, and the passion of the incredible Memphis Horns. It made "Take Me Away" sound like a weedy little preprogrammed tune on a cheap Bontempi organ. Sex versus impotence. Scotch on the rocks versus orange squash through a straw.

I sang along, but Sam was silent again. I sensed something brewing in her, and waited for her to tell me about it.

We barreled through yet another tiny picturesque village, this one with a quirky little square church tower peeping over the rooftops, pinnacles on only three of its four top corners.

Sam finally spoke. "There's something I need to tell you."

She turned down the volume on the CD.

"I thought so. What is it?"

There was a brief pause over the top of the muted Memphis Horns.

"I didn't say anything to you before, but I saw my specialist at the hospital yesterday. My lungs aren't ever going to get better on their own. In fact, they're packing up. He says I'm going to need a lung transplant."

I got a funny swimmy feeling in my head and had to grip the steering wheel hard. All I could think of to say was, "When?"

"Whenever I decide to go on the waiting list, and then as soon as they find a donor. That could be three days or three years."

The swimmy feeling turned into a sick feeling. "One lung or two?" I asked, as if I were at some surreal organ-donors' tea party.

Sam laughed, catching my thought, but she had tears in her eyes. "Just one should do the trick."

I didn't want to ask—but I couldn't *not* ask. "What are the success rates like for this . . . kind of thing?"

"If you mean what are my chances, the survival rate is about forty percent in the first year."

This figure whirled around my brain for a while in a useless way, not sticking anywhere, like the algebraic formulas we had to do in school. I didn't understand what it meant, and that time I didn't ask. It didn't sound at all promising to me.

"But do you have to do it?" I was almost pleading.

"No, not immediately. But I should do it before I get too weak to cope with the operation. If I don't have it done eventually, I will probably die."

She sounded so calm, but also slightly numb, as if it hadn't sunk in yet. Her last statement shocked me even more—I knew it wasn't good, but I hadn't realized her health had gotten *that* bad. I suppose I hadn't wanted to realize.

We were out of the village, but suddenly the countryside looked drab and uninteresting. I pulled the car into a lay-by, buried my face in my hands, and burst into tears.

"Oh, don't, please," Sam said, "you'll start me off."

But she didn't cry. She stroked my shoulder as if it was my life under threat, and then pulled out a packet of fruit Polos, offering me one. "Go on, it's red, your favorite."

I took the Polo but I couldn't look at her. It was too painful to think that something might go wrong and I'd never see her again. The sharp sweetness of the Polo hit the back of my tongue, and I clung to the taste as if someone had thrown it to me, a mini red life belt.

I tried hard to think of what I'd learned over the years, in my various flirtations with different sorts of spirituality: Christianity, Buddhism, Transcendental Meditation—they all said the same thing, that the soul was eternal, and death of the body meant nothing, not in the grand scheme of things. But not Sam's body! Sam's body had *Sam* inside it!

Cars whizzed intermittently past us in a whining crescendo of painted metal and engine noise, the wake of their momentum making my BMW rock slightly.

Sam leaned her head on my shoulder. "Listen, Helena, I'm not going to go on the list just yet. I'm going to think about it for a while and then decide. In the meantime I really want to enjoy this holiday, okay?"

"Okay." I blew my nose and after a minute we drove off again. I still felt stunned but I tried to be optimistic, to look at it as a piece of good news.

"Just think what you'll be able to do with a new lung—run, swim, shop. It'll change your life totally. I'll make you get up early with me and help me with the show—in fact, why don't you come and live in my house with me?"

"I hate getting up early. And thanks for the offer, but there's no way I'm moving in with you if Vinnie's still on the scene," said Sam grumpily, taking advantage of my vulnerability.

"Then he's history, definitely this time. I would happily never see him again, for you to be better, and close by. Oh God, Sam, it would be so wonderful to have you back to your old self."

Sam sighed. "What is my old self? I really can't remember."

* * *

It was late that evening when we finally got settled in our apartment in Santorini, which was basically a luxuriously furnished cave, carved from the side of the cliff. Even in the dusk we could tell that it was utterly beautiful, but it was also probably the world's most un-wheelchair-friendly place. There was a short but very windy walk up steps and round corners from the road to the apartment, so I left

Sam and her wheelchair waiting in the car while I puffed up and down the path with all our stuff. When I'd finished I was sweating like a cart horse, and worried that it might finish me off altogether to have to give Sam a piggyback, but thankfully she was able to walk unassisted. She collapsed peakily on one of the beds as soon as we made it through the door.

"Why didn't you rent an apartment that we needed to abseil down to? At least that might have been less tiring to reach."

She wasn't cross, just being sarky, but I still felt stricken.

"I'm sorry, Sam, really. The brochure made out that it was just by the road. I had no idea."

"Oh, don't worry. It's just nice to be here. Let's sleep on it, so I've got the energy to face some retsina and sunshine tomorrow."

* ✳ *

We did very little that holiday, except lie on our begonia-bright terrace, gawping at the stunning view around the dramatic horseshoe-shaped cliffs and over the black volcanic island. Sunset was our favorite time. We sat companionably in our deck chairs in the charged silence, as the massive sky before us changed into every outlandish shade of red we could imagine. The volcano got blacker, the clouds pinker, and finally the sun slunk down in a blaze of orange into the dark Aegean waters of the caldera. It was so far away from everything: perfidious boyfriends, the sound of my voice echoing out of cafés and cabs and offices all across London, scarred lungs. To both of our delight, Sam felt better that week than she had for a long time.

"It's all the negative ions in the air from the volcano," I informed her one evening when we were out for a "walk" (I was pushing Sam in her wheelchair). "Apparently the health benefits are well documented. It says so in the guidebook."

"Wish we could stay for longer," she said wistfully as I propelled her chair with difficulty up the steep and ill-kept road, struggling womanfully until we got to the brow of the hill.

"Me, too. But I tell you what: Healthy, it might be; flat, it ain't," I puffed, before deciding that perhaps we shouldn't go down the other side, as I might not be able to control the speed of our descent.

I laughed out loud as something occurred to me. "Hey, Sam, this reminds me of the Great Continental Quilt Bob-Sleigh Race—you know, heaving like mad to get into position, then losing all control on the corners and down the stairs—we nearly killed ourselves!"

"Oh God, yes! I used to be so terrified when you were dragging the quilt, but I couldn't get enough of it. Hey, how about a quick turn down the hill now? I'll sit on your lap in the chair!"

I started protesting, horrified at the thought, until I saw she was laughing. I gave her a friendly slap on the shoulder, and we looked out at the beautiful view of the sun shimmering across the flat turquoise sea instead, an act much more befitting our age and status.

* * *

Later that evening, both of us glowing pink from the day's sunshine, we were polishing off a bottle of retsina and flicking olive stones off the balcony wall in the hopes of starting our own cliffside olive grove.

"We need more wine, and some music." I jumped up and ran to fetch a CD and a fresh bottle. "I want to hear Ann Peebles again."

I came back out with my Discman, setting it on the wall next to us and inserting the CD. The introduction to "I Can't Stand the Rain" quivered, somewhat more tinnily than from my deluxe car stereo, out of the tiny little Discman speakers, filling the ionized air around us.

"John Lennon thought this was one of the greatest songs ever," I started to say, but about halfway through the sentence, my voice stuck and unexpected tears flooded my eyes.

"What's the matter?" Sam asked with alarm.

I shook my head and gesticulated at the Discman. I found that I had just proved my own theory of music and memory. "I forgot we'd been listening to this song when you told me about your lung transplant."

I knew at that point that forever more when I heard Willie Mitchell's orchestrated drum "raindrops" at the start of that song, I would relive the feeling of driving through a Hampshire village with the trees in bud, and Sam telling me that she had to have a life-threatening operation.

We sat listening to the track in silence, holding hands, me dripping tears all over the begonias. It was such an instinctive reaction: "I Can't Stand the Rain" equaled tears.

Eventually Sam opened the new bottle of retsina. "Come on, get some more of this down you. Let's enjoy life while we can, eh? Nobody else can do it for us. It's too short to waste."

I nodded, held out my glass, and swiped my hand over my face.

"I tell you what, Helena," she added. "You don't half cry a lot, for an international pop star." She grinned at me.

I gulped down half the contents of my glass. I wasn't sure whether I was quite ready to be teased or not, but the strong bite of the retsina reassured me that perhaps I was.

"Hey, you know me." I managed to grin back. "Some people have weak bladders; I have weak tear ducts. It's a quirk of nature, that's all. Top me up again, would you?"

Sam obliged, and this time we clinked glasses in a toast.

"To enjoying life."

* ✳ *

My other enduring memory from Santorini came on a day when Sam had been feeling a little tired and had decided not to venture off our terrace. I had set off alone, to find a swimming spot I'd heard about right at the bottom of the cliffs at the highest point of the island.

I wound my way down three-hundred-odd shallow and uneven steps, overtaken constantly by knock-kneed donkeys bowing under the weight of lazy tourists, to sea level, past a neat little seafront bar and round a corner. Here the path petered out, and I had to clamber over heaps of jagged rocks to a small secluded place where a group of locals and a few tourists in the know were sunbathing and diving off a selection of bigger, flatter rocks.

About twenty feet out into the sea was a tiny, tiny island—less an island, really, than one huge stone jutting out of the water. Perched on the side of it facing the volcano was a stone shrine, simple but beautiful in the way that rural Greek architecture always was, merely an arch with a bell, a small altar, and steps leading from a crude stone mooring place. I thought it was a shrine to the Virgin Mary, but I couldn't clearly remember.

What I did recall, though, was swimming out alone round the
island to where the sea suddenly became deeper than I could possibly have imagined. This was where the volcano had blown out the
center of the main island, sometime during the second millennium
B.C. When I dived down even a few feet, the water became much,
much colder and darker, and it frightened me. Suddenly I experienced a sensation of unutterable loneliness. It was as though I
could feel the sadness of Santorini's Bronze Age inhabitants as
what they must surely have dreaded came to pass: In a vast evil
plume of molten lava their beautiful civilization was buried, frozen
forever in time. What was not blown up or covered in many feet of
pumice was flooded out by the sea, which had rushed in to fill up
the vacuum left by the subsequent collapse of the volcano's magma
chamber.

In the silence of the water's depth I felt the grief of a lost people,
perhaps even the mighty Atlantean race; this could conceivably
have been the furthest Western tip of Atlantis. The air was so
vibrant there that anything seemed possible.

But being under the water was too frightening, too much like
death, and I shot back up to the surface to where I could once
more hear my breath and feel the hot sun warm my chilled face.
Seagulls wheeled reassuringly around my head, and I de-misted
and replaced my goggles before turning to swim back to the shore,
unable to shake the feeling that something might grab at my legs
from the ineffable depths. As I'd struck out for the rocks at a brisk
crawl, my face alternately in the water and to the side for air, something caught my attention and I stopped. Just ahead of me a sharp
ray of sun had pierced the water's surface and was shooting down
through the blackness, lighting it like a laser beam. I put my face
back down in the sea and stared at it underwater.

It was unspeakably beautiful. For the first fifteen feet or so,
where the water was still light, it made an effervescing cauldron of
blue-green with sparkling white speckles; intense, but the subtlest
thing I'd ever seen. Then as the water got darker it ceased to have
that transformative effect, but the ray itself kept penetrating as
strongly as ever. I followed it with my eyes as far as I could, which
appeared to be to the very center of the earth. Its pull on me was so

pure, so forceful that I could almost feel myself being sucked down, compelled to go with it. I *wanted* to go with it. At that moment I believed that never in my life had I felt so much joy, or so much peace. The black water was no longer threatening. It was a part of me.

It's okay to trust life, it seemed to tell me. Take it, it's yours. Don't waste it.

Sam was right, I thought, coming back up for air. It was all up to us, as individuals. I was the only one who could make my life truly worthwhile, to find the value in what I had been given. I supposed I'd spent so many years being dependent on others for my success and happiness: our fans, Sam, Vinnie, even Ringside and Mickey, and now New World. It was time to be more self-sufficient. It was time to be myself.

"I LIKE STINGS"

SEEING CRYSTAL LASERS IN THE SEA AND BELIEVING EVERYTHING would be all right was all well and good. But nothing was all right, was it? Sam was dead. Vinnie had betrayed me. I'd lost my eye and my job. The only person I felt remotely like seeing, apart from Sam, was Toby, but there hadn't been a peep out of him since the riverside debacle.

Admittedly, he didn't have my address or phone number, and he *had* been hanging round Richmond on the off-chance of seeing me—but that was pretty lame, as far as I was concerned. He could have found out that Ron was my agent easily enough, and contacted me that way. For the sake of my dedication to the Plan, therefore, I persuaded myself that, in the cold light of day he'd probably decided that he wasn't interested after all. It could never have worked out between us, not with all our respective baggage. But I still wanted to see him once more, even if just to say good-bye.

The manuscript was nearly finished, with just a couple more chapters to go, and I felt ready to tie up a few loose ends.

I was going to give Ruby the Hel-Sam box.

* * *

I drove slowly through Fulham, peering at the street names until I found Larchfield Road. For some reason I had been expecting number twenty-seven to be a sizable period house, not this narrow-shouldered anemic cottage, sandwiched like an apology between two similar ones.

I parked, badly, a little way up the street, behind a large white van into whose bumper I reversed. Since losing my eye, my previously pristine BMW was acquiring more knocks and scratches than a toddler's knees. Still, who cared? I wasn't going to get sentimental about the bloody car.

I gathered up the Hel-Sam box, locked the car, and headed for the pale cottage, trying very hard to swallow down a bubble of excitement at seeing Toby again, despite the inauspicious circumstances of our last encounter. I'd have telephoned first, but there'd been so many creases in the balled-up receipt when I'd finally picked it up from the floor of the car and straightened it out that the scribbled phone number was illegible. I had only just managed to decipher the address.

It was a strange feeling, being excited and suicidal. I hated using the word *suicidal* but decided that it was about time I started to. It was a step toward making the Plan more than just typed words on a page and a playlist.

Another step was this meeting. I banged the door-knocker twice, with a briskness that I didn't feel inside, and waited to see Toby's familiar smile.

The door opened. A woman stood there, my age, with Toby's eyes but a more angular face. She had a pierced eyebrow and the Middleton curls, only hers were dark brown.

"Are you Lulu?" I stuck out my hand to be shaken. "I'm a friend of Toby's. Is he still living here? I'd have called, but you're ex-Directory." Nerves made me sound aggressive.

Lulu shook my hand, more of a twitch really, and stared at me. "You're Helena Nicholls." I couldn't tell if this was a good thing or a bad thing.

"Yeah."

Lulu blushed suddenly, and I realized that she wasn't being unfriendly, but was phased by my sudden and unannounced appearance at her house. "I'm sorry. Toby is still staying here, but he's away on business tonight. He had to go and meet a client in Dublin."

"Oh." I'd timed the visit for early evening with the assumption that Toby would have finished work, but I'd never considered that he might be away. I was such an idiot. "Sorry to bother you, Lulu. I shouldn't have just turned up. Actually, I brought something for Toby to give Ruby. Can I leave it with you?"

We both looked down at the battered old hat box in my arms. Lulu's expression read, *And you want to give that to Ruby why?* I resisted the temptation to tell her that this was my last true link with Sam. My last true link with life.

"Ruby's here, though," Lulu continued. "She's just getting ready for bed. Why don't you come in and give it to her yourself?"

I tried and failed to smile, allowing Lulu to usher me into an open-plan living room. I was clutching the Hel-Sam box tightly against my abdomen, its curves comforting me. When I released it there were speckles of glitter on my hands and down the front of my sweater, and grief made my head spin.

"Cool house," I managed eventually, looking around. It was much more spacious inside than its exterior suggested, and beautifully decorated in muted earthy shades. There was nothing extraneous, no clutter. Sting's voice drifted out of two state-of-the-art hanging egg-shaped speakers. A staircase rose from the middle of the room, stairs carpeted with a nubbly cream sisal carpet. "It's hard to believe you have a small child staying with you."

Lulu grinned. "I've just tidied up. "She indicated a closed cupboard door with a jerk of her head. "She's going home tomorrow, and I'll miss her—but I'm looking forward to having my social life back again. Would you like a drink? I was about to open a bottle of wine."

"Thanks, I'd love one."

Lulu headed toward the kitchen, stopping en route at the foot of the stairs. "Ruuuu-by! Can you come downstairs, please? You've got a visitor!" She turned back to me. "Make yourself at home. I'll just go and get Ruby's milk, and the wine. Back in a second."

"I cleaned my teeth," said a small voice from the top of the stairs.

I walked over to the staircase and looked up. Ruby was sitting on the top step, a white tidemark of diluted toothpaste crusting around her mouth. Her hair had corkscrewed into a whole new layer of curls, and even her feet looked bigger. I was overjoyed to see her. "I can see that you did. Aren't you clever? Will you come down and talk to me?"

Ruby bumped slowly down, step by step, on her bottom, until she was sitting at my feet. She was wearing red Teletubby slippers and a yellow hooded dressing gown over powder blue flowery pajamas, a small riot of color against the pale carpet. I wanted to hug her but thought it might scare her. Instead I crouched down and sat on the step next to her.

"Do you remember me, Ruby? From the hospital?"

"Mmm, you're the pirate," she said, gazing at my eye patch. "Where's your eyebrow gone?"

I usually shaded in the few sparse hairs remaining with a brown eyebrow pencil, but I had forgotten that day, what with all the tension of planning the visit.

"Um, it sort of got lost in my accident." I glanced toward the kitchen in the hope that Lulu wasn't following the exchange. I didn't like to draw attention to my missing body parts.

"Never mind, I get my daddy to buy you a new one." Ruby patted my shoulder in consolation. "A black one," she added firmly.

Lulu, laughing, came back into the room with two glasses of wine and a beaker of milk, which she handed to Ruby. She had obviously overheard the conversation. "It doesn't work like that, Rubes. Helena isn't Mr. Potato Head, you know."

Lulu mistook my frown for incomprehension. "He's a character from *Toy Story*. Ruby's got the toy, and all his bits come off—you know, ears and eyebrows and stuff. . . ." Wisely, she tailed off before she dug herself any deeper, but it was too late.

"I know who Mr. Potato Head is," I said, frostily, and Lulu blushed.

She changed the subject, wiping the chalky ring from around Ruby's mouth with a spit-dampened thumb. "Why did you clean your teeth already, Rubes? You'll only have to do it again after your milk."

Ruby sucked at the bottle. "Because I cleaned my teeth," she said. Then she cocked an ear toward the nearest eggy speaker. "What's this music?"

"It's Sting," said Lulu.

"I *like* Stings," Ruby announced mournfully, shaking her head.

Lulu laughed again. "That means she *doesn't* like Sting. It's all in the intonation."

I smiled, deciding after all that it would be churlish to hold the potato-head comment against anyone. Life was too short. "Her language has improved so much—I can't believe it. She doesn't even lisp anymore! It's like she's a whole new person, in just a few months. How old is she now?"

Ruby drew herself haughtily up to her full height of almost three feet. "I not a new person. I Ruby Tabitha Middleton. I'm twoana-harf."

"Going on fifteen . . . Helena's brought you something, Ruby Tabitha. Why don't we all go and sit down, so she can show it to you?" Lulu passed me a glass of wine and steered us both over to an immense cream sofa, Ruby jumping up and down on the way.

"Present! Present! It's my birthday!"

"No, it isn't your birthday. Now calm down, please. It's bedtime in a minute, and I don't want you getting overexcited."

"Sorry," I said to Lulu. "I shouldn't have come at such a bad time. Actually, I didn't think she'd go to bed so early. Not having kids, I don't really get how these things work. . . ."

Lulu grimaced. "Don't worry. It's fine. No, *calm down*, Ruby. You'll knock over someone's glass in a minute."

I lifted Ruby onto my knee. For a second she looked as though she wanted to squirm off, until she remembered that a gift was soon to be forthcoming, and stayed put, drinking her milk and leaning expectantly against me. She was heavy, a great plump bundle of yellow terry cloth and smooth pink skin, more like an oversized baby than a little girl. Her hair smelled delicious, of poppies and warm towels and baby soap, and for a second I couldn't speak. I had an overwhelming urge to touch her soft skin. The baby I'd never have. I gently squeezed one of her bare chubby calves, feeling it give and mold squashily to my hand. Why was it the beautiful minutiae of life that made it so hard to leave: the downy blond hairs on Ruby's shin, a dog-eared collection of teenage sentiment in a box?

"Ruby." I turned her gently around so we were face-to-face again. "This present is something very special. In fact, it's my favorite thing in the world because it reminds me of a very old friend, and, you know, the best presents are the things that we love most ourselves."

Ruby nodded, dropping the now-empty beaker onto the sofa, and Lulu sipped her wine, looking embarrassed. I saw her gaze longingly at a magazine lying on the coffee table. Fortuitiously for her, a telephone rang at the far end of the room, and she leapt up to answer it, slopping a little white wine on the table in her haste to escape this strange display of sentiment.

"That's probably Toby, ringing to say good night to Ruby."

"My daddy," said Ruby to me, lifting up her head. I tried to eavesdrop on the conversation, but Ruby continued to chat to me and I couldn't. "Daddy come back 'morrow, and we go to live with Mummy again."

I started, and a small strange noise came from the back of my throat.

"Got hiccups?" asked Ruby blithely.

"With Daddy? You're all going to live together again?"

Ruby nodded vigorously. "Yeah, my daddy and my mummy and me. I got all my toys there too, an'—"

"Ruby! Daddy wants to say good night!" Lulu called, holding out the receiver. Ruby slid off my lap and ran to the telephone. "Toby wants to talk to you, too," she added.

I stood up miserably and trailed over to join the queue for the telephone. After Ruby's revelation, Toby was the last person on earth I wanted to speak to, but I could hardly refuse.

"Na-night, Daddy. Any fireworks, any scaries?" Reassured, Ruby made kissing noises. "I shout you in the morning, yeah?"

Lulu pried the receiver out of Ruby's hand and passed it to me. "I'll just take Ruby up to clean her teeth again, and then we'll come and say good night," she whispered to me.

I nodded. "Hi," I said blankly into the phone.

"Helena! God, I'm so gutted I'm not there! I mean, I'm so glad you're there! I've been going mad trying to track you down—you will leave your number with Lulu, won't you?"

There was an embarrassed pause, which I felt physically, a small dropping sensation in the pit of my stomach. This was all a mess. I was tired of everything, too tired to challenge Toby on his hypocrisy at wanting my number if he was about to get back with Kate, too miserable that once again my timing was up the spout. . . .

But hold on, I told myself: It was entirely academic whether or not he got back with Kate. It made no difference to me, nor was it the reason I was there, in Lulu's front room, surrounded by bronze buddhas and artfully arranged piles of smooth stones. My sense of perspective was, as usual, twisting away from me. I should be happy that at least one of us had a future.

"You were a good friend to me in hospital," I blurted, unable to think of anything else to say.

"Not more than that?" Toby asked, hopefully.

Another pause. "Under the circumstances, I think not," I said, not elaborating on which specific circumstances: Toby's marriage, my bereavement, our joint vulnerability.

"Oh." His disappointment swelled into my head, as palpable as the crackling from his mobile phone. "Is everything okay, Helena? You sound a bit . . . strange."

I tried to close the lid on my disappointment and frustration, imagining it as an overstuffed suitcase that needed to be sat on before being zipped up. Toby had been a good friend and a good listener. I didn't want his final impression of me to be of an obstreperous old harridan yet again giving him a hard time. What we both did with our lives was entirely our own business.

"I'm fine. I'm sorry if I sound a bit off. I guess I'm just disappointed not to see you." I rushed on, before he could suggest another meeting. "Actually, I came over to give something to Ruby. I've been thinking a lot about . . . her, and, you know, now that I've recovered and I'm about to start work again, I figured that it might be a nice gesture to pass something of mine on to her. It might seem a little weird to you, but I really want her to have the box of letters and bits and pieces that Sam and I first started keeping as kids. There's quite a lot of mementos of the band in there, old fanzines and photos, that kind of thing, as well as the letters."

Another pause, but this time a reverential one. "Are you sure, Helena? That's . . . that's just an incredible gift! Why do you want to get rid of it? I mean, those are memories of Sam. Surely you want to keep them?"

"No," I said firmly. "Actually, I really don't. I've spent far too long dwelling on them. I need to move on, stop living in the past. I would be honored if you'd accept it, on Ruby's behalf. If you could just keep it for her until she's old enough to decide what she wants to do with it. Maybe people can come to her when they need to do research on the early days of Blue Idea, or whatever. I don't know."

"Why wouldn't people come to you if they need to do research on Blue Idea?"

I hesitated, feeling caught out. "Yeah, of course they would, and do. I'm talking ten, twenty years down the line here—you never know, maybe there'll be a huge Blue Idea revival in 2020, and who knows where I'll be then? I just thought it might be something Ruby would like to have, one day."

Toby still seemed overcome. "What can I say? Thanks, Helena. This is the most amazing present Ruby will ever receive. I promise we'll take care of it for you."

Ruby and Lulu came back downstairs, and Lulu hid the Hel-Sam box behind a large cushion before Ruby saw it.

"Just one more thing, Toby. Can I trust you not to look in it yourself? I mean, of course you can one day, but . . . not just yet, eh?"

"I promise that, too. Ruby should be the one to open it, when she's old enough."

"Thanks. Listen, I'd better go. Ruby's off to bed now. We'll be in touch, okay?"

Toby started gabbling. "I'll be back tomorrow, leave your number, I'll ring you then. Why don't we go out next week? Just as friends, of course, but I'd love to see you—"

"Bye, Toby." I put the phone down, sick at heart. *Have a nice life. I wish things could have been different. . . .*

Ruby was sitting on the floor by the sofa, one of Lulu's feet in her lap. When I came back over to join them, I heard her say, "I'm the lady, you be the man. I wash your feet, yeah?"

"Bit young for a Mary Magdalene complex, isn't she?" I said to Lulu, relying on flippancy to push down my anguish.

"Yeah. I keep telling her that she should stop reading that Bible so much," Lulu agreed, and I managed a laugh. For a second we exchanged a look that said, loud and clear, we could be friends.

Ruby stopped pretending to anoint Lulu's foot with tears and dumped it unceremoniously back on the floor. "Where's my present?"

"Oh, yes. We got interrupted by your daddy on the phone. Oh, Ruby, I hope you won't be too disappointed. It's only an old box full

of letters and stuff, but one day I hope that you'll enjoy looking
through it and owning it." I retrieved the Hel-Sam box from behind
the sofa cushion and put it on the floor in front of her.

Lulu squinted at the faded label and smiled, reading it out loud:
"'The Hel-Sam Box of Important Stuff! Keep Out! Unless you are
Helena Jane Nicholls Or Samantha Grant! In the event of the
untimely death of either of us, this box is to go immediately to the
other one's house and stay there. No one else is ever, ever, allowed
to look inside. It's all Top Secret.' So how come it's not at Samantha
Grant's house, then?" As soon as she'd said it, she bit her lip, and I
realized that Toby must have told her about me and Sam.

I grinned faintly and painfully, through gritted teeth.

"I'm sorry," said Lulu.

"It's okay. Don't worry. I hope you don't think it's weird, but I
want Ruby to have it."

Ruby was tugging at the lid of the box. "Are there sweeties
inside?"

"No, darling," said Lulu.

"How 'bout *Toy Story* video, then?"

We shook our heads sadly.

"What, then?"

Lulu put an arm around her. "Sweetheart, it's just a special box
for you to keep for when you're older. It's a bit hard to explain for
now, but it's really a very special present. Say thank you to Helena."

Ruby stuck out her bottom lip and rubbed her eyes. "I like special box," she whined.

I wished I'd had the foresight to bring her some chocolate buttons as well.

Lulu picked her up. "Okay, tired girl, now it really is bedtime. Say
good night and thank you to Helena." She leaned toward me so
Ruby could give me a kiss, and for a brief intoxicating moment
Ruby nuzzled in the side of my neck, her hair tickling my cheek.

"Tanks, Ellna. Any fireworks, any scaries?"

I glanced at Lulu for the answer, and she shook her head. "No,
Ruby. No fireworks, no scaries. Sleep well, sweet dreams."

Ruby waved at me as she was carried up the stairs, finger in
mouth, her head already drooping on Lulu's shoulder.

* * *

By the time Lulu returned several minutes later, I had regained my composure. She offered me another glass of wine, some supper, a coffee, but I declined. We did chat for a while longer, and again I marveled at what easy company she was, but it felt like a snare. The Middleton way of drawing me into their family so I wouldn't want to leave—God, they all did it! If I stayed any longer, I'd be tempted to ask about Toby and Kate—if it was true that they really were getting back together—but I was desperate not to. It would be so demeaning, and the truth was that I simply didn't need to know.

"I've taken up enough of your time already." I stood up. "I really have to go now. I've got tons of things to do."

This was true. I had to start thinking about getting my affairs in order: canceling my next outpatient checkup at the hospital, the smear test I had booked for October, all my standing orders.

At least Toby and Ruby had been dealt with, anyhow. I expected to feel less guilty, now that I'd closed the book on that episode, but to my horror the guilt merely transferred itself to thoughts of my parents instead, which was far worse. I felt like the biggest, yellowest coward that ever lived.

But as I said good-bye to Lulu and left the house, I changed my mind. I wasn't a coward. It was surely more courageous to end a worthless life than to live in misery. Anyone who truly loved me would have to understand that.

THIS IS A LOW

WITHIN SIX MONTHS OF OUR RETURN FROM SANTORINI, SAM'S health had deteriorated even more dramatically. She couldn't walk more than a few steps without getting exhausted and breathless, and had to have constant recourse to an oxygen mask and cylinder. Her need for a new lung finally became extremely pressing—it was no longer a matter of choice. She agreed to go on the waiting list, so the hospital gave her a pager, and she was on twenty-four-hour standby for a call to say that a donor lung had been located.

I still went down to Salisbury every weekend, and spoke to her on the phone every day. I'd have stayed down there permanently were it not for the fact that I had to do my show. My heart was torn to see her getting thinner and weaker every week.

On my last visit, she was just sitting hunched on her sofa, gray-faced and skeletal, with the oxygen tube now permanently fixed to her nostrils, a slave to the heavy metal tank next to her. She looked so sad and ill that all I could do was sit next to her and hold her in my arms like a child, rocking her gently against my shoulder. I couldn't stop tears from rolling down my face, and she frowned at me faintly.

"Crybaby," she whispered. Then she wrapped her arms around my waist, sighing heavily. She was so thin that I could feel all the bones in her shoulders and back as I rubbed them gently with my hand.

Everything in her little flat was as bright and cheerful as ever: the crisp blue and white stripes of the sofa, the pictures on the wall, the thick, colorful rug on the floor. I always used to think how well she fitted this little basement. Like dogs who resembled their owners, Sam's flat was the essence of herself, full of light and color and energy. Now she looked incongruous in her own place, almost inappropriate, like a gray vase full of wilting flowers in the middle of a florist's shop, surrounded by a riot of fresh-colored blooms. I couldn't bear it.

I tried to push the image away, and talked to her in a low voice about how wonderful things would be once she'd had the operation, reminding her again of all the things she would be able to do and see once more. How she'd have to lose the disabled sticker on her windscreen, and take her chances with the city's traffic wardens like the rest of us. How she could come to gigs with me, and we could stay out till four in the morning, if we wanted. We'd live together, and cook, and try finally to bag ourselves a couple of decent blokes.

Sam just leaned against me and listened until I ran out of steam. Then we sat, in an undeniably depressed silence broken only by the soft hissing of oxygen from the cylinder into her poor, useless lungs.

Finally she fell asleep, and I maneuvered her into a horizontal position on the sofa, lifting up her feet and swinging them gently around and up onto the cushions. I covered her with a quilt, kissed her forehead, and crept upstairs to tell Cynthia that I was leaving.

When I climbed into my car, inhaling its faint plastic and air-freshener smell, I was overcome with a feeling—empathic, perhaps—of utter exhaustion and desolation. I leaned back and closed my eyes, trying to fight away the emotions of frustration and grief at seeing Sam that way and not being able to help her. I would willingly have donated one of my lungs to her then and there—both, if it were possible—and I cursed the fact that she didn't need an organ I had spares of. For the first time ever I really thought that she might die, and the sensation overwhelmed me with pain.

Then suddenly, out of nowhere, the fog in my head lifted and all my senses sharpened up completely. Everything around me felt hyper-real, and I experienced a huge rush of adrenaline. The leaves on the tall trees across the road became a green so deep that they took my breath away. I sat bolt upright, surprised and stunned by this emotional transformation. Into the empty palette of my focused mind sprang five distinct words: *She's going to be fine.* They stayed there, so clear that I could almost read them in bold black letters, for several seconds, until my grief was replaced by euphoria. I almost rushed back into the house to tell Sam and Cynthia, but changed my mind when I realized that I didn't want either of them to think I'd ever doubted it. Instead, I drove back to London feeling a deep sense of calm, and a cautious joy.

* ✳ *

One freezing November day a couple of weeks later, for want of anything better to do, I was cleaning the outside of my bathroom window with balled-up newspapers (the cleaner, who didn't speak English, had indicated via a sketched window with a big X through it that this was a task she declined to incorporate in her routine; I'd felt that it was time to do something about it, since there were ribbons of bird crap festooning the panes, courtesy of the family of pigeons who lived in the bathroom gutter).

I was sitting almost in the sink, with one arm hooked around the closed side of the window, when the phone rang. Cursing, I extricated myself and went to the top of the stairs so I could hear the machine pick up the call. I didn't want to talk to anyone except Sam or Vinnie. With a click and a crackle, I heard Cynthia Grant's voice come onto the line, so I bounded downstairs two at a time and lunged for the receiver, my fingers numb with cold and terror.

In one sick moment I had a flashback to the time I'd called her from Ringside's offices ten years before.

"Cynthia! What's the matter? Is Sam okay?" I picked up the phone's body with my free hand and started pacing around the room with it, leaving black newsprint all over its cream trunk.

"Now listen to me, Helena, don't panic. She's all right, but she was having so much trouble breathing that they've taken her into hospital, to put her on a ventilator until the donor lung comes through. She needs to get her strength up for the operation—she was using too much of it trying to catch her breath the whole time. This is the best thing for her; she needs the rest. But she's fine, and in good spirits."

"Can I have a phone number for her? When can I see her?"

I was horrified and relieved at the same time. I sat down heavily on my pale armchair and, before I noticed, left more sooty fingerprints on the arm and seat.

"Well, there's no point you phoning her—she can't talk. She's got a tube in her throat from the ventilator."

"Oh my God, poor Sam," I said, appalled.

"She shouldn't really have visitors, either, but I've spoken to the nursing staff and told them that you should be allowed to come and see her regularly. Only once or twice a week, Helena, mind, and just for a few minutes. She won't be able to cope with more than that."

This felt terrible, final and deadly serious. I knew then that if Sam didn't leave that hospital with a new lung, she wouldn't leave at all. It was, I supposed, what people called "make-or-break time." After I hung up from Cynthia, I sat in the chair taking long deep breaths and wishing I could do the same for Sam. Then I remembered what I'd heard the day I last saw her, and repeated it softly out loud, over and over again, until my fears were calmed. "She's going to be fine, she's going to be fine."

Eventually I decided that the only thing I could do was to go and visit her immediately. As I left the sitting room to conduct my habitual pocket-rummaging for keys, in coat-cupboard and wardrobe, I happened to glance back over my shoulder, the black marks on the chair and phone finally catching my eye. I ignored them.

* * *

Sam was on the ventilator for four weeks, every moment of which felt measured by the rise and fall of each of her machine-manufactured breaths. I carried on doing my show, on autopilot, crying quietly off-mic every time someone requested a song for a sick friend—a sick anyone, really. Someone mourning their dead hamster would've set me off just as easily. I could have claimed any number of other people's records for myself: "The Bitterest Pill," "Bridge Over Troubled Water," "Us and Them." The requests all seemed to feed my grief and worry, plumping them up like raisins in milk, the pain of others mingling secretly with my own.

I commuted to Sam's hospital in Oxfordshire as often as the staff permitted, even if I could only see her for a few minutes at a time, and I monitored every little change in her condition, for better or worse. After a week, I decided that I was going to talk to Geoff and Gus as soon as I could, and ask for some compassionate leave so I could be with her until she had the operation. I didn't care how long she had to wait for it—they could fire me if they didn't like it.

Of course, as soon as I announced this to Sam, she wouldn't hear of it. Her thin fingers picked up the felt-tip pen beside her right hand and wrote on her notepad in surprisingly firm letters, "It might be months before they find me a new lung." I had argued with her, but she retaliated by scribbling, "If you don't stay at work, I won't tell you when I have my op!"

"Blackmail!" I said—but felt much better about it. She placated me further by adding, "You know I'm much stronger now."

It was true—although she still had an ethereal, almost ghostly quality about her, she had put on a little weight and her eyes were regaining some of their old spark. The doctors were very pleased with her progress and had told us that should a donor lung become available, she would be strong enough to have the operation immediately.

"You just don't want me around because I'm better at crosswords than you are," I whined. She rolled her eyes and grinned at me.

* ✳ *

The message from Cynthia came through in the fourth week, just as I was finishing the show one December morning. A donor lung had turned up for Sam, from a young biker killed on a patch of black ice the day before. She'd had the operation immediately, and was in Intensive Care, very ill, but alive.

* ✳ *

I must have wondered whether it was the last time I'd ever see her, but my brain would not allow the thought to articulate itself. I created a huge roadblock in my head, complete with armed soldiers barring entry to the enemy territory. It was four days after the operation, and I'd been at the hospital as much as the nurses allowed me to be, catching a few hours' sleep whenever forced to at a nearby hotel.

I had made two phone calls: One was a message I left for Geoff, to say that I was taking compassionate leave, and that I'd keep him posted, and one to Vinnie, to ask if he would come and be with me at the hospital. I was desperate for the solid reassurance of his body, a real human body to ground me, when it seemed like Sam's might be slipping away. I'd given him the address and phone number of the hotel, but two days later there was no word from him. I wasn't surprised.

Initially, Sam's new—"nearly new"—lung had taken, and the operation tentatively declared successful. But then it all started to go wrong.

Within four days, an infection had crept into her vulnerable body, tearing at it, trying to oust the unfamiliar interloper crammed inside her rib cage. She was fighting hard, but her body was so weakened from the surgery that drugs and oxygen were having to do what her poor, struggling immune system could not.

That hospital room became my universe, a small, horrible, painful cosmos with bland textures and tension in the air. There were no flowers in the room—their superficial fussiness would have seemed too trivial amid the far more important business of preserving an existence. All around were pale colors; unadorned walls were framed by plain curtains and colorless lino floor. Even though Sam was hooked up to all kinds of breathing apparatus, barely conscious, there was a full jug of water, an inverted glass, and a box of Kleenex on the locker next to her bed.

It was a totally functional room, and despite all the expensive lifesaving equipment and the awful scent of hospital detergent, it smelled of sickness and despair, heartbroken love and rage. Inexorably, it smelled like a room in which to die, not to get well.

Sam was the room's focus, lying still under a thin, nubbly yellow hospital blanket, her legs and feet defined like a skeleton's under a sheet. She was hanging on to her poor, cut-up body by the merest of threads, and even as I watched she seemed to drift away and back again. The room was silent except for the mechanical *huff* and *thunk* of the ventilator. I wondered if she was alarmed by our appearance, as we were all masked and gowned up to prevent our germs from tipping her precarious balance. I felt that my mask had an additional purpose—to hold my own pain deep inside my body, to prevent it from spilling out of my mouth in a huge, jagged scream of frustration and fear.

Nurses bustled in and out, their rubber-soled shoes squeaking on the linoleum. They adjusted the equipment, took readings, gently plumped the pillows under Sam's blue face, flipped the pages of her chart up and down before replacing it in its holder at the end of her bed. The writing on the pages did not appear to be in any language I'd ever seen before.

Sam's eyes were closed, and she looked like a very old woman, or a wizened sick child. Cynthia and Mike hovered around, too, talking gently to her and to each other, and Dylan and his wife were outside drinking vending machine coffee from Styrofoam cups. I walked past them all on my way back from the ladies'; Dylan's mouth was twisted up and trembling so much that he could hardly swallow his coffee.

There was a sign on a door across the corridor that read, ELECTIVE SERVICES DIRECTORATE. MATTRESSES AND PILLOWS STORED IN HERE. I did not understand what that meant any more than I understood the squiggles on Sam's chart.

Every now and again Mike absently patted my shoulder, but he couldn't look at me. He seemed fixated by the various items of hospital paraphernalia pushed or carried past by the nurses: yellow-wheeled trolleys, stainless-steel kidney trays, boxes of nonsterile latex gloves.

Later, back in Sam's room, her jovial uncle, of whom I had heard but never met, came up to her bedside. His joviality was supposedly his strongest characteristic, but he was really fighting to find it at that moment.

"Hello, Sam, love," he said to her quietly, passing a weary hand over his eyes. "Your Christmas roses are blooming a treat. You've got to hurry back and chase that damned neighbor's cat out, mind. It's trying its best to dig 'em up."

Last summer Sam had started cultivating a section of her parents' large garden, and it was her pride and joy. Until it turned too cold, it had become nigh on impossible to reach her on the phone; she was always out in her wheelchair on the lawn, surrounded by hoes and pruning shears, either fiddling with her sweet peas and marigolds, or giving orders to her sweating father, who handled the

more backbreaking tasks. But she didn't give a flicker of acknowledgment now.

Her uncle stroked her still hand. "Well, I just wanted to come
and see you, you know. Get well soon. Auntie Pauline sends her
love—she'd have come, too, but her hip's been playing her up
again. Good-bye, love."

He got up abruptly and lumbered out of the room. Sam stirred
and moaned. She seemed frightened and disturbed. Her parents
and I leaned forward, as though our proximity could chase away
her fears. Tears spilled from Cynthia's eyes.

"It's all right, Sam darling, we're here. Shhh now." She held
three of Sam's fingers, gently but as though she would never let
them go.

The doctor came in and asked us to leave for a minute. As I
walked numbly out of the room, he took me aside. He had thick
tufts of bristly reddish hair coming from his ears and nostrils that
moved gently when he spoke, like sea anemones in a rock pool.

"Listen," he said kindly. "I think it's important that she gets some
rest now. Really, the less people around her, the better. And I'm
sure you could do with a break, too. You've been here all day. Why
don't you get a good night's sleep and come back in the morning?
She's had a lot of visitors today. I really think it would be best
for her."

I didn't want to leave, but I did want to do what was best. "Can I
say good-bye?"

"Yes, go in now. Be as brief as you can, though."

Cynthia and Mike stood aside to let me reenter the room. They
looked the way they had all week—blank and stunned, as I'm sure I
did—like shipwreck or inferno survivors.

I walked over to Sam's bed, alone with her for the first time all
day. I held her hand and stroked her hair; she was so familiar, even
in these unnatural surroundings. I thought about that new strange
lung inside her, which had not yet proved whether it was friend
or foe.

The walls felt as though they were pressing in on me, and I had a
fleeting desire to see something bright and colorful—a Matisse

print, or a child's building blocks—something happy. The bed-sheets looked like hard white plywood. I gazed into her face but could not see any peace there.

"I've got to go now, Sam, but I'll be back tomorrow. Hang in there, okay?"

I paused, but there was no reply. I stood up and started to turn away. As I did so I felt, rather than heard, a tiny movement. I turned slowly back around to see Sam's eyes flicker open, and with all her strength she lifted her arms a tiny way up toward me as though for a hug. I rushed back to her and embraced her gingerly around the tubes, feeling as though my head and heart would simultaneously burst with pain and grief.

I stumbled out of the room and walked in a daze back to the hotel up the road. That hotel seemed to have been built for people like me, guests all wandering around the corridors looking anxious and haunted. I sat numbly in an overstuffed armchair in the hotel's big lobby, surrounded by a litter of low coffee tables and the hulks of marooned sofas, while a small washed-out waitress brought me coffee. I couldn't really think what else to do. I didn't want to go to my room, because I didn't want to be alone.

Just then, the revolving doors spun around and deposited Vinnie right in front of me. Unshaven, a bit whiffy, and smoking, but Vinnie nonetheless.

"Hi, baby," he said as I stood up to meet him. "It's okay. I'm here."

He wrapped his arms tightly around me, and I thought, Whatever else he's done to me, I'll always love him for this.

"Thanks for coming, Vin."

He ordered a beer from the peaky waitress, and after I'd filled him in on the details of Sam's condition, we sat in silence together.

"Strange old hotel, this, isn't it?" Vinnie commented, looking around him.

I nodded. He was right; it was a very odd place. Presumably the effect was meant to be that of a large, friendly living room, but it felt to me like a plush dream version of the ICU's waiting room. Perhaps the proximity of the hospital's grim suspense had rubbed off on the designers, I thought with antiseptic-drenched imagination. I still could not speak, but Vinnie didn't seem to mind. He swigged his beer as I grimly concentrated on the pale china of my coffee cup.

I was aware of what was going on around me, but I just kept seeing Sam's face, hollow and betrayed-looking. The hotel seemed very busy—perhaps a lot of people were dying at this time of year, winter's inevitable victims.

A mother walked by, crying, two small boys trailing behind her. The boys were making cawing sounds, like wheeling seagulls. They weren't sounds borne out of grief, more from the boredom of their mother being so distracted. I wondered who she'd lost, or was losing, and saw Sam's face again.

The two receptionists were chatting loudly and vacuously behind their impressive mahogany counter about a party one of them was planning.

"Spiffy-*cahj*," she kept saying, shortening the word *casual* in an affected way. "I told him it's going to be spiffy-*cahj*; spiffy-*cahj*, I said. If he's not going to come spiffy-*cahj* like the rest of us, he needn't bother coming at all."

Vinnie leaned over to me from his end of the sofa. "That's one party I *really* hope I'm not invited to," he whispered, and I even managed to smile for a split second.

"I wish I still felt so sure that she'll be okay," I said.

He took my half-full coffee cup from me and put it down on the glass-topped table. "Come on, sweetheart," he said. "I think you need to go and have a lie-down, you look wrecked."

I stretched my hand out toward him and let him lead me up to my room and steer me over to the bed. As soon as we were through the door, Vinnie was peeling off his clothes.

"I'll just grab a shower, if you don't mind. Haven't had the chance to have one yet today. Back in a minute."

He vanished into the bathroom, and I lay staring at the ceiling. I was thinking how unfair it was that I could just jump up off the bed any time I wanted to, and Sam couldn't. I was so tired that I began to think that I was hallucinating; the slippery brown bedspread underneath me seemed like a vast card table on which my mind was turning over personalized Tarot cards: Sam holding up scales; the

Grim Reaper; Sam, Sam, Sam; Vinnie holding out his hands. I felt cold, chilled to the bone, and all I wanted to do was to get warm again.

Before I even realized it, I had slid off the bed and into the bathroom, the hot splash of Vinnie's shower calling me. I stripped and stumbled in to join him, falling into his wet arms, crying more than I had thought it possible for even me to cry.

Vinnie hugged me so hard my bones cracked, and I buried my face in the space between his neck and shoulder until the pounding water nearly suffocated me. I kissed him then, all salty and sobbing, as if he were a lifeboat on a stormy sea, and he kissed me back, hard and distracting.

He was so warm against my iced-over soul that I just wanted to get closer and closer to him. After the shower we crawled beneath the chilly bedcovers and he held me, pressing his body against mine, heavy and warm and curved, almost indistinguishable from my own; the only thing in the world that might possibly stop my pain.

We lay in silence, my grief occupying every ion of the air around us, rendering speech redundant. Vinnie was obviously not finding it easy to be naked in bed with me, but for once in his life, he had the sensitivity to realize that what I needed from him at that moment went much deeper than sex. To his credit, he didn't even try to instigate it.

Eventually I fell into a dreamless black hole of sleep, as suddenly and violently as falling over a cliff. The last thing I remembered was the feel of my cheek on Vinnie's chest, and my head lulled by the gentle rhythm of his breathing.

I was woken some time later by the sound of a match sparking as Vinnie lit a cigarette. He was sitting up in bed, drinking a beer from the minibar and watching television. It was dark outside, but he hadn't drawn the curtains.

"Hello, gorgeous," he said, kissing my nose. "I've got to make a move soon, you know. Things to do."

I sat up groggily. "Really? I thought you were going to stay."

"Sorry, baby, I can't. I've got this big project to finish. I just wanted to make sure you were okay."

"Thanks again, Vin, I really appreciate it. How did you get here, anyway?"

"Borrowed a mate's car. That's another reason I have to get back. He'll be wondering where I've got to. I didn't actually tell him I was coming this far."

He put out his cigarette by dropping it in the dregs of his beer, and then got out of bed, picking up and putting on the clothes he'd discarded earlier. I felt bereft that he was going but didn't have the energy to stop him—my deep sleep had left me with a woozy kind of hangover, as though I'd taken a sleeping pill. Once dressed, he came and lay back down on the bed next to me, stroking my breast thoughtfully.

"Oh, by the way, Helena," he said, matter-of-factly. "The machine swallowed my card, and I'm completely strapped for cash. You couldn't do me a huge favor and lend me a few quid, could you? Say, two hundred?"

I stared at him open-mouthed. I felt that nothing else had the power to hurt me, not while Sam was fighting for her life—but it didn't stop me from feeling angry.

"So that's why you came up here?"

Vinnie looked hurt. Predictably. "No way. You're my baby. You keep kicking me out, but I'm always there for you when you need me. I was just hoping you could do the same for me, that's all."

"Me and my checkbook, you mean."

"Is that okay? I mean, I know this is a really bad time for you, and I wouldn't ask unless I was really stuck, honest. . . . I'm sorry, H."

I wearily hauled myself out of bed and extracted said checkbook from the depths of my handbag. Two hundred pounds was nothing to me; Vinnie was nothing to me. Sam was all that mattered.

"No, it's not okay, Vinnie." But I gave him the check anyway.

* ✳ *

I lay motionless on my bed for the rest of the evening, not watching the flickering muted television, not listening to the mutterings of the radio, which I'd switched on for company.

It was eight-thirty P.M. when the call came from Cynthia at the hospital to tell me that Sam had died. Before I even picked up the receiver I was already wondering how my positive thought could have been so wrong, how *She's going to be fine* could have dissolved into these final, terrible words across a phone line.

When the brief call was finished, some impulse made me turn up the volume on the radio by my bed, willing there to be a song on which I could hang my grief. Something fitting, something dignified, something for Sam.

It was a gift. Blur, "This Is a Low," the opening trippy acoustic chord sequence climbing up my emotions: E, F sharp minor, G, A, just as I began to listen. The most emotive song about shipping forecasts ever written. It was like a tornado whipping all its power round and round into a tiny deadly funnel. I poured everything into that song. Volume up and up and up until the little speakers of the radio quivered and shook . . . I let it lift me up, too, and take me away from there. Away from the feeling of utter and complete loneliness and desolation, the feeling that nothing would ever be right again.

Damon Albarn almost howled the chorus out: *"This is a low, but it won't hurt you / When you're alone, it will be there with you / finding ways to stay solo . . ."*

It did hurt me, though. God, it hurt me so much. But for the next five minutes, at least for that long, I could survive by letting the song take on my pain for me.

I couldn't feel the light rising of Sam's soul up toward a different world, but I imagined that this song was escorting her there, the chords and words, sentiment and volume, and my own feelings for her along with it.

As the song's final bars faded out, it made it easier for me to understand that *She's going to be fine* held much truer when it was not limited to a broken shell of a body.

FIFTY QUID

BY COINCIDENCE, OR PERHAPS SOME STRANGE SYNERGY, GUS FROM
New World phoned and left an urgent message for me to ring him
back, on the day I was writing the final chapter of the manuscript.
Whether it was urgent or not, however, I was utterly incapable of
returning his call until the next day. By the time I'd completed the
last words, about Sam's poor broken body, I was absolutely *hammered* on vodka and was in no fit state to speak to anybody.

The only reason I even heard the phone's distant ring was
because I had just spilled an entire glass of vodka and pulpy orange
juice all over my keyboard and had had to take a break from my
frenzied weeping to try to wipe it up.

Drunkenness was essential to the operation. It was the only way I
could bear to relive those memories without having "This Is a Low"
to act as a dock-leaf on the sting, and I couldn't play the record
before the show. I'd set myself a strict embargo on all the tracks
accompanying the manuscript, until the actual broadcast. When I
listened to them all together for that one last time, I wanted them
to have the maximum impact on me, in case I needed an extra spur
to assist me in carrying out the Plan. They were not just little irides-
cent plastic CDs. They were computer disks with my memories
stored on them, and I wanted them to remain as new and shiny as
was possible under the circumstances.

Nonetheless, writing about Sam's operation nearly finished me
off. The vodka acted as an anesthetic, but not a particularly effective one. I had to keep drinking and drinking it, trying to remember the details objectively, and failing miserably.

On reflection, alcohol and sorrow never did go awfully well
together. My brain-drilling headache informed me of this the next
day, when the room had finally stopped spinning enough for me to

locate the telephone and dial the number Gus had left on my machine.

"Gus? It's Helena Nicholls. How are you?"

"Helena! I'm great, thanks—but more to the point, how are you? Why are you whispering?"

"Hideous hangover, that's why. But otherwise fine, thanks. I got your message. What did you want to talk to me about?"

"Right, well, I understand you sent Geoff a letter a couple of months ago, registering your interest in the two-to-four A.M. slot. He wrote you back, care of your agent, asking you to confirm a date, but we haven't heard from you. Have you changed your mind? Or didn't you get the letter?"

I guiltily remembered the letters I'd dumped unread in the bin, that day when Vinnie was lurking in the undergrowth.

"Um, no, I haven't changed my mind. . . . Yes, I got the letter, I just, er, forgot to ring him with the date."

"Not to worry. We've been having a reshuffle here, and if there's any chance of you starting next week, Monday the twenty-eighth, that would be terrific. It would get us out of a hole, and it would just give us enough time to get your name in the listings."

"I said I didn't want any publicity!"

Raising my voice, even just to a faint, indignant squeak, caused the pressure in my head to build up still further, until I thought that steam would come out of my ears. I vowed not to drink another drop of booze until the day I died. Ho-ho.

"No, no, honestly, we won't make a song and dance out of it. It's just that we need a name to stick in the *TimeOut*s, and so on. Can't leave a blank space, can we? Besides, no one'll notice. Hardly anyone listens at that time of night, anyw—Well, what I mean is—"

"Oh, never mind, Gus. I know exactly what you mean."

I could just see the headline: DISGRACED DJ DEMOTED TO GRAVE-YARD SHIFT. Still, maybe a little bit of advance publicity for the Plan wouldn't hurt. . . .

My feet suddenly turned into two immobile blocks of ice, at the realization that the endgame now had a date: Monday the twenty-eighth. The day I was scheduled to disappear off the face of the earth.

"All right, I'll do it. Do I need to come in for a debriefing or anything?"

"No, you know the score. You've done it enough times. It'll be just like the morning, only nighttime and without requests."

What a wag.

Gus continued, "The security code is currently eight-one-five-seven. Don't forget it, because no one else will be around at that time, unless you bump into Pete Harness and his producer on the way out. He's taking over the eleven-to-two A.M. slot."

"So who's my producer, then?"

An important question, since he or she would be the last person to see me before I left. I found I'd stripped off a jagged piece of cuticle with my teeth, leaving a long white gash of flesh that instantly filled up with red spots of blood, which then dripped mercilessly onto the leg of my favorite combat trousers. Oh, well, I thought, won't need to wash them again.

There was an embarrassed silence at the end of the line.

"I thought Geoff told you in his letter, Helena. You won't have a producer at that time. Nobody does. Pete only has one that late because he does phone-in quizzes and things on his show."

I wasn't quite sure how I felt about this. If I'd planned to do the show long-term, I'd have been hideously affronted. It was like expecting Elizabeth the First to get dressed up for a state banquet on her own, with no one to lace her stays or hang jewels in her hair. It also meant that nobody would be manning the phones. It was just as well that I wasn't intending to do a request show.

Gus must have picked up on my disgruntled train of thought. "No point having anyone taking calls at that time of night. We'd get all the axe murderers and child molesters ringing in if we did."

"Oh, great," I said, trying to sound like someone who cared who'd be listening. "My target audience."

Maybe not having a producer was a good thing, if I could get over the humiliation. Practically speaking, it meant that I'd have the studio to myself.

I tried to be brisk. "Right, then, I think I'm set. Monday the twenty-eighth it is. I'll give you a shout if I think of any other questions."

"Good girl. Are you excited?"

How incredibly patronizing, I fumed. Were it not for the fact that Gus had given me my first DJ job, I'd have seriously gone off him by this point.

"No, Gus, to be honest, I can't say that I am wildly excited by having to do the graveyard shift. But it's a job, I suppose, and I'll guarantee you this: It'll be a show to remember!"

Gus laughed uncertainly. "You bet, Helena. Well, best of luck, then. I'll check in with you after the first show, all right?"

* * *

On Saturday the twenty-sixth I donned my sunglasses, even though it was raining, and set off to Richmond for a very specific shopping mission. Sainsburys Home Shopping would probably have balked at delivering the items I wanted, so a personal expedition was required. I parked at a meter on the edge of the green and strolled cautiously into the town center, noticing how much less paranoid I felt being out in public—probably because I knew it was the last time. Oddbins was my first port of call, where I purchased a large bottle of gin—I didn't care for gin, but the hangover was still too fresh in my memory to even think about vodka without retching.

Next I went into Boots and bought a jar of paracetamol and a Bart Simpson hot-water bottle cover (to try to make the pills look less suspicious). I'd planned to repeat the exercise in every other chemist in Richmond—minus the novelty hot-water bottle covers, of course—but after an hour of walking around, I had failed to locate any other pharmacies at all.

Bugger. I'd have to drive round instead, looking for those big green crosses outside buildings that signified chemists' shops.

It struck me that buying booze and headache pills, and gathering together my favorite CDs, made it feel more as if I was planning a hen party with a bunch of girlfriends. Not that I *had* ever gone anywhere with a bunch of girlfriends, though. My girlfriends hadn't come in bunches, like grapes, but as one perfect piece of fruit. Sam the Starfruit.

My meter was about to run out, so I headed back toward the green, going via W H Smith's to buy a purple folder for the manuscript. The girl at the till got annoyed with me when I flung the money at her without waiting for my change, but I was paranoid about getting a parking ticket. It was funny how I could still be worried about such trivialities, I thought.

It began to rain again, just as I was circumnavigating the bald muddy patches of grass on Richmond Green, wondering once more why I bothered—I was planning to kill myself, but it was of paramount importance not to get mud on my Patrick Coxes or a parking fine before I did?

Head down, thinking aspirin, I was muttering to myself, "Only one bottle, well, that won't get me very far, will it? Where else have I seen those big green crosses? Oh yeah, there's that one in Twickenham, the Maple Leaf, and I'm sure there's a couple in St. Margarets, too. . . ."

"A couple of what?" said a familiar voice from behind my car.

I stood on a loose paving slab, and water squirted up my trouser leg. There appeared to be no escape from Vinnie.

"What are you doing here?" I glared at him as jaws of cold water sank into my left calf.

"Waiting for you, of course. Good thing you got back when you did; only a minute left on your meter, and a soggy, cross-looking traffic warden heading toward us as we speak. I'd hate to see you get a ticket, now."

Vinnie tutted with mock-concern and leaned on my bonnet. As usual, my shock turned to fury.

"You're happy to make a few hundred grand by selling pictures of me to the press, but you'd hate to see me get a parking ticket? Just go away, Vinnie. You make me sick."

"Ah, but that's where you're wrong—I'm not happy to make money out of you, Helena," he said, brushing a stray leaf off my windscreen. "That's why I'm waiting for you. I've got something to tell you."

"Well, I don't want to hear it," I said shortly, pressing the button on my key ring to unlock the BMW. The little *pip* it made sounded as grumpy as I did.

"Oh, but you do," said Vinnie, dancing round the driver's side and putting his hand over mine as I tried to open the door.

I snatched it away. "Piss off, Vinnie, I'm not in the mood."

Vinnie delved into a damp backpack and pulled out a hardback brown envelope. He thrust it at me. "There you go."

"What is that?" I asked wearily.

"Prints and negatives. All there, none missing, I promise you."

I stared at him. "None missing except the one you sold to the tabloids, right? When's it coming out, then? I've been checking the papers, but I haven't seen it yet."

Vinnie laughed. "No, straight up. They're all in there. I haven't sold any of them. I'm giving them back to you."

He dropped suddenly to his knees on the wet road and wrapped his arms around my thighs. "I've been a complete arse, Helena, I'm so, so sorry. You have to forgive me. For everything: Miyuki, Natalie, the photos—everything."

Who's Natalie? I thought.

"I miss you so much. Please take me back. I swear I'll never let you down again. Marry me, Helena, please? I love you."

My jaw dropped so far that even with its recently broken limited movement, it was close to clunking Vinnie on the top of his head as he groveled beseechingly before me.

I didn't know what to say. No one had ever proposed to me before. Marry him?

It was lashing with rain now. I disengaged his arms and collapsed speechless into the car. Vinnie rushed back around and climbed into the passenger seat. We both sat there, dripping, until he turned and threw the envelope, Frisbee style, onto the backseat.

"What's the matter with the photos? Were they all blurred or something?"

Vinnie looked hurt, more, I thought, because I was doubting his technical prowess as a photographer than because I was doubting *him*. He like to excel in all things.

"Of course they weren't blurred. They're great, as it happens, crystal clear. I'm telling you, I just feel like a heel for doing something so horrible to you. I was desperate, man. I got into a spot of bother with a dealer friend of mine—you know, I owe him some cash, and he's not happy with me. That's why I did it. If I'd been thinking straight, I'd never have done anything to hurt you."

"But you didn't sell them?"

"No. Look, I realized I was out of order."

"So do you still owe him the money?"

Vinnie lit up a Gauloise, but I reached over, extracted it from between his lips, and threw it out my door. We watched it roll away across the tarmac, sparking red, to lie disconsolately in the gutter.

"I can't stand you smoking in my car," I said.

"Sorry," Vinnie replied humbly.

I decided to make a generous gesture. He was obviously in trouble. "Listen. I don't mind if you want to flog all that equipment I bought you—the computer and stuff—to pay off your debts."

Vinnie looked away, and I realized that he'd sold them long ago.

"Oh, right, I see. Cheers, then," I said.

I hadn't realized he had such a bad drug problem. Or perhaps he owed money because he was dealing? I wouldn't have put it past him. Either way, I didn't really want to know.

"I was desperate, H. Please forgive me. You were the only good thing in my life, and I let you down."

I leaned back against the headrest and watched a little boy heading our way, three or four years old, followed by his mother. The boy was dressed in yellow galoshes and one of those really cute yellow duck raincoats, where the peak of the hood was the duck's beak. He was carrying a small translucent umbrella decorated with a frieze of tropical fish, which he held down low over his head. I could see his baby breath misting up the inside of the plastic. His mother was carrying car keys and looked harassed.

"Come on, Timmy, hurry up, the car's parked just across the road," I heard her say.

Timmy broke away, ran a couple of steps, and jumped with both feet into a deep puddle by the curb, soaking himself and his mother. I waited for her to yell and drag him off to the car, and for a second she looked cross. Then suddenly and unexpectedly she skipped forward two steps, too, and jumped into the same puddle. They stood there laughing with glee, and even in the midst of Vinnie's machinations, I couldn't help smiling as well.

Suddenly I wished, with a fierce, fearful yearning, that it was Ruby splashing under a duck's beak hat in front of me, and Toby clowning around with her. I could have gotten out and joined them, and forgotten all about Vinnie.

"You've always let me down, Vinnie," I said. I'd always thought it was a cliché, when people's voices were said to sound "very far away," but mine did. Probably because it was off somewhere with the rest of me, jumping in puddles with Toby.

"Whenever I needed you, you let me down. You've cheated on me, taken advantage of me, sponged off me. When Sam was dying, I thought for once you were there for me, but you weren't. When I had the accident, you never visited me in hospital; you never came near me until you decided that you could make some money out of me. Why on earth would I want to marry *you*?"

Vinnie made one last-ditch effort. "I only didn't visit you in hospital because you said you never wanted to see me again."

"But I'm always saying that. It's never stopped you before."

I grinned very slightly, and Vinnie sensed that I was weakening. I couldn't help it. I began to remember all the good things about him: his sense of humor and adventure, his amazing prowess in the sack. How he kept me company. How he made art for me.

"Please, Helena, let's give it one more try. I really want you. I'm so sorry about everything."

Then I remembered the Plan and snapped back to reality. "Sorry, Vin, no can do," I said briskly, putting the key into the ignition. "We can't get back together because I'm leaving in a couple of days. I'm going away, and I'm not coming back."

"Where? Let me come, too!"

I laughed shortly. "You can't. Now, if you don't mind, I've got preparations to make."

His expression turned from peachy wheedle into purple tantrum. So much for contrition, I thought.

I started the car and put it into gear. If I looked straight ahead, I couldn't see Vinnie at all, since he was sitting on my blind side.

"Bye, then, Vinnie. This time I can promise you that you won't be seeing me again."

Vinnie opened the door, narrowly missing getting it torn off its hinges by a passing car. "Aren't you even going to thank me for not selling the photos?"

I cackled again. It felt quite liberating. "Er, let me think. . . . No. Do you really expect me to be grateful to you for that? Now please go. I'm not even going to wish you a nice life this time, because your karma is probably so rotten by now that it's very unlikely that too many more good things will happen to you."

I twisted my head so that I could see Vinnie get out of the car, dragging his backpack like a petulant child. Before closing the door, he stuck his head back inside. There was an extremely nasty expression on his face, worse than any I'd seen before.

"I've got news for you, Miss 'I'm a Pop Star,'" he said. "You think you're so fucking famous that you don't like to go out in case you're mobbed? Well, that's just a joke, because I know for a fact that nobody gives a shit anymore. No one cares that you had an accident, no one cares that you lost your job, no one cares if you never work again. Blue Idea are naff eighties has-beens."

He continued, talking almost to himself. "Of course, I should've realized that it was all in your head long ago, but you had me fooled, too. All this talk about paparazzi and stalkers and people hassling you—I went out with you for a year, and I never saw you get hassled for being famous. I never even saw you sign an autograph!"

"You always made us stay in because you were afraid of Miyuki seeing us together!" I protested, half afraid, half amused by Vinnie's lame attempt to get back at me.

"It's all in your head, Helena," he hissed, tapping the side of his forehead with a nicotine-stained finger. "God, I feel sorry for you. You're living in a fantasy world. I only came near you because you're rich. Why else would I bother? You're a loser."

I noticed that the car parked across the road contained a uniformed child propped up asleep in the backseat, alone, her face compressed and melted in sleep against the window, her school hat slipping off the side of her head like a little clown's. The front window had been left open for her, just a crack, as if she were a dog on a hot day.

"If you say so, Vinnie. But I think you're the one who's imagining things." I tried to sound bored, but his voice was so scathing and venomous.

"Ah, but that's just where you're wrong, Miss Barking Mad. I've got proof. When I rang up the *Daily Mirror* to say I had exclusive photos of you after your accident, know what they said? They laughed in my face. 'Give you fifty quid for them, mate,' they said. 'No one's interested in her these days. We only ran the shot of her accident because her mate Justin Becker was involved.' So now do you see? It's *all in your mind.* You aren't famous at all anymore."

He slammed the door and walked away from me for the last time, whistling a vindictive little tune, which sounded a lot like a Blue Idea song. The sleeping child stirred and stretched out in the backseat of her car, disappearing from my view.

The Sundays

HERE'S WHERE THE STORY ENDS

TWELVE-THIRTY A.M. ON MONDAY THE TWENTY-EIGHTH. I WENT around caressing all the walls of my beloved house, thanking it for its indefatigable support and hospitality over the years. I turned the radiators on low, just in case an unseasonal frost should happen to nip at the gutters before anyone got back to check on it. I emptied the larder of perishable foods, put the rubbish out, switched off the water, made sure all the windows and doors were locked. It was like going on holiday, that silent, dark, creeping-around time before the start of a long journey to a nice, warm, relaxing destination. Yes. That was a good way to look at it.

My carefully assembled props consisted of the following:

1. Three jars of paracetamol, a half-full jar of Valium, an unopened bottle of gin, and a picnic tumbler in my Kate Spade giraffe-print shoulder bag.
2. Box of CDs.
3. Manuscript, with letters and *Bluezine*s and diary entries glued carefully in, sitting proudly in its purple folder on the dining-room table.
4. Letter to Ron in my coat pocket, addressed and stamped and ready to drop in a post box on the way to the studio:

Dear Ron, By the time you read this (*etc., etc.*). Keys to house under mat (*etc., etc.*). Please come to house and collect purple folder (*etc.*). Any advance you receive on publication of manuscript, feel free to keep fifteen percent for yourself. The rest is for my parents, at this address (*etc.*). Please also forward the enclosed letter to them. Have informed lawyers, all should be in order. Thanks for everything, Helena. P.S. By the way, I'd really like it if you could suggest to publishers that a

CD of the songs from the show accompany the book. Kind of a new idea, but why not? *(Etc.)*

5. Difficult tearstained letter apologizing to parents, enclosed inside Ron's envelope.

I was ready. I went to put the CDs into the car, but when I picked up my giraffe-print shoulder bag, the bottle and jars all clinked and rattled together so excessively that I felt compelled to do something about it. I went back into the kitchen, pulled a Ziploc bag from the drawer, unscrewed the tops of the pill bottles, and emptied their contents out into the bag.

Small as it was, this unforeseen hitch threw me, and my hands started to shake. I'd have had a swig of the gin, only I couldn't take the risk of being stopped by the police while driving to the studio—being thwarted by a Breathalyzer test at this late stage was too terrible to contemplate.

So I remained sober and did some yogic breathing instead. This involves pinching one nostril shut, breathing slowly through the other side to the count of four, holding your breath for the same count, exhaling for eight, then repeating with the other nostril, ad infinitum. I'd always suspected that the reason this actually worked was that you felt such a prat doing it that it took your mind off why you were stressed in the first place.

After several breaths, I did feel better. Everything had begun to feel super-real, like my "revelation" in the car outside Sam's flat that time, when I was convinced that she was going to be fine. Now I was convinced that I was going to be fine, too. I was going to be free of my one-eyed, less-than-perfect body. It was an ending and a new start, simultaneously.

* ※ *

I arrived at New World and parked the car on a yellow line right outside the building. After climbing out, I retrieved the box of CDs and the giraffe-print bag from the boot, locked the car, and headed slowly toward the studios. It was 1:45 A.M.

I pressed the number pad outside the front door, 8-1-5-7, and the door buzzily invited me to push it open. It sounded so inviting and businesslike, I felt like kicking it. If I come in now, I'm never going to leave—don't you know that? I thought. The door didn't care. I barged my way in, all elbows and sharp cardboard corners, and it shut behind me with a heavy, ominous click.

A security guard I didn't recognize sat at the front desk. "Name, please?" he said unsmilingly.

"Helena Nicholls."

"Two o'clock show. Right. Studio One."

I wasn't going to thank him, not if he didn't even know who I was. I walked over to the wall of pigeonholes and looked up to mine to see if there was any post. It was stuffed full of letters, but when I reached up and took them down, the security man said, "That ain't your box. That's Millie Myers's box."

I peered at the letters, pink, brown, blue, and white envelopes in all shapes and sizes, decorated with stick-on hearts and curly schoolgirl writing or the scruffy hormonal scrawl of the adolescent male, addressed to Millie, Gorgeous Millie, Miss. M. Myers, I Love You, Mills.

None for me. The label on the pigeonhole bearing my name had been peeled off unceremoniously, and a smart new *Millie Myers* sticker slapped over the top of it.

Crushed, I shoved the fan mail back into the box. Perhaps what Vinnie said had been right. Perhaps I wasn't half as famous as I thought.

"Where's mine, then?"

The security guard shrugged. "Try the bottom right. That's usually where they put stuff for new DJs."

"I'm not a new DJ."

"Oh, wait. I remember. Mr. Hadleigh left something for you behind the desk here. This is it."

He handed me some sheets of printed paper with a memo from Geoff clipped in the top right-hand corner: "Dear Helena, Here's your show. As per my letter to you, please stick to the format. Speak soon, all the best, Geoff."

It was a printout from Selector, the computer that programmed all the music and ad breaks and timings of live links for the station. I scanned it frantically, a line jumping out at me here and there:

. . . 2.04:00	Bon Jovi: "Living on a Prayer"
. . . 2.18:00	*Ad: Persil*
. . . 2.18:40	*Ad: Kingsmill*
. . . 3.10:10	Live link
. . . 3.11.00	Spice Girls: "Mama"

No. No way. There was no way, after all this, I was playing the fucking Spice Girls and Bon Jovi! None of my records were here, not one. Geoff had completely ignored my playlist. How dare he! My teeth were clenched, and I was having trouble swallowing. Don't lose it, don't lose it, I kept telling myself. This is too important.

I sank down on a sofa in reception, causing the neck of the gin bottle to peep out from between the handles of my bag. The security guard noticed, and looked at me with an expression of casual disdain, but I didn't care.

I'd been stitched up! Bet Geoff had never even sent that letter— he must have known I wouldn't do the show if I couldn't play my own records. Oh, God, what was I going to do?

"Five minutes till you're on air. Shouldn't you be in your studio by now?" the guard asked boorishly.

"Mind your own damn business." I was still reeling from Geoff's bombshell and this awful, preprogrammed, bolloxsy, brain-dead excuse for a show that they seriously expected me to do.

I jumped up, grabbed my things, and headed down the corridor, punching in the security code again as I passed through another door, and again as I finally entered the studio. It was my old break-fast-show studio, looking exactly the same as it had the morning of the UKMAs, when I'd done my last request show.

I sank down in the swivel chair behind the desk and, out of habit, slid off my shoes. Putting my handbag on the carpeted floor by my feet, I let the bag of tablets flop out slightly, so I could feel its soft bulk with my toes.

Three minutes to go. Through the thick window, the glass fuggy and brown as if all the DJs chain-smoked, I could see Pete Harness and his producer finishing up in Studio Two. Surreptitiously, I unscrewed the gin bottle, poured half a glassful into the tumbler, and downed it in one gulp, my throat constricting with the effort of not gagging.

Next door they were letting Pete's final record ("Walking on Sunshine" by Katrina and the Waves—one of my least favorite tunes) play out while they put on their coats and gathered their things. Pete waved tentatively at me through the window and gave a thumbs-up signal. I could tell that the producer, a pretty young black girl, was scrutinizing me slyly, probably trying to see how different I now was from the photos she'd seen of me before the accident. I hoped she hadn't seen me swig the gin.

Two minutes. I hesitated over the Selector printout for a moment and then swiveled around and lobbed it into the bin by the door. What was the worst thing Geoff could do—fire me? I was only planning the one show, anyway, and besides, probably no one would even notice. Feeling giddy with rebellion and adrenaline, I unpacked my box of CDs and lined them carefully up in order, cueing up "The Ballad of Tom Jones" first. I watched as the CD slid into the machine with a metallic skid, thinking, Here goes. I was going to completely override Selector.

One minute. It felt so strange, flying solo. Strange but liberating. Pete and the producer disappeared, waving foolishly at me again. I got the impression that they'd wanted to come in and say hi, but my closed-down expression had put them off.

The Selector screen to my left was showing the supposed running order of my show, the same as the printout, but because it was to my blind side it was easy to ignore.

I found a minidisc with the New World jingle on it and shoved it in the machine, followed by one of my old breakfast-show idents— why not, I thought.

Thirty seconds. I reached beneath the desk for the bag of pills, selected ten paracetemol to be going on with, and arranged them in a daisy-petal pattern around the base of the tumbler. Taking them throughout the show would mean less to swallow all at once at the end. The pills looked inviting, and I imagined them soft and sugary like sweeties on my tongue. I decided on two per record, and none of the Valiums until the final track—I wanted to be awake to finish the show.

The clock hand swept gracefully north, toward two o'clock, and I took a deep breath, clamped the cans on my ears, adjusted the microphone, and hit the on-air button to take control. No turning back now.

"Good morning, London—those of you who are unlucky enough to be awake at this time, anyhow. Helena Nicholls here; yes, it's me. Remember me from a few months back? Well, as I expect you heard, I had a rather nasty accident, and they had to get someone else to cover for my breakfast show. Millie's doing a great job, isn't she? And to be honest, I'm more of a night owl myself, so I thought I'd give this a try. I've got some fantastic music lined up for you tonight, twenty songs in all. It's kind of going to be a request show—but not in the way that you remember my show from before. Sorry, folks, but you can't ring in—tonight is going to be my songs, from my life. Don't worry, I do have quite good taste, so don't touch that dial. . . . I've got some Elvis Costello, Blondie, Dexys, Jimmy Cliff—so stick around. Ten songs in a row coming up after these messages."

I bunged in a trail and ran an ad break—better make at least a minimal effort to do the right thing, I thought. There was a tap on the window, and I looked up to see the little producer girl standing there waving a white envelope at me.

I swiftly moved the tumbler, leaned my elbow on the pills so they were hidden, made sure the gin bottle was out of sight, and reluctantly waved her in.

"Hi, Helena, I'm Vicky. Are you really playing ten songs in a row? Won't you get in trouble? That's not the running order, you know."

She sounded concerned, but her eyes were secretly scanning my face in the hope of seeing a scar close-up. I had a sudden urge to rip off my eye patch and loom ogreishly up at her, shouting, "Grrrrrr," just to see if she'd scream and run away.

"I know. Thanks. I'll deal with it."

She handed me the envelope. "Sorry, but this was stuck between the pages of Pete's show. I think it's been floating around for a few days, but you didn't seem to have a pigeonhole."

"Thanks," I said again. "Better crack on now." I gestured back to the desk.

"Good luck, then." Vicky edged backward out of the studio, as if she was worried I might take a bite out of her ass on the way out. I faded up the mic, planning to talk up to the vocals:

"Right, first up we've got the only recent song from this show. It's the song that was playing when I had the accident—macabre, you might think, but I couldn't leave it out. I think music's like everything else in life. Even the tough things have to be faced up to. They never go away on their own. Here it is, then, the lovely Cerys Matthews with Space, and—"

Damn! Tommy started singing, catching me out. I'd crashed the intro, a cardinal sin for a DJ. Off to a great start, then.

"'The Ballad of Tom Jones,'" I added hastily.

It was the first time I'd heard the song since the UKMAs, and it was even harder than I'd imagined. I instantly felt high again, foolish, the metallic taste of coke numbing my teeth and the rush of the bright lights spinning my head. I thought of poor Justin, having to heave me up and down on his back, and . . . no, I couldn't bear it. Despite what I'd just said on air, I still couldn't face up to that particular song. I lowered the pre-fade to a nonintrusive hum, poured myself some more gin, popped two paracetemol in my mouth, and downed them, retching almost immediately. This was not going to work. I'd have to take the tablets with water instead—one more mouthful of gin and everything would be coming straight back up again. I should have stuck to vodka.

Dashing out to the water cooler in the hallway, I rinsed out my tumbler and filled it to the brim with icy water, gulping it down gratefully to wash the bitter juniper taste out of my mouth. Not to worry, I had heaps of pills, and after the show, I could just hold my nose and pour the gin down my throat like medicine. Filling up the cup with water again, I returned to my desk and glanced at the envelope Vicky had brought in.

It was addressed to me, care of New World, in a strange plump handwriting. I slit it open and flipped the four sides of paper over to see who it was from. I suspected a nutter, writing that amount. Fan letters these days were usually just brief requests for signed photos.

At the very end I saw "All my love, Toby," and for a split second, everything in me turned to water, from knees to nose and all the bits in between. I thought I might just dissolve right there onto my desk, fusing all the electrics in the studio and bringing my show to a premature climax. But I forced myself to remember our last meeting: Toby swaying and running off to puke, calling me "she" and sucking lager off his arms. Then I remembered Ruby telling me how they were all going to live together again as a family. . . .

I was so distracted that I nearly forgot to cue Jackie Wilson. With no link at all, I segued into "Sweetest Feeling," knocked back two more pills, and devoured the letter, skimming at first through its contents.

> Dear Helena
>
> . . . fantastic to talk to you when you were at Lulu's . . . can't believe you didn't leave your number. I had been trying to get hold of you ever since you left hospital, via your agent, but you didn't reply, so I suppose you never got the letter.

Damn, I must have thrown it away along with Geoff's letter

> . . . forgot to mention it when we spoke on the phone, and when you saw me drunk that day. So, so, sorry about that; I'm mortified. I made Bill come with me to Richmond in the hope of bumping into you—what a twat, eh? As you noticed, I was hardly at my best. I gather that Bill told you why. . . . miss you very much . . . think about you all the time . . .

Omigod! I read the final page more slowly:

> It might seem to you like I'm running after you because I'm on the rebound—but I'm not, I promise. Things hadn't been right between Kate and me for ages, but because I'd already been walked all over by one woman (Lorraine, the one you met), I just wouldn't allow myself to see that it was happening again. It's been a nightmare, but Kate and I will stay in touch—we have to for Ruby's sake. Ruby doesn't understand what's going on, although I think she'll be fine. She was happy staying at Lulu's, even when I was away on business. Kate did most of her recovering at her lover's flat, where there apparently wasn't room for Rubes. Kate and Giacomo (prat!) have now bought a house together, and Ruby went to live there a

few weeks ago—in fact, the day after you went to Lulu's.

So Ruby was mistaken when she thought Toby was coming back to live with Kate, too—jeez! That would teach me to take the word of a two-year-old as gospel. I couldn't believe my idiocy.

. . . The Italian Prat is actually a fairly reasonable guy, and Kate's keen to be "mature" about access (so I should bloody well hope!), so I'm sure I'll still see lots of Ruby.

Anyway, listen, I'm worried about you, Helena. It's fine if you've decided that you don't want to pursue a relationship with me (well, actually, it's not fine at all, but I'll live with it), but you seemed upset when we spoke on the phone. Even though she hadn't met you before, Lulu thought you were acting a bit strangely, too. I still can't believe that you really wanted to give away something as precious as your memories of Sam. You aren't planning anything stupid, are you??

Whatever you think of me now, please do me one last favor and call me to let me know that you're okay. It's 0171-386-9162 (Lulu's number—I'm staying there until I find a place of my own. We're selling the house in the country).

I've been scouring *TimeOut* ever since the girl in your agent's office told me that you were going back to New World, and I was delighted to see your nighttime show listed. I'll be tuning in, you can count on it. It will be fantastic even just to hear your voice again.

All my love,

Toby xxx

When I looked up from the letter, I saw that there were only two seconds left of Jackie Wilson. I'd been intending to talk a little bit about Sam, and how we first met, before I played "Route 66," but I was too flabbergasted. Leaving three unprofessional seconds of dead air, I hastily pulled down the fader to start Sandie Shaw and flopped back into my chair.

This truly was radio at its worst—I hoped that nobody was listening. And this was the show that was supposed to be going down in history. I'd have to pull myself together and concentrate harder.

It also occurred to me that I hadn't once even thought about

Sam while the record was playing. Perhaps my theory about music and memory wasn't so infallible after all.

Still, there was a long way to go. Three down, seventeen left. I touched the Ziplocked stash of tablets with my toe, rubbing them affectionately against my sock. I had never felt so confused. I took two more tablets. Then another two, quickly, to prove that Toby's revelations weren't going to change my mind.

Damn you, Toby, I thought through the jolly brass of "Route 66." It's too late. I can't go back now. This show sucks so badly that even if I hadn't ditched the format, I'd probably get fired for it.

I replaced the cans and listened to the end of Sandie Shaw before opening the fader on my mic again.

"That was a little-known but fantastic track from the great Sandie Shaw, her version of the classic song '(Get Your Kicks on) Route 66.' I know I said these were my songs, but that one's for my dad, over in New Jersey.

"Hey, it's a good thing this isn't my old show, isn't it? For those of you who remember it, I used to never play a song unless the person requesting it could practically write a thesis on the reason they wanted it played. And I have to tell you, right now I wouldn't play any of these records if I was that punter, ringing in for them. . . . But I do have an excuse. I knew there wouldn't be enough time to talk much on air about why these tracks are important to me, so I wrote it all down instead. And if any of you care enough, perhaps one day it'll be made into a book, and you can read it. It's a thesis about my life, I guess."

I paused. "Who thinks that I maybe ought to be just a little less self-obsessed?"

I faded up "Wichita Lineman," determined to talk up to the vocals without crashing them: "And here's a song that reminds me of being a kid, hanging out with my best friend, fighting with my mother—the way you do when you're nine years old. I thought that it was about a linesman, you know, like they have in tennis matches."

Bingo. Got it right that time. Suddenly love-struck linesmen and my own self-obsession seemed terribly funny, and I began to laugh. The show wasn't going a bit like I'd imagined it would. All those months, writing and planning and being serious and grief-stricken—and now these songs were making me laugh? Perhaps I was losing it. Or maybe it was the medicinal cocktail starting to take effect.

Well, since Toby had had the decency to write and declare himself worried about me, the least I could do was to ring him. I liked the idea that he would be the last person I ever spoke directly to.

I dialed Lulu's number, feeling a ridiculous heady sensation that I couldn't quite identify.

The phone rang and rang, but there was no answer. Just my luck. Eventually an answering machine picked up and curtly instructed me to leave a message. I spoke quietly, guiltily, in case I woke up Lulu.

"This is a message for Toby. I'm really sorry to call so late. Anyway, I got your second letter, but not the first one—oh, by the way, it's Helena here. Call me back at the studio, if you like. I need to tell you something. I hope you get this message, but it's two-fifteen and you're probably in bed asleep. But if you aren't, then ring me on"—I peered at the number of the XD line written on the studio phone—"0171-935-6906—that's a direct line into the studio. Bye, Toby. It was really great to hear from you."

Not speaking to Toby had pulled me back to earth again, and I felt like I was getting down to business as I played "Sunday Girl," "Sitting in Limbo," and "Home Again." I concluded that it probably was the pills making me feel weird, so I decided to ease off them for a while, to stay alert.

I talked a lot in between each record, more than I'd intended, but kept it to generalities: when, why, what. Inside, I waited to be overwhelmed by memories of Sam and me on magic carpets, of the visitor's pink ribbon and the preacher with the bouffant hair, of my first bedroom sessions on the rickety bass—but it didn't happen. Yes, I remembered Sam, and saw her face, and relived the feeling of the love that bounced off the high tapestried walls of the Freehold Baptist Church, and heard the flat thud of my bass strings before I knew how to properly play it—but the odd thing was that I felt it all quite *fondly*.

It was like watching a much-loved movie, the way you go, "ooh, I love this bit!" but you aren't particularly glued to it because it's too familiar. You've seen it too many times before. The revelation I was expecting never occurred.

By revelation, I mean a defining moment, some sort of *It's a Wonderful Life*-esque catharsis; that by seeing my life unfold before me through those songs, it would make me appreciate its value, and I'd want to live again. This was not happening, but something else was.

Slowly, slowly, as each song shook out and laid before me its patchwork memories, I realized that, yes, these were indeed my memories, for better or worse—but frankly, I'd spent so much time dwelling on them in the past few months that they were no longer quite so interesting to me. The funny bits still made me laugh, but not out loud. The sad bits brought tears to my eyes but didn't destroy me. I had become an observer instead of a participator.

I'd thought that playing the music would tip the balance, but it didn't. My memories had, in the writing of them, become downgraded from Top Priority to Day File. By osmosis and obsession, they had become part of me. Suddenly I didn't even *want* to share them with the rest of the world. I didn't want a bumper sticker announcing to anyone that I'd Told London My Song—I wanted to keep my songs. Now that I'd given away the Hel-Sam box, they were all I had left of Blue Idea, of Sam, of the past. They were mine.

I galloped seamlessly through "Oliver's Army," "There There My Dear," and "Ghosts," and before I knew it, I'd done my first ten in a row. I switched over to the news desk for a bulletin and then ran a few more ads just to use up a bit more time.

During "To Be Someone," the XD line on my phone started flashing, indicating a call. I just happened to glance down and see the little green light blinking at me, and I lunged for the receiver, my heart in my throat.

"Toby?" I said loudly and breathlessly, over The Jam.

"No, this is Geoff," came a cross and crackly voice from a mobile phone. "I'm in a car in Crouch End coming back from a party, and this is what I hear? What the hell do you think you're playing at, Helena? I gave you express instructions that you were to stick to the format, and you're totally pirating it!"

"I've played the ads and had the news," I said lamely.

"So I should bloody well hope. Get back to Selector, now!"

I swallowed. "Geoff, listen, I haven't been straight with you. I only ever planned to do the one show. I'm really sorry that I've messed you around, but either you let me continue with my own records or else I walk out of this studio now. It's going to take you a while to get down here from North London, so unless you want forty minutes of dead air, you'd better let me keep going."

I waited for the staticky spluttering to commence, but there was just a brief pause. "I don't respond well to blackmail, Helena. We'll speak about this in the morning."

I segued into "Shipbuilding" without missing a beat, headphones pressed against one ear, an irate passenger in a car in Crouch End connected to the other ear. It was still such a marvel, being able to do two different things with two different ears.

"If you like, Geoff—but before you bother to fire me, consider this my resignation. I'll put it in writing and get it to you by ten A.M. I've decided that I don't want to be a DJ anymore."

Or a rock star, or a pushover, or a recluse. I realized then, with complete certainty, that I would still be around at ten A.M. to type up a letter of resignation. I knew that I would leave the building as hale and hearty as when I'd entered it. I knew that Vinnie was right, that no one really cared anymore. And instead of that fact making me shrivel up like a salted slug, I saw that it was all the more reason why *I* had to care, in a positive way. A looking-forward, new-life kind of way, not a wallowing-in-the-past way.

I just wanted to be me, Helena Nicholls, making a new start, hopefully with a new boyfriend, and maybe even a few new friends. Sam wouldn't mind. In fact she'd be cheering me on.

Vinnie had done me a favor. Who'd have thought?

I kept the tracks coming, wash after wash of music and faith and recollection flowing over and through me—but then out the other side again. Not sticking around clogging me up but rinsing me. And then, as if my body was echoing the sentiments in my head, a great wave of nausea rose up from my stomach. I only just made it to the ladies' in time to vomit out the gin and the eight paracetemols.

Back in the studio in time to cue the next track, I felt cleansed inside and out. It didn't prevent me from feeling sad during "Deep Blue Dream," though, remembering how Sam had seemed to shrink just a little more each time I crossed the Atlantic to her bedside—but at the same time, I was thinking about the future. How I didn't have to run away, or plan my death. Who cared? Nobody. Instead of panic and depression at the idea that I might be forgotten, I felt liberated. I could do whatever I liked!

My XD line flashed again, just after I'd cued up "Lovesong." I answered, more cautiously this time.

"Hi, Helena, it's Toby."

I couldn't speak. I was so surprised at how amazing it was to hear his voice again that it took my breath away.

"Helena? Are you there?"

I gulped. "Yes. Hello. Thanks for ringing me back."

"I've been listening since the start, only I was in the loo when you rang and didn't notice there was a message until just now. Are you okay? You sound fine on air, but . . . Oh, look, tell me I'm being daft, but I really am worried about you."

I lowered the pre-fade volume on The Cure, realizing as I did so that I'd picked "Lovesong" because it celebrated the first time Toby and I ever met.

"You're being daft. Honestly, I never felt better. Hey, this is the track that reminds me of you, you know. They were onstage at Brixton that time when you were interviewing us downstairs."

"I know. I'd hoped that was why you were playing it. Does that mean I'm in the book that you've written?"

I grinned sheepishly. "It sure does. So, are *you* okay? I know I didn't mention it when we were on the phone last time, but I couldn't believe it when you said that Kate was cheating on you."

Toby sighed.

"Yes, I'm fine now. Four days of being roaring drunk in Richmond helped get it out of my system. Except, once I recovered from the hangover, I thought I'd blown it completely with you. I was gutted when you didn't call. And then when I talked to you at Lulu's, you sounded so . . . *off* with me."

"That was because Ruby had, just that second, informed me with total conviction that you and she were moving back in with Kate the next day, to play Happy Families again."

Toby laughed. "Haven't you ever heard of wish-fulfillment? You really don't know much about kids, do you?"

I wasn't even offended at the criticism. "I could learn."

I could hear the grin in Toby's voice. "I know a great little teacher—a bit of a bossy one, though." He paused, and I was convinced that we were both sharing a mental image of Ruby wagging her finger sternly at me.

"So, you said in your message that you needed to tell me something. What is it?"

"Ummm . . . " The word dropped into an ever-deepening chasm of revelation somewhere down the phone line, like a pebble into a loch. I swiveled my chair around to face the wall, picked up the Ziploc bag of pills with my toes, and kicked it as hard as I could across the studio.

I'd wanted to say good-bye to him. What had I been thinking? Toby's voice brought my complete idiocy even further home to me, right up the garden path, in fact, and into the attic. There were still people who loved me: Mum, Dad, Cynthia, Mary Ellen. Jus, David, Joe. And now it looked like Toby did, too.

"Oh, it was nothing really. I just wanted to say that . . . I'm really, really sorry about the way we left things at the hospital, and then not ringing you after that day in Richmond. . . . I've been sorting a lot of things out in my head."

Toby laughed, in a relieved kind of way.

"I'm surprised you ever wanted to clap eyes on me again, after that day in Richmond. Anyway, stop apologizing. It's all been my fault. I behaved really badly—I felt so guilty, leading you on. So, can we meet up soon?"

I looked at the crumpled sack of tablets, destined for the same U-bend as the contents of my stomach.

"Yes, please."

"How about tomorrow?"

"Yes, please—hang on a second." I faded up "Kinky Afro," and cued "I'll Be Home."

"Sorry, I'm back. Hey, guess what—I've already quit this job. That was quick, wasn't it?"

"Why?"

"It's a long story. Suffice it to say that I don't want to be a DJ anymore, especially not at this godforsaken hour."

"Excellent!" Toby said. "Perhaps that means that you and I could go away somewhere together, for a little holiday. What do you think?"

I wrapped the spiral lead of the telephone around my finger, feeling my own excitement coil up inside me in the same way.

"That would be lovely. Can Ruby come, too?"

"I hoped you'd say that, but I think we need some time on our own, don't you? Perhaps we could have a weekend in a hotel in the U.K. first and then take her away somewhere warm afterwards. We could all do with a break. Oh, and one last thing before I leave you in peace to get on with your show: Can you play me a request, please?"

I laughed. "Didn't I already say this isn't a request show? Besides, I'm not sure that I can get access to the record library at this time of night. What is it?"

"Don't worry if you can't. I just had an urge to hear "Here's Where the Story Ends" by The Sundays, because it reminds me of you."

I was surprised. I couldn't remember that song figuring in any of our previous exchanges. "Why?"

"It was after our first kiss, you know, outside the lifts that time. I was driving back to Fulham, and the day before I'd bought a load of albums that I'd never owned but always thought I ought to. The Sundays was one of them, so I bunged it on in the car and went straight for that track, track two, cranked it right up. All through the song, I couldn't get you out of my head. I'd never felt so many different emotions: attraction, love, guilt, worry, euphoria, stress, grief. . . . It was terrible, but wonderful at the same time. And that song just seemed so perfect, even if I wasn't listening to the words. It sounds daft, but I knew right then that whenever I heard it in the future, I'd think of your smile, and the smell of the hospital, and me rubbing your poor nose, and your arms around me, and I'd remember driving home wondering how it was all going to turn out. . . . Are you still there? I'll stop now."

I was beaming so widely that I dislodged my eye patch. "Sure, stop," I said, readjusting it. "As long as you carry on again later."

The next track was "Safe from Harm," and now that I no longer wanted to kill myself, memories of Vinnie were the last thing I needed. I used the five minutes to rush down the corridor to the record library, discovering that I only needed to key in the code once more to open the door. To my joy, New World did own a copy of *Reading, Writing and Arithmetic,* and I seized it and ran back upstairs to the studio just in time to fade up "Nothing Compares 2 U." Another "Vinnie song," but to my surprise I had no trouble whatsoever about not even thinking about him. I was too busy day-dreaming about splashing around in azure shallows somewhere with Ruby in a frilly swimsuit and water wings, and Toby snoozing on the beach behind us, worn out by our weekend of passion. . . .

The last two records were my difficult ones, my Starfruit Sam ones. "I Can't Stand the Rain" and "This Is a Low." It was impossible not to sob throughout those, as impossible as sneezing without blinking, or eating doughnuts without licking one's lips. An involuntary, inevitable reaction.

But it felt different, better. Not agony, just a dull, sad ache.

I realized that the real catharsis throughout this whole exercise lay not in the songs, as I'd thought, but in the contents of a shiny purple folder on my dining-room table. All those months of writing it down had begun to heal me, and I was ready to start again. To add some new songs and new memories to my well-played collection.

Somewhat snotty and hiccuping from crying, I opened the mike for the last time as the final bars of "This Is a Low" faded out.

"So my time's nearly up, folks. I hope you've enjoyed the show. I haven't said as much as I intended to, but I wanted the music to speak for itself. Perhaps something momentous happened to you tonight, and you can claim one of these songs as your own. Be my guest—just because they belong to my memories doesn't mean they can't belong to yours, too. That's the great thing about music, isn't it? It's for all of us. Anyway, this is probably the last time you'll hear me on the radio, so, it's been a pleasure. Have a great night, what's left of it. I'm going to play you out with one final request: It's The Sundays, 'Here's Where the Story Ends,' for Toby Middleton. Good night, London.'"

I packed up my CDs, Toby's letter, the bag of pills, the cup and the bottle, and left the studio to the sound of jingly guitars and Harriet Wheeler's sweet voice telling me that I had a future after all.

Just as I got to the end of the corridor, I heard the early break-fast-show DJ come into the lobby, and I nipped into the ladies' to avoid him. My face was all puffy and tearstained, and I felt too wrung out to make small talk with a stranger. One step at a time on the sociability front, I thought.

The gin bottle nudged me in the side, reminding me of its exis-tence. I took it out of my handbag and deposited it in the waste bin underneath the sink. Then I went into a cubicle, removed the Ziploc bag, unzipped it, and dumped its contents into the toilet bowl. Booze and pills—it had been a ridiculous idea, anyway. If I'd had the courage to blow my brains out all over the desk, then yes, that would have made headlines. But swallowing tablets was such an untidy ending, like a sheet of wrapping paper someone had tried to tear instead of cut, ripping a slash across it whose jaggedness defeated its original decorative purpose.

Besides, now that I thought about it, I had always hated making the headlines.

I had to flush the toilet three times to sluice away the tablets from the bottom of the porcelain.

I finally left the building, surprising the dour security guard with a half-friendly wave good-bye, and turned up my collar against the chill of the shut-down city. As I stepped toward my car, a figure wearing a Walkman and a big red puffa jacket startled me by walk-ing out of the shadows toward me.

The figure removed his earphones, held out his arms to me, and hugged me hard. "Thanks for playing my record for me."

I dropped my box of CDs, and they all spilled out on the pave-ment, jewel cases cracking like ice breaking as I hugged Toby back.

"You look beautiful," he said, prising my face away from his neck and cupping it with his two cold hands. "You've been crying. No wonder. That can't have been easy."

I broke away from him and started picking up the bits of scattered CDs. "Sam was always telling me that I was a great big crybaby," I said. "You'd better get used to it."

Toby crouched down and helped me collect the pieces. "Fancy walking over to Soho, for a coffee at Bar Italia?"

I nodded, grinning. "Let me lock this lot in the boot first, then we can go."

* * *

Ten minutes later the sound of our footsteps echoed down a sleeping Charlotte Street, drizzle giving the streetlights hazy golden haloes. Our arms were wrapped around each other and our feet easily in step.

I put my free hand in my coat pocket and pulled out the envelope containing the letters to Ron and my parents. I'd forgotten to post it.

Author Note

Louise Voss has been in the music business for ten years, working for Virgin Records and EMI in the UK, and then as a label manager at Caroline Records in New York City. For the past two years she has been Director of Sandie Shaw's company in London. She now lives in south-west London with her husband and three-year-old daughter.

Voss is British but has lived in the U.S.A. three times: for a summer nanny job in Miami in 1984; a year at Kansas University in 1986–87 (as part of her U.K. degree course); and in New York City from 1995–97, for the aforementioned job at Caroline Records.